The Godwits

ROBIN HYDE

The Godwits Fly

Edited and Introduced by
Patrick Sandbrook

AUCKLAND UNIVERSITY PRESS

Auckland University Press
University of Auckland
Private Bag 92019
Auckland

First published by Hurst & Blackett 1938
First published by Auckland University Press 1970
Reprinted 1974, 1980, 1984
Second edition 1993
This edition 2001

ISBN 1 86940 245 6

Typeset in Goudy and printed by
Astra Print Ltd, Wellington

Contents

Acknowledgements

I would like to acknowledge with gratitude Derek and Lyn Challis, for making manuscripts and biographical information available to me, for reading drafts and offering advice, and for their generous hospitality and encouragement over many years. To Mary Paul and Michele Leggott I am grateful for sharing ideas from their own research which I incorporated into this introduction and notes, for giving me access to useful materials, reading drafts and advising on technical matters. My understanding on a number of points was clarified by having access to Lisa Docherty's PhD research on Hyde's letters. Support from the Royal Society of New Zealand Marsden Fund has enabled Derek and Lyn, Mary, Michele, Lisa and me to undertake research on aspects of Hyde's work and to share ideas and a passion for her writing along the way. I am grateful also to have had the assistance of Lucy Broadbent from the Massey University Library, Taiarahia Black from Te Putahi a Toi at Massey University, and staff from the Palmerston North Public Library, Auckland University Library, Auckland City Central Library and Henry Field Library, Christchurch College of Education. Thanks to Elizabeth Caffin and the staff at AUP for their dedication to the production of the book and commitment to Hyde's work. I am grateful to have had encouragement and support from Tom Prebble, and practical assistance from Tina Hilliam. Thanks to my wife, Cathy Sandbrook, for assisting with research, reading drafts and above all for sharing my journey through Hyde's writing from the start.

Patrick Sandbrook
Massey University

Introduction

A life short as you like, but vivid

> 'Dr G. M. Tothill
> *This imperfect part of truth*
> *Robin Hyde (Iris Wilkinson)*
> *April 1939, England*'

This is the inscription on the flyleaf of the brand new copy of *The Godwits Fly* that Robin Hyde sent to Gilbert Tothill, the psychiatrist whom she had also regarded as her mentor and friend. When she wrote the words she was half a world away, broke but writing hard; battered and ill as a consequence of months spent at the battle-front in China resisting Japanese invasion. She was still pitching all she had into the cause of humanity and justice as Europe too slid towards war; and about to cross swords with some hard-nosed English play producers over terms for a script she was just then completing. Four months later, at 33 years of age, she would be dead – of 'benzedrine poisoning and suicide while of an unsound mind' (*AHome*, xx).[1] But at that moment in the northern spring of 1939, she held success in her hand.

Gilbert Tothill's copy of *The Godwits Fly*, held in the Auckland City Library's archives, was donated by him in 1965. Its inscription, 'This imperfect part of truth', still gestures towards the things about a life that have to go unsaid – or that can only be understood imperfectly by those who have not lived through them. They are like the knowledge that war veterans cannot put into words. Hyde had glimpsed that painful knowledge in Starkie and his generation and written it into *Passport to Hell*; she had lived her own hell in the war zone of China in 1938 and recorded it in *Dragon Rampant*. The same kind of knowledge dwells in the contours of the 'steep blue country of melancholy' as they appear in this novel. Eliza Hannay's experience of loss and alienation is a terrain familiar to Hyde herself and to Tothill, who had been with her on part of her own journey through it.

Robin Hyde had recovered her mental health and self-esteem under the care of Dr Tothill and his colleague Dr Buchanan after a breakdown in 1933. On 1 June she had jumped off an Auckland wharf in a desperate rejection of a mentality and a set of circumstances that had made her life not worth living. Fished out, she was put in Auckland Hospital's DT (delirium tremens) cells, had a rebellious and unhappy period at Avondale Mental Hospital and then left Auckland briefly under her mother's care. From Wellington she went to Northland then back to Auckland where she appeared in court in early December to face a charge for the suicide attempt. The next day she collapsed again in the middle of a busy street and begged to be taken back to Avondale Hospital where she was admitted to the Lodge as a voluntary patient. There her condition improved; she gradually rediscovered the power to write and began to forge new terms on which to live.

The impulse to write directly about her own experience led Hyde first to produce an autobiography, which she completed in 1934 for Tothill. About a year later she returned to the subject of the intimate course of her own life and wrote *The Godwits Fly*. Getting the story down as she wanted it to be was a long, hard struggle, involving rewriting the draft, thinking and reading about style and authorial control, and seeking advice from friends. By the time it was finished two years later, she felt she had succeeded in representing human experience meaningfully and honestly using the pattern and texture – 'imperfect parts' though they were – of her own individual life.

The main elements of Hyde's life have been described in a number of other places, but for readers encountering her work for the first time, the main outline is as follows. Iris Wilkinson (Hyde's real name) was born on 19 January 1906 in Capetown. Her parents moved to New Zealand shortly after she was born, the second of four daughters, and she was raised in Wellington. While at Wellington Girls' College she gained local notice as a poet. From about the age of fifteen she also knew a young man named Harry Sweetman. She fell deeply in love with him and dreamed of a shared life of travel and adventure. Her strong attachment to Harry endured, even though it was mixed with bitter disappointment when he set off alone for England, where he died shortly afterwards. She became a career journalist, working during the 1920s and 1930s on the *Dominion* in Wellington, the Christchurch *Sun*,

NZ Truth, the *Wanganui Chronicle* and the *New Zealand Observer* in Auckland. She also had freelance articles, stories and poems published widely in newspapers and magazines throughout New Zealand, in Australia and Britain. She earned respect as a hard-working and independent-minded journalist. She was inquisitive about what made her culture tick – sharply observant about the position of women, prepared to get actively involved in radical politics and economic debate at a time when New Zealand – and the rest of the world – was gripped by Depression, aware of taha Maori and informed about international politics.[2] By the mid-1930s Hyde was also an accomplished poet of the new generation and a novelist of great promise.

At a personal level, her life was difficult and tragic. An injury to her knee in 1924 left her lame and in the long course of medical treatment she began a dependence on drugs that persisted to the end of her life. There were two unwed pregnancies; the first baby (Robin) died at birth in Sydney when she was 20, the second (Derek), born four years later, had to be provided for discreetly. The experience of motherhood with its complex economic and emotional pressures also took a toll of grief and anguish. Unmarried motherhood stigmatised her socially, strained family and other relationships and threatened to undermine her chances of a steady career in the respectable world of work.

She was driven to reckless forms of behaviour. Two breakdowns were followed by periods of convalescence, first in Hanmer in 1927, then from 1933 to early 1937 as a voluntary patient at the Lodge (she invariably referred to it as 'The Grey Lodge'), a residential clinic attached to Auckland Mental Hospital in Avondale. In the relative security and serenity of these surroundings her creativity flourished. From her time at Hanmer had come poetry; from her attic room in the Lodge came a torrent of poetry, autobiography, novels, stories and plays. *The Godwits Fly* is part of this extraordinary burst of activity in 1934–35 that gave rise to almost half of her total output of creative writing. As she regained health, she was able to come and go more freely from the Lodge and get involved in the social and literary life of Auckland. She became a well-known figure in the town and kept in close touch with the current scene.

By 1936 the Depression was over and the national economy was rebuilding. A Labour government had swept to power in November

1935 with a fresh vision for New Zealand's economy, society and place in the world. The local literary establishment was feeling confident too, and was already forging monuments to itself. There was a New Zealand Authors' Week held in April and plans were already being laid for New Zealand's Centennial to be celebrated in 1940. Younger writers did not have much of the limelight – Hyde was invited to speak at Authors' Week only at the last minute – but they were stimulated by the issues nevertheless. There was a good deal of talk in the air about the Great New Zealand Novel and other prodigies. Hyde celebrated that energy and innovation in an article for *Art in New Zealand*, seeing great potential in the emerging talents of her own generation. Poet and personality Rex Fairburn, for example, whom she knew and admired from their period of common interest in Douglas Social Credit in the early 1930s, might be able to combine his radical politics with the energy and power of his exceptional lyric gift to produce 'the New Zealand novel about which New Zealanders still moan'.[3] The prediction was also a challenge to produce the goods – and it was directed at herself as much as at Fairburn and their contemporaries.

Hyde was optimistic about her own chances of achieving recognition as a clear and strong voice for her generation, as she set to work to revise and complete *The Godwits Fly* in the winter of 1936. She felt she was writing with maturity and discipline. *Journalese* (1934) had already been published locally by the National Printing Co. in Auckland, but her big break had come when Macmillan's of London accepted *The Conquerors* (1935), her second book of poems, as part of their prestigious Modern Poets series. Shortly after, *Passport to Hell* (1936) was taken by the English publisher, Hurst and Blackett. Now she was an international writer with a literary agent in London; and publishers wanted more of her work. *Wednesday's Children* would soon appear under Hurst and Blackett's imprint and they also had a collection of her short stories called 'Unicorn Pasture' for consideration (though it was not subsequently published). America was in her sights too. *Check to Your King*, the product of her ground-breaking research in Sir George Grey's sprawling archives, had been submitted for a competition run by the *Atlantic Monthly* and was commended by the judges.

Could *The Godwits Fly* now put her firmly on the literary world map? Was the 'schoolgirl poetess' of six years earlier, with two slim volumes of verse from a small corner of the world about to hit the trans-Atlantic big-time?

She readied herself for greater independence. As a kind of trial flight, she made several short stays away from the Lodge on the North Shore and elsewhere, then a much longer trip in September to Dunedin and on to other parts of the country. But it was a complex set of events and motivations that finally prompted her to leave the Lodge altogether in early 1937. Now there was a difficult year of living precariously from her writing on the North Shore in Auckland before she left New Zealand on 18 January, the day before her thirty-second birthday. In Hong Kong she abandoned her intended trans-Siberian trip to Europe and went instead into war-torn China. Months later she travelled on to England but by a different route. New work was being published in England and she carried works in progress with her. Still writing prolifically, but now seriously ill and relying on friends for cheap lodgings much of the time, she survived in and around London for about a year. Then on 23 August 1939, as Europe too stood at the brink before plunging to its destruction in world war, Iris Wilkinson took her own life.

A decade before, Hyde had written to Harry Sweetman's brother, Hardy, advising him to 'Paint your own dreams – of a life short as you like but vivid' (29 May 1928). The advice was her manifesto and perhaps her requiem: a determination – almost a desperation – to make every moment count.

An individual living in the world

How are we to read Hyde's life in relation to her fiction? Since her death, almost every one of the publications of her work has had biographical information attached to it by its editor. As a result Hyde has always been 'present' alongside the work itself, like another character, needing to be read into our understanding of the fiction in some way. Boddy and Matthews's approach in *Disputed Ground* is an interesting example. Where they had no other available information, they incorporated events and descriptions directly from *The Godwits Fly* into their biographical essay on Hyde to produce the most directly biographical reading of the novel to date. Other readers have had a variety of reactions. Some have been passionate admirers. Some have wanted to read about her life with less indirectness; others have reacted to her 'hysteria' and 'lack of control'; still others have not been able to find their expectations about fiction readily fulfilled because of their sense of the writer's active presence. The prevailing critical taste after her death was also unfavourable to her writing. A new definition of New Zealand's 'high culture' was being forged in the post-war years of the late 1940s and 1950s. A modernist style and national themes were the vogue, cast in small, highly crafted forms – lyric poems and short stories – preferably with the artist, as in James Joyce's words, 'invisible, refined out of existence, indifferent, paring his fingernails'. Looking back across the war years as a divide of time and sensibility, Curnow, Bertram, Brasch and other priests of the high culture had little sympathy or space for other ways of framing experience. Hyde was problematic: she wrote 'too much' and in unsettled forms; her sense of 'New Zealandness' was too prone to fuse and interlock with the supra-national, the mythical and the archaic; her 'life' bled through into her 'art'. She was considered as a specimen of an unsuccessful branch on the tree of New Zealand's cultural evolution, and was bypassed.[4]

For a considerable period, her work remained largely unknown and unread. *The Godwits Fly*, in print continuously since 1970, has in fact been the most available point of access for readers, apart from the selective glimpses offered by the poems included in various anthologies. Then in the 1980s, there was a remarkable recovery of her other writing. Bridget Armstrong's solo drama *The Flight of the Godwit* (1982) was the prelude to a burst of renewed interest in her spectacular and tragic life story.[5] In a span of less than ten years following Armstrong's solo dramatisation, Hyde's work achieved a publishing prominence matched by no other literary figure of her generation. All of her known prose work was brought forward from the 1930s to a new audience and a new critical climate; together with enough fresh information about her life, the depth and range of her writing and her creative process to re-make her place in the national literature.

A unique feature of Hyde's work is that a significant amount of previously unknown work has appeared long after her death, alongside the re-published texts, and much more is yet to be published. There is still a remarkable freshness to the work as well. Her nonconformity in matters of genre and style – considered odd or perverse in her own time – now reads as a rich and insightful engagement with ways of inscribing experience and opening up the text.[6] The collection of articles, reviews and social commentary in *Disputed Ground* re-contextualised her non-fiction writing. Completely 'new' works by Hyde have included *A Home in This World and The Book of Nadath*, both of which show new facets of her work and also invite a re-reading of the previously known canon. Other unpublished work comprises more poems, autobiography, almost a hundred short stories, half a dozen plays, the verse chronicle 'De Thierry's Progress', a novel called 'The Unbelievers' and the incomplete start of at least one other called 'Come Away, O Human Child'. Yet other of Hyde's teeming offspring are missing, presumed lost: novels called 'The Windy House' (1929), and 'These Poor Old Hands' (1935); and the playscript based on *Wednesday's Children* (1939). A considerable body of letters, journals and other evidence of Hyde's life and craft also remains to be fully explored. Academic research interest is growing both within New Zealand and beyond. A biography and a Collected Poems are currently in preparation. Filmmakers and screenwriters continue to be drawn to the dramatic possibilities of her writing. We haven't heard the last of Hyde yet.

Each of the new editions and new texts has been accompanied by further insights into the writing, its context and its authorship. The availability of more information about both Hyde's personal life and her writing career has stimulated exploration of the political, social and literary tensions at work in them. Feminist and post-modernist ways of reading the literature and the life have contested the older modernist approach – though at their most reactive such readings have risked simply privileging Hyde for the same marginality that had caused her to be disregarded in the cultural construct of the 'Curnow generation'. Pondering that literary-historical about-face, Mary Paul offers a useful corrective in her reminder that the work needs careful reading, not special pleading. 'To understand Hyde's narratives only for their pathos is to reduce their significance . . . Hyde wanted a new way of showing an individual living in the world, and at the same time of questioning the boundaries of self and world. [She was] interested, not so much in subjectivity for its own sake, but in sites where social ideologies and forces were busy playing out their effects' (*Her Side of the Story*, 174, 157). *The Godwits Fly* is one such site.

Concerning godwits

It is remarkable how poorly Hyde's use of the godwit motif has been received by critics, despite the strong readership the novel has continued to have. The title of the novel had evidently been the first thing Hyde decided on. Rawlinson, looking through Hyde's papers, noted the 'sudden decision recorded in her journal 2 March 1935: 'Settled: I'm going to write a faintly autobiographical novel called "The Godwits Fly"' (Rawlinson, intro. to *Godwits*, xiii–xiv). Joan Stevens is representative of critical opinion in passing lightly over the godwit theme. Instead she preferred the Mansfieldian depiction of 'crystalline impressions of childhood days' in the first half of the novel, adding: 'Unfortunately, the adult portion of the book is less effective, distorted possibly by its intimate relation to her own life' (Stevens, intro. to *Check*, ix). Rawlinson took the same view (Rawlinson, xi, xvi–xvii). More recently Stuart Murray is also equivocal: Hyde is 'clearly a successor to Mansfield's analysis of an emerging settler society', he says, supporting this with some of the major correspondences between *The Godwits Fly* and Mansfield's New Zealand stories in *never a soul at home* (1998) (189). He finds Hyde unable to sustain fully realised characters in the larger form of the novel, however. Timothy Cardew he sees as a 'stock character': 'the decade's composite poet/tramp/scholar'. In his view, that Timothy should 'command such an investment on Eliza's part unbalances the novel, and Hyde struggles in particular to find an adequate ending to this narrative' (Murray, 192). These readers' presumption that the novel is to be read primarily as a picture of childhood in suburban Wellington leaves a great deal unexplained. The key to avoiding reductiveness is the godwit motif itself, which needs a more complex reading.

Hyde herself draws attention to things that are *wrong* with the godwit motif, in the Author's Foreword. First: 'many people do not know what a godwit is'. Then 'godwits, flying north, never go near England. They fly to Siberia'. Finally, having flown away, 'logically . . . they ought to have the same compulsion to come back'. The Foreword offers no easy resolution of these difficulties. But by deliberately confronting us with the fact that the literal migration of the godwits is not a good fit with the events of the novel, Hyde is suggesting that we read with our wits about us.

Taken most directly, the godwit's flight is intended to be read as a metaphor for an emerging post-colonial state of mind. It depicts the 'white' New Zealanders' (as she called them elsewhere) 'Colonial England-hunger', or over-easy reliance for cultural sustenance on their stock of canned and preserved culture, imported from Europe – and past its 'use by' date – which had retarded their effort to cultivate more wholesome homegrown forms. The lack of a sense of community in contemporary New Zealand society had already emerged as a theme in *Journalese*, written just a year or so before she began *The Godwits Fly*: 'If society consists of a body of individuals with some real tie of feeling between them, we have no society in New Zealand as yet: there are ties of prejudice and self-interest, but of genuine feeling, no' (*Journalese*, 113).

But that tricky Foreword also clues us in to look at Eliza's emerging powers of thought and action rather than simply the idea of a geographical journey to England or even an exploration of social themes. In the novel Eliza realises that it is 'ourselves we reach out for, our own undiscovered selves' (*Godwits*, 137). To be a godwit in these terms is to go in search of oneself; a search which is without end, since the self is in part defined by the journey it makes – as the godwit is defined by its endless, instinctive migrations around the world.

'A wild jumble of scenes': traces of Hyde's creative process

The Godwits Fly was the novel that Hyde re-worked most extensively of all her prose writing. Evidence of her creative process remains in the collections of her manuscripts and archives; and these traces provide insight into how she worked and how *The Godwits Fly* came to be in its present form.[7] The Hyde archives are physically disparate, and much remains to be done to establish bibliographical coherence among the various collections. Other lost pieces of the puzzle may yet come to light. Looking at the *Godwits* material, we can partially resolve the interrelationships of the surviving fragmentary drafts but questions inevitably remain because of that fragmentation. Bearing these limitations in mind, the following is a brief outline of the novel's construction.

Hyde had written the autobiography for Tothill in 1934, about a year before she began on *The Godwits Fly*. The broad outline of the 'faintly autobiographical' *Godwits* was clear in her mind from having written the earlier text. The First Version (as Rawlinson named it) was written quickly and evidently with very little in the way of planning or other preamble before the 2 March journal entry: 'Settled: I'm going to write a faintly autobiographical novel called 'The Godwits Fly'. . . . telling about the Colonial England hunger, and they that depart, and they that stay at home – Girl to be called Eliza Hannay, God knows why – But there she is – Like me but very much pleasanter and I think a sense of humour would be a help.' A week or so later Hyde was at chapter four, but then she paused for about six weeks to write *Passport to Hell*. By 12 May the *Godwits* draft was finished. In the space of about four weeks' writing time, in the attic at Avondale, she had completed 300 pages. But she was unhappy with the result and put it aside for further reflection (Rawlinson, xi–xii). This typescript is still substantially complete, though it lacks a title page and possibly an Introduction. It is currently located partly in Challis's collection (261 pages) and partly in the Auckland University Library collection (38 pages). The story is structured in two parts. While the title page of the first Part is missing, a separate title page for Part Two is headed 'Success' but then crossed out by Hyde and in her hand renamed 'The Middle Distance'. As well as this structural division, the First Version has significant differences in arrangement and treatment from the later drafts.

Hyde wrote prolifically after she had put *Godwits* aside. Between 12 May 1935, when the First Version was finished, and the autumn of 1936 she produced an abundance of poems, short stories and articles as well as re-writing *Check to Your King* and working on three other novels: 'These Poor Old Hands', 'The Unbelievers' (both still unpublished) and *Wednesday's Children*. Images, incidents, themes and stylistic approaches from the First Version recur in various ways in these other works. Letters from this time and passages in her journal and notebooks show her actively experimenting with ways to overcome the problems that had left her dissatisfied with *Godwits*. Then, in a letter dated 8 May 1936, Hyde told John A. Lee she had begun redrafting *The Godwits Fly*.

What had spurred her to action? Finishing other work, particularly *Wednesday's Children*, left her desk clear. External events such as the April 1936 Authors' Week also energised her with the feeling that the moment was right to gain from a broadening public interest in local writers and themes – Lee's own *Children of the Poor* impressed her as a model of fictionalised autobiography. But probably more personal pressures dictated that she would now turn her attention to the autobiographical novel, in preference to the many projects she either had started or had in mind. There is for instance a long description in her journal on 13 March 1936 of the emotions recalled by a letter received years before from Harry Sweetman, when she visited the family home in Wellington at Christmas. The letter made ghosts walk: 'Twelve pages of it and tonight lying next to my heart! If that seems childish, so was he – he had a curl of my hair, and says in the letter that to sleep without it gave him nightmarish dreams'. It is strong emotions like these that may have been the driving energy that took the novel in a new direction.

Hyde returned to work on the novel in April 1936. Dialogue at this time with her closest friend, Gwen Mitcalfe (née Hawthorn), seems to have helped her to rethink the novel's approach and in particular to focus on the relationships between Eliza, Simone and Timothy. It was this focus, and the playing out of the events of Eliza's '21st year', which was the 'breakthrough' to resolving her dissatisfaction with the form and structure of the First Version.

Major changes to the First Version were the result. She removed an extensive treatment of Augusta's godwit journey before Eliza is born. She rounded out John Hannay's character – he had been killed off at the beginning of the First Version. Other friends of Eliza's, who competed with Simone's characterisation in importance, also disappeared. Most importantly, the final third of the novel was reshaped to remove both interpretative comments on the society and politics of the day, and an account of Eliza as a successful journalist travelling and working around New Zealand, living in Christchurch, visiting the Marlborough Sounds and the Wanganui river valley and other events. Other characters – a travelling companion called Hildred, Marlborough residents, a spiritualist called Shadow – were also removed from the novel. Hyde also abandoned the (literally) 'cliff-hanger' ending of the First Version, which has Eliza drive off the road to avoid hitting a mob of sheep as she contemplates a destination either at a lonely farm called 'Solitude' or at Spirits Bay in Northland.[8] Part of her dissatisfaction with the First Version may have been that so much of the lived experience in the novel was displaced onto other characters or handled obliquely, leaving Eliza's character weakly motivated.

There is no surviving complete draft of *Godwits* from this period; but there are some fragments of typescript. Specifically, there is a 40-page typescript of the 'Little Ease' chapter (AU-B12b, fragments 1, 2) and another collection of 81 pages of typescript in the Challis collection of episodes corresponding to the beginning of Part Two of the First Version. These are distinctive in having handwritten annotations by both Hyde and her friend Gwen Mitcalfe. [9] Mitcalfe was the person on whom Simone is based in the novel and these passages are the ones involving Simone and Timothy most directly. This is the only case where anyone other than Hyde herself worked directly on the actual drafts of *The Godwits Fly* as it was being composed. It is evidence that Hyde sought Mitcalfe's advice and that these passages of the novel at least were receiving particular attention. Further work remains to be done to determine the exact date and compositional order of these 'Simone' passages; but most likely they are from May–June 1936, when Hyde was recasting the novel in a significantly new shape.

The other surviving materials from this period are two notebooks containing, among much else, handwritten notes and drafts for the novel. Rawlinson ordered and named these Exercise Book 14 (Ex 14) and Exercise Book 15 (Ex 15). The Ex 15 notebook of about 100 pages contains a total of 11 pages of notes and a list of chapter titles for the novel. Hyde dated one of these pages 'July 22nd 1936'. One end of Ex 15 starts with the 13 March journal entry, quoted above, and a group of poems. Ex 14 includes a redraft of part of the text. She was evidently working in both Ex 14 and Ex 15 at the same time; and old themes were taking a new focus. [10]

The outline chapter list and 'phrase shorthand' notes in Ex 15 are very close to the sequence of the First Version, suggesting that these plans at least are from very early in the revision. Interestingly, this Ex 15 outline gives the novel a three-part structure. This may be the moment at which Hyde went back to the typescript of the First Version, crossed out the Part Two title 'Success' and replaced it with 'The Middle Distance', which implies a third Part to come. But the idea of a three-part structure was not pursued. In fact, the whole idea of splitting the story into parts was dropped after this point, possibly because such internal divisions are at odds with the thematic concern for unity and integration.

The next stage in the development of the novel is a manuscript draft (which I have called MS version) that survives in an almost complete form, spread across three more notebooks in the Challis collection (Ex 16, Ex 17, Ex 18). This draft establishes the final shape of the novel, though there is still a great deal of detailed change to be made to the text and to the chapter divisions and titles between this and the final published version. The MS version lacks the first two chapters (and possibly an Introduction or Author's Foreword), which must have existed either as loose pages or in another notebook There is also a chapter and a half missing between the last two notebooks.

It is unusual for Hyde to have handwritten a revision of such a long work. She commonly worked directly onto her typewriter. She must have worked from an earlier typescript however, since large parts of this text follow word for word passages in the revised sections of the First Version. One reason why this draft was handwritten is that Hyde was working on it while she was away from the Lodge, perhaps on weekend stays with friends in Auckland at first, then while travelling further afield.[11] She went from Auckland to Dunedin by train in late September 1936, staying in a boarding house on George Street in Dunedin and spending time as the guest of the Hon. W. Downie Stewart, writing in the tranquillity of a balcony in his house on Heriot Row. The first of this set of notebooks containing the draft of *Godwits* also contains notes made in the Hocken Library and notes of discussions with Stewart himself about political history.[12] There is also material about Charles de Thierry in this notebook, suggesting that Hyde had first used it before she left Auckland and while she was at work on *Check to Your King*, which she had completed in 1935. It is possible therefore that the MS version was begun before Hyde set out for Dunedin.

There is no known complete draft of the novel after the MS Version. There are, however, the first 137 pages of a typescript draft, which currently exists as two fragments, each in a separate collection. The first, of 49 pages, is in the Auckland University Library (AU-B12b fragment 1); the other, of 84 pages, in the Challis collection. This partial draft appears to belong to the revision made over the summer of 1936–37. While it is possible that it is the remains of a full late typescript draft which is no longer in existence, the short timeframe makes this unlikely. Hyde told Lee the novel was finished in a letter from the Lodge dated 16 January 1937 and that she knew it would 'crisp out' in the final typing. This she undertook, probably on her new portable typewriter purchased on 25 January, in the baches she stayed in at Whangaroa and elsewhere over the next month or so. The completed typescript of the novel was to be sent to her agent in London 'next week', she wrote to Stewart on 5 March 1937. It is not possible to determine when or in what form the Author's Foreword was added to the text, due to the incomplete state of the drafts. The final typescript sent to A. P. Watt and Son, Hyde's literary agent in London, does not appear to have survived.

A sliding picture of the days

It is characteristic of her style that Hyde should have settled so fixedly on the phrase, 'the godwits fly' when she began the novel. As a newspaper journalist as well as a poet, she had an ear for a telling phrase. Elsewhere she described her ability to recall events in vivid detail by attaching them to a single image. 'I used a kind of phrase shorthand, very simple, unintelligible unless I explained it myself' (*Dragon*, 281). The godwits evidently rang true as a piece of 'phrase shorthand'. Hyde also had Wednesday Gilfillan warn us that perception is shifty; things that appear to be simple truths have 'second selves, split personalities, double faces' (*Wednesday*, 273). These comments point to a symbolic – she would have said poetic – way of layering meaning and perception, which Hyde applied to her writing across genres. Initially she may not have fully grasped what the godwits meant for her, but she was confident that she could enable its significance to emerge.

Hyde was determined to find a way to write 'artlessly' or lyrically, to let objects or incidents reveal their particular form and yet, by techniques such as juxtaposition and repetition, to make each image radiate meaning into larger rhythms and patterns. Her notebooks and letters to friends show her constantly on the lookout for new and different approaches. She admired Joseph Roth's writing, for example, because of its qualities of texture: 'His stuff is so detailed that at first it looks solid – then it breaks into pattern, like little leaves . . . I've tried for that – the rounding out of things, picture, person, until their separate existence is coherent in the pattern too' (To Schroder, September 1935). She was also pleased when – too rarely – her own skill as a writer was appreciated. Thanking Lee for his review of *Passport to Hell*, she wrote, 'You were the first to do what I wanted, to pay some attention to the actual structure of the book' (To Lee, 7 August 1936).

So one of Hyde's major stylistic concerns was to realise images fully in her work to convey the kind of 'crystalline impressions' that Stevens remarked. We can trace this concern a long way back in her writing career. Over the summer of 1927–28 she had been commissioned by the New Zealand Publicity Bureau to write 50 articles on places of interest to tourists. For a short, exciting period she also wrote screen titles for silent films made by the Bureau. She wrote to Schroder: 'I go in and watch a wild jumble of scenes which might mean anything. I have to try to make them into [a] titled sequence' (28 November 1927). That movie-making experience occurred to her later as a vivid way of describing her style in the autobiography she was attempting to write in 1934. It was, she explained to Schroder, 'a sort of sliding picture of the days . . . utterly sincere and true, not just my halting truth but the truth of all the faces, tormented and inarticulate and quelled by life, that slid past' (August 1934).[13] When she wrote *The Godwits Fly* Hyde used the technique with mastery. To take only one example, Eliza's emotional battle with Simone involving jealousy over Timothy and the need for, and value of, marriage is conveyed entirely by using this filmic technique of a 'wild jumble of scenes' in the 'Business Girls' chapter. Hyde even foregrounds the method, heading one of these quick scenes 'A last shot' – the scene is Simone sitting in the 'Fleahouse' watching a 'picture show' (*Godwits*, 138).

'21 years of a life'

The most relevant formal context for *The Godwits Fly* is the bildungsroman, or 'novel of education', though the novel has more commonly been read as simply a lightly fictionalised autobiography. Whatever its origins in the material of Hyde's experience, the novel stands on its own terms as a work of art. A good deal of the work she put into planning and shaping the draft from mid-1936 to early in 1937 went into paring it down, she told John A. Lee, to '21 years of a life' (2 April 1937). Big sections of the early drafts of the novel were cut or rearranged, as described above. The first person narration was transformed into predominantly an omniscient third person point of view, which removed the constraint of a single consciousness within the narrative. The result is a strongly realised set of events and characters arrayed around Eliza so as to set up symmetrical tensions and patterns of conflict and resolution which reflect and define her progress. As bildungsroman, it shows Eliza to be marked out for her special role, her world to be in a troubled state and her education ('the growth of a poet's mind') equipping her to engage fully with that turbulence.

The detailed naturalistic texture of the narrative contains the key thematic patterns of the novel. An example is the way Eliza is marked out as the key character. She is not the oldest child in her family, but from very early in the story she makes herself the focus of attention. In the opening pages she and her older sister Carly compete at story telling. Carly has the natural advantage of age: her 'memory stretched back' further; but Eliza can 'tell things better' (*Godwits*, 2). This first encounter prefigures their later relationship as well as setting Eliza on her course as an artist with words. Carly's dislike of lentils, referred to three times in this first chapter, echoes the archetypal story of sibling rivalry from the Book of Genesis. The elder son Esau sold his birthright to his younger brother Jacob for a pottage of lentils, fulfilling the prophesy that 'the elder shall serve the younger' (Genesis 25:34; 25:23). Symbolically it will be Eliza, not Carly, who leads the way to the novel's meaning.

Eliza's worthiness to lead the spiritual quest for understanding is embedded in the larger structure of the narrative as well as in its allusive detail. In chapter twenty-two, titled 'Carly', the older sister vicariously experiences the traumas Eliza has lived through. Her missed chance of marriage to Trevor Sinjohn and the death of her friend Kirsty Blake parallel Eliza's lost relationship with Timothy. Witnessing a painful childbirth, she confronts the experience Eliza had endured with the stillbirth of her baby. Carly is moved to tears, but doesn't have the 'courage or the strength' (*Godwits*, 224) to go beyond that. The following chapter, 'Absalom, My Son', shows John Hannay's vicarious pride in Eliza's success as a poet. He pays deference to her having reached a community with mankind which he had only been able to prefigure in his impulse 'to get into the masses who have no consolation but life and death' (*Godwits*, 82). In Eliza's poems John recognises 'a language . . . which all could speak' and 'a child could understand . . . or an ageing man' (*Godwits*, 229).

Eliza's apprenticeship to her art involves her learning to be a poet, and also learning what her subject matter is to be. From being able to 'tell things better', she advances quickly – 'Half-way through the war, Eliza became a poet' – and at first comically, rhyming 'Hun' with 'gun' and 'Verdun' (*Godwits*, 70–71). In the 'Little Ease' chapter she is engaging seriously with poetic form and subject. By the end of the novel she has been published. Her 'humble little book', 'Stranger Face', takes its place among the greats, when it is raised with John's aid to 'the middle of the top shelf' at the bookshop Poetry Counter alongside 'a nice set of Browning in vermilion leather covers' (*Godwits*, 226).

Eliza's discovery of the subject matter she is to express unfolds from the experiences and ideas she encounters. Her formal education begins under the tutelage of Mr Bellew, who 'talked about the godwits' and their mysterious ('secret') journey far away ('to Siberia . . . . north . . .'). Even in her childish imagination Eliza is able to sense something beyond Mr Bellew's simple account of geographic distance. She connects that mystery and remoteness with the here-and-now of her own place, sensing 'something delicate, wild and far away' which has been obscured by jingoistic nationalism: 'You didn't really have to think about it – Maoris, godwits, bird-of-my-native-land' (*Godwits*, 33). Later, in 'Little Ease', Eliza goes further and rejects an education system which is bent on division and dismemberment. She sums this up in the image of a dissected buttercup: 'we never do anything by wholes, it is all dismembered, like the buttercup, and nobody has the energy to stick it together again' (*Godwits*, 95).[14] In her own family Eliza sees the same pattern of isolation, conflict and division in the discord between Augusta and John. The fact that a world war rages in the background of her childhood suggests that this is a universal condition.

Alongside Eliza's formal education are more natural growth processes. Her sixteenth birthday at Day's Bay, described in 'Reflections in the Water', is a coming of age. The motif of a journey and arrival is picked up in the picture of the *Cobar* at the Day's Bay wharf. In the dressing-shed Eliza observes pink flesh, now with 'patches of dark, frizzy hair' (*Godwits*, 117) and has an insight into how Carly's sexuality is a vulnerability that will be exploited (*Godwits*, 115). She is then led by her mother along the 'up-path', beyond a waterfall like a 'white bridal veil', past 'two lovers . . . lying in the fern' (' "And only man is vile", says Augusta'), then on to the 'lazy serenity' of a street full of 'old houses'. This is her initiation into the world of 'man, woman and child' (*Godwits*, 118–19). As they all journey back to the everyday world on the *Cobar* Eliza recognises in the snatches of community song the subjects with which she must engage.

The characters in the novel ring true to life, but in this aspect of the novel too, what appears to be simple documentary realism resolves unobtrusively into form and structure. The interaction and juxtaposition of characters creates a pattern of figures and 'journeys' surrounding Eliza that reflects in various ways on her central 'journey'. The major figures in the pattern are two women, Augusta and Simone, and two men, John and Timothy. Together the women reflect Eliza's exploration of the personal and introspective, while the men reflect her exploration of the social, political and sensory realms.

In Augusta's life Eliza sees the domestic realm upheld. Augusta's values of motherhood, security and conformity find their doomed extreme in Carly. Her unfulfilled journey to an idealised England was strongly realised in the First Version of the novel but here it is pushed further into the background. Eliza's father, John, who was a shadowy presence in the First Version and had been killed off by the end of chapter two, now plays a strong role as a foil to Augusta's values. The depiction of their fractious marriage is highlighted as essential to the novel's thematic structure. Augusta's pride and desire for respectability hold her aloof from her partner and those around her. These negative qualities are the legacy which Eliza has to be able to renounce in order to see value in 'the spawning-ground of life' (*Godwits*, 234). On the other hand, Augusta's 'genuine toughness of spiritual fibre' (*Godwits*, 82) is her positive legacy to Eliza.

In Simone Eliza sees the emerging artist imperfectly reflected. Simone's experimentation with personal style attracts Eliza but is ultimately empty of real engagement. Simone lacks Eliza's bravery and willingness to take risks – in relationships as well as in other spheres:

'What's the good of love without marriage?' she asks, to which Eliza responds, 'What's the good of marriage without love?' (*Godwits*, 139). If Simone's negative quality is her timidity, then the positive lesson she has for Eliza is her strong and intact sense of herself and her own needs as a basis for action. Eliza is disappointed that Simone chooses to marry Toby at the end of the novel, until she is able to recognise that Simone and Toby may need the complementary qualities they sense in each other: 'she was looking for her lost daemon . . . Queerest of all if Toby turned out to be the daemon. Inside marriage she'll have a new face, a stranger face' – the last phrase echoing the title of Eliza's book (*Godwits*, 234). In their marriage, at which Eliza is bridesmaid in the last chapter, there is the hope of true union and equality in contrast to the isolating tensions between John and Augusta.

John Hannay's faith is rooted in the socialist brotherhood of man. So in her father Eliza sees the world through a political frame. His failure to connect this faith with his daily life makes him by turns angry and sentimental. His fantasy of martyrdom for Tom McGrath, his union boss (*Godwits*, 154), is pure sentimentality and his anger is comically parodied in the oafish Olaf. The positive side of John's legacy to Eliza is his desire 'to rejoin the whole' (*Godwits*, 82), his conviction that the positive driving force of human nature is generated at its most instinctual level.

Timothy drags Eliza at a gasping run into the physical and sensual world. Physical exertion and sexual energy are shot through the various worlds he encounters with Birkett, Damaris Gayte, Shelagh and others.[15] His idealism prevents him, however, from being able to participate unselfconsciously in the everyday world: 'he was disappointed when the tramp called him "Sir", instead of "Digger" or "Mate"' (*Godwits*, 123). As if her own energy has been earthed by his, Eliza risks being trapped in a state of suspended animation under the influence of his keeping her 'white, for an ideal' (*Godwits*, 123). But his zest for life in all its forms and his willingness to commit without hesitation to the great cause of humanity is a positive influence on her. Eliza reflects this influence in her own discovery that 'It doesn't matter much' what course of life she follows because she is capable of being a 'stock now of various goods . . . for everybody' (*Godwits*, 235).

The central journey that Eliza makes in the novel is through the experience of alienation ('loneliness') and loss – first Timothy, then her stillborn baby – to disintegration and beyond these to an integrating self-knowledge. The redemptive possibility she struggles towards is foreshadowed in Timothy's mythologised journey to the seat of Empire as a 'Barbarian for Caesar'. Here he is imagined not as a colonial subject who goes to pay tribute, but as a free citizen of the world in full command of himself: 'I have been afraid and made others afraid' (*Godwits*, 182). He finds his true identity paradoxically by placing himself in the service of a cause greater than just his own. Eliza herself pays a tribute to the Kingdom of the Defeated. Her stillborn baby is the 'delicate thing' chosen by the 'gods of beauty' to be taken from this world into their realm (*Godwits*, 209). It is after her baby is born dead that she rediscovers her 'old power' to write – now with 'a stronger face, an estranged face' (*Godwits*, 210). Like Eurydice in Rilke's poem, 'Orpheus, Eurydice, Hermes', with which the novel concludes (*Godwits*, 235), Eliza is taken apart from the mundane world and metamorphosed paradoxically into her 'undiscovered self'. Rooted now in 'the wonderful deep mine of souls', she can be 'given far and wide' as if from an inexhaustible source.

After '21 years of a life',[16] the bildungsroman leaves Eliza rooted in a deep understanding of the human condition and poised to face a future that is unknown but no longer feared. And she need no longer suffer loneliness, since she shares her fate with all other human beings whose 'odd disjointed thoughts about their homes and life's work were the hermitages in which they dwelt' (*Godwits*, 236).

Part of the reason Hyde was content to concentrate the scope of *Godwits* was that she intended to connect it to a larger thematic architecture in her subsequent work.[17] There is a direct line of succession from Eliza's self-containment at the end of *The Godwits Fly* to the 'centre of equipoise' Hyde describes in *A Home in This World*, and elsewhere in her later work (in the poem 'The Balance', written in 1936, for instance). This is a creative and restorative state of mind freed from partisan feeling and divisiveness, and in touch with the most fundamental level of human nature. Individuals in this state are capable of functioning at a high level socially, acting as what another of Hyde's characters, Macnamara, calls a 'stabilising agent' (*Nor the Years Condemn*, 309). In *The Book of Nadath* (1999), written very shortly after

The Godwits Fly was finished, the section called 'The Far Flyers' adds resonance to the godwits' migratory cycle – now two-way – between geographies of the human spirit.

The godwit motif exemplifies how Hyde constantly recontextualised key images and patterns to show evolving thematic preoccupations at work. This 'phrase shorthand', so much a signature of her writing style, draws attention to sites where a particular 'effort towards understanding' (*Dragon*, 13) is being made – always for Hyde a joint enterprise between the writer and the reader. The effort is directed at opening up the text rather than pinning it down to a final 'meaning', since, as she wrote in the Foreword to this novel, 'Passing judgements . . . is no use at all'.

So when Hyde inscribed *The Godwits Fly* to Gilbert Tothill, 'This imperfect part of truth', she was inscribing her respect for the things that can be known and not known about a life. She was also inscribing her fascination with ways – as a writer and as a reader – of reaching out imaginatively to 'our undiscovered selves', so that the absence of certainty or closure in dealing with our own lives and the lives of others is not alienating but boundlessly integrating and creative. She was also placing herself in the company of other poets and writers whom she felt had the privilege and the duty to be 'the organ of the voice, given back to the body, which is the people',[18] to express the fundamentals of existence in the world of 'man, woman and child'. In the words of a fellow poet, Edna St Vincent Millay, to whom she alluded in the Author's Foreword:

> Down, down, down into the darkness of the grave
> Gently they go, the beautiful, the tender, the kind;
> Quietly they go, the intelligent, the witty, the brave.
> I know. But I do not approve. And I am not resigned.

Hyde's own words live through the power she had to set down sincerely and memorably what it means to be alive.

Footnotes

1   For abbreviations of Hyde's published book titles see Works Cited, page 257.

2   This aspect of Hyde is best seen in Boddy and Matthews's *Disputed Ground: Robin Hyde, Journalist*, (1991).

3   Robin Hyde, 'Poetry in Auckland', *Art in New Zealand*, 9, no. 1 (1936), 80.

4   Michele Leggott's 'Opening the Archive: Hyde, Duggan and the Persistence of Record', *Opening the Book* (1995), remarks on an aspect of 'what happened to women poets and their work as literary codes were altered just before mid-century by a cultural nationalism inimical to previous competences' (266).

5   In 1984, along with the reprint of *The Godwits Fly*, there appeared Wevers's edition of *Robin Hyde: Selected Poems*; *Dragon Rampant* was reprinted with an introduction by Derek Challis and Linda Hardy; and Tony Isaac's video telefeature *Iris* was screened. Derek Challis also published for the first time *A Home in This World* in that fabulous year for Hyde readers. In 1986 *Passport to Hell* was reprinted with an introduction by Don Smith and *Nor the Years Condemn* reappeared with an introduction by Phillida Bunkle, Linda Hardy and Jacqueline Matthews. Shortly afterwards, *Wednesday's Children* was reprinted with an introduction by Susan Ash. The Golden Press *Check to Your King* also made a reappearance in 1989. *Disputed Ground* (1990), edited and introduced by Gillian Boddy and Jacqueline Matthews, collected much of Hyde's journalism, but is significant not least for its two substantial essays on Hyde's life and her writing career.

6   Opening up the text has been interpreted as an editorial strategy in Michele Leggott's editions of *The Victory Hymn 1935–1995* (1995) and *The Book of Nadath* (1999). Both exert a gravitational pull back towards the poetry on which Hyde staked her reputation. With sensitivity to Hyde's synthesising imagination, they employ multi-layered and open ways of presenting and reading textual variants. Leggott's innovation is strikingly appropriate and relevant to Hyde's work – so much of which, like Wednesday Gilfillan's 'truth', has 'second selves, split personalities, double faces' (*Wednesday*, 273), all of which need to be seen and to interplay dynamically, not to be resolved. 'It's also development of a textual strategy to fit the writing practice as encountered in an extensive archive. We are abolishing (as she did) the (Modernist) notion of a single, authoritative text. Whatever rolls through the typewriter next is the text' (Leggott, email to Sandbrook, 6 February 2001).

7   This material was annotated and ordered to some extent by Gloria Rawlinson and Derek Challis during the 1950s and early 1960s, when some items were placed in the Auckland University Library by Challis. The material continued to be used, arranged and annotated by Gloria Rawlinson up to about 1970, when her edition of the text was published as part of the Auckland University Press/Oxford University Press 'New Zealand Fiction' reprint series. There is a detailed description of the material in Patrick Sandbrook, 'A descriptive inventory of some manuscripts and drafts of the work of Robin Hyde', *Journal of New Zealand Literature*, 4 (1986), 21–47.

8   There is some evidence in an interpretation of Hyde's 1935 Journal that there was a further 'coda' to this ending of the text; but the text of a 'Part Three' to the First Version is not with the rest of the draft and has not been identified elsewhere. The Journal says: 'I'll have to rewrite some of *The Godwits Fly*, I'm not sure how or why it dissatisfies me, but it just does, except the first book [= Part?] and the very small one which is at the end – the ending is really good, I think, and the whole book mustn't be wasted.' (2 June, p. 78). There is nothing in the extant text of First Version that clearly fits the description of a 'very small [Part] at the end.' This passage from the Journal also supports the view that Hyde's particular difficulty lay in recasting what would become the latter part of the novel in its published form.

9   One of Mitcalfe's marginal notes on Hyde's draft reads: 'in this book I would like *more* Eliza and more real Eliza. In satisfying your secret desires by making her more heroic you make the story less real & herself less a person + less appealing. 'Tout comprendre c'est tout pardonner' + her faults revealed in truthful narrative draw only sympathy' (AU-B12b, Folder 4 (fragment 2) 154). There was an extensive correspondence between Hyde and Mitcalfe over many years, but little of this remains. The Challis collection has seven letters and some excerpts in transcription included in notes made by Gwen Mitcalfe for Challis (not sighted in preparing this account).

10 This description is different from Rawlinson's account of events leading to the next known full draft of the novel. Rawlinson highlights a handwritten notebook draft of the chapter, 'Reflections in the Water', dated by Hyde 'June 22nd 1936', as the moment when Hyde made a 'breakthrough' which enabled her to reframe the novel (Rawlinson, xiii) – a milestone event as significant in Rawlinson's reading as Hyde's 'sudden' decision taken on 2 March 1935 to begin the First Version. The view expressed here is that Hyde began the redrafting earlier – about April 1936 – and that it was the subject matter and structure of the latter half of the novel that was being re-worked: there was no single 'breakthrough' to the new version.

11   'Hyde had overnight or weekend stays with Elsie Stronach in Castor Bay
at least three times early in 1936 (19–22 Feb, when she *handwrites* first
draft of "In a Silent House" into a little *notebook* [11.5 x 14 cm] which is
otherwise blank, 33 pp in total; 12 April, when she wrote a letter to
Eileen Duggan from there, and 8 May when she also addressed a letter to
Lee from there. She felt very secure there (see "At Castor Bay", in
Persephone; maybe "Digging" in *Houses*) . . . going to live on the North
Shore in 1937 was no accident' (Leggott to Sandbrook, 6 Feb 2001).

12   Stewart was then working on his biography *The Rt. Hon. Sir Francis H. D.
Bell; his life and times*, Butterworth: Wellington (1937). There was a vague
understanding that Hyde would assist Stewart with research but this did
not happen.

13   Again later, she describes *Dragon Rampant* as having been written with
'few politics and no art' to illustrate 'the agony of the drops which show
human faces for a single moment before they go over the waterfall'
(*Dragon*, 12).

14   As Hyde later wrote in 'Journey From NZ':

> Our city had doorways, too many shut.
> Morning and evening, facing the rampant crimson brutes of the light,
> Nobody had the beautiful strength to decree:
> 'Leave your doors open morning and evening —
> Leave your gates wide to the stranger.'

15   Timothy's characterisation owes a good deal to Edward Marsh's portrait of
Rupert Brooke in his 145-page memoir in *Rupert Brooke: The Collected
Poems* (1918). Many of Brooke's poems are present in the text of *The
Godwits Fly* in the episodes about Timothy.

16   Hyde wrote to Lee that the novel covered autobiographical events from
her life until she was 'only 22' (16 Jan 1937); then in a subsequent letter
to him described the novel as 'fiction ... twenty-one years of a life', adding
'. . . I liked the ending all right' (2 April 1937). The difference in these
accounts is subtle but crucial. It indicates that she had deliberately
rearranged the chronology of events based in her own life to produce a
particular pattern in the fiction: she wanted to have Eliza 'come of age' at
the end of the novel.

17   She projected two other novels, she wrote to Lee: ' the first about *here*
[the Grey Lodge], and the second about the last three months [in which
she had travelled extensively around New Zealand]. But I'll never do
them unless I can do them so gorgeously well that they won't be Iris and
her blunders, but phenomenal martian things' (16 January 1937).

18   Robin Hyde, 'The Writer and his Audience', unpublished text of an
address for New Zealand Authors' Week, April 1936, Auckland City
Library, NZ MSS 542 folder 6.

Concerning Godwits

BUT many people do not know what a godwit is. And the dictionary says sourly, a kind of marsh bird. Of the immense northerly migrations that yearly in New Zealand, when summer is gone, shake wings into the sky as if from a giant's salt-pot, nothing is told. But this is true: every year, from sandy hollows in the north of the northernmost of those three islands, the godwits set out on a migration beside which the swallow's blue hither and yon is a mere stroll with wings.

And it is true, too, that the godwits, flying north, never go near England. They fly to Siberia. But to a child in this book, it was all more simple. A long way was a long way. North was mostly England, or a detour to England.

Later she thought, most of us here are human godwits; our north is mostly England. Our youth, our best, our intelligent, brave and beautiful, must make the long migration, under a compulsion they hardly under-stand; or else be dissatisfied all their lives long. They are the godwits. The light bones of the mother knew it before the chick was hatched from the eggshell.

England is very beautiful, she thought, staring at a tree whose hair . . . not properly flowers . . . was the colour of fire. And this also is very beautiful.

'Where is Mowbray? Where is Mortimer?' whisper the old leaves of their history. 'Nay, and more than all these, where is Plantagenet?' But ours, darker, might cry, 'Where is Selwyn? Where is Rutherford? Where is Katherine, with weeds on her grave at Fontainebleau, when what she really wanted was the dark berry along our creeks? (Don't you remember? We call them Dead Man's Bread.) Nay, and more than all these, where are our nameless, the beautiful and intelligent who went away and died, in wars and otherwise, the beautiful and intelligent who went away and hopelessly failed, or came back and were never themselves any more?'

Passing judgements on any circumstance, compulsion, fate, is no use at all, she thought. England is beautiful: this also is beautiful. They are the godwits. Still, I think it odd, because I know this country. Think not without a bitter price. . . . That's for the easy brittle plough, that wants our hills.

We are old and can wait, said the untamed soil against which she pressed her fingers; although it, more than anything else, was awake and aware of its need to be a country . . . the integration of a country from the looseness of a soil. Maybe, responded the girl; though logically, living or dead, they ought to have the same compulsion to come back . . . the godwits, I mean. And, of course, there's something fine, a King of the Castle feeling, about having the place almost to oneself. Fine but lonely. . . .

Only fools, said the sparse-ribbed rock, are ever lonely.

ROBIN HYDE

CHAPTER ONE

Glory Hole

UNTIL the year after the war, life for the Hannays always meant other people's houses, and they wore out a long line of cats, invariably and irrespective of sex named Tam. Perhaps there had been some Tam the First to whom they were genuinely attached, and the rag, tag and bobtail merely stepped into his name, as into the place left vacant by his little white boots. The cat-stream, at all events, was ceaseless. The dog is a gentleman's animal, demanding licence fee and collar, but the tribe of Tam came from nowhere, and mostly shifted for themselves. Whenever one of them died (which they generally did in the cellars, requiring to be excavated by John, with great pains and blasphemy, when they had begun to smell), Augusta, his wife, skewering her auburn hair with a grim vigour intended to show that this time she had made up her mind once and for all, declared, 'Well, that's that, and good riddance to bad rubbish. The last time one of those strays shows his ugly face round my kitchen door! You children eat up your porridge, and don't let me catch you encouraging kittens to follow you home. Filthy things, with their vermin and their diseases.'

In a week's time there was always another stray showing his ugly face wherever he liked, except on the dining-room cushions, which were sacred. At night Augusta would put down a saucer of milk for him beside the stove. When the Hannays moved, part of the ritual was clasping a struggling tom against somebody's bosom, while Augusta buttered his paws. Complaining bitterly of his uselessness and the nuisance he would be in their new house, she creamed his pads until wherever he stepped he made messy little footprints on the floors she had scrubbed stark for the incoming tenants. Then he was immured in the dress-basket, which had been Eliza's cradle on the voyage from Cape Town; and Carly, the sentimentalist, stood by mourning over him. 'Tam, Tam dear, don't miaow so. It's only so that we can take you on the tram. Oh, Mummy, are you sure he can breathe in there? He won't suffocate?'

For the Hannay children (Carly and Eliza, joined by Sandra about the time they moved from old Captain Puckle's to the house in Oriri Street) their migrations were no trouble, but adventure. Carly, who was three when they came to Wellington, could go back in memory to the Sampson house, where Mrs Sampson used to stand on the stairs, talking

1

too much and too loud, her hair all down in rats' tails over a red kimono which wasn't even properly done up in front; and she didn't wear a camisole underneath. That was the real reason they moved. Augusta didn't think it decent, with a strange man (John) liable at any moment to come out of the bathroom and feast his eyes on Mrs Sampson. In their first New Zealand years, many things shocked Augusta, especially the way people, instead of bleaching their linen snow-white in properly secluded drying-grounds, pegged out meaty-coloured combinations and underpants to flap balloon legs and arms right under anybody's nose. But she hid her feelings, except from the family, and when they left the Sampson house, Mrs Sampson thought it was on account of having to carry the children's bath-water up all those stairs.

Carly could tell most of this wisely and graphically, as if scoring a point against Eliza — and so she was, for remembering things after dark in their bedroom was much their most popular game. But if Carly's memory stretched back into dimmer recesses, it was Eliza who could tell things better, and she knew it. Of Cape Town she remembered nothing, neither the mealies nor the old Kaffir women who used to follow Augusta about because Carly had such beautiful long hair. But she hung about, gathering crumbs of information from her parents' table, and at the critical moment she could nearly always squash Carly. 'Anyhow, it was me who went to sleep in the big bulldog's kennel. You were afraid — so there.'

Eliza's first real recollection was of the Puckle house. If she shut her eyes in the dark, and waited until the twirly pictures beneath the lids had faded away, she could see ferns growing under a doorstep, fine as green lace, and above them a little window of sad blue glass. She knew she was sitting at Captain Puckle's back door, and that in front of the big house, if she ran round, wind would be stooping shiny yellow grasses and veronica bushes all one way, in a garden so steep that it had to be climbed by many flights of wooden steps, called 'The Zigzag'. The Zigzag was a public right-of-way, and people in black clothes climbed up it, bending nearly double. Sometimes their umbrellas blew inside out, and they stood and swore. If she waited long enough in the memory-dream, she could see the furniture-van drawn by two old horses, straining slowly uphill. Suddenly one of the horses slipped and fell. It lay plunging about, and two men in blue overalls leapt down and ran to the back of the van, while a woman in a near-by garden shrieked: 'Mind that pianner! — you dratted, lazy stots, mind that pianner!' Then Eliza was standing in the little crowd who had thickened around the accident, and the furniture man said hoarsely, 'You'll 'ave to sit on 'is 'ead, Bill.' Obeying this strange command, Bill sat his short thick body — like a broken-off clay pipe — on the horse's head, and its legs stopped plunging. The crowd shouted encouragement, and Bill's mate sang out, 'Yo, heave away!' and presently the old horse was on its feet again, trembling all over, but ready to be yoked and pull the van. Its brown eyes behind the blinkers had long powdery lashes, and looked so very sad.

And she had diabolos, but she threw them too high and they got stuck in the telegraph wires. And John bought her miniature bagpipes, the squeak part of which looked like a black sausage when blown up; but Mrs Puckle said she couldn't have those things about the place; her poor head, her poor head. So much was perfectly clear. The shapes of Captain and Mrs Puckle took on identity much later, though to Carly Eliza pretended she could remember everything straight through. But in her heart she knew that the old people were only real because often, after leaving them, Augusta took the children back from Oriri Street to visit them. She liked old Mrs Puckle, and said of the Captain, 'At least he's a gentleman.' Eliza thought they were like the toy couple who pop in and out of cardboard weather-houses, the little man holding out an umbrella for the wet, the little lady with a parasol if today will be fine. Captain Puckle had a very long white beard, and his wife was dumpy and tiny as an outsize fairy. She made lace on bobbins, great yellowish cobwebs of lace, to be sewn into shawls, coats, babies' christening-robes and quilts for the best bed. While she was talking, she never took her eyes off your face, and it was uncanny to watch her yellow fingers making minute loops, swiftly and stealthily, as if they worked without her connivance. On the walls of her sitting-room, whose great bay windows looked down on Wellington Harbour, photographs framed in red plush were arranged in fans. Young men, top-hatted and with greyhound waists, stuck out horizontal legs, the spokes of the fan. There was a cabinet filled with seashells and dusty mushrooms of coral, rose and white. Sometimes Captain Puckle, who was very deaf and said, 'Speak up, speak up,' took out a shell and thrust its polished lip against Eliza's ear, saying, 'Hark to the sea a-murmuring, a-murmuring.'

The greatest curiosity in the cabinet was a dried Maori head. Eliza always hoped he wouldn't show it, for its lips were drawn back in such a queer, implacable grin from its long yellow teeth, and its eyes had dried up, but you could see them between the lashless eyelids. On a satin cushion in the room sat a small liver-coloured pug, who cried perpetually, both from his eyes and from his negroid black nose. He made Carly and Eliza uncomfortable; Augusta said that children with runny noses were dirty, and not to be played with, and when they sat near him they were seized with a desire to sniff. But Mrs Puckle was most attached to her pug. The steadiness of the thread worming its way over the bobbins, the horizontal legs, the tears of the pug, all made the big room rather frightening, even on the days when old Mrs Puckle didn't produce her legend.

This was about the time when she was bitten by a katipo spider. The katipo, a tiny black spider with a red spot on his back, is almost the only poisonous thing in the country, though the boys called the rose and indigo blobs of jelly washed in with the tides at Lyall Bay 'stingarees', and said that once a little girl was stung to death by them. But Mrs Puckle had really met her spider, and been bitten. She didn't die, though she might have; but her arm swelled up the size of a bolster and turned purple as a damson plum, and for three days and nights she cried with the pain of it, without so much as a wink of sleep.

If she told the story with sunset pouring in through the faded slats of Venetian blind, light livid and dust-moted in her yellow room, Eliza could see her sitting there with a huge purple arm, and had to draw her breath down very deep and hold it tight inside her chest, to keep from running and running when she got outside into the tessellated hall. She knew she was a coward, though John still joked her about going to sleep with the fierce bulldog. But she had already thought that out; she was only one when it happened, and probably she didn't know then how much bulldogs bite.

The Puckles' house, enormous if very old-fashioned and decrepit, was the most pretentious of their stopping-places. At Oriri Street they had a dingy little bungalow, and almost no garden. Tomatoes grew over the wall from the house next door, and Augusta said it was theft to pick them; but John said, 'Rubbish, finds were keeps,' and little enough he ever found, worse luck, so he had the tomatoes with bread and butter for his supper. The children very seldom had bread and butter. Augusta wouldn't buy margarine, which she considered Cockney and horrible, but they spread slices of bread with dripping, and when they came to the brown-gravy parts, it was really nicer than butter.

At Oriri Street the Glory Hole was Eliza's adventure, and Sandra's was the earthquake. It seemed a shame to waste the earthquake, for Sandra was only a baby, too little to understand or remember. The walls growled, and the lights in the house started swinging violently from side to side. Sandra's cradle, which stood outside on the portico, was upset, and she rolled all the way down the steps to the asphalt path.

Augusta, with a face like death, tore out to retrieve her, while Eliza whimpered, 'Oh, look, Mummy — Daddy's moustache cup is broken.' There was nothing much wrong with Sandra but an indomitable, ferocious yell, which she could supply without any earthquake when the mood was upon her. But Augusta sat with the baby on her lap, fingering the skin beneath the ringlets of pale Scandinavian gold, and repeating, 'It's a great bump the size of an egg . . . the size of an egg.' John, who was working night-shift at the office, came home excited about the stone ball that had rolled off the top of the Post Office and crushed a man standing underneath. But Augusta didn't care about the crushed man. She would only cry fiercely, 'Stop talking, can't you, and think about your own. She might have been killed.'

John rubbed Sandra's bump with his brown, clumsy fingers, and smiled sheepishly.

'Nothing to worry about, old girl. Stick a lump of butter on it and she'll be right as ninepence in the morning.'

Augusta, shivering from head to foot, tossed off his hand.

'Much you care. If it had been Eliza, you'd have wanted the doctor in.' She rocked Sandra fiercely in her arms. At moments of family crisis, Eliza knew, either John or Augusta was likely to accuse her of being the Pet. And Carly always said it. . . .

But John was right, John with his queer, brown, hurt face. Of course it was far more interesting about the man who got crushed by the big stone ball than about Sandra's little bump, which hadn't hurt her much, anyway. The earthquake was like the old nursery tale. (*'Oh, Goosey-Loosey,' said Henny-Penny, 'the sky has fallen on my poor bald head, and we're all going to tell the King.'*)

It was Bob Malley who owned the Glory Hole. For one brief day, that made him more important and beautiful to Eliza than any King. He lived next door, not on the tomato-growing side, but in a low, ramshackle bungalow whose cream paint, like that of most Wellington houses, was thick-pelted with dust. He was nearly fifteen, a tall boy, long-legged as a giraffe, and with a forelock falling over his freckly forehead.

Eliza sat on their garden wall, swinging her legs and watching him smooth a plane over crisp white pieces of wood. He threw one piece aside, and started making thin puddles of sawdust under his father's sawhorse. She stared at him, feeling defiant and lonely. She was glad when he looked up and spoke to her.

'Hullo, little girl next door. Come along over; hurry up, and I'll show you the Glory Hole.'

'What's the Glory Hole?'

'Where the fairies live. Hurry, this is just the time to catch them at afternoon tea.'

Bob's hands, firm under her armpits, swung her from the wall. They went into Mrs Malley's wash-house, Eliza holding tightly to Bob's hand. It was a very tidy wash-house, and Mrs Malley had a new rubber wringer. Augusta was always asking Providence for one, and saying it broke her back to wring the clothes out by hand. Bob pulled aside the matting on the floor, and there lay a great hole, a square filled with black velvet darkness.

'Down there is where the fairies live.'

She stared at him. Suddenly she knew that all her life she had never really believed in fairies, and always she had wanted to. Little sheeny iridescent wings, bodies like floating bluebells. . . .

'Truly?'

'Want to come down and see?'

She nodded, unable to speak. 'Then come on,' said Bob; and at that very moment they heard Mrs Malley's voice outside.

'Is that you, Bob? Where are you?'

'Bother women!' muttered Bob.

Mrs Malley came into the wash-house. She was a dark woman, her navy blue print frock very clean and well-pressed over her firm bosom, and her hair drawn straitly back. She said at once, 'You're not taking Mrs Hannay's little girl down your nasty, dirty hole, Bob Malley, I'll tell you that. I'd like to know what her mother would have to say — her pinny all dust and webs when she goes home. The very idea!'

Eliza, shivering as her mother had shivered when the earthquake tipped Sandra out of her cradle, wanted to explain that she would risk all the clean pinnies in the world, all the scoldings, or even the hairbrush, for one moment to watch the fairies, one glimpse of their blue wings through the spy-hole Bob Malley had dug down under the earth. But words wouldn't come; she was tongue-tied, a silly baby in the clutches of a grown-up.

'A dear little soul,' said Mrs Malley, firm-bosomed and speckless.

Bob said, 'Never mind, Liza. I'll bring you back a present from the Fairy Queen.' He swung himself over the edge of the Glory Hole. At one moment his freckly hand gripped the floor-boards, then they had vanished, and Eliza was left behind. Mrs Malley took her on her knee.

'Bob's a big rough boy,' she said, stroking Eliza's hair. 'You mustn't mind him, he doesn't mean to tease. Your mother keeps you neat as a little picture, that I'll say. My, what pretty curls. I'll bet those get combed out morning and night. I could do with a little girl of my own. Would you like to live here and be Mrs Malley's pet girl?'

Live with the Glory Hole. . . . And yet Mrs Malley didn't care, she wasn't wondering where Bob was now, downstairs in the dark earth. Perhaps the big spiders had got him. Perhaps there was a stair that twisted up and up.

'I want to go down the Glory Hole.'

Mrs Malley laughed.

'You'd get cobwebs on your pinny that your mother's ironed all nice and fresh for you. You're lucky little girls to have such a good mother.'

Presently Bob's freckled hands swung into sight again, and a moment later the rest of him doubled over the edge of the Glory Hole. A strand of web lay dusty on his cheek, and he looked tired, but to Eliza his eyes seemed full of mysterious light.

'There you are, Liza.'

He put into her hands a lavender china shoe, filled with wet new violets. Their scent made a pale streak in the wash-house.

'The Fairy Queen sent you some violets in one of her shoes, and she hopes you'll come yourself next time.'

Mrs Malley's face brimmed with half-laughing, half-compassionate mischief, the face of a grown-up fixed in the attitude of being grown-up.

'There now, do look at your trousers, all dust and webs. You'll wait a long time before you get another pair, my lad, I can tell you that. How you can be bothered with your nonsense, and putting ideas into her head. Run along and brush yourself, do. Eliza, dearie, wouldn't you like a piece before you go?'

'Eliza 'ud rather have a tikky,' said Bob, and Mrs Malley's mischievous smile streaked out again. South African children say 'tikky' for threepenny-bit, and Carly, stickler for old customs, branded them as outlanders by sticking to 'tikky' even now.

Mrs Malley could smile; but one night, perhaps when the moon floated like a white terrifying balloon over the fences, Eliza was coming back to the Glory Hole; she wanted to see the Fairy Queen for herself; she wasn't afraid of dirty spiders in Fairy Land. Once, in the Magic Cave, she had been taken to a sparkly place and told, 'This is the Fairy Queen and her fairies'; but they weren't, they weren't. They were only big girls dressed up in muslin, and their faces were pink and hot, and the stars on their wands were cardboard silvered over. They smiled and looked apologetic. They didn't know. Little bodies, littler than *little*; and her voice was like a pale chime of bells.

That night, when Carly and Eliza were in bed, and Carly quite asleep, her hair spread like a branch of moonlit brown leaves over her pillow, Eliza heard Mrs Malley's tinkling laugh.

'I can't think where she's put it,' said her mother, vexedly.

'Maybe she's gone to sleep with it, the poor dear. Leave her be till morning. I wouldn't have her waked for worlds. I wouldn't have troubled you, Mrs Hannay, but it's one of a pair, though not worth sixpence, and it does come in handy for my primroses and the little things with short stems. What that boy will be up to next — tunnelling between my wash-house and my own bedroom, drat him.'

'You should put him into engineering,' said John's deep voice, sombre, and with its usual accompaniment of crackling newspaper pages. Just then it was a grievance with him that he had three daughters and no boy.

'A grave-digger would be better. At digging holes in the ground he's the beat of a rabbit, and there's a trade won't go out of fashion.' Mrs Malley's light, rainy laughter sprinkled the dark, like the scent of the dying violets in the shoe beside Eliza's pillow.

Bob tells lies, thought Eliza. That's nothing, so do I, and Carly if she's frightened. But he was pretending, like a grown-up. Littler than little. . . . She saw his serious grey eyes, his freckled nose, and the sawdust slipping down to a thin, fine puddle as he flicked the saw. 'Sissy,' she said to his image, and fell asleep.

In the morning she came in from the garden, where she had broken the lavender shoe and hidden it away in the ash-can, right under the scraped cold porridge, where nobody would ever look, and told Carly she had just seen a fairy.

'You shouldn't tell stories,' said Carly. She was shelling broad beans, and to make her taller she stood on a stool, her white apron, embroidered with a red running-stitch duck, pressed against the kitchen sink. Her hands, very neat and dextrous, made the green beans jump like tiddleywinks out of their white, felt-lined houses. Sometimes she ate one raw; she thought they tasted like kidney. She couldn't bear lentils, because they looked so pulpy-yellow.

'It's not a story. I saw it on a fuchsia, so there.'

'Mummy,' called Carly, 'Eliza's telling stories again.'

Eliza burst into tears. Between her fingers, steepled across her eyes, she saw her mother come into the kitchen, flour smudged across her cheek, one auburn wisp straggling on the forehead which was marked deep between its eyebrows by two vertical lines.

'Carly, whatever is it? Eliza, don't cry like that, you're not a baby. Carly, you're the eldest.'

'She's telling a story,' said Carly, her own soft pink mouth beginning to quiver. 'She said she saw a fairy outside on the fuchsia. You said she wasn't to tell any more stories.'

'I did see it, I did see it.' Eliza faced round, tears channelling her hot cheeks. 'Mummy, aren't there any fairies? Daddy said there were. And I did see it.'

Her mother, speaking indirectly and over her head, said, 'You should remember she's only little, Carly.'

'She's always telling stories.'

'Aren't there any fairies?' persisted Eliza. 'Aren't there, Mummy?'

'Run outside and play,' said Augusta. 'You can have a piece of bread and dripping if you like.' Eliza stopped crying, abruptly, as if she had turned off a tiny tap behind her eyes. She had never really wanted to cry, anyhow, except to find out; they fooled and fooled, and wouldn't answer when you got them in a corner. She heard her mother's voice saying, 'Carly, you'd better soak some lentils for tomorrow,' and knew how Carly would hate that. She sauntered outside. A privet border, low and scanty, cut off the oblong of grass, over which white clothes were drying, sprinkled like great snowflakes. One cypress bush was a hard, compact oval of colour, and a white butterfly made a folded triangle of its wings over the serrated leaves. The underwing had a tear in it, and the butterfly opened and shut its wings very slowly, and moved its feelers as if the effort were far too much for it. Presently it fell to the garden path, and couldn't move. She picked it up and put it back on the bush. Sun stroked its feeble body, but all the colour and passion, the ecstasy with which it had first tossed itself against the spring wind, were fled away. Eliza decided that she would make Carly pay for everyone; for Bob Malley, and Mrs Malley's laughter, and Augusta, and the tired butterfly. 'Because she told,' she thought. That night, when they were together again in the dark, she recited 'The Spanish Mother'.

The woman, shaking off his blood, rose raven-haired and tall,
And our stern glances quailed before one sterner far than all;
"Ho, slayers of the sinewless! ho, tramplers of the weak!
What, shrink ye from the ghastly meats and life-bought wines ye seek?"

'Eliza, stop it, you're frightening me.' Carly's plaintive little voice.

"Poison? Is that your craven fear?" She snatched a goblet up,
And raised it to her queenly head, as if to drain the cup.

'Mother,' shrieked Carly. 'Mother, come quick. Eliza's reciting 'The Spanish Mother' again. Mother, make her stop it.'

Sobs, the dark quaking hummock under the bedclothes that was Carly, a shine of light from the blue enamel light, cutting the shadows in halves. The little flame, flat as a snake's head, wasn't enough to light up the whole room. It showed only the towel-horse, with white towels over it, and Eliza's mother's hair, down and dark red over her shoulders.

'I ought to take the brush to you, young lady.'

But the voice bore no relation to the wild, somehow tameless and beautiful dark red hair, on which the lamplight crept like a rusty moth. Eliza sat up, straining her arms through the darkness.

'I love you, Mummy. I do love you, better than anything.'

'Talk's cheap. Why are you such a naughty girl?'

'I do love you, I do.'

'Oh, I suppose you do.' Eliza's mother sat on the edge of the bed and felt Eliza's hands. 'I can't think why you're so hot; you feel like a burning coal.'

Carly, lying flat and still in the other bed, felt tears round and slip down her cheeks, but she made no sound. It was just like Eliza. But she herself loved their mother best, better than anyone in the world did, much better than Eliza. Carly made even her fingers and toes still, and shut her eyes; when her mother moved away from Eliza's bed, and looking down at her, said, 'Asleep?' in a half-questioning voice, she made no answer. She couldn't bear to be listed second. Yes, she was asleep, asleep, folded away still, not asking for anything. But she made up her mind to get up early in the morning, put on her apron, and polish out the grate, and do all the forks and spoons for a surprise, and mix the porridge without any lumps, so that her father wouldn't growl. When her mother got up, everything would be done. And she would eat the lentils, great soapy yellow chunks of lentils, without a word. Carly's bed rose gently on an enormous, beautiful wave of sleep, and slid her down into a dream as she ticked off the things she would do tomorrow.

When Eliza next saw Bob Malley, she sat on the fence and swung her legs, but never said a word about the Glory Hole. Instead, she sung a derisive chant:

> Giddy, giddy gout,
> Your shirt's hanging out,

over and over. Bob's grey eyes were hurt and surprised. When she wouldn't stop singing, he turned his back and sawed away at a carefully balanced plank, making the pinkish dust fly. A curious white scent, resiny, stained the air, and the steel ribbon flashed and flashed. 'Giddy, giddy gout,' chanted Eliza, until she was tired of it. Then she clambered down and went to the front garden, where the irises pierced up in hard purple spikes, their flags furled. She felt she had paid Bob Malley out. After that, he didn't matter any more, and she could even like him.

Across the street was a row of houses, their tops almost level, gabled, but so small and uninteresting that they looked nowhere near so fine as the wonderful, unpurchasable dolls' house they saw every Christmas Eve, in the Toys Department at the D.I.C.

Every Christmas Eve, John said fretfully that he wasn't going to drag kids into that crowd again, and every Christmas Eve they went. This year, with Sandra on the map, Eliza would have to walk all the way, instead of riding home pick-a-back on her father's shoulder. But they would put a penny in the slot of the gold cage where a jewelled bird broke into a sparkle of song; and when their mother wasn't looking, John would buy them each a penny squeaker, which when blown up and then allowed slowly to expire shrieked like a dying pig. Inside the taut red silk of the squeaker, a little drop of spit would run round, and come out pink through the nozzle. Carly and Eliza would say in a secret whisper, 'What are you going to have?' and Carly would choose the very biggest Teddy Bear, the thirty shilling one, but Eliza would have the dappled grey rocking-horse with the scarlet nostrils. Of course they couldn't have them, but standing at the open mouth of the Magic Cave, where the floor was a litter of purple papers torn off the sixpenny presents given by old red Santa Claus with the false beard, it felt almost the same as if they had bought the shop.

The sky behind the flat houses and the taller brick shape of the Old

Men's Home dipped softly down, a perfect round. It was pale blue, not shiny, not cloudy, but shot with streams of tiny bubbles, all moving upwards in an unending stream. Suddenly Eliza felt awed and happy. She thought, 'Isn't it big . . . isn't it big . . .' She tried to imagine anything bigger than the sky, and failed. The blue curve dipped down far away, just a little beyond shops and houses, and the foam-daisied harbour, and the brown hills. Because it was so big, there was nothing in the world unhappy or uncomforted; they were all streaming and shining up toward it, like the bubbles.

A great Scotch thistle grew inside the gate. She pulled out the thick silk of its thistledown, and ate the white nut underneath. Then she arranged the purple silk in a pattern, making it into a doll's dress. Presently Carly came out, and Eliza showed her what she was doing. Carly fetched her doll, Mrs Trimble, and made her a thistledown dress as well, though her pink rag limbs showed oddly through the rich purple. Carly said, 'When I grow up I'm going to have a white silk dress with silver leaves, right down to my feet,' and Eliza said, 'Mine's going to be crimson lake.' She loved the sound of crimson lake, though she did not know what it meant.

Their father came home, passing the big white hopscotch bases on the pavement, and the other children who were playing French skipping. The Hannays were not supposed to play with them. The little ones, with short thin legs the colour of marigolds, showed their white drawers as they bounced up and down; but the girl Jauncey, who was nearly fourteen and had curly dark hair and a pink dress, skipped in a self-conscious way, though she was very good and it was hard to get her out. John thought, 'Next year she won't skip on the pavements,' and his eyes filled with a vague, transitory regret. He flung his bicycle against the coprosma hedge, and Carly and Eliza came running out to meet him.

'Good for once,' he said, and kissed them, his cheek harsh and rough with its little sprouting bristles. 'Good as good,' said Eliza, rubbing her face against the sandpaper cheek, 'Did you bring us home anything, Daddy?' He laughed, and let her grope about in his pockets. There were two chocolate Teddy Bears. 'Don't tell your Mother,' he said. Carly's eyes stung; she loved chocolate Teddy Bears with an almost holy devotion, but was too shy to say so, so it was purest accident if she ever got one. Clasping the beast, she bit off one foot, then wrapped it up in her handkerchief and put it carefully in her pocket. She was going to make it last — perhaps all night, perhaps for two days. Eliza had eaten hers.

CHAPTER TWO

Little Houses

CARLY showed Mrs Hostler the doll's bed she was making as a present for Sandra, when Sandra came out of the hospital where Dr Porteous had sent her because she had shockin'-tonsils-and-adenoids. It was only two halves of a cardboard box, the lid fitted into the bottom, but Carly had covered it with mauve sateen, and made little looped curtains; her stitches were so small that you couldn't see them on the right side. The penny doll between the sheets had white drawers that you could put on and take off. Mrs Hostler thought it was lovely. 'My, what a clever big sister we have!' she said archly. '*Somebody* will have to take lessons.' Eliza said, 'I think it's silly, drawers on when she's in bed,' and ran outside down the steep path and into the orchard. This belonged to the Hostlers, and the Hannays, who shared the house, were supposed to have no part or lot in it. Mr Hostler had painted the apple-trees rough white. Loganberries grew between them, their little fruits still tart but edible, squashing into purple stains on the fingers. Eliza took some, knowing that Mrs Hostler would notice, and say when they met in the hall, '*Now* I know the little bird who's been stealing my loganberries.'

Carly was Mrs Hostler's pet, especially now that Augusta went down every afternoon to see Sandra in the Children's Hospital; Mrs Hostler taught her to cook, and Carly topped and tailed all the gooseberries for jam, and was called 'the little housekeeper'. Eliza would rather have liked to make big preserving-pans bubble and froth into scum, then clear, dark colours as well; but everybody took it for granted that she wouldn't, and she was too vain to ask. She was half afraid of Mrs Hostler, half-contemptuous. Mr Hostler was a carpenter, a meek-looking brownish little man, who spent most of his time underground, like a goblin, in his cellar workshop. Sometimes he let Eliza play with the peeled shavings, and called her Old Hostler's Beauty, but he seldom went against his wife. They were both very religious, and their house was hung with huge illuminated texts, saying, 'Behold the Lamb of God', and 'Though thy sins be red as scarlet, they shall be washed whiter than wool'. (Scarlet . . . lovely word. Carly was religious too.) On the wall in Mrs Hostler's bedroom hung a pale-blue silk brush-and-comb bag, and net hair-tidies in which she collected the bits of hair that fell out, to make them into a switch. Her little Swiss clock ticked dark and

13

stealthily, and had a painted cuckoo that stuck his head out when the hours struck.

Below the orchard spread the crinkly azure and cream shawls of Lyall and Evans Bays, with Island Bay right far away, a blue dent in the sky; a sheer drop of yellow cliffs and sultry-smelling gorse came in between, and Eliza could nearly pick out the strange house which had greenstone on its chimneys, and for its gate the white jawbone of a whale. The lions in Newtown Zoo gave their desolate yawning roar, a browny-gold sound that turned black as night came on. The house was so near the Melrose cliff-tops that the children weren't supposed to go out at the back, in case they should fall over. But now Eliza said loudly, 'I don't care,' and marched through the latchet gate into the wilderness where brown gorse arched above her head. Everywhere came the fusillades of the spitting, crackling seeds. Sometimes she could persuade Carly to come too, and they built whares, little secret houses among the gorse, and lined them with the soft flamy petals. And she ran such a fierce gorse-prickle into her finger that it had to have a bread-poultice two nights running, though Mrs Hostler had wanted to Christian-Science it, the same as she had with little Carol Kissin. The Kissins, who lived three houses away, were the only children the Hannays were allowed to play with. Loveday, who had silvery hair and was ten, older than Carly, went to Sunday School, and made herself rather superior, except when they lost themselves playing hide-and-seek in the lovely dark green wilderness of Tonks' old place, which had up a 'Trespassers Will Be Prosecuted' notice, but which nobody ever visited except the children and the footraces of undersized wild daffodils. Loveday's brother, Carol, was only two. His curls were beautiful, as pretty as Sandra's, but silvery instead of pale gold. But he was fat and stupid, and used to sit still like a little pudding, only laughing when you rolled something shiny at him — the lid of a tobacco tin, or a glass alley. Mrs Hostler and Augusta used to talk about him, in those hushed voices which at once made you want to listen. 'It's pitiful, that's what it is,' would say Augusta's voice-you-are-not-supposed-to-hear; and Mrs Hostler, 'If only his mother would read the works of that blessed woman, Mary Baker Eddy!' One day, Carol Kissin disappeared from his place in the melting sun; it was strange, as strange as if the top layer of garden, where the fowl-run used to be, had suddenly been transposed with the lower streak of wallflowers. At table the Hannay children were told they must be kind to poor Loveday, because her little brother was dead.

'What did he die of?' asked Carly, awed. Her mother said, 'He was just taken quietly away to Jesus,' but John snorted behind a newspaper, and ejaculated, 'Water on the brain.'

John was one reason why Mrs Hostler wouldn't ever be allowed to Christian-Science Eliza's prickle or Sandra's tonsils-and-adenoids. Lying on her stomach, with the brown hot earth beating up at her in little flakes of grass, little crawling stiff-winged things, jewel-flies and beetles, Eliza thought she wouldn't mind dying at all. She wished the ground would capsize in one great landslide, carrying her far down into the sea, whose blossoms of foam tossed and tossed on the scalloped beaches. She went as near to the edge as she dared — just to show them. But though she didn't mind the idea of being dead, the idea of pain terrified her. She cried all night when she had the gorse-prickle, cried at the top of her voice, until she hadn't the faintest idea where the pain left off and just crying began. Then John behaved, as Augusta said, like a raging lion, storming about the house and shouting: 'You've got to get her something. You've got to stop that row. I don't care whether it's good for her or not, I won't have that howling. I have to get up in the mornings and work for your children. A man might as well be dead as live in this house, with a lot of damned women and lunatics.'

Old Mr Hostler was working in his cellar when Eliza climbed up the garden path. She slipped quietly through the cellar door, and shut her eyes for a moment before she looked at what he was making, half hoping that it would be, half that it wouldn't be; but of course it was — the Wonderful Dolls' House. Mr Hostler was making it for his nephew, Young George, who lived in the country and had girly ways, owing to a weak chest which kept him home from school. The bathroom with the real little lavatory was finished, and now Mr Hostler was making the flagstaff. There was a penny Union Jack lying on the bench, ready to be hoisted. He whittled a little knob at the top of the flagstaff, and talked to Eliza without turning round. 'Ah,' he said, 'don't seem natural for a boy, this don't, sickly and all as he is. But flesh and blood's flesh and blood, kith and kin's kith and kin, you can't get away from that.' Eliza said, 'What colour are you going to paint the tower room?' She hoped it would be green, although Young George was getting the dolls' house. The stair to the tower was a spiral, wonderfully made, some of its steps so narrow that even the feet of penny dolls would have a hard time edging up it. Mr Hostler's back, in its striped shirt and dingy waistcoat, looked almost humped as he bent over the plane. White sunbeams came down through the dusty window, queer, like potatoes that have just sprouted. She picked up a shaving-curl, and threw it over her left shoulder, making the initial of her future sweetheart. 'It's G,' she said, staring at it, 'I hope it's not George.'

'My name's George, as well as the young feller,' said Mr Hostler. 'Wouldn't you have me for a sweetheart? Who's old Hostler's Beauty?' After a moment, Eliza smiled and said she was, but the spiral staircase and the unpinned Union Jack left a pain across her chest.

John in these days snorted more and more behind his newspaper. He disliked the Hostlers, because they were too religious; and besides that, he had to get up at six in the morning, cycle all the way to town, and push his bicycle up the Melrose hill again after dark. At first, when they left Oriri Street, he was all eagerness and plans, as he always was at a new place; but the cycling had worn him down, and he called Mr Hostler a damned old sanctimonious fool. He didn't mind Mrs Hostler's religion quite so much; but then, Eliza had noticed, Daddy always seemed not to mind women, while Augusta, though she gave young men the rough edge of her tongue, was inwardly tolerant towards them.

John's swearing started at Melrose. Carly said it was awful, but the children were fascinated by it, though Carly afterwards spent distracted hours warning Sandra, 'You mustn't ever say that, or the Devil will get you.'

'Damn and blast your bicycles,' he shouted, 'I'm sick of riding your damn-and-blasted bicycles. Damn and blast your hills. I won't go on living on a precipice to please you. We're going down to the flat.'

'Before your own children . . .'

'Damn and blast my children. I didn't ask to have children.'

Augusta changed her tack. 'We can't live in town. You know perfectly well the rents are too high.'

'Then we can live in Newtown.'

'That slum . . . I suppose I can bring your children up in a hovel, with a public-house next door, and a lot of dirty, drunken loafers hanging over your gate. Or perhaps you'd like Haining Street? The hill air's healthy for your children.'

'Then bring up your children on your damn-and-blasted precipice. I'm going out.'

Slam of a door, and John was gone; during these quarrels, Carly, Eliza and Sandra automatically became 'your children' to both sides. Augusta said dramatically, 'You're responsible for bringing them into this world,' and their father, darkly, 'Oh, I am, am I?'

'Where's Haining Street?' Eliza asked Carly. Carly looked important and nervous.

'It's the place where the Chinese dens are. Don't tell Mummy I told you. We're not supposed to talk about it'

'What's a Chinese den?'

'Don't talk so loud. You always go and blurt everything out.' Carly was on the verge of tears, so Eliza said, 'Oh, all right,' and sauntered away, trying to imagine the man who came round at the back door, selling French beans and wilted lettuces, sitting on a concrete floor like a lion with slim steel bars blackening his face. She found Carly's doll, Mrs Trimble, lying on the steps above the wallflower patch, and shook it gently, so that its round scarred head wagged from side to side. 'Damn and blast my children,' she said, 'I didn't ask to have any children.' But she said it softly; Augusta would use the hairbrush if she knew.

Strife among the Hannays made the illuminated texts rattle, and little Mr Hostler, in his meek and mild way, protested to John. That gave him the excuse he was looking for. He wouldn't stay another day under a roof where he'd been insulted. He looked fierce, all red and thin and flamy-eyed, when he was in this mood, and Augusta gave in.

Immediately John was charming again. Carly, Eliza, and Sandra were 'the children', and even 'our children', and he said happily that in Newtown he could take them to the Zoo and the pictures.

'And bring home a lot of germs. And where's the money for pictures coming from, may I ask?'

'Oh, look on the bright side for once,' demanded John, impatiently. Again Eliza felt secretly that he was right, and hoped they were going to live in Haining Street, among the Chinese dens. But there were no Chinese at all in Newbold Street. Rows and rows of grimy little streets and terraces, mostly very flat, crawled listlessly from the shopping centre and the big concrete block of the hospital to the green garment's hem of the bay. Newtown in its half-century of life had contrived to get itself very dirty: and it was static, nothing there would change. Always little houses, little shops, the tramway sheds, the Heddington Arms, with a tower on top and orange paper flowers showing through unwashed windows. Where it fused with Town, near the Basin Reserve which had been under water until an earthquake tossed it up, it was a melting-pot of Asiatic shops and quarters, narrow wooden houses in which old Chinese smoked opium and cut greasy cards, or thin-legged, great-eyed Hindoos carried on their business as small fruiterers, ripening bananas under their beds. The

Orientals were merely Oriental, and too poor for elaboration; white slatterns had settled down among them, like a covey of gulls on ship's waste.

Stepping down from the hills was a blow from which Augusta took years to recover. It used up all her softness, all she had in hand besides fortitude and pride. Whenever she won some little advantage, a neighbour who could be called 'nice,' a patch of lawn, a few yards of garden which John refused to dig, something went wrong; and the furniture-van, drawn by the sage old heavy-breathing horses, pulled up outside their doors again. Sparrows picked at the heaps of manure, children bright-eyed and feckless as sparrows ran past with bare legs and drippy noses, while Augusta stood on the pavement shrieking 'Mind that table!' John lost the bicycle, but on the flats caught rheumatism, bibliomania and politics, none of which he could afford. Augusta's children were never slum children: she dominated John where his pay envelopes were concerned, though it cost her her youth. They caught minor diseases, measles and scarlatina, and Eliza cried terribly at the slightest pain. But Augusta, usually severe with them, could not bring herself to shut Eliza's mouth with a strap. Once she said, 'I believe it's because I made such a fuss when she was born that she goes on like this.'

Eliza neither knew nor cared. All she understood was that when she was in pain it hadn't any special place; it wouldn't stay in her tooth, or in the little finger Sandra broke with a cricket-bat, but spread in great waves, until it occupied every cranny of her. And she couldn't remember a time when it had not been, or imagine another time when it would have gone away. When it left her she sobbed and sobbed herself into exhaustion, and the pillows felt lovely, and the dark room with its blinds drawn was full of wavy blue light, rolling towards her like a sea; or sometimes the process was reversed, and the blue light-cords streamed outwards from her temples. At this stage she was very passive and obedient, never likely to blame anyone because she had been hurt, but looking up at them with swollen eyes, sure that they would bring relief. Her father, who was proud of her when she was gay, came in sometimes to stand at her bedside, muttering, 'I can't make you out at all.'

The empty houses, when they moved, had a kind of fascination; shells, with sunlight rippling and fawning in oblong patches on their naked floors. Augusta's sticks of furniture never quite fitted the new place. There were days of paring and patching worn linoleum, and always another auction sale, where she bid in sixpences for odd chairs and tables; the auctioneer, stout and red-faced, seized the handle of the chamber, and shouted, 'And what am I bid for this 'ere jerry?'

At the auctions Eliza was allowed to wander about, to see the restless unhappiness of old houses turned inside out, like the baby octopi fished up by swart Italians at Island Bay. They were turned inside out like gloves, and their stomachs were cream bags. . . . There were things she wanted, ticketed on round red labels — cabinets whose curly drawers shot out at pressure on a lacquer knob, a rocking-chair creaking dimly as if ghosts sat in it, queer-titled books done up in bundles. Once she saw a dark-varnished thing, like a little towel-horse, but with a wheel attached.

'What is it, Mummy?'

'It's a spinning-wheel.'

'Oh.' The idea of spinning-wheels dipped back into fairy books, into the tower of the Sleeping Beauty, with thorny white roses nodding through her windows. 'Can you spin, Mother?'

'My mother could,' Augusta said; then, as if unawares she had entered the sleeping forest herself, she added softly, 'Her christian name is Leonora. She had lovely little hands.'

Eliza wanted to ask if her grandmother had any other romantic qualifications. Augusta said, defensively, 'When I was born, she had only one neighbour within twenty miles, and that was an old Irishwoman, ignorant as Paddy's pig, who smoked a black pipe. To this day I remember her with her black pipe in her mouth. Once she took me to a wake. That was near a great lake, with thousands and thousands of black swans. You never see them in such numbers, except in Western Australia. And the boys used to be called "the Mallee Giants".'

They didn't buy the spinning-wheel, but took home a wringer. 'It'll be such a mercy,' said Augusta, stopping in the garden, out of sight of red faces and red labels, to scoop up a root of mignonette. Stealing plants from derelict gardens, or pods and clippings when they swarmed over her fences, was her only form of dishonesty.

But when a municipal edict changed the shape of their world, transferring them from Newtown to Oddipore, Augusta broke the law. Carly had been going to school for three years, and Eliza had just started. Their headmaster, Mr Forrest, was a quiet man with a pointed grey beard, and Augusta pinned her faith in him. She said, 'At least he's a gentleman,' and the children knew that this meant he could do almost anything, if he liked, without being permanently in the wrong. He could even drink. . . . Not that Mr Forrest ever did. Of the new district and its mandatory new school, she would hear no good. What prejudiced her was a tramwayman's poem, published in the evening paper:

> But the thing that makes me sore,
> On the tramcar — 'lectric tramcar —
> Is the kids from Oddipore;
> Wipes their noses on the windows,
> Licks the glass — that makes me sick. . . .

'It's bad enough living where we do,' she said, 'but to that school they're not going.'

John protested lazily about the Truant Officer, but she said sharply 'Hold your tongue. It's you who dragged us here, but whether you like it or not, my children won't be brought up with gutter-brats.'

Carly and Eliza got up at seven, their usual hour. It was pitch dark in the winter-time, and so cold that they slept with John's old coats thrown over their beds. But they washed with yellow soap in cold water, and Carly helped Eliza to dress — combinations, knickers, bodices, flannelette petticoats with herringbone stitch around the necks, and finally their frocks. All the other children in the district still wore long white drawers, and when Carly, bending over, accidentally revealed that she had red knickers, matching her frock, she was mortified by yells of 'Red Trousis, Red Trousis,' from the rough Macartney boys. Carly's straight brown hair was tied behind in a pony tail, but Eliza's had to be curled round somebody's finger. They blacked their boots, which did up with twenty buttons to each boot; Carly helped Eliza with the silver buttonhook. At table John, though already at the beginning of his atheistic stage, bowed his head and said rapidly, 'For what we are about to receive the Lord make us truly thankful, for Christ's sake, Amen. 'Gusta, for the love of Mike, can't you change to another oatmeal? This porridge is full of lumps.' 'It suits the children, and the children come first,' Augusta retorted. The children, their porridge sprinkled with brown sugar and channelled with thin milk, ate silently, Carly thinking of the day when she would have a shilling a week pocket money and buy nothing but chocolate Teddy Bears. After cocoa (Eliza's in a lustre mug which showed the face of an angel when she had drunk the last sugary brown drop), they stood up for final grooming, and said, 'Please may we leave the table?' Augusta kissed them gravely, saying, 'Carly, mind Eliza doesn't lose those mittens. And see you go straight off to school.' John, who had rushed to the bathroom and was making sandpaper noises against his golden-brown bristles, shouted, 'So long, kiddies!'

At school the Hannays went to Mr Forrest's office, and, gazing timidly at their old headmaster, asked, 'Please, Mr Forrest, may we stop at school to-day?'

The law was the law. They were none of Mr Forrest's any more. He could only jut out his sharp little beard, and say gravely, 'I'm afraid not. You see, you have been transferred to the Oddipore roll.' To this Carly's strategic move was, 'Please, Mr Forrest, our mother said to give you this note.' Mr Forrest read the unvarying contents.

Dear Mr Forrest,

I do not want my children to be transferred from your school, as I am satisfied that they are well off where they are. I hope you will arrange for them to continue with you.

Yours faithfully,
Augusta Hannay.

When Mr Forrest dismissed them, like a couple of privates strangely sent off to fight for the wrong Emperor, they didn't have to present themselves at the new school, that profane institution where kids wiped their noses on the windows and licked the glass, making tramwaymen sick. Nor were they to go home, because the Truant Officer might catch them. Within the bounds of the Museum, the Park or the Zoo, they were free.

The Museum was upstairs, above the Children's Library, to which Carly belonged. At the foot of the staircase sat an old man in a skullcap, with white whiskers, red cheeks, rheumy blue eyes — a Union Jack face. A notice against his severe profile read 'Children Not Admitted Unless Accompanied by Adults.'

Carly, holding Eliza's mittened hand, remarked in her deferential way, 'Please, we won't touch anything.'

Pale eyes peered out under bushy brows, like whelks from their shells.

'Can't you read, Miss?'

'Please, we'll be very careful, and not touch anything.'

'Passel of children romping. . . . Up you go, up you go, and just listen to this. Don't let me find any dirty fingermarks on my glass cases, or I know who's going to catch What For.'

Carly loved the gold-painted chunk of wood that pretended to be the biggest nugget ever found. She didn't know why, but love it she did. Eliza stared at the bird; albatrosses strung on wires, their great wings snowy over the arches between room and room. In one case two olive-green birds hung over a baby lamb, its woolly back all thick and sticky with painted blood. They had torn its kidneys out. The notice read, 'New Zealand Keas and Lamb'. But the humming-birds set among mossy branches were the littlest things in the world, some soaring through space, some drinking with needle bills. On bodies small as sovereigns, the wonderful plumage, purple, green, rose, sparkled and shone. Wherever you stood to look at them, they sparkled afresh, sparkled behind your eyes and in your heart. As you went down the stairs, they flew in a wreath after you, little and calling to one another. This was well; for at the stairhead stood the Reconstructed Moa, higher than a tall man, tailless, almost wingless, but mighty, and armed with striking spurs broader than a man's hand. Eliza was scared, though the notice said, 'This Bird Is Extinct'. It was hard not to run down the dusky stairs, but running and noise were forbidden, so they crept like mice past the old man, who mumbled, 'No messy fingerprints on my cases, that I do hope.'

Outside, the wind took ragged bits of paper and threw them up like a boy flying kites. The streets ran flat and straight to Newtown Park and Zoo. They could play in the cricketing grounds, and in the Zoo on week-days, when it was free, but not in the pine-tree part, or the wilderness of grasses beyond the rosery; because there they might meet a man.

Eliza asked why they shouldn't meet a man, and Carly replied, 'Because he might be drunk.' But when they really did meet a drunken man, crossing a stile in a permitted stretch of the park, Eliza liked him at once. He couldn't climb over the stile, and stood bowing and wobbling on the top step.

'Come on, let's run,' breathed Carly. The drunk man bowed from his middle, and shouted, 'L'il girl, like half-crown?' He flung silver on the path — not one half-crown, but a whole pile. 'Come on,' urged Carly. Eliza said, 'Wait a minute,' and picked up the half-crowns. The drunk man called, 'Good-bye, l'il girl!' and she waved her hand at him. Half-way home, she saw a wonderful rainbow, dipping like silk over dusty Newtown, and stopped in her tracks.

'Carly, look. It's a rainbow It's lucky to see a rainbow.'

'Will you come on?'

'But it's such a lovely one, rose and green; wouldn't you like to have a silk dress that colour?'

'You're always stopping,' said Carly, the tears beginning to trickle, 'You just do it to get me into trouble, because I'm the eldest.'

When Augusta saw the half-crowns, she seized Eliza's hand and dragged her back, at a rapid trot, to the Park. For an hour she hunted about, looking for the drunken man, but he had vanished like the rainbow. Eliza thought then that they might keep the half-crowns, but Augusta dropped them in a coldly gleaming little pool beside the stile.

'I wanted a rocking-horse,' sobbed Eliza.

'I want you to be a good little girl who doesn't talk to horrible drunkards.' Their points of view didn't fit in. Eliza whined, 'Don't go so fast, I've got a stitch in my side.'

'You should have thought of that before. My dinner's on, and I've no time to loiter.'

'Daddy got drunk once, and I hit him over the head with my hobby horse,' said Eliza. Augusta's profile went bleak and set, though she only said, 'Trust you for remembering.' Eliza wondered, 'What is the little jumpy thing that makes you talk out loud when you promised you weren't going to?'

On Sundays, where the pines sloped towards turf and bandstand, the Highlanders came marching up the Park road, and the pipes, far away, started a dancing feel in one's body. The bandstand was a wooden octagon; so many people had sat on its plank seats that they sagged at both ends. Rusty, rusty needles, and the blowing pipes mixed up, and the lions roared yellow. Children weren't allowed by themselves in the swinging-boats, but if John was in a good temper, he climbed into the boat and worked it up until they were the highest, higher than any of the other children, glancing down on a floating green and brown world, with lions roaring in great sagging voices on the other side of the barbed-wire fence. Their mother stood by, saying, 'Be careful when you get out — there was a little girl who got her head cut open, running under one of these wretched things.' John only laughed, and pulled the creaking iron stays higher still, and freckled light, in tiny rainbows, streaked through the lashes of tight-shut eyes.

Then they went to the Zoo, where the camel had moulted in patches, and mangy lions rubbed their galled sides against the bars, and stared out with blank desert-coloured eyes. Eliza didn't mind old King Dick or Queen Mary, but always wanted to run away from Blackmane in the other cage. He roared so, and the bars were so thin. But when the keeper dragged great purplish shanks of dead horse up to the trapdoors, and thrust them through with an iron pole, she pressed close with the rest, and pretended to be pleased as the lions pawed and growled. It was a great attraction at the Zoo, special notices told the feeding-times; and nobody would ever know that she hated it. 'If I could only do something awfully brave,' she thought, knowing that she never would. The lion cubs were ginger footballs, to be rolled over and cuffed; they had silly, knowing, pathetic faces, like Louis Wain kittens. Sometimes when the big lions were feeding, the keeper went into the cubs' den, and held them up, grinning from ear to ear. He was a thin boy, sickly pale under a peaked cap, but Eliza thought him braver than Dr Livingstone.

Often Carly and Eliza wandered off together, while Augusta sat on a bench and sewed, and John took Sandra walking among the Sunday crowds. She was dispossessing Eliza, in public, anyhow; always some woman remarked, 'Oh, hasn't she got the sweetest little curls?' and John beamed. Sandra's solemn eyes were like bluebells. She was dressed in cream, short little corduroy velvet jacket and kilted skirt, and when Grandmother-Hannay-in-China sent money at Christmas to buy the children muffs, Carly and Eliza got commonplace brown ones, but Sandra's was silky white, like Polar bear.

Carly pulled at her sister's sleeve and said, 'Come along. You're not to stand looking at the monkeys, Eliza.'

'Why not?'

'Because monkeys are dirty. Besides, if you do, people look at you. Come and see the bear.'

'But I don't want — '

'Mother says so,' pronounced Carly. There were several other things at the Zoo that mustn't be looked at. If they saw men coming out of the Gentlemen's Only, they must look the other way; then there was the Fire-Bellied Newt, which lived under a soggy green mass of reeds and branches in the stone caves called 'The Aquarium.' 'Mother says belly's a rude word,' said Carly simply. 'Come and see the sea-lions.' They saw the sea-lions, which gulped down live gleaming fish and waddled about on amusing flippers, but had no fiery bellies. When they got back, John was encouraging Sandra to roll down the grass bank, heedless of the dark-green stains she made on her white pants. 'It's Mother who has to wash them,' said Carly. Over and over flashed Sandra's fat legs, their short cream socks crumpled. A lean man at John's elbow said, 'That's a proper little hard case you've got, Hannay,' and John laughed his best-pleased laugh. The daisies had the primmest of shocked blushes on their round faces, and the air smelt of bitty grass. Eliza, furiously jealous, climbed the stone pillar at the foot of the steps, and sat down in the sort of jampot left for geraniums, a hard weedy square. Her legs stuck out over the sides. It was quite a long way down, and she thought, 'I might fall and break my arm, I might easily.' But John was too much taken up with Sandra to notice her, and it was Augusta's voice that said tartly, 'Get down, and don't show off.'

There grew up a difference between Carly and Eliza. First it was only that Carly was the eldest, but then it grew wide and authoritative. Carly liked doing the things she was told; Carly didn't see little pictures in the dark. She would play, but she had to be told, she didn't originate; and she was far happier left alone with her dolls, or helping Augusta.

Augusta said tragically over the back fence to Mrs Protheroe, their really nice neighbour, 'I don't know what to do with Eliza. She finds old men behind bushes in the Park, and asks them home to tea.' 'A good, hearty smack,' said Mrs Protheroe, and indicated where. John roared with laughter. 'Yes,' said Augusta, 'but you'd be the first to carry on like a lunatic if anything happened to her.' 'Oh, 'Gusta,' inconclusively replied Eliza's father, and left it at that. To Eliza, who was playing in the backyard, their queer talk only made her old men seem more interesting.

Old Mr Boad started behind a bush in the Park, a pink escallonia with sticky little rose-pink flowers and dark, poisonous leaves. But he was such a quiet, inoffensive old man, and rambled so much about the England he had known in his youth (Augusta's beloved, unattainable England) that he was not only allowed to stay for tea, but became for a brief while a domestic pet. Then, one day, Augusta said, 'If you meet that old Mr Boad in the street, don't you go talking to him.'

'Why mustn't we talk to him?'

'Run along, and don't ask questions.' The children never met old Mr Boad in the street; but once, when he was first ill, and begged to see them, Carly and Eliza were allowed to visit him together, just for five minutes. He didn't seem changed, except that when he was saying goodbye he kissed them, and told them to grow up like their dear mother; and he gave Carly a tiny white-and-gold cup, marked 'Souvenir From Brighton', which Eliza thought unfair.

When he was dying in hospital, he sent for Augusta in the middle of the night, and she got up at once. They heard her saying, 'Give me my stole, John,' while their father grumbled, 'Might wait till morning.' With the clipped astrakhan stole pinned round her shoulders, she marched off to the hospital, and old Mr Boad told the nurses she was an angel of God, and died quite peaceably. Years before, his wife had divorced him for adultery: and someone had passed the story on to Augusta, after he began to visit their house.

Adultery was a fantastic and disgraceful disease, like ringworm. It was all very well to cry and be sorry, but if you had it, then you must be isolated. Old Mr Boad, at the bottom of his heart, not only respected Augusta's point of view, but shared it. It gave him a melancholy satisfaction to be an incurable sinner, not merely a lonely old cancer-ridden man with a walking stick, trailing about the streets of Wellington. Sin is better company than none at all.

There were still Eliza's drain-men, who came every week, halting their blue dray outside the windows. They lifted the gratings of the street sewers, and dug down with long-handled shovels, making plopping sounds and a horrible, penetrating stench as they splashed dollops of mud into their dray. Once Curly Adams' bag of marbles, glimmers and chalkies, came up on the shovel, and the drain-men gave them to Eliza. 'Here you are, Topsy.' She wished they would take her for a ride on the blue dray, out and out, trundling into nowhere, past the rim of little dusty streets. But when she asked the drain-man, he only turned to his mate and laughed.

'Here's a little 'un wants to come along of us, Bill. What price the Missus?'

Bill said, 'Aw, I'm tired of me missus, anyhow,' but they never took Eliza, and the dray rumbled off, leaving the drains clean and empty. Augusta bobbed her head out of the window. 'Eliza, come away from those smelly drains this very minute. Do you want to catch a fever?'

The Hannays never caught a fever, but the Macartney children did, which according to Augusta was no wonder, for the way they lived would have disgraced an ordinary, decent-minded pig. They lived three doors down the street and had great brown freckles, running together all over their splayed features; and Katrine Macartney had Things in her red hair. When they took the scarlet fever in a batch, and were sent off in the ambulance to be isolated at the Tin Shed — the fever hospital — Augusta sent them custards and jellies, though ordinarily she didn't talk to Mrs Macartney, who stood with shiny red arms akimbo, talking about Holy Jasus and the Blessed Mother of God. When the Macartneys came back from the Tin Shed, they were thinner and temporarily cleaner, but wilder than ever. Katrine had holes in her bloomers, which oppressed

Carly with deep vicarious shame. All day long they skipped on the footpath, singing:

Handy-pandy-sugary-candy, French-almond-*nuts*,
Bread-an'-butter for me supper, that's all ter put in guts,

or:

House ter-let, apply within,
People turned out fer drinking gin,
I saw Peter hanging out the winder,
Bang, fire, *pop*.

Sometimes what they sang was much worse, so Carly gave them a wide berth, dragging Eliza at her heels.

Augusta, the Truant Officer, Mr Forrest and John were all getting weary of the change of schools war, though Augusta, having started it, wouldn't give in. For a whole month the Hannays had been outlaws. Once they were stopped in the street by a tall, serious man, who wrote their names down in a black book. When they told Augusta, the frown between her eyebrows grew deeper, and she said, 'That was the Truant Officer.' The children were awed, though Eliza played an after-dark game in which they danced round the Truant Officer and put out their tongues, like the Macartneys.

It was John who settled the war. One night, after supper, he opened fire from behind his newspaper.

'Well, 'Gusta, I hope you like the new house.'

'New house? What are you talking about?'

'Number Nine, Calver Street. I've rented it for a year. It's nearer the children's new school.'

'John, my children aren't going to that school.'

'Their names are down on the roll. I had a chat yesterday with the head — Bellew. He's a perfectly decent fellow, and the building's up-to-date. There's been no occasion for all this ridiculous fuss. Besides, there's too much din about the house. I won't have the children brought up like street arabs.'

'That's like you, after all the trouble I take, slaving day in, day out, over your house and your children.'

'Well, look at Eliza.' (That was mean, Eliza thought; there was no need for her father to look at Eliza, when half the time he had a hand in Eliza's doings himself.) 'They're not going into that dirty street.'

'Then settle yourself where the rent money's coming from. I gave notice here a week ago, and I've paid down a month's rent at the new place. You should have married a millionaire, while you were about it.' John folded his paper, and strolled out. He didn't have to argue any more. Money always had the last say, with £1/19/- a week to keep three children, and nothing to help out but occasional packages or postal notes from Grandmother-Hannay-in-China.

For a week Augusta returned white and tired from the Calver Street house, firing off little strings of questions at supper.

'I suppose you know the bottom's nearly out of that kitchen sink you picked at Calver Street?'

'Not a chimney fit to use, except the one in the kitchen, and that smokes. No fires this winter. We can sit over a stove.'

John, puffing his short pipe, said, 'We'll see.' Until he got really uncomfortable, he would stand by the new house, because he had picked it behind Augusta's back. Parents, parents were funny people.

Mrs Protheroe came in to help with their packing, while the children sat on boxes in the hall. Sandra had been crying with toothache. Her short fair curls glistened wet, and her cheek smelt of vinegar. The little glittering ice-ship, sent by Grandmother-in-China, still hung on the gas-bracket. They had often used it for playing Explorers, and nobody had the heart to take it down. Augusta, outside in the back garden, scraped at her stolen ice-plants and pansies. Her voice came through the door, odd and choky.

'It's no use. They'll never grow again. There's no garden, only an asphalt yard.'

'There, dear; have you remembered to butter Tam's paws? *Such* a nice gentlemanly cat.'

'I used to sit up in the old fig-trees, with a vineyard in front of me a mile long. And the birds. Little did I think I'd ever come to this. Why did I get married?'

'You wouldn't be without the children, dear.' When Augusta came in, the lines between her brows looked as if they had been carved with a sharp knife, but she tidied the children's coats and bonnets without a word.

They were sent to the school that was no longer theirs, to knock on Mr Forrest's door. 'Please, Mr Forrest,' Carly recited, 'Mother said we were to

thank you for all you've done, and we're very sorry to leave your school.'
Mr Forrest shook hands with them. His face looked grey and solemn.

On the way back, Eliza tried hard to remember she was very sorry; she
liked to be sad, except when she actually *was*; then it was unbearable. But
she could think only of the time Laurie Helmer accidentally cut a little
girl's head open with his cricket bat, and the wound had to be stitched.
And that other day, when three of them cheated, and she was one.
Standing out in front of the class, with 'I am a Cheat,' chalked up on a
slate; standing all the afternoon.

It was harder for Carly. She was older, and worshipped Miss Calman,
whose hair blew into little light-dusty rings as she hurried across the
playground. Carly sniffled as she walked. She was sure she would never
like any other teacher so much. Perhaps the new teachers would be men;
she hated men, and was afraid of them.

The house in Calver Street was square and empty. It looked little as a
matchbox. The sun had gone, and no patch of white light rippled
laughing on the floor. Augusta said, 'You children will sleep in here,' and
opened a door. The bedroom was ordinary in every way, except that
outside its window leaned a wattle tree — not the Australian mimosa
kind, but the powder-puff tree, its greenish-gold brushes heavily laden
with pollen.

Eliza plumped down on the bed. 'This is my tree,' she said.

'You always want everything.'

'I said it first. It's my tree.'

'Oh, I don't want your old tree. You can have it. I don't like wattle
trees, anyhow. I'm going outside to help Mummy unpack.'

Carly ran out of the room. Eliza, left to herself, felt curiously lonely.
She wouldn't follow Carly, but she wished she had thought of unpacking
for herself. Opening trunks was fun.

On the opposite side of the street a lamp suddenly went on. It was
electric, though the houses had only gas. The light clung on its wooden
post, like a cold little luminous bug; she peered through the window, and
could see nothing but dusk and one great daisy-bush. Beyond that ran
Calver Street.

CHAPTER THREE

Bird of my Native Land

Drift, logs, drift, down the shining stream,
Drift, logs, drift, down the shining stream —

Then some lines Eliza couldn't remember; but after them came:

Batyushka gosudar,
Wan wanes thy setting star,
Fallen art thou, the Great White Czar.

Lovely, with the memory of a thousand deaths packed into it; almost the only lovely thing that had ever been printed in the school journal. Batyushka gosudar. . . . She thought of Mr Duncan, who took the classes for mathematics and singing, and called him 'Batyushka gosudar'. It had to mean something good enough for Mr Duncan. He had a round face and a little red moustache, rather like a cat's, and a round bald spot on the top of his head. Nevertheless . . .

Carly nowadays stopped late at cooking-school, bringing home little piedishes and basins filled with bright-green arrowroot jelly and awful macaroni cheese. Her mouth drooped if after the first spoonful Augusta said, 'I don't think I will to-night darling. I haven't much of an appetite,' and John always growled, 'Why can't they teach girls something sensible?' But John and Carly didn't get on, that was an established household fact.

Carly's cooking-lessons left Eliza free to go home alone. She was old enough now to cross the flat little streets and the tramlines by herself; nearly eight years old. The school cloakroom smelt of wet mackintoshes and Jeyes' Fluid, and outside, the playground was chalked with big white rings for marbles, squares for hopscotch bases. Girls and boys, though sometimes they joined in ring games, played marbles quite differently. The girls rolled their marbles gingerly up against the school walls, but the boys knelt at the side of the big rings, and very deliberately cannoned one another's rosies and glimmers out of the way. You could practise it when they had gone, and nobody was about, but somehow the trick never came off; besides, the other girls preferred their own way of playing. There wasn't any set reason why it should be so, it just was, like wearing pinafores and frocks instead of trousers, and the fact that boys could collect cigarette cards, but if they saved the coloured cards you got inside Toblerones, they were sissies.

Funny, darkling world of boys. Once two were nearly expelled for writing things on the cloakroom wall. Carly and Eliza didn't know what things, the chalk had been washed off before anyone had a chance to look. There were four sorts of boys; the ones Mother called nice, like Arnold Newbigin, who played on his mouth-organ at St Monica's Church social, and wore big round specs; the hoarse-voiced, growing-up ones, with patched pants and large raw knees, like Bill Tybolt, who had to sit beside Eliza in class as a punishment for being so bad at arithmetic, and who kicked her ankles when Mr Duncan wasn't looking; the seven Orphans, who were industrious, but wore hideous yellow trousers and marched away in a little procession every afternoon, somehow isolated and queer; and the Duffel Street boys, who were like the Macartneys, only much worse. They had great cowslip freckles, sprawling together, and nits in their hair. More than one of them had been scrubbed with carbolic over the school lavatory basins, and once the nits had escaped into the ranks of the righteous, and every child in class had to be carbolic'd and kerosened. Augusta wasn't satisfied with that. She shut her family up in the porch and blew sulphur fumes down their throats from long paper spills, until their eyes wept and their lungs wheezed. Eliza wasn't ever to take the short cut home through Duffel Street, where the slatternly little houses, squeezing close together, belonged to The Micks. But it was fun to look down from the white handrail above, and imagine what was going on down there; the fiery spit and crackle of red-headed life. Only you mustn't stare too long, or the Duffel Street boys came out and threw manure.

She passed the duckpond, brown and slimy, but leafily overhung by a great old willow. In spring its leaves were as minute as the tips of jade arrows. The duckpond and its big tree were The Willow Pattern Place, and it was satisfying to see the draggled white breasts of the ducks against the dirty water.

Mr Bellew, the headmaster of their school, loved trees, and tried to fight the emptiness of the raw clay around his brick building by getting the children to dig their own little garden-plots, where they could grow everything from potatoes to sweetpeas. Gradually he weaned them to trees and shrubs, and gave them long lectures about the duty of preserving their heritage of native bush — which they never saw, as it lay miles away over the hills. His favourite day in the year was Arbor Day, when he always managed to conjure up a Member of Parliament, like a whiskery watch-chained rabbit out of Mr Bellew's top hat. The Parliamentarian, having cleared his throat and rasped away at the children for twenty minutes, would scratch the ground with a trowel until the hole was deep enough for a sad-coloured, skinny little native tree to be planted. It didn't matter if he stuck it in lop-sided, because Mr Bellew would make the big boys replant it when he had gone.

Rear view of black trousers bending over: then the Parliamentarian came up to blow, and the Top Girls, Standard Six, of whom Carly was smallest and shyest, trebled:

> Bird of my na-tive land, beau-tiful stranger,
> Perched in the kauri tree, free from all danger.

Bird-of-my-native-land was supposed to be the tui, but none of the children had ever seen one, or a kauri tree either. Sparrows hopped everywhere, living as the Lord provided, on spilled crumbs and dust and chaff leaking from the nose-bags of patient old reddy-brown horses, who stood stamping and shuffling their feet. And there were thrushes, if you had a coprosma hedge with fat little orange berries to tempt them. The Hannays had, and used the berries for sovereigns when they played Shops.

It was a lie to say that bird-of-my-native-land and the thin trees stuck in holes in the playground were sacred and beautiful, half as sacred and beautiful as the thin, clear flame of the English trees, which came out such a surprised green in spring. Somewhere, far away in real wildness, it might be different; but here the native things looked only grey and sad, and covered all over with dust. And the cabbage-palms and tree-ferns people grew in their backyards — like beasts in a zoo — looked cowed and sick.

Funny, the bird and tree business. Sometimes the school journal called New Zealand 'Maoriland' or 'Ao-te-aroa'. There, again, you hardly ever saw a Maori, and if you did, it was in town. A dirty old wrinkled brown woman, with a black shawl over her head, sat on the steps of some indifferent building and puffed at her short pipe, while around her the sleek Wellington pigeons hopped, their breasts flashing emerald and proud opal. A few of the Island Bay fishermen were darker than the Italians; they were called half-castes, and there was something just faintly shady about them, though their babies had apricot cheeks, and great eyes and eyelashes you could only envy.

Occasionally, on holidays, the school went by train for a picnic. There were red-painted stations, stinking of freezing-works and sheds where tallow is rendered down, and the excursionists sang lustily:

> Kaiwarra, Ngaurangha, Petone,
> Kaiwarra, Ngaurangha, Petone,
> Kaiwarra, Ngaurangha, Petone,
> The next stop is The Hutt.

The Hutt was a little river, willow leaves and sunlight dropping into it like tarnished coins. In its pools were electric eels, and if you trod on one it would electric-shock you to death. Also, though the wide pale water looked very shallow, its ripple broken by banks of gravel, there were places where the current pulled you under and drowned you. Lots of people had drowned in the Hutt. It was the nearest to real *wild* that the children ever got.

If you took a branch line to another station, there was a great azure curve of sea scalloped with foam, far beneath the highest bluff in the world. So high and airy it stood that on it you felt light and unreal, and looking down caught your breath away. This place was 'Paekakariki', a Maori word meaning 'The perch of the green parrakeets'. But no green wings broke the air there any more . . .

Sometimes in class Mr Bellew talked about the godwits, who fly every year from the top part of the North Island to Siberia, thousands of miles without a stop. They fly north, they fly north. . . . They lined a dell one night with secret olive wings, and next morning were gone. Mr Bellew said, with melancholy satisfaction, 'And the eye of white man has never looked upon their flight.'

Something there had been, something delicate, wild and far away. But it was shut out behind the doors of yesterday, lost beyond the hills, and sticking a dead twig of it into a hole in the playground, or a rotten poem in the school journal, only made it sickly and unreal. You didn't really have to think about it — Maoris, godwits, bird-of-my-native-land. Attending to it at all was a duty call to a sick-bed. History began slap-bang in England. 'At the Battle of Hastings, in 1066, William of Normandy defeated King Harold.' A picture showed King Harold very angry and frightened because William had tricked him into taking an oath on the bones of the Saints. You were sorry for him and didn't want him to be beaten, but of course he was; especially you wished the arrow had hit him anywhere but in the eye. Normans in England said 'Bœuf' and 'Mouton' at first and the old Saxon tongue struggled and died out, till nobody understood it, any more than people here understood Maori. . . . You had to know that much, or you failed in your examination.

You were English and not English. It took time to realize that England was far away. And you were brought up on bluebells and primroses and daffodils and robins in the snow — even the Christmas cards were always robins in the snow. One day, with a little shock of anger, you realized that there were no robins and no snow, and you felt cheated; nothing else was quite as pretty. The tall sorrel heads of the dock-plants were raggedy under your hands, and the bush of daisies with brown centres stuck out from under the bedroom window, its roots somehow twisted into the asphalt of Calver Street.

Chalked on the pavement, just below the Silly Boy's house, Eliza read, 'Lizzie Hannay is Mad. She is stuk on Old Burgoo.'

She considered the white letters for a moment, before scrubbing them out with her boots. Bill Tybolt had written that. He never could spell, and he was wild because Mr Duncan made him share her desk. Mr Duncan was Old Burgoo. 'If I tell him,' she thought, 'Bill Tybolt will get six cuts. Perhaps he'll be expelled.' But there was the possibility, too, that Bill might be sent to the Head. On the surface that looked worse than being caned by Mr Duncan, but all the big boys knew that Mr Bellew wouldn't really hit them. He just couldn't. When they came to him in his office, first he slammed the door and took out his cane. Then he roared, so that you could hear him all down the corridors, 'I'll make you dance, sir — I'll make you smart,' and jumped about, hitting chairs, tables, even vases, anything except his pupils, who dug their knuckles into their eyes and whimpered, pretending to be terrified. When he was worn out, he said, 'Let us hope that will be a lesson to you, sir,' and the victim trotted back to the classroom, grinning from ear to ear.

She would manage Bill Tybolt herself — somehow. Besides, next year his father was taking him away from school and putting him on the milk-rounds, and Eliza had vague dreams of persuading him to let her ride on the milk-float. Once he had given her a conversation lolly, lettered pink, 'I Luv U'; but when she said, 'Do you really, Bill?' he replied, 'Sucks.'

Mr Duncan was different. He really whacked. Ruahine Doane had a striped palm for two days after getting six mistakes in her spelling. He only caned Eliza once, for saying with unnecessary emphasis, as they ploughed their way through *Macbeth*:

> Wake Duncan with thy knocking;
> I would thou could'st.

Then, when she got home, she had cried so much that she couldn't go back to school, and John said he would call the police to her. In the end Mr Duncan had to come to No. 9 Calver Street, to ask, in his gruff voice, 'May I ask what all this nonsense is about, young woman?' By that time the room was filled with wavy blue light, and Eliza was so pleased to see him that after a gulp or two she stopped weeping, and forgave him on the spot. Later she explained, with what dignity she could muster, that she was crying not because he caned her, but because he had hurt her feelings in front of the whole class. Mr Duncan replied that young women with feelings had better stay out of his class, but often he called her into his study for special coaching in arithmetic, and gave her chunks of the almost inedible plum cake with which his landlady stuffed his lunches. Carly, who was jealous, said it was only because Mr Duncan was so Scotch he wouldn't let the dogs have it.

'Why do I like him, when he's got such a temper?' Eliza wondered. In singing-class he was worse than ever. He made them sing things written by Bobbie Burns — Eliza hated poems in dialect — and caned them if they didn't get the pronunciation right. His tuning-fork quivered like a little striking asp, struck the side of the desk. And he said, 'Swallowed a potato, have you?' with a crimson and sarcastic face.

It wasn't for his scalplock of red hair, or his broad, stubby face with the bright grey eyes. It was because he was clever, clever and miserable, and not in the least soft. She was soft herself, and she hated people to be. . . . Besides, on the whole, she felt worse if she didn't love somebody desperately than if she did. It had been like that since the very beginning. And once on the hockey-field, a dank green fen with rickety goal-posts and boys shrieking like gulls as they swiped at one another's huge muddy knees, Mr Duncan had made Eliza into what she wanted to be: Little Heroine. It was a complete accident. The girls played matches, too, higgledy-piggledy, amateurish affairs which none the less alarmed her; a crack over the ankle with a hockey stick could hurt. Just that happened. Somebody hit her on the shin, and blind with rage and pain she swiped out. Her stick collided with that of the girl who was dribbling the ball up the field . . . lovely clean smack of wood on wood, shooting the ball away down-field. Mr Duncan's whistle shrieked. He came panting up.

'This little girl is the only one in the pack of you who'll tackle anything.'

The coiled-up feeling in her chest warned her that if she didn't say, 'Please, Mr Duncan, it wasn't on purpose,' she would pay for it after dark. At the same time George Washington's 'Father, I cannot tell a lie,' slid into her mind. She said nothing. Sylvia Rainer, waiting till Mr Duncan was out of earshot, called softly, 'Teacher's pet.'

Sylvia had fawn-coloured hair, long as Carly's, but daintily frizzed up at the ends, and real lace on her pinafores, and an amber-eyed collie dog who met her at the school gates and trotted home with her to her house in Westacre Street. It was the Rainers' own house, with Irish Elegance roses in the front garden. Irish Elegance . . . lovely sound. Sylvia was an only. Her parents had some sense, Augusta said. Eliza on the hockey-field held her head high, and smiled the exasperating smile which could always make Sylvia wild, lace-edged pinafore or not. All the same, she wasn't perfectly certain that she was cleverer than Sylvia, and pretty sure that she wasn't so good-looking.

On the upstairs iron balcony of his house, the Silly Boy stood as usual, swaying and smiling, ludicrously polite. His head tipped right back, so that he seemed to have no chin at all, and he always smiled foolishly, bending over double as the children passed him. He was quite grown-up, with curly dark hair, but he didn't know how to talk. Every morning his parents dressed him and stood him out in the sunshine, where he remained swaying quietly all day. Eliza had never seen him sitting down. He leaned out, as if vainly waiting for someone, and one of the trapped cabbage-palms came just level with his head. Its stiff blades, choked with dust, were tongues on which the spittle has dried. He wasn't as mad, though, as old Mrs Flint, who lived right opposite the Hannays, and every full moon became what Augusta called Very Queer. She was a minute woman, all wrinkles and flying grey wisps of hair, and from their bedroom window the children could hear her swearing and crying out. Sometimes she was taken away to the Asylum, but always she was home again in a few months. She had four children, tall and serious, with rather nice brown eyes.

Mr Potocki, who had a gymnasium class, and got drunk, thought he could fall off the roof without hurting himself. Every time he had been drinking, he climbed up to his roof and said he was going to throw himself down. His wife came to Augusta, crying and wringing her hands, but John said it would be a good thing for everybody if Mr Potocki broke his damfool neck, and Augusta ought to advise Mrs Potocki to take out an insurance policy on her husband. The only other queer person in Calver Street was old Nigger Jack, who drove about with a dusty sack round his shoulders, chanting, 'Bottle-oh, bottle-oh,' in his strong, sad voice. He lived at the top of the street, next to the brickyards, and had a white horse and a white wife, neither of them anything much to look at.

Augusta had forgotten the fuss she made about coming to Calver Street and sending her children to the new school; for it was quite a good school, and Mr Duncan said that Carly, though a nervous little idiot, was safe to get her Proficiency. And Mr Bellew was a gentleman, as much as Mr Forrest. The only difference was that he had a spade beard, and Mr Forrest's was a little grey fork. Mr Forrest, Mr Boad: old beards jut into your life, and go away, and are forgotten.

The tables had been turned on the Hannays, though Augusta didn't seem to notice. Next to the Silly Boy, Mrs Flint, Mr Potocki and Nigger Jack, they were the worst people in Calver Street — the poorest, anyhow, and not well thought of, since John had become a Red Fed and started spending his evenings in Carl Withers' bookshop. Mr Vaughan, their next-door neighbour, travelled in pianos, and had the use of a car on Sundays; Mr Mosley was in insurance, Mr Peters was retired, Mr Curnow came from England and had a tailor's shop, and the old Miss Whitneys had a lovely house with a white tower on top, and blue panes of glass in their windows. When Eliza once asked her father what his occupation was, he said, 'Licking stamps and boots,' which sounded so menial that she let the matter drop.

In their after-dark games the children could bring in Grandmother-and-Grandfather-Hannay-in-China, who seemed somehow more exciting than the Devlins, their Australian relatives. Grandfather Captain Hannay sat on the mantelpiece, photographed in uniform, with a tiger-skin draped beneath his long legs and poker back, and a white moustache bisecting his face. Grandmother-in-China was photographed in a long verandah closed in with wire-netting, and filled with tiny flying birds. She was the only one who sent presents, ten shillings for every birthday, five shillings each at Christmas, and sometimes a Wonder Box. The Wonder Boxes were miles the best, because usually the money got spent on something useful; but in the boxes were wee

Christmas puddings in enamel basins, Chinese lanterns painted with silky birds and butterflies, scrap-books, snake bangles, wooden animals. Only Eliza was the one who came off badly, because John had written to Grandmother-in-China saying that she was very studious, and after that, she nearly always got little books of views, or John's old school prizes, marked in a fine crabbed handwriting, 'For dear Eliza.'

Ngaio and Jock Vaughan, the children next door, had pale, pointed bunches of green grapes hanging from the V-shaped roof of their greenhouse. But they never invited the Hannays to eat any, and when Mrs Vaughan realized that Carly, Eliza and Sandra were playing in her garden, she called Ngaio and Jock indoors, and shooed the Hannays away to their own place, the Back Yard. Then they could hear the steady drumming of a piano, as Ngaio did her five-finger exercises. Sandra mimicked, 'Ping-pang-pong-Pung,' drumming her fingers on the fence loudly enough for Mrs Vaughan to hear. But that didn't alter the fact that the Hannays had no grapes and no piano.

The Back Yard was a broken square with a clothes-prop, and at one end a wash-house. There wasn't any bathroom inside the house, and Augusta said the children were too big now to be tubbed in front of the kitchen fire, with their father sitting there behind his newspaper. So every Saturday evening the copper was heated, and robed in coats over their nightgowns, they trotted across to be boiled. At first it was fun — bright crayfish-coloured bodies poking up wet heads over the rim — but Carly, the incurable innocent of their tribe, let things out to the Vaughans, and little boys used to hang about the back fence, calling, 'There go the copper kids.' The Back Yard, as Augusta had complained from the first, had no privacy. By keeping right against the brick wall which surrounded it on three sides, they could be out of sight; but that was impossible, because in the wall lived the Red Insects. They had translucent wings and lacquered bodies, and to be attacked by one was the end. 'They fly down your neck and sting you to death,' Carly explained.

It was Sandra who settled the copper question — Sandra, so delicate that in her first four years, the others always thought of her in terms of missing teeth, tonsils and adenoids, and a bottle of syrupy red medicine which nobody else must touch. Because she had pale gold hair, velvety blue eyes, Sandra got all the spoiling, and took herself very gravely. At first she couldn't realize that the street boys were making fun of her, but when she did, one evening, with perfect calm she removed her coat, nightgown and combinations, and stalked quite naked across the Back Yard. Carly and Eliza stood stricken dumb; Eliza, after a moment, wishing she had thought of it herself. Outside sounded a long, surprised whistle.

'Why did you do it? Mummy will nearly die,' Carly wept.

Sandra's head, tufted with its pale ringlets, showed above the copper. 'Give them something to look at.' Eliza thought, 'Sandra's not an angel, not one bit; she's just angel-coloured.'

Augusta, when she heard of it, did nearly die. But after that she came out to shepherd them over to the wash-house, and if the little boys were about, she sent them away with a flea in their ears. They were frightened of her stinging tongue. A good many people were frightened of Augusta. Green grapes and piano notwithstanding, Eliza much preferred her mother to Mrs Vaughan, who had a purplish skin and a bobbly sort of neck.

And just sometimes — once in a blue moon — the Back Yard was lovely. On moonlit nights, when they played that the clothes-prop was a maypole, and dressed up . . . John could join in beautifully, when he liked, much better than Augusta, who was tired and busy, and said abruptly to her husband, 'It's well to be you.'

They wandered in dusk as far as the edge of the Park, to find wild poppies and cornflowers for wreaths, or sometimes right over the grey hills, where on scrubby bushes grew the pale-starred clematis, traveller's joy. John had an old flute, though it bubbled rather horridly when he tried to play it. They danced, and were witches and fairies and grown-ups, and the street floated calm ebony and silver, until Ngaio and Jock slipped away from Mrs Vaughan and said, 'Please, Mr Hannay, can we play too?' and the Collie boys from the bottom of the street joined in. One of the Collie boys had a glass eye, because his brother shot the real one out with a pea-shooter, and he was always hiding the glass; once he put it in Carly's apron pocket, and she screamed as if a red insect had got on her. But night was lovely for the most part, warm and lovely. . . .

Augusta called, 'Eliza, don't go over my soapy floor. Take off your shoes, and go round the front way.' She obeyed, slipping silently into the empty, tiny room which was left to the children for their games. In a way, this was distinction; they were the only children in Calver Street with a special playroom, though it was only because there wasn't enough furniture to make it into a sitting-room, as Augusta reminded John when they were quarrelling.

Quarrelling. . . . It was what made everything in the house seem funny and strained, a tone too loud.

'Tonight after dark,' she thought, 'we will play we're in the bush.' Years ago, they had picnicked in the bush with the Harris family; and Nellie Keller was there, Nellie with her white, flat face, who had anæmia. She was dead now. And a fantail came and flirted with his fan, and Bob Harris made a supplejack bow and arrows. There was a stream, amber-brown, smelling of wild mint. The high fennel arched above their heads. They would take off their boots and socks and turn a blackberry corner. She didn't quite know what happened next, but it always developed after dark: only she had to general Carly, who was getting very religious since she went to St Monica's, and said such long prayers that she was sleepy when she got into bed. . . .

'Eliza,' called Augusta, 'you'd better get on with that homework. You know what your beautiful Mr Duncan says about your sums.'

Eliza sighed. Loving Mr Duncan had its drawbacks.

CHAPTER FOUR

O Rome, My Country

'YOU'RE putting more coal on that wretched stove. How do you expect me to pay the bills, and Sandra with the soles nearly dropping off her shoes?'

Sometimes, with a rumble of protest, John would drop his book and come to bed. Sometimes he swore, slammed the door, told the world that it was his house and his money, and stretched out his long legs again in front of the stove. The book war was much more difficult for Augusta that the coal one, because she couldn't localize it in the house, where a whisper was audible through the jerry-built walls and lumps of coal rattled like falling bricks. When John was in his early political and atheistic stage, he spent even his tobacco money on books, and then went about looking so miserable that Augusta had to scratch out housekeeping items, and give him his two ounces of Navy Plug Cut.

He wanted to know; eagerly, obsessively he wanted to know the insides and contents of things settled for Augusta by Providence and the British Constitution. Once John had read his books, he was usually through with them. He didn't care to keep and touch them, as the children tried to keep everything they had once liked, even the baby sparrow that eventually had to be buried in a cardboard box under the coprosma hedge. (And then they had tried to play Lazarus, and Sandra, her blue eyes solemn as an angel's, had informed Carly, 'Lord, it is the third day, and he stinketh,' which was true.)

Augusta, though she grumbled whenever a new book appeared, and called most of them either filth or seditious rubbish, bought a bookcase at an auction sale, and conscientiously dusted the green and gold bindings. But John buttoned them under his greatcoat and sneaked them out, to be sold at fourpence each to his friend Carl Withers, who was an I.W.W. ('I won't work,' Augusta translated.)

The book-raids meant another cry in the night.

'What's happened to those Waverley novels? Don't say you've gone and sold them for more of your trash. The miserable few pence you get for it, and then bring home some awful thing. . . .'

It was useless; the Lake poets, the pepper-and-salt philosophers, made their brief appearance on the bookcase, were gutted in a night by John, and then returned to Carl Withers. Some, which Augusta said weren't fit to be in the same house with children, lay in the top of the high dresser,

41

behind the money-boxes and Sandra's codliver oil and malt.

Eliza dipped into the bookshelf. Almost everything was incomprehensible, but one book, gold-lettered, made waves splash into the room, sharp, angry and strong.

> O Rome, my country, city of the soul,
> The orphan of the heart must turn to thee,
> Lone mother of dead empires . . . And control
> In his shut breast his petty misery. . . .
>
> Dost thou flow
> Old Tiber, through a marble wilderness?
> Rise, with thy yellow waves, and mantle her distress.

Waves, yellow Tiber waves, and a black-cloaked man standing with his arms flung out, while they hissed greedily around his feet. Eliza liked reciting the verses. At school Miss Curzon, the senior lady teacher, said with her buttoned-up smile: 'And I wonder how much of that our little Eliza understands?' as if understanding descended on you, like the Holy Ghost, when you had gone into thick ankle-length tweed skirts and turned sour. And Mr Duncan advised her to leave poetry alone and stick to mathematics. But at home, sometimes she could be almost impenetrably lonely, hedged about with a blue-and-gold thicket of gas-flames.

'Eliza, don't recite while you're washing up the dishes. Don't leave those forks to the last, they'll get all cold and zamzoid. How often have I got to tell you?'

In the quick dark of winter, the kitchen was filled with broken flames, rather stingy flames, dancing on shale coal, shining back from brass hooks on the dresser, where all the cups hung in a row, John's big rose-flowered moustache cup jutting out at the end. In the dining-room, which was never used for meals, but had the bookcase and sham leather chairs, Carly and Eliza did their homework. To make up for being away from the stove, they had a kerosene heater, a long, sad animal in blue enamel, with a little flame that twitched up and down behind a yellow pane if one moved a lever. Carly, her long brown hair brushed and sedate for the night, heard Eliza's tables; but Eliza was always finished first, and ran to the bookcase, to mutter poetry which sounded like rubbish to Carly, angry, incomprehensible rubbish.

'If you don't do your homework properly you'll fail in your exams, and they'll put you back,' she said. She looked like an owl — not the big owls that hoot and chase mice; the very little ones, with fluffy feathers and wide, scared eyes. In her owl eyes was caught the shine of the gas-light. Eliza only answered, 'No, they won't,' but to Carly the examinations were nightmares. If she failed to get her Proficiency, she thought, if her name were called out before the whole class, 'Competency', or just 'Failed', she would die.

Only one thing could be worse — the thing that made her run home as soon as cooking-class was out. She liked wearing apron and cuffs and baking things in little pie-dishes, she liked the warm feel of flour on her fingers; but all the time, at the back of her mind, Carly was thinking, 'Suppose anything has happened to Mother? Suppose she's dropped dead?' Sometimes pictures came, and she could see her mother lying beside the stove, with a big blue mark on her forehead. Then a great terror and loneliness filled her. If Augusta was close at hand, peeling potatoes, or making the old hand-machine whirr as she ran up hailstone muslin for Sandra's new best dress, she could creep in and look at her mother, or put a hand on her arm. But if it happened while Carly was at school, she couldn't concentrate. She could only sit crouching, waiting for the bell to ring and let her go. And sometimes then they kept her in.

Augusta never said anything about her children's looks except 'As good as many, and better than some,' though everyone knew Sandra was pretty. But of herself she said frankly that she was no beauty: a tall, spare, sad-faced woman, with dark red hair, grey eyes, and lips that turned down. She never wore anything in the house but print frocks, and for going out a costume called 'my pepper-and-salt', and the fuzzy strip of astrakhan, 'my stole'. Those were detachable bits of her. When she was in street dress, her red torch of hair went out under the 2/11d straw hats she got at Mr Ebery's, and a thick black veil was tied under her chin. Mr Ebery came to New Zealand on the same boat as the Hannays, and had done very well with his bargain store. He was a waxen-white, smiling man with a tiny dark moustache, and often came out from behind his counter to chat with Augusta. But though Carly often pretended that Mr Ebery said magnanimously, 'Here, Mrs Hannay, take one of my rose-coloured 15/11d hats,' he never did.

Carly liked to ask her mother about the dresses she had worn when she was a little girl, especially if the hand-machine was running; that was such a smooth, whirring, pleasant sound, a sound of puckered dreams, falling into rows of even stitching. Augusta said the prettiest she ever had was a sage-green delaine, with little jet buttons all the way down the back, from neck to hem, and a black velvet sash. And she had an eighteen-inch waist. 'Everybody had, in those days. But I thought myself somebody, I can tell you,' she would finish, with her dry little laugh.

To think of her mother in the sage-green delaine reassured Carly. It made her feel less as though she might come back any day to an empty house, and stand there crying, quite uselessly, sickeningly, because when people are dead you put them in a box and throw clay on them, like the baby sparrow Eliza had found fallen from its nest, opening and shutting its beak to show a tiny flat pink tongue inside, before its eyes glazed and its head dropped over sideways. Its beak wouldn't shut, so they put a nasturtium flower into it when they buried it. She would have liked to play talking-games after dark about their mother's girlhood, but she was slow at putting her ideas into words, while Eliza could rattle off at once, 'We're invited to Cressil Burns' party, and we're taking her a yellow satin hanky sachet with violets on between us, and there's hundreds-and-thousands on her birthday cake and pink candles, and green jelly in cups, and crackers, mine's got a ruby ring inside, what has yours got, Sandra?'

Carly was certain which one of her parents she loved best. Even when she was little, she knew that she hardly loved John at all, and he didn't love her. It was because of Mummy. . . . For Eliza it was different, and Carly found that hard to forgive, because you had to be on one side or the other. If you were Carly and heard John putting more coal on the fire after ten, you had to call out, 'Mummy, Daddy's doing it again.'

When Eliza brushed out Augusta's hair in the dark, she had no doubts. Under the long, smooth strokes of the whalebone it crackled and crisped, and gave off pouncing sparks of blue, and Augusta talked about the black swans in Western Australia, and the honeybirds dipping their long bills into stiff flowers on Table Mountain. Or if you were sick, as Eliza was when she took the medicine by itself instead of three drops in a wineglassful of water, Augusta was the one who helped. But it was John who understood about poetry, though sometimes he laughed at it.

When he heard her saying, 'O Rome, my country,' one day, he gave her his queer, whipped-dog look.

'You love that, don't you?'

'Yes, Daddy.'

'Then keep it. It's all we've got.'

He never sold Lord Byron to Carl Withers, or *The Heroes*, or any book Eliza said she specially liked. And she loved him, too, when he played soldiers with the Calver Street boys, and had them all round him, listening to how he won his medal in the Boer War; or when they went mushrooming in the steep, stony hills behind the reservoir, and there was one great rock called 'the Druid's Stone', because sunset ran on it like blood, and all over the grey scrub-bushes hung the fragile foam-wreath of clematis.

But when he quarrelled it was hateful. His voice got too big, filling the house like the smoke-djinn that escaped from the bottle. Everybody joined in, blinded and frightened, and Carly wept, 'Don't you dare to bully my mother,' and Augusta, standing at bay, said, 'Don't look like a devil at your own children.' The veins stood out on his forehead, and he swore at God and the British Empire; half the time it was some tiny thing that set him off. He seemed to be two people rolled into one — the thin, brown one who laughed, and the thin, red one who quarrelled.

How can you hate? How can you properly take sides? It was Eliza's father who took them over the hills to fly kites in the evenings. The long thin tails of the kites lay on the air, wriggling like great serpents, and their flat diamond-shaped heads dragged hard, trying to escape. Summer smelt brown and lordly in the grasses. But when the two working-men came to mend the kitchen door, and Eliza was reciting, and Augusta sat at her sewing-machine, one of the men opened the door. They stood there listening, and she felt as if she were on fire — proud, making the bells ring and the skies burn, in an old poem that went out of her head afterwards. And Augusta, though as a general rule she didn't like working-men, and was most annoyed if Eliza smiled at the tram-conductor when she gave him her penny, let them stand listening. Then one of the men said admiringly, 'She's a fair little wonder, Missus,' and Augusta agreed, 'Not bad.' The corners of her down-turned mouth twitched. She was actually pleased.

Augusta and John couldn't have been more different, Eliza thought. Augusta said, 'Dear old England,' and had been longing and longing to go there ever since she was a little girl, and sat in the crotch of the great fig tree in the West Australian orchard. And she had worked her way half across the world, to Africa; but then she got married, and had Carly, Eliza and Sandra instead of finishing up in London. John, though he had been in England at school, and would show them pictures of forests and cottages if he felt in the mood, said, 'Curse your bloody British Empire,' when he was angry. John was an atheist, and read all the books about it that he could get from Carl Withers. Augusta sent the children to Sunday School every week, and Carly brought home texts illuminated with puffy silver letters, lilies and lambs.

On Sunday evenings, Augusta took them to Saint Monica's, a wooden building with a pointed, raftered roof, made fierce and dignified by its shadows, and the enormous carved eagle whose yellow eyes blazed from the lectern. Eliza liked the fused, singing voices, always accompanied by funny little froggy croaks from the church-warden, Mr Herring, who sat at the end of their pew. But when they sat down, she began to dream, and Carly, pinching her arm, would whisper, 'You're not allowed to go to sleep in church.'

She wasn't quite asleep. She could smell new kid gloves, and violets, and see the round of Gertie Carstairs' cheek. Gertie was the prettiest girl in Sunday-school, she looked so smooth and finished off. . . . Eliza could hear the Zoo lions roaring, far away, lonesome and grim, and before she knew it slipped into pretending that Blackmane had got loose, and the only way to escape was by crawling out along the rafters, right to the middle, where it was too high for Blackmane to jump. You could do it by swinging from the cord that held back the red plush curtain. In the body of the church, Blackmane growled and ate people.

The minister said suddenly, 'The Prince of the Power of the Air'; and there were dark, dark eyes, eyes she had always known, looking at her. He was like the black-cloaked man who had written 'O Rome, my country', but much taller and sadder.

'Eliza, put your penny in the bag.' It was a deep red bag, and pennies fell louder than threepenny bits, which made a thin, smirking jingle.

'You'll drop it if you don't wake up.'

'Anyhow, you were sitting on your foot. You were squatting, like an old nigger woman.' You could always get back at Carly over that; she had a trick of sitting with her feet curled under her, like the Kaffirs in Africa.

Cold outside: black cold, pierced by heavy winds. People in blurred coats said, 'Good night, Mr Harcourt,' and shook hands with the minister. They moved away through the night to their houses, their edges melting into darkness. It wasn't possible to think of them separately, as having babies and bicycles and offices, they were just shapes. The Prince of the Power of the Air. . . . His country was all low thorn-bushes, nuggets of dark.

John got the parts of a *History of Mankind*, which ran in small print and coloured plates through a weekly magazine. Carl Withers sold them to him for sixpence, and bought them back for a penny. Some of them upset him dreadfully. He came rushing in and slammed the door, his hair standing up on end, his thin face flaming.

'Look at that. That's your capitalist system. That's what they do to men. Look at that, I tell you.'

Augusta looked. 'It happened two thousand nine hundred years ago,' she said tonelessly.

'They're all the same. Capitalists — murderers. Look, Eliza, that's what your mother wants me to put into Parliament. That's what she votes for herself.'

'Must you defile the eyes of your own children?'

'Let them see what the world is. Look, Eliza!'

Eliza looks, and sees a picture of some slaves flayed alive by an Emperor. They lie huddled, not unlike the raw pink rabbits that have to be soaked overnight in the sink before they can be stewed. The Emperor stands over them with his whip, looking rather like Daddy in a temper.

'Yes, Daddy.'

John fires off his parting shot.

'That's your Imperialism. That's your *God* for you.' Augusta, hard tears forcing themselves between her eyelids, continues to pare very thin rings from the potatoes.

Two people, solitaries, dreamers, winning out of their first environment, find a dog-chain twisting their ankles together. Still they fight for their escape; one lonely, shy, suffering under a sense of social injustice, for escape into the steaming companionship, the labouring but powerful flanks of mankind: the other fights for what blood and tradition have taught her, fields of bluebells ringing all on the one exquisitely lengthened note, courage, craftsmanship, the order which for her has existed only in a dream, so that she cannot know if its grey stone pile be crumbling today. They are young when it begins; their words, like their veins, are hot and full of passion. They share a double bed, and have children. One day an ageing man looks round, and finds himself wrestling with an ageing woman, her face seamed with tears.

Mrs Rainer asked Eliza to tea after her eighth birthday. Eliza thought Sylvia's mother very wonderful — a small, dark, Frenchified creature, with fluttering white hands and no household coarseness. When Eliza asked if she liked poetry, she clasped her hands and cried, 'I pulse to it — I pulse to it.' On the table stood a great crystal dish of orange jelly, which wobbled as Mrs Rainer pulsed. Her dark eyes turning reproachfully on Sylvia, she added, 'Sylvia breathes a different air. She doesn't pulse, as I do.'

'Oh, come on out for a walk,' said Sylvia. Mrs Rainer said, 'Show Eliza where she can make herself comfortable, dear,' and Sylvia led the way to a closet papered with pictures of tiny snarling dogs, bulldogs in hunting pink. As they went out of the garden to the flanges of the sharp hills, green with winter's short, frost-bitten grass, Sylvia said, 'Don't pay any attention to Mother. She's like that.'

'I think your mother's wonderful.' Eliza wanted to add, 'And your lavatory,' but it didn't sound quite nice. They came in sight of a brown pond, corralled by hawthorns on whose boughs still hung a few shrivelled berries, hearts for daws to peck at. Behind rose a crenellated building of sour grey stone.

'That's the Home of Mercy,' said Sylvia. 'They've got babies there with two heads.'

'How do you know? Have you seen them?'

'I know a girl who did. She was a Mick. Are your family Micks?'

'We go to Saint Monica's. Carly's in the Bible Class.'

'Oh, that's C. of E., same as us. That's all right. I thought you mightn't be, because such a lot of Micks live down near Calver Street. They believe if you bite the wafer at Holy Communion, it bleeds. They've got to swallow it whole, even if it nearly chokes them. Kathie James is a Mick, and once her cousin kept the wafer till he got home, and bit it, just to see, and blood fizzled all over the stove. He had to confess to the priest before it stopped fizzling.'

'Ugh, how horrid.'

'Well, that's what Kathie says. And the nuns eat frogs. This is their frog-pond. They catch them and eat their hind legs.'

They lay flat in the mud beside the pond; the weedy water slipped through their palms. Certainly there were frogs, some like commas, some kicking lustily with inch-long legs. Sylvia found an old jam-tin, and they put the frogs in water.

'Catch a toad and you'll get warts,' she said. Over the saddle of the hills, so high that sunset balanced there like a red sword before burning down into the valleys and the creeks massed with watercress, the last of the afternoon light slid coldly radiant.

'Eliza, do you like Mr Duncan?'

Better to be offhand. 'He's all right,' said Eliza. 'He's a bit bald on top, isn't he?'

'I think he's silly,' said Sylvia, pirouetting. 'You do like him, Eliza; you're fibbing. If you were a Mick you'd have to confess, and the priest would make you do something awful.'

'What?'

'I couldn't tell you.'

'You're only saying it, because I beat you in essay. I'm going to climb the hill.'

'A man hanged himself up there.'

'Where?'

'Over in the Happy Valley. On a tree. And there's a haunted house; look, you can just see it. One day a boy was going past its windows, and he saw a terrible face looking out.'

Suddenly the pink and fawn that was Sylvia, the glints on her curled hair, shattered into pieces of laughter. 'Silly . . . Silly . . .' she called, and raced away down the hill. On the top of a hummock she stood and shouted, 'Mary Bray knows how babies are born, and so does Isabel Yoland, so there.'

Eliza climbed a little way by herself, over a creek where cows' hoofs had made huge squelchy prints in the mire, and buttercups shone like painted tin. If you put one under your chin and it made a yellow reflection, you stole butter; but she didn't, only the dark streaks from gravy dripping. There were no paths, and the hills looked as though no one ever climbed them, only cattle and sheep, whose uneven grooves spiralled towards the top. Beyond lay the Happy Valley, and the man who hanged himself jerked and thumped softly against the wind, so that the rope, which had worn a white place for itself, creaked on the bough. Why was the face looking out of the window terrible? If you said a horrible face, it only meant tongue out and eyes crossed, like Billy Rames made. But terrible was different. Very white, very white, and always smiling.

And she did like Mr Duncan. And babies being born was one of the things Augusta said you must never talk about, a kind of little curtain dropped down hard in the mind if anyone even spoke of it. But not knowing as much as Mary and Isabel was silly, when she was top of the class. Sylvia had scored all round.

Going towards Calver Street, she thought suddenly of the Glory Hole. Wherever you went, you came to the edge of it.

That night, Augusta and John had a thunder-and-lightning row. Eliza didn't hear it all, but part of it was about the British Empire. A few days later, the corded tin trunks were out in the hall again, and Sandra was told she couldn't take her hobby-horse, it was too clumsy to pack.

'Where are we going, Mummy?'

'To Australia,' said Augusta. 'Your Uncle Rufus sent the passage money.'

John said, 'If you insist on making a fool of yourself,' and slammed out of the house. Carly ventured timidly, 'Is Daddy coming, Mummy?'

Augusta looked at her, with grey eyes perfectly blank, like stones in water. Eliza had seen them like that before, but not Carly.

'Hold your tongue, Carlotta.'

Carly's mouth quivered. She crept away silently to tell her dolls, Mr Trinkle and Mrs Trimble, squatting like an old Kaffir woman beside the green packing-case doll-house. John had got tired of making it, so it had no front, but stood wide open. In the apex, which Eliza should have kept clean, strands of cobweb puffed, filtering dust. Eliza's dolls, though christened with grandiose names — Athene, Andromeda, Perseus, Cressida — were unwashed, unsmacked and irreligious. But Carly loved hers. She told Mr Trinkle and Mrs Trimble that they were going to Australia.

'And we've got lots of uncles and aunts and great-uncles and great-aunts, and grandmother-and-grandfather, and all the little cousins, and the second cousins. And one of our great-uncles was an Admiral and the Shah of Persia gave him a sword. And people in Melbourne said they'd rather have old Dr Devlin drunk than any other doctor sober, and Great-Aunt Christobel is very witty.'

The polite Japanese faces of the dolls looked unimpressed; a sunbeam flew in, making a patch of wobble against blue walls. Carly tried to feel, 'Poor Daddy,' but in the curled-up place, inside her heart, she couldn't.

That night they played they had fowls, and had to leave them behind when they went to Australia.

'Mine was called Speckly,' said Sandra. 'She used to lay lots of eggs every day; an' we had her boiled.'

'Mine was Whitey,' said Eliza. 'She was a Leghorn.'

Sandra's inexorable little voice said, 'An' we had her roasted.' Inexplicably, Eliza's heart felt torn in two.

'No, we didn't,' she said. 'You can't roast Whitey.'

'Yes, we did,' said Sandra. 'We chased her and wrung her neck and cut her head off and had her roasted for dinner. She never laid any eggs, anyhow.'

Eliza choked out: 'She did,' and began to cry in great sobs. A patch of cold at the back of her head told her, 'You know if you start you can't stop,' but she didn't care. She heard her own sobs louder and louder, and they seemed quite separate from herself. Carly pattered across the floor, a ghost in her nightgown.

'Don't Eliza. You know you're only putting it on to make a scene, and

Mummy'll hear you. I promise we won't kill your fowl if you stop before she hears, I promise truly. Your fowl does lay eggs.'

'She hasn't got a real fowl,' said Sandra dispassionately.

'*Don't*,' Carly implored. But their voices, and the restless knuckle-tapping of the wattle tree against the window, and the small flame when Augusta, her hair down, held up the lamp and said, 'What is this?' were all irrelevant. Then John came in, and said he couldn't understand her. 'Stop that row, you're making my head ache.' Blue waves slid easily out, rippling into dark, and John was a rough shadow at the bottom of the bed.

'It's cold,' he said miserably. 'I'll put another coat over you.' She felt the soft, thick weight of cloth flung down. It was time to go to sleep, time to let sobbing become monotonous and soft as the waves on a still day at Island Bay. There were prawns in the pools, green prawns with transparent bodies like wave-colour, and they caught them in nets made out of canary-seed bags.

CHAPTER FIVE

Follow the Boomerang

Mrs Protheroe, who had come over from Newtown to see the Hannays off, said, 'With men, you never can tell.' Augusta, wearing a new veil with black velvet spots, as well as my-pepper-and-salt and my-stole, cried, 'He can't have meant us to miss the boat, when I've bought the tickets. That would be waste — wicked, shameful waste.' Mrs Protheroe shook her head and refused to know what men would do, and half an hour dwindled by, the children sitting in their new brown velvet cloaks on the boxes in the hall, sunlight dancing on the worn Chinese matting in their bedroom. Their father had refused to let the house, saying they would be back again, like the black cat, as soon as Augusta came to her senses.

At last Augusta called one of the Collie boys, and gave him sixpence to run out and find a cab, as the one John had promised to order hadn't come. The boy came back, spitting on his sixpence, and said there weren't any cabs anywhere, only old Nigger Jack's bottle-oh cart.

'Well, you certainly can't go through the streets of Wellington with that awful darkie,' pronounced Mrs Protheroe, who secretly felt that Augusta was in the wrong. Augusta clenched her hands.

'Can't I? John did this on purpose. He wanted us to miss the boat, after I'd spent money on the tickets. It's downright dishonest.'

'But a darkie — '

'Or no Australia.' To the Collie boy, Augusta said, 'Tell Nigger Jack to bring his cart here this very minute.' Carly began to sniff. She was frightened of black men.

Nigger Jack had his sack round his shoulders when his cart pulled up outside, and Mrs Protheroe said sharply, 'For goodness and consideration's sake, driver, can't you take that off?' His eyes rolled at her mournfully, funny treacle eyes with a spot of mist in each pupil. There was a big dip in his horse's back. Augusta said, 'Come, children,' but Eliza remembered that she hadn't said goodbye to her wattle tree. It was almost the first time she had thought of it as hers, since the night they came to Calver Street. Now she ran back into the bedroom, and breathlessly patted its thin brown branch, which rapped hard knuckles against the window. 'Goodbye, my tree!' 'Eliza, come *on!*'

Nigger Jack put his hand under their boots as they jumped up to the seat. Eliza felt her cloak swish against the harsh sack. They all started to remember things, as if this were darkness instead of broad daylight. Sandra cried, 'Once I found a big walking-stick insect,' and Carly, 'Once I made some scent, but when I opened it, it smelt horrid, and I threw it down the drain.' The cart was moving, jolting and hurting you where you sat down; but you could only hold tight, seeing the little houses jump past. From high up, they looked uncanny. . . .

Dancing on a whale washed up at Lyall Bay. Hundreds of children were taken to see it, and they danced up and down. Underfoot was nothing but slippery black, gashed with the yellow clay from their boots. 'Now I am dancing on a whale.' Once they had a lovely picnic-day there, and cut huge doorstep sandwiches in a tiny hut on the beach. Sand drifted over the crusty bread, little grains fine as silver. They called it 'Hunks House', because the bread doorsteps were so thick, and the waves came curling, but they never went there again. . . .

And white, quivering egg-plants grew out of the wet ground, and felt like slippy flesh. Once there was an egg-plant in Ngaio and Jock Vaughan's backyard. The boys said, 'If you leave an egg-plant grow, a little horse'll come out.'

Mr Duncan and Daddy.

Instinct was too strong for Nigger Jack. As the cart rattled, his strong, sad baritone chanted, 'Bottle-oh, bottle-oh, bottle-oh.' Augusta said, 'Oh, driver, must you do that?' and his muddy eyes stared at her, frightened. For a moment he was silent, then began chanting again, under his breath.

At the last moment, Daddy was a wet-looking red face down on the wharf, with forests of streamers bumping against it. He brushed them off impatiently, and their coloured ends dangled in the air. 'Goodbye, old girl — goodbye, kiddies; come back soon.'

'Mummy, isn't it a funny little room? Mummy, our beds are stuck on to the wall,' said Sandra, tumbling about, enchanted. The noise of the engines was a soft thrumming. Then a green streak of water widened, and Eliza thought, 'I'll jump overboard.'

'Mummy, I feel sick; awfully, terribly sick.' Carly spoke in a whisper, her face drawn. Sandra bounced on the edge of a bunk.

'Carly's sick already. Carly's sick already. Sandra isn't sick. Mummy, can I sleep in the top little bed?'

Augusta pulled off her hat, tearing the new veil on a hatpin. She said loudly, dreadfully, 'Children — flesh of your flesh, bone of your bone,' and put her hands over her face.

Little bubbles, invisible except to eyes half-shut, streak up like dense steam from a kettle. They are going to Heaven. The sun writes in big, white letters and Morse flashes on the green uneven waves; Carly is drawing chalk hopscotch bases on the deck.

'The captain is going to throw you overboard for making marks on his clean deck,' Carly looks up with grey, startled eyes, sunlight cleaves the water like a great gold fin, a creasy wing settling.

Eliza says, 'I was only making it up. I'll play hopscotch if you like.'

'It's horrible to tell stories.'

'You should have seen your face. It was pasty, like when you were sick.'

Eliza from the deckrail, or from the invisible funnel through which the yeasty bubbles are sucked up to God, watches them both. They are happening a long way off, and yet inside her. If she tries to explain this, she can only say, 'I feel as if they were growing inside me,' and people laugh. For how on earth can yourself grow inside yourself? How can tall, dank pillars of stone in a strange city, pillars with little dark bruises of spit, curl right through you, like fern-fronds?

Eliza, raising a white perspiring face from the pillows, thinks, 'I was sick on curried crayfish crossing the Great Australian Bight.' It turns into the first line of a ridiculous comic song. Her inside feels perfectly empty, and she is better since Mr Steward brought her a Nip. Sandra, in spite of her boasting, has been sick all the time, so sick that Augusta, tied to the cabin, has trusted Carly and Eliza to go to table with Mr Steward, a nice man in a white coat, who brings them things to eat; first bread-and-milk and plain broth, then, when they say they aren't a bit sick, Bombay duck and crayfish and a wonderful whole pineapple whose inside has been taken out and put back in pieces, mixed with other things. They fish into it with long silver spoons rattling slivers of ice.

Carly whispers, 'Don't take so much, Eliza, and don't spill anything. Everybody's looking at us.'

A man at the table sits swallowing raw grey oysters.

'I wonder if he swallows their pearls?'

'Sssh,' from Carly.

'I wonder if he swallows them while they're still alive?' But then the pop eyes of the portholes swim round and round, Eliza feels the crayfish coming back and presses her hand to her mouth, while the oyster man says, 'Ugh! — little girls! little girls!' and Carly, agonized, wails, 'Mr Steward — oh, Mr Steward.'

Tasmania drips with tiny waterfalls, like fringes of glass beads. Then it has vanished, and one-of-the-uncles is finding seats on the train. He has red hair and freckles, and kisses Augusta heartily.

'Well, old girl, it's high time you came to us and got some flesh on those bones.'

Life bustles through high grey arches.

'Mummy, where are we?'

'In Melbourne. At the railway station.'

'Are we going to stay in Melbourne?'

'Not now, we're going out to the farm with your Uncle Martin.'

'Where's the farm, Mummy? How far do we go?' Uncle Martin comes back with slotted pink tickets.

'Oh, Martin, never you go and have a pack of children. My head spins round with them.' Uncle Martin says, 'Tell that to the missus,' but he eyes the Hannays questioningly. Queer, peaky pestiferous brood. . . .

Sandra was the one on whom Australia beamed. The fruit was so cheap, barrows and stalls of piled-up, luscious colours, raw orange, slashing purple and gold.

'Like old times,' said Augusta, biting into the warm cheek of a pear.

'Williams pears, tuppence a pound,' boasted Uncle Martin. Sandra crept on his knee like a white rabbit. She chanted softly, 'Williams-pears, Williams-pears, Williams-pears;' her gold head lay against Uncle Martin's waistcoat, and she looked so angel-coloured that Carly wondered whether she ought to warn him, 'Sandra has our father's temper.' But at the last station, where just after dusk-fall they were met by another uncle, and had to choose whether they would ride in the gig or the buggy, Sandra gave herself away.

'I don't want to ride in the bug or the giggle. . . . I don't want to ride in the bug or the giggle. . . .' 'She can keep up that shrieking for hours,' said Augusta hopelessly. The new uncle said, 'Hop up, kiddies,' to Carly and Eliza, and they were tucked under a rug on the high seat beside him.

Countries on the map are misleading. True, Australia was coloured plain red, like New Zealand, but it was so large, and the names of such odd products, pearl-shell, molasses, trepang, were printed in little letters round its coast, that somehow you would have expected it to jump out at you like a Jack-in-the-box, saying, 'Here I am, I'm Australia.' Instead, it was plain, indifferent and lonely, with a few startled night-birds flying out of its armpits, and the high gig-wheels turning in deep ruts.

When they got down, the strange uncle said soberly, 'I'm your Uncle Will. Do you want to give me a kiss?' They did, without excitement. Out

of a little wooden house, with a lantern swinging in its porch and a great
kerosene lamp buzzing inside, came a woman in a print gown.

'This is your Auntie Rosalind.'

Aunt Rosalind kissed them, and gave them bread-and-milk, but as
soon as the buggy-wheels scrunched outside, she said, 'Come along now,
and I'll show you your bed.'

Carly and Eliza had to sleep in the same bed, tops and tails. In the dark
was caged a sizzling sound, like a minute drill.

'Carly, can you hear it?'

'Yes, it's a mosquito. Go to sleep, Eliza.'

'I'm awfully hot. They might have let us stay up, our first night.
Sandra's still up.'

'She's probably asleep. Besides, she's the baby.'

'I hate Australia.'

'How can you hate it yet?' began Carly; and then, illogically, 'So do I.'

Australia kept coming clear in bits and pieces, seemingly unrelated to
any whole. The Hannays had many uncles and aunts, but these, instead
of being clustered together in a colony, were so widely distributed that it
took days to go by train and buggy to their little wood houses. Aunt
Rosalind and Uncle Martin had a daughter, who was the Hannays' cousin
Katrine, the first they had ever met. She had freckles, and red hair so like
the Macartney children that at first they watched her surreptitiously to
see if she scratched her head. Uncle Will was a bachelor. The only other
thing that impressed them in the first little house was Carly's terror of the
spiders. Cousin Katrine said, 'Sometimes a tarantula gets into the house.
They're as big across as that' (measuring a foot in the air with her hands),
'and they're all black and hairy. You look up at one side of the door, and
you see a beady eye winking at you; and when you look up at the other
side, there's the other beady eye winking, too.' After that, Carly wouldn't
even go to the lavatory alone. She was too scared of beady eyes winking.

Grandmother and Grandfather Devlin lived twenty miles away. When
the children were driven over to stay with them, Grandmother Devlin
turned out to be little and severe, in a black dress, but Grandfather, so
brown and earthy that he looked like a potato, had jujubes in one pocket
for good children, and blackballs in another for bad ones.

There was a yellow dog named Sandy, who used to steal loaves and
bury them in the sand. After tea, Grandmother said that the children
could go and help separate the milk. They had tried milking, but they
couldn't make anything come out of the cow's hard pink teats, and the

farm-boys laughed at them. Eliza found herself sitting beside a red-painted machine, turning a handle. Thin streams spouted from its sides, one milk, one cream. This was rather magnificent; in Wellington they never had cream except on Christmas Day and birthdays, when it was whipped into fuzzy masses on the fruit salad. Eliza liked hearing the machine purr, and watching her thin freckled wrist revolve with the handle. By and by Grandfather Devlin came back laughing, and said, 'Quite good — quite, very good,' pulling the jujubes out of his pocket. She wanted to try churning the butter, but it wouldn't come lumpy behind the little thick window in the churn, and Grandmother Devlin called, 'Bring the children in for their supper, Sammy, it's high time they were off to bed.'

When they were getting undressed, Eliza remembered what Augusta had once said about Grandmother Devlin. 'Her name was Leonora. She had lovely little hands.' She stopped and stared, standing in her flannel bodice and white frilled knickers. But Grandmother Devlin's hands in the lamplight were spotted the colour of rust, and their inside skin was wrinkled up like washerwoman's fingers. She wasn't a bit like Leonora. . . .

Next morning they went to let the horses out of the stables for a drink at the dam. They came out with such a tossing of manes and stamping of proud hoofs that to Carly's eye there seemed to be hundreds of them — a heaving convulsion of red-skinned, rolling-eyed, autocratic horses. She hung back behind the stable door. There were so many things in Australia of which everybody said, 'You mustn't be afraid, Carly. You're the eldest.' She hated horses, hated the way they showed their high yellow teeth and whickered; but not Old Bill, the blind horse, who stayed in the stable-yard drinking in sunshine through his mud-matted hide, and dribbling green at the mouth. He looked so patient and blind that Carly made herself stroke him. His nostrils felt like grey velvet, and he didn't open his mouth, just moved his head a little in the sun, as if he liked being stroked.

Sandra fell in love with the pigs. She ran about hatless in the sunshine, all her little ringlets wet gold from the comb; mud squelched over the tops of her sandals, but she didn't care. 'Pigs are horrid,' said Carly, to whom the sows looked massively naked and unclean. 'And they smell — ugh.'

'This one's nice,' said Sandra, staring at a huge sow on a pillow of mud.

'She's not. She's dirty, lying in the mud when there's plenty of clean places.'

'She's sad,' said Sandra, unmoved. Her pale-blue velvet eyes were fixed in their own vision. The pig was sad and good, Sandra knew it, and nothing could alter her knowledge.

After lunch, they had to stand patiently and be fitted by Aunt Coral, their single aunt, who was making them brown velvet frocks and poke bonnets to match their cloaks. Sandra wept, 'I don't want a poky bonnet,' but Aunt Coral only replied, 'Don't fidget, Miss, and don't be a cry-baby-cry.' She had a wooden model bust which could be screwed creakily up and down, making it taller or shorter, and her work-basket was lined with rose sateen. Carly longed to beg some of the work-basket scraps to make new clothes for Mr Trinkle and Mrs Trimble, but was too shy to ask. Sandra shuffled from foot to foot, and had to be spoken to sharply; as soon as she was fitted, she raced out of the room, and they could hear her singing under the window, 'Hate Australia — hate my poky bonnet.' Aunt Coral said, 'There's gratitude for you.'

Rock melons were piled up outside, streaky, stripey piles. Cut through their green hides, which felt like glossy water, and you came to rosy flesh studded with dark-crimson pips. The children found tiny unripe grapes under the leaves in the vineyard, and one huge one, quite ripe. Eliza said, 'The birds 'ull only get it,' and popped it into her mouth. Carly and Sandra both said she was greedy, and at table Carly told on her. 'A nice little unselfish girl might have brought it home to poor Mother,' Aunt Coral remarked. Light trembled like diamonds in the dusty water carafe set between them, and Eliza felt that she hated Aunt Coral. But afterwards Augusta said she didn't mind at all about the grape, and took Eliza for a long walk over the paddocks. Birds made swift little blunt-edged holes for themselves in the crystal air, and plunged through. A black cat was just a cardboard shape cut out of the afternoon, with dark emptiness pasted behind the place left by his absence. If you stared at him, you could easily see that he wasn't there. Augusta stopped at a fence, and imitated a magpie. Sure enough, a real one answered, gurgling in his throat with a pleased, liquid sound. 'Oh, it's like a dream hearing the old fellows again.'

In Australia there were emus, kangaroos, dingoes and blackfellows, but quite useless, for they lived in other parts of an enormously large continent. Once the children saw a mottled brown-and-gold thing limp over a fence, and squalled, 'Snake, snake,' but it was only a dead one, that one of the ploughmen had hit on the head and skinned. An old farmhand with skim-milk blue eyes told them of an island where, when the rains swelled the creek, thousands of snakes came swimming along, their backs up in pothooks and hangers.

Australia should really have been Carly's night out. So often she had fitted her great-aunts and grand-uncles into games of Lords and Ladies. Great-Uncle Peter, who was an Admiral and got the sword from the Shah of Persia (but he was dead now); and Great-Aunt Christobel, who was so witty, and Second-Cousin Daisy, who had said she wouldn't be in the least excited if the King asked her to dinner at Buckingham Palace. 'I should behave myself as I usually do — as a lady.'

Great-Uncle Gervase Devlin was the first indication that Carly's Lords and Ladies were really a terrible have. A bachelor, he lived all alone in a tiny bark-roofed hut among bluegum trees, with great bars of light crashing down on him from their motionless horizontal branches. From the trunks hung strips of bark, reddish and grey; underneath the wood was perfectly smooth, clean and shiny, and the trees looked solemn. Out of Great-Uncle Gervase's chin protruded a whisker so fine and wavy that it looked as if he used it to feel with, like the antennæ of a moth. Otherwise he was very brown, more like a goblin than anyone the children had seen before.

Augusta left the children in his spotless little house while she went to see if she could find a kookaburra among the gum-trees. Although the goblin gave them moist chocolate biscuits from a tin, he seemed quite to have forgotten who they were and why they sat looking at him, and Carly had to explain. He went off into fits of gap-toothed laughter.

'Dearm, now — that Augusta's children. The freckles she did have on her nose, and the temper of her, to be sure. One of your high-and-mighty, hoity-toity sort.'

'I think we'd better go and find Mother,' said Carly, as politely as she could, but with eyes that watered from anger and smoke. Eliza and Sandra obeyed her 'Come on' a little reluctantly, and they stepped out into the bluegums. Sun gleamed and splintered on a kerosene tin, at which scraggy fowls were pecking. A hundred yards from the hut, they heard cries and saw the goblin hobbling after them.

'Dearm, now,' he wheezed, 'if I didn't forget to give you the mushy-rooms. You tell your grannie to fry those brown in the fry-pan. But there, she'll never learn, them might as well be twoad-stools.' The button mushrooms, with white tops and pink frilled pantalettes, were wrapped in a red bandanna handkerchief. The children went down the road, until all they could see was a plume of smoke from Great-Uncle Gervase Devlin's tin chimney. So old . . . so old . . . and one whisker like a white filament.

'I don't believe he's real,' said Eliza, in a hushed, dreamy voice. She liked pretending that people were not real, or else they were going to change and disappear.

'He's horrible,' said Carly, 'He's a horrible Aussie.' Sandra piped up, 'What's an Aussie?' but Eliza said, 'You'd better not tell her anything you don't want her to come out with; you know what she is,' which was truth. When they met Augusta, she added to the disorder of the day. Her hair was bark-rough, and she looked somehow as if she had been splashed all over by the mist of waterfalls. The trap had to ford a shallow stream, and Augusta, the bandanna of mushrooms in her lap, said, 'Slappy reared once, coming across this ford. I had your Aunt Coral on my lap, and over she went. If her baby clothes hadn't floated her up, she might have been drowned.' Eliza didn't mind much if Aunt Coral had been drowned, because of what she said about the big grape; but somehow she liked the goblin, and the bright, streaming day.

Cousin Druce and Cousin Mabel, Aunt Patricia's children, were to play with them in the Melbourne Botanical Gardens. Stiff palm-fronds rattled on the air, with hard little slapping sounds, and they had grapes in a brown-paper bag.

'Don't you skin them and spit the pips?' asked Druce, his brows astonished over his hazel eyes. Mabel added, 'Our mother *never* lets us eat grapes with their skins-an'-pips. We might get appendicitis. Besides, a black man might have handled them.'

Carly and Eliza felt ashamed. Like cream, grapes were something you hardly ever had in Wellington. But Sandra said unexpectedly, 'I had appencitis.'

'Go on!' Druce was sceptical. 'Did you have the doctor?'

'Yes,' said Sandra, with her far-gazing blue look, 'an' he cut me open and took a little baby out. Let's play doctors.' Druce sat up hastily. 'That's not appendicitis. Come along, Mabel, we'd better go back to Mother.'

In the Zoo you could go on riding the elephant for ever and ever. He lurched from side to side, vast but gentle, and looking over you could see the huge prints he was making in the yellow gravel. 'Give him a bun, little lady.' The elephant curled his trunk back, and for a moment you saw right down inside. It was pink and wrinkled, like the inside of a hose-pipe but a different colour. Make yourself touch it. . . . The elephant took the bun, and everybody laughed and seemed pleased. Eliza could feel her panama hat slipping from its elastic, and her cheeks were burned, but she didn't want to get down from the seat that had tassels of red and dusty gold.

Cole's Book Arcade. . . . Mirrors making you thin as a spoon-handle, or enormously, waddlingly wide. Breath-catching, because they are what you dream sometimes, and then you have to pant hard, and say, 'It's a dream I will wake up it's a dream I WILL WAKE UP,' with tremendous, increasing momentum as you swing up from the pit to safety. A curly iron stair twisted, and the notice said, 'To the Roof-Garden, Adults Only.'

'I know what adults are,' said Sandra loudly. 'They're in the Catechism.' Everybody stopped, and Aunt Patricia said, 'What?' before Carly could pinch Sandra's arm. 'They can commit adultery,' said Sandra cheerfully. Aunt Patricia's eyes pecked like two crows, but Sandra stood unmoved, her bee curls clustering under the white velvet cap that matched corduroy jacket and short socks. An old lady said, 'What a sweetly pretty little girl,' and Carly thought, 'I wish you had her, and you were the eldest and everybody blamed you, that's all I wish.'

In the middle of the hot night a light shone, and a man walked into the room where the children were sleeping three in a bed. He was like the other Australian uncles, and yet unlike.

'You'll wake them up,' protested Aunt Patricia's voice over his shoulder.

'Nonsense. Do them good. Let them look at their Uncle Brendon.'

Eliza sat up.

'Ah, ah,' he said, 'there's the one for me.' He fished her out of bed like a winkle, smoothed down her nightgown, and said, 'Come on, I'll tell you a story.'

'Brendon, at this hour.'

'This is my girl, and she's hot as a coal, and she's got a bung eye from the mosquitoes,' said Uncle Brendon. Tucked in his coat, Eliza sat in the dining-room, listening to stories that were absurd and not absurd, so real that she knew they had really happened, happened in this short house under the fig-tree, which he said was the biggest fig-tree in the world. Once he poured a purple jewel into a glass for her. It made a hot little patch in her chest, and she apologized. 'I'm afraid I've got the hiccups.' 'Hold your breath and count twenty,' said Uncle Brendon. When the hiccoughs had gone, he told her she mustn't listen to him, as he was the bad lad of the family.

'I love you,' said Eliza sleepily; Uncle Brendon kissed her, and she thought, 'That's the first time I've been properly kissed in Australia.'

Their Aunt Bernardine was matron of the Agricultural College at the Yalla, and looked much more like Carly's Lords and Ladies than the others. She wore a rainy tremble of amethysts on her fingers and her long white throat, and had a house with a long screened verandah and garden of blowsy old roses and blundering bees. The college grounds were a huge farm. Sandra, asked what she liked best, said, 'Oh, the pigs first, and then the students,' and the students, tall young men with clean-shiny, slippery faces, crowded round and laughed.

There was no need to ask Carly what she liked best, once she had unfastened the heavy gilt clasp on Aunt Bernardine's photograph album. There they were, the people she had imagined; women with narrow oval faces and ringlets to their shoulders, men in uniforms. But she was sad about them, because the interesting ones had happened and been brushed out of the way long ago. 'And now we're all plain, ordinary, common-sense country folk,' finished Aunt Bernardine, briskly, 'except poor old Arthur Storey, who's as mad as a hatter and on his last legs, though musical people thought a lot of him in his day. Keeps violins by the dozen under his bed, in a dirty little flat, and thinks his family's in league to rob him.'

Even the faint, reflected light of the faces in the photograph album was better than no Lords and Ladies at all. Carly was never unhappy at the Yalla, except the night when the bat flew into her hair; then she screamed and screamed, spinning like a top, until Aunt Bernardine called sharply, 'Keep still at once, or I'll cut off your hair at the roots.' Then Aunt Bernardine's hard white fingers caught the bat, and chucked it out into darkness, a squashy little brown bogy.

Once they saw a whole hill alive with rabbits, brown-squirming, and Eliza felt a new respect for Australia. Its bareness was different, after all. Strange things were shaken out from under its armpits. . . . The students fraternized with the children, and mostly Augusta and Aunt Bernardine encouraged this, except for the morning when Sandra asked, 'Mummy, why do Australians always say, "God stiffen the crows?" '

But Eliza hated the Yalla after Mr Rush and the baby rabbit happened. One of the young students gave it to her, trembling and warm between her hands, its little nose wabbling suspiciously, its eyes large and startled. Mr Rush came up smiling, and said, 'What's that you've got, Tuppence?'

Eliza showed him the rabbit.

'That plague.' He caught the rabbit by its hind feet, and knocked its head against a tree. He did that three or four times, just a streak of brown and a crackle. When he dropped it, its face was all a bloody mash, and one of its eyes had come out. She felt streams of salt in her throat, and tried to swallow them back, choking. Mr Rush laughed. She threw herself straight at him. He said, 'Here, here,' and easily caught her wrists in one hand, but she bit his arm. Aunt Bernardine came out and said Mr Rush was quite right, rabbits were a plague and a destruction to thousands, and she screamed, 'You're a bloody murderer, Mr Rush,' until she was shut up in a room.

It seemed strange afterwards that Uncle Rufus, who had paid their fares to Australia, was the most obscure in memory of all. But his farm was far away in mallee country, scrubby and grey. The children knew from the conversation of the grown-ups that Uncle Rufus, who was a bachelor and quite well-off, wanted to adopt them all.

'That means we'd always live here, with Uncle Rufus, and never go back to Wellington any more,' Carly explained. Sometimes their mother's eyes were red-rimmed with weeping, and the uncles, towering over her, urged her, 'Think it over, old girl.' Not believing in God and the British Empire were very serious offences to them. They looked so different — so square-set on earth, with their red, healthy hair and their big freckles. John, when Eliza tried to call his picture back to mind, looked like a cut-out man of leather, with no thickness through at all.

Quite suddenly the talk of the grown-ups changed, becoming faster, harder, agitated, curiously proud. Life filled up with voices, everybody asking questions, nobody willing to stand still and explain. In a few days, Augusta came running in with a cablegram. She looked on the point of tears, and yet triumphant.

'We must go home at once, by the next boat. John's enlisted as a private.'

For a moment there was silence among the grown-ups. Then Uncle Martin said awkwardly, 'Well, old girl . . .' His red-brown face was embarrassed and sympathetic.

'Shows all that clack about the British Empire wasn't anything but a pack of man's talk,' cut in Aunt Rosalind. Uncle Will nodded.

'Many a man who's apt to rant a bit till the time comes shows up all right when it comes to deeds. Actions speak louder than words.'

'Three children to keep on a private's pay,' said Augusta. Her mind was a battlefield of ideas. She had been unfair to John. . . . John had enlisted. . . . John might be killed fighting for his King and country, which seemed paradoxical, after all the row he had made . . . she must get home at once, and see him off . . . three children to keep on a private's pay would mean bare existence. Automatically, she repeated the last fragment aloud. Money was not the most important thing in her life, but since she had had the children, it had become the most pressing and worrying one.

'Well, old girl, there's still Rufus's offer. He wants to give you and the kiddies a home, and he'd want it more than ever now.'

Augusta, hardly thinking, disposed of Rufus in one sentence.

'Oh, no,' she said, 'He'll be going too.' It was Uncle Rufus's epitaph. The children never saw him.

Still the long tin-roofed sheds at Wellington; still the screaming gulls, the towering cranes dipping their limbs patiently into the horizon. But John, when he met them at the wharf, hadn't yet got his khaki uniform, and the romance of him fell a little flat. When they got back to Calver Street, tired and dusty, Augusta soon forgot to be excited about the war. John while she was away had done the unspeakable, and got into debt. 'Look at these bills,' she cried, between rage and tears, 'your children can do with bread and dripping, I suppose; but for you, the moment my back's turned, tinned asparagus and strawberry preserves.'

Carly, Eliza and Sandra gazed at their father, with eyes round and bright as new pennies. Even in Australia, where the red machine trickled milk at one end, cream at another, and Uncle Brendon's fig-tree swelled into bursting purple fruits, they had never had tinned asparagus or strawberry preserves.

CHAPTER SIX

Toy Town

RAIN swelled and darkened in the sky. Eliza practised the complicated French hop, thinking that at last the Hannays had scored over the Vaughans. Mr Vaughan, it had come out, was traveller for a *German* firm; everybody had envied his Sunday car, but now they said, 'Look how he gets it,' and when Jock Vaughan cheeked Carly, Augusta marched up to the Vaughan door and gave Mrs Vaughan a right-down piece of her mind. 'The idea of your children calling Carly the Kaiser. The cap fits nearer home, Mrs Vaughan, the cap fits nearer home.' Her voice carried down into the backyard, where Carly and Eliza and Sandra sat listening, Carly still a bit tearful, and gave them a delightful sense of triumph. Eliza repeated it as she hopped: 'The idea of you calling us the Kaiser, Ngaio and Jock Vaughan, the very idea. The cap fits nearer home.'

Unnaturalized Germans were interned on Somes Island, in the middle of Wellington Harbour. Three of them swam for the mainland one night, and one was left dying of cold on the rocks. 'Just like Germans to leave their friend in the lurch,' said Augusta; the others were soon caught and sent back, so it didn't matter.

And in all the butcher-shops, pink-rinded German sausage, with the delicious little triangles of bacon fat, had become 'Belgian sausage'. Belgium is brave little Belgium, one of our Allies.

Half-way down Calver Street, standing on his iron-railed balcony, the Silly Boy swayed and smiled, dipping from his middle to the dusty-headed cabbage tree. His smiling face sagged back, chinless; his body, in its good black clothes, bent in a rickety way at the waist. His hands were like queer white creepers clutching the balcony rail, and down on him poured hard sun, the red oil from the cruse of clouds. Sometimes in Calver Street you could hear the military bands flare forth from Island Bay; then the main-streets looked exactly like torn brown-paper bags, with peanuts rattling out, men in khaki. But the Silly Boy never took any notice. Smile and sway . . . smile and sway. . . .

The Flint boys, whose mother went backwards and forwards from the Asylum, had lumbered off months ago in their khaki, serious and nice. Not long afterwards, Mrs Flint came screeching over to the Hannays' door, her grey hair flying, and cried that Augusta had killed her Joe and buried him in the backyard. It seemed so funny, because the backyard was covered over with asphalt, and anyone could see it would be impossible to bury even a cat there. A policeman had to be called when Mrs Flint started waving the chopper about, but afterwards Augusta, instead of being furious, only put her hands over her eyes. 'The poor thing. The poor thing.'

Rain began to fall in bouncing drops like marbles, down on the Silly Boy's bare head and the cabbage tree dying of dust. Eliza heard her mother calling for her to come home at once and do a message. She answered, 'Oh, all right,' and dragged one foot after another up the gutter. She hated going home. It was all right for Carly, but Eliza didn't like babies much.

The back door was open, and Augusta stood peeling potatoes over the sink. Behind, Eliza could see the dim and gentle outline of Carly, sitting in the kitchen with the blinds drawn down, rocking the cradle. She tiptoed in, but Carly, looking up, said instantly, 'Sssh, you'll wake him,' and she saw that, as usual, Kitch had gone to sleep with Carly's little finger in his sea-anemone mouth. He had a red little face with waxy nostrils, and he cried too much, but Carly adored him. She had known that he was coming. When Eliza and Sandra were so surprised, Carly wrinkled up her face in superior wisdom. 'I knew all the time.'

'Mother always favours you,' Sandra complained. But for the first few weeks, while Augusta was in bed, they were too busy intriguing against Mrs Maguire to care how the war-baby came, or why.

Mrs Maguire was supposed to be the housekeeper and Augusta's nurse, but she stacked the dishes in great greasy piles for the children to wash when they came home from school, strained and jerked their hair into tight pigtails that took all the curl out, and read German atrocities out of the newspapers when she was supposed to be bathing Kitch. She could read with her mouth half-full. Nearly always she said, 'Well, I think I'll just have a snack,' and they met her coming out of the pantry with a carving-knife and pink hunks carved off the joint for tomorrow.

'She's a cockroach,' said Sandra, 'a big, damn cockroach.' Carly said patiently, 'You mustn't say Damn, or God won't look after Daddy at the front.' She was very logical about God; no good behaviour, no pie. Every night they knelt down by their beds, and when they had finished their ordinary prayers said in chorus, 'And bless dear Daddy and keep him safe, and bless-all-the-poor-soldiers-and-sailors-on-sea-and-land-and-bring-them-all-safe-back-home-again-for-Christ's-sake-Amen.' Sandra was always in a hurry to finish her prayers — she got chilblains — and the poor soldiers and sailors ended in a little slither.

They were all glad when Mrs Maguire went away; Augusta threw the dummy out of the window, and said her baby must never touch that filthy thing again. Kitch howled and howled, until Carly discovered that if he sucked her little finger he went off to sleep quite as well as with the dummy. She was his godmother when Mr Arden baptized him at Saint Monica's in the name of the Father, the Son and the Holy Ghost. He was Kitchener for Lord Kitchener, John for Daddy, and Louvain for a town in Belgium that the Germans had burned down.

Kitch at first was very bald, but the down came in golden-brown streaks on his skull. 'He's got lovely hair,' said Carly proudly. 'You can touch it, if you like, but whatever you do, don't wake him up.' Eliza stroked the golden-brown. 'It *is* silky,' she said in a whisper, and Carly looked so pleased; but really Eliza didn't like him or want him, she thought he was like a little pink slug, and hated the way he opened his mouth and cried whenever he liked, even when he'd got everything he wanted. It was different to cry when you were hurt or sorry or enraged, but how could that pink formless thing feel troubles?

'Eliza,' said their mother, 'I told you I wanted you for a message, not to hang about. You can do the blind alphabet, can't you? Well, just run down the street and tell old Miss Pyritt the war news. I'm too busy, and I know that niece of hers has gone gadding off to town again, I saw her through the window.'

Eliza lingered.

'I don't like going there, Mother. She's got a funny smell.'

'If you were as old as that, you'd have a funny smell. She's got her two nephews fighting for you, all she has in the world. You do what I tell you, and look smart about it.'

Straggling yellow weeds grew in Miss Pyritt's garden, and the door had panes of opaque pink glass. The real reason Eliza didn't want to go inside was that one night she had had a terrible nightmare about this place. She stood on the doorstep and pressed the doorbell, and something — not Miss Pyritt, something big and flat and round — came flopping down the stairs to meet her. She could see its shape, like a vast jelly-mould, through the opaque glass, before she fled shrieking. . . . In real life, it was no use ringing the doorbell, Miss Pyritt couldn't hear. Gingerly Eliza turned the key and walked in. Miss Pyritt sat in her kitchen before the stove, which had a softly-smouldering mouth of flame; her black cat rubbed softly against the thick black wool of her stockings, which were gnarled like the bark of a tree, on account of her rheumatism. When Eliza touched her on the shoulder, she lifted her face. Both her eyes were covered with pearly cataracts, and she couldn't hear a word. She was very thin, sallow as old parchment, and her hands were all knuckles.

Eliza knelt down, and taking Miss Pyritt's right hand pressed her fingers against it. Miss Pyritt, who could speak, repeated letter after letter as Eliza made them. Double loop of first finger and thumb for B, knuckle pressed into palm for R, touch third finger-tip for I. Slowly the necessary words, 'British victory,' were spelt out. Carly was much quicker at the deaf-and-blind alphabet than Eliza, and often in class the big girls used it if they wanted to talk secrets.

'Many dead?' croaked Miss Pyritt. Eliza spelt, 'No — not ours; big German losses.' With minor variations, this was all the war news Miss Pyritt got from her neighbours. The cat's purring was growly, a little thunder in the deaf and blind room.

'Thank you, my dear, thank you. That is news we must be grateful for. We must all thank God.' She pressed Eliza's hands between her two palms; their skin was yellow and detached, like your heel when you have been in bed for a fortnight with the measles. 'A child's hand,' she said, 'a child's hand.'

Rain fell hard in oblique sharp lines on the other side of the pink glass doors, but Eliza was glad to get out in it. Her face drank the rain, she even tasted it on her tongue. She cried, and did not know why she cried. She walked in the yellow brim-full gutters and cried, and did not want ever to go home.

War is long, slender rows of names between two black lines in the evening paper. Some of the names have a star against them. War is little pictures.

Lord Kitchener is drowned. Carly cries softly, for pity, and because Kitch is his namesake. But Augusta puts her head down on the kitchen table, rests her face on her outstretched arms. The children have never seen her do that before. Kitchener's picture, brass-framed, scowls severely down at her.

'My poor country. Oh, my poor country. What *has* she done to deserve it?'

'Stand up, the girls with more than three spelling errors. This is your imposition. You are to write twenty times, "I am a German."'

Young Mr Gillan, the third master, who is only twenty and has already enlisted, thinks he's smart. Soon he is going into camp at Featherston.

Eliza feels heroism making a hard knob in her throat, and rises.

'Please, Mr Gillan, we won't write that.'

Mr Gillan stares hard.

'Won't you?' His cane cuts soft swishes in the air.

'No, Mr Gillan, we'd sooner have the cane.'

The other girls with more than three spelling errors get caught up into drama. 'We won't write it, Mr Gillan, we'd sooner have the cane.'

'Very well. You can write "I am a Britisher" fifty times instead of twenty.'

He catches Eliza's eye. He has a devilish little twinkle, and a black moustache.

'Please, Mr Gillan, we'd love to do that.'

Auckland is further ahead with the Copper Trail than Wellington, and that is a disgrace for Wellington. The Copper Trail, a huge snake of pennies, has to cover the whole length of the North Island. Then it will be spent on comforts for the wounded soldiers and sailors. The children do not realize that its length will only be measured on the map; they see actual pennies laid end to end, shining through bush and ti-tree, over stubborn hills, and Wellington's disgrace sticks in their throat. Wellington is only about up to Featherston, Auckland is right down to Cambridge. They are allowed to do anything to collect — black their faces and go round in wheelbarrows yelling, 'Guy Fawkes, Guy,' collect bottles from house to house, or wear red, white and blue cockades, and be appointed Ticket-Sellers, after an interview with a very grave gentleman who impresses on them that they must be careful not to lose the tickets.

Carly is too shy, though she has knitted two and a half balaclavas, and is now sobbing over the heel of her first khaki sock — trying to knit on four needles is terrible till you know how. But Eliza and Sandra make fine ticket collectors. In town, hurrying people sometimes brush them aside, or give beggarly pennies and threepences, but down on the wharves they are a huge success. The wharfies sit with backs against the tin sheds, their legs sprawled out, red handkerchiefs crusted round their heads. Some chew steadily on great hunks of bread and meat. Through cracks in the wharves you can see green water sparkling and sliding, and feel the whole wharf shake slightly as the piles move in the tide. Big horse-wagons lumber along, the wharves are all sprinkled with chaff and horse-dung. A man lives in an iron house above the wheeling, patient cranes. The wharfies pull half-crowns and florins out of their trousers, and fling them to Eliza and Sandra. 'Here, little codger.'

One says, spitting clear into the sea, 'What'll yer give me?'

'A kiss,' Eliza suggests, her brown hair blowing madly about her head. She feels light and strange, happy as the seagulls. 'Aw ri,' says the wharfie, and she kisses his cheek. A roar of laughter goes up.

'Five bob for that one, Bill. Come along, be a sport.' Bill fishes out two half-crowns and hands them over. Another wharfie corners Sandra.

'What'll you do for 'arf-a-crown, kid?'

'I'll sing *Three Cheers for the Red, White and Blue*,' offers Sandra, and pipes up, while the wharfies laugh and keep time. Afterwards she says to Eliza, 'I wasn't going to kiss that one. I saw him blow his nose on the back of his hand.'

'It's for the wounded soldiers and sailors.'

Sandra looks doubtful. 'Anyhow,' says Eliza, 'I made £2/9/7d. How much did you make?' They forget all about the wharfies, counting up Sandra's pennies and threepences and half-crowns.

Half-way through the war, Eliza became a poet. It happened in a white dinghy down at Island Bay, where Augusta used to take them in the summer evenings, Kitch in his push-chair. The boat looked safe and tired; there was a little dirty sea-water in its bottom, but not enough to count. She slid into it and curled up.

She heard the fishermen shouting, their oars splashed as they rowed out to drag the ends of their huge nets from the buoys. They were an Italian colony, who ate fried octopus and hung strings of garlic and red-gold onions in their huts. Once a hermit had lived on Island Bay's little Island. He was dead now.

But always . . . the sand had splayed out in fawn-coloured drifts, and the pale paraha bells had trembled their taut mauve silk, elastic to the touch, against the wind. It was a cold sea, hurt and tired.

The nets were in, it was nearly dark, and she knew Augusta would be buying three fish cheap. Tiny soles, shark, sea-urchins, fish like bursting kelp-pods, fish with flopping silver bodies and round red mouths.

Another voice mixed with the loud fishermen-voices, calling. She shut her ears to it, it would have broken the spell. At last, when a few pale stars sprinkled the sky, silver daisies on a stiff-standing dark blue taffeta gown, she clambered out of the boat, stiff all over. There was a crowd at the other end, and when they saw her everybody started at once. Her mother caught her by the wrist.

'Do you know the Boy Scouts are out looking for you? Where have you been?'

'I couldn't help it. I was writing a poem.'

Eliza felt that if the cliffs came tumbling down in a spoil of yellow sand, still she must say it. Men started calling back the Boys Scouts, who were enjoying themselves scuttling like crabs about the rocks; Eliza was wicked, selfish and ungrateful. When Augusta had finished apologizing for her, they went home.

Presently, Augusta was not cross any more, and they were all drinking macaroni soup at the house in Calver Street. Augusta said, 'Now let's have this blessed poem.' Eliza repeated it without a hitch. It rhymed ocean with motion and weather with feather.

Augusta said, 'Humph . . . Not so bad. But you let me catch you hiding in boats again, that's all, my lady.' With the same queer inconsistency she showed towards John's books, she bought Eliza an exercise book, and Eliza drew a palm tree and a Union Jack on the inside cover (somehow she always imagined John as sitting beneath a palm tree and a Union Jack, and besides, palm trees were easy to draw) and started writing poems with the regularity of a model Orpington mother laying eggs. Often when the poems were done she cried over them. John lay buried all over the world, in burning tropical sands, in Flanders mud, in English soil, on mountain-tops. Augusta sent him copies of the poems, but he didn't like them much, and wrote, 'Eliza really ought to improve her handwriting.' Mr Arden, the young curate of St Monica's, was enchanted, however, with 'The Soldier's Babe'.

'But this is delightful, Mrs Hannay. The others are childish — this has the true spirit of poetry.' His long fingers were clever with the piano, and once at a church social, little girls in white cashmere frocks and open-work stockings sang Eliza's:

> Hush thee to sleep, O gentle babe of mine,
> Hush thee to sleep, beneath the southern vine;
> Hush thee to sleep, holy and undefiled,
> Hush thee to sleep, thou art a soldier's child.

There were several other verses, rhyming 'Hun' with 'gun' and 'Verdun'. Sandra said, 'There aren't any southern vines in Wellington, except in the Vaughan's greenhouse, and they're dirty Germans, so you oughtn't to put them into a poem about a soldier's babe. And besides, you don't do any hushing Kitch to sleep.' But Eliza was happy, not so much in the concrete results — those horrifying little jingles with Union Jacks on their breasts and laurel-leaves in their hair — as in the mysterious sense of power and satisfaction that lay behind them; a daydream power, which slips through the eyes of all children, sometimes through the brooding eyes of meadow-beasts as well, but which is only rarely held and formulated. Eliza had no name for this feeling but 'it'. Sometimes for weeks it would stay away, and she felt a petrifying conviction that it never would, never could come back again. She tried to bribe it by being incredibly good; then her mind swung to the opposite pole, and she thought, 'Perhaps if I'm bad it will. I don't care, then, how bad I am.' Then, without forcing or pleas, it was there, and with it peace; it was the first thing she had ever had that she could call truly her own.

Carly took Eliza's poetry hard. Once, at school, she went to the length of telling a fantastic lie about it.

'Huh,' she said scornfully, 'Eliza doesn't write all that rosy-posy stuff. Mr Arden makes it up.' Eliza stayed dumb with wounded vanity. After school, she cornered Carly alone.

'That was a lie, Carly. Nobody makes up my poems for me.'

'I don't care if they don't.'

This wasn't soft Carly. Eliza groped in holes and corners for an explanation.

'Carly —'

'I don't care. You can go home and tell Mother.'

'I'm not going to tell on you. I know why you did it.'

'Huh.'

Eliza proceeded gently, 'You're in love with Mr Arden, aren't you, Carly?'

For a moment Carly's grey eyes looked as if they were going to pop out of her head.

'I'm — I'm *what?*'

'In love with Mr Arden.'

'I'm not in love with anybody. I never was, and I never will be. You ought to be ashamed of yourself for talking about such things, Eliza Hannay, so there.'

'Then why did you give him my poems?'

Water stood in Carly's eyes. She said, 'Oh, you and your damn' poems — don't be so smug about your damn' poems,' and raced away downhill, evidently forgetful that because she had said 'Damn' — she said it twice — God might let their father be killed that night. Eliza stared after her with vague eyes. She was too much interested to be hurt any longer by Carly's lie, and besides, she felt now that she could write another poem. So she did, sitting among high dockplants in the empty section opposite the Willow Pattern Place. The dark-green leaves were stained foxy, and mottled with death, and the rusty spores, green at the base of their little octagons, shook down lightly on her face. She loved the feel of *things*, even hard, common things, like lumps of yellow clay and broken brick in the section, and the two halves of a white china cup somebody had thrown out. She had a game of trying to stare them out, and could look at them for a very long time without her eyes watering. And sometimes *people* changed in the same way. Some of the girls at school had boys; Eliza never did, but once she went up to the brickyards with Jim Burstle, just at sunset, and the red light poured over the reddish dusty bricks. All she could think was, 'I am sitting in the brickyards with a boy.' It didn't matter a bit who the boy was, or that neither of them said a word.

Then in a winter's morning Augusta was saying over and over again, 'It's gone, I tell you it's gone. I've looked everywhere.'

'Sit down, Mummy, you know you're always putting your bag in funny places,' said Carly, who since Kitch arrived and became her nursling was faintly authoritative with Augusta.

'I didn't lose it. I put it on my dressing-table last night. It was there when I went to sleep, and now it's vanished. Fourteen pounds — what shall I do? We'll all starve.'

'It's sure to be somewhere.' But it wasn't. The children hunted in old teapots, under the mattress in the cradle, even in the street drain, which the Collie boys eagerly poked with long sticks.

Sandra announced, round-eyed, 'We had a burglar.' Secretly, she was bubbling over with pleasure and importance; having a burglar was far more tangible in her mind than losing the £14. The children never had any money of their own but a halfpenny a week, paid on Saturdays, and if they did anything specially naughty, this was stopped. But Augusta, never helpless except in the hours of childbirth, sat half-collapsed in her rocking-chair, muttering, 'Fourteen pounds — what shall we do, what shall we do?'

At school everybody was far more interested in the burglary than they had been in the war-baby, and Mr Duncan put a reward for information notice in the papers. But it was young Mr Arden who brought Augusta round. He wanted to take up a parish subscription for the Hannays; his kindliness got her right up to the last fence, and then she baulked. Her body became rigid, her mouth set.

'No — no, thank you very much, Mr Arden. We'll manage.'

She managed, and the children never noticed the difference. But ten years later, at a vaudeville show, when a clairvoyant in a black velvet mask offered to tell the secrets of past, present and future, Augusta got up.

'Where did my fourteen pounds go?'

The clairvoyant said that the Union Steamship Company got it.

'Too big to search,' said Augusta grimly, and sat down.

Carly, Sandra and Eliza were to go straight down to the hall, where the spraying-machine was, and when they had been sprayed, to hurry back without stopping to play with anyone. There wasn't any school; school was shut up, and many of the Duffel Street children were dead or dying, and Augusta, who was a V.A.D., said she did wish the Roman Catholics weren't so religious.

'The moment they have a nose-bleed they start seeing Saints and angels, like a game of snakes and ladders, and have me out of my bed for nothing. If they spent half the time cleaning their houses on earth as they do white-washing their souls for the Hereafter they'd have more chance when they really are ill. I haven't had my sleep for the past four nights.'

But though Augusta grumbled a little, she was in her element, and her red hair won back its old defiance, marching with the red-lettered V.A.D. badge on her arm. Mr Duncan was nearly dead. He had broken into the Boseley house, and found old Mr Boseley (according to Sylvia Rainer) stiff as a board and black all over, and stopped on to nurse Mrs Boseley and her son, even after he caught the influenza himself. Then he had staggered out and collapsed near the Rainer gate, and Mrs Rainer was nursing him, for which Eliza would once have envied her almost to death. But now the silent streets and ugly little match-box houses looked so deserted that, in a negative way, they were exciting. They were a dusty mouth that had opened and swallowed everything up. . . .

The formalin with which they were sprayed smelt sweet-sticky, clinging in vaporous, fine-beaded mists to skin and hair. The old people who owned the Willow Pattern Place had died of the 'flu, and their ducks paddled about, dirty white breasts and yellow bills on the weedy pond. A line in a poem she had read came into her mind:

Toy Town is covered up with weeds.

In the real poem it was 'Troy Town', and went on beautifully to tell of the Atlanteans; but she liked 'Toy Town' better. The houses were so little, and the empty sunlight straggled and bloomed over them, itself like a great golden weed.

Half-way down Calver Street the Silly Boy still stood, swaying and smiling. Eliza thought, if all the confetti of the wrong Armistice Day, when the grown-ups went mad, came down on his head, rose and blue and little bits of rainbow green, still he wouldn't have cared.

They were meeting Daddy at the wharf; and after hours in a crowd tight-packed, John was off the gangway; John, thinner and a little browner, was kissing them all, his rough hairy khaki brushing against faces and hands. From Cape Town he had sent them presents — silver leaves, bright hankies, and for Carly a crocodilite brooch in a golden filigree setting, though the filigree soon tarnished, proving it was not real gold. But Carly thought then that she might love him, after all, and had gone through spells of remorse like toothache. They took a taxi going home, the first they had ever had. Carly stood up, wanting to watch the scattered world of khaki clothes and crying pink faces. He grabbed her by the arm, and jerked her back to the seat.

'Sit down, can't you, sit down? What do you think you're doing?'

Carly thought, 'I still don't properly love him, and he doesn't love me.'

The real end of the war happened up in the little grey hills behind the waterworks. It was an easy walk from Calver Street, and sometimes the boys used to fly kites there on Sundays. The Hannays found and played in an enclosed space, planted like a garden with shrubs. Dark trees with sticky pink flowers hived multitudes of slumbrous bees. At first Carly was nervous of the trees, because they might meet a man or a cow — cows nowadays seemed to her just as bad as men; but it turned out a reliable place, and they were sitting cross-legged under the pink-flowered shrubs when the music began.

Carly said, 'It must be the wires,' and they listened intently. But there weren't any wires, no fine spider-web catching in these hills; and besides, the music was far too large for them. It seemed to swell out of the ground, out of a magically opened doorway in the hillside; deep and vibrant it talked. Afterwards Eliza thought, 'It was like a windharp,' though she had never heard one. The low hills vibrated gently, and none of them could say how long it lasted. Dying traveller's joy lay spun on the bushes, masses of gauzy filaments. The children dropped their pine-cones, and stared at one another. Their faces were round and pale, like the puff-balls of blossom they used to call wild clocks. Odd little things, they looked, suddenly raught away from the world. When the music trembled no more and they could catch no least echo of it, they went down over the hills to Eliza's Toy Town.

CHAPTER SEVEN

Laloma

AFTER the war, when it was decided that their father's gratuity, helped out by the State Advance mortgage (another little Government treat for the returned soldiers), should buy the Hannays a house of their own, the children sat round the kitchen table, chanting, 'Buy Laloma, buy Laloma, buy Laloma.' They had never seen Laloma, but they were afraid that if it weren't bought they would get no house after all. John was tired of house-hunting, of the way Augusta went mousing in the drains and cooking arrangements of his prospective castles. Besides, to get to Laloma from Oddipore they had to change trams twice, which made it seem far away and romantic, and Eliza visioned it spotted all over with little flakes of falling snow. The children sang 'Buy Laloma' till Augusta gave in. 'Anything for a quiet life.'

The name of the house was a Samoan word, meaning 'The Abode of Love'. Laloma had its points; an ugly rickety house of white-painted wood, on a slope so steep that where in front it started life as a two-decker, at the back it had only one floor, the odd space going into cellars dominated by cats, rats, spiders, and the children. But its over-the-hills-and-far-awayness rang true. Most of the view glowed and kindled with gorse. In front was a clay precipice which Augusta called the garden, at the back a tiny lawn and a veritable native tree, a ngaio. Its branches were too thin to bear a swing, but its oily leaves, pin-pricked with gilt light, were pleasant when one lay beneath on curt grass and dandelions.

From the front you could see the old gravestones of a disused cemetery, jagged and yellow as decaying teeth. Between them at night slithered phosphorus, sometimes a mere glow-worm, sometimes long sheets of blue; behind, the hills curved softly and darkly into the bush, wilderness reached by five-mile tramps along lampless roads of brambles and little creeks. Laloma was half a mile inside civilization's fringes, and had the water laid on. The outpost was Bawder's Farm, with nothing beyond but bright broom and gorse, and stony valleys where Bawder's bull grazed, shaking its great head impatiently if the children approached. Mr Bawder supplied milk and duck-eggs, and was also the nightman for the houses without water services. His cart went rumbling along like something from Black Death days, and Mr Bawder, in a rabbit-skin cap and a red lantern at his belt, shamelessly waved and called out, 'How's yer Ma? Tell yer Pa

I could let him have that sitting of duck-eggs dirt cheap,' causing great shame among the adolescent girls of the district, who did not quite like to recognize him, as they stood in their dusk-billowy, daisy frocks outside the gates with their boys. Mr Bawder had no remorse, and did not believe in the cleanliness of the world. 'Eee,' he once said of his poultry, 'duck's a bird lays her egg in the moock, and then does something on top.'

Nearly everyone in the new district was sedate, except old Tim O'Keefe, the harness-maker, who was a Bolshie, and had in his shop window a large, unsteadily lettered notice, 'No Bushrangering Done Here'. He had a silver mop of hair, like an albino golliwog; John immediately made a friend of him, and Augusta, on principle, hated him all the way down from whiskers to shoe-leather. In an Irish way, he was good-natured, and tried to heal the Hannays' family strife. 'Ah,' he'd say of John, 'the big gob he makes on his face for throuble, like a thrush would be swallowing worms.'

Quietly, leaving hardly a slender pencil marking behind it, Calver Street had melted away; that happened almost overnight, as the returned soldiers, one moment arrogant and united in their rough khaki, in the next were shabby nothings in navy blue, back to their old pigeon-holes — the gentlemen (ex-merchants, or merchants' sons), the clerks and shopkeepers, the labourers, the tramwaymen, to whom you couldn't talk, because they were cheeky. John's lean face had hardly lost its khaki hat, his body hardly decided that the fierce northerlies tearing down from the hills to Laloma were going to give him rheumatism, when he started to 'make a big gob on his face for throuble.' And here there were no Silly Boys, no drunken Mr Potockis, no Nigger Jacks, to take the edge off his dissension. He had come amongst the respectable. The respectable, in their way, enjoyed him tremendously. Within six months John was a branded man.

At Laloma the sitting-room was called the drawing-room, the kitchen was the breakfast-room, and the scullery was the kitchenette. John, who had ceased to sleep with Augusta in the double bed, had a little blue room to himself at the back of the house, his window opening on a dank pit known to Augusta as 'the fernery'. Augusta and Kitch, Carly and Sandra, shared bedrooms, and Eliza had a tiny green room of her own, technically because she was studying for her senior scholarship, actually because she was restless and made things unbearable for everybody.

In the drawing-room stood the upright piano on which Augusta had spent more than half of the money left her when Uncle Rufus was killed

on Gallipoli. His photograph, in a frame with crossed Union Jacks, stood
on top. The children were to have music, piano-lessons, culture. . . . In
their first two years at Laloma, girls and boys, according to the custom
of the country, came visiting and sang sentimental ballads. Carly very
soon learned to play; she had a soft little voice, like a singing mouse,
and would secretly have loved to sing solo in church. But in the choir
Miss Blair and Little Miss Blair (one like a frog, the other like a tadpole)
had cornered the solo work, and Carly was pigeon-holed as relieving
organist, shiner of church brasses, holder of stalls at St Kevin's bazaars,
good girl generally. Nearly all the important people at St Kevin's were
related, or connected by marriage. One built the church, another held
the mortgage on it, a third was Sunday School superintendent, two were
churchwardens, and the broken reed of the family worked in as janitor.
When they died, their brass tablets stared from the brick walls healthy
and aggressive, and Carly helped to keep them clean. The women of the
clan married, no matter *what* their teeth looked like, exchanged recipes,
and didn't go wrong.

Carly spread her fingers on the keyboard of the piano, which she loved.
She took great trouble with her hands, rubbing them with lemon and
cucumber rinds, and at last she had broken free from the awful,
overwhelming shame of biting her nails, a trick which had come on her
in her first year at college. Her finger-nails now were little pink discs. She
had entered her third college year. Though she was in the B classes — C
for arithmetic — she was popular, in a mouse-coloured, quiet way. She
liked listening to the other girls talk, giggled when they giggled, and kept
her troubles to herself.

She pressed the keys, and ballad notes trickled out, honey from a hose-
pipe. The boys' voices joined in, Trevor Sinjohn's loudest. Hose-pipe
. . . Sandra had been caught prancing undressed under the hose-pipe, in
the front lawn, where any of the boys coming home from school might
have seen her; Trevor Sinjohn might have seen her. She was so glad
Trevor Sinjohn hadn't come by; she would have died. A faint red warmed
her cheeks at the thought.

> 'From my fond lips the eager answers fall,
> Thinking I hear thee — thinking I hear thee call.'

Trevor's hand turned the pages; she knew it, detached from the rest of
him, as well as though it were a piece of herself. She smiled at him,

without looking up, and joined in the next song. But her voice was only a murmur under the louder voices.

Augusta loved them, the boys and girls. She went to the expense of cutting sandwiches for them without a protest, and Carly had a birthday party their first year in Laloma. Contact with frosty-cheeked youth, neither too clever nor to weary. . . .

But the youths and maidens came less frequently now. Either at nine o'clock Tim O'Keefe arrived, with a cargo of ale and politics on board, and talked his rubbish into the small hours; or else, after stewing thunderously in the back bedroom, with the window jammed down, John appeared, his hair ruffled up on end and some book in his hand.

'Ever read this?' (To any one of the white-flannelled youths.)

'No, Mr Hannay.' The youth's dark eyes, lean slouch, refrained from insolence, but did not get so far as deference.

'Time you did. Time you got to know what this bloody capitalist system means.' Seeing Augusta crinkle up, he repeated the word slowly. 'A boy with no convictions is no bloody good to himself or anyone else.'

'No, Mr Hannay.' The boy, who probably had definite convictions that he loved life, that he must earn a living in some vague, rosy way unassociated with grind, that the girl Simons was gone on him, that his sister had better remember to press his bags because he would want them for the cricket tomorrow, stared with bird-bright eyes, thinking, 'Old fool.'

The life of the district was vigorous and orthodox. The older men were a little like seed-pods, a little like sly brown animals. Religion (church, choir, Bible Class, bazaars) were focal points. So were the Sunday afternoon walks to the bush, sauntering past Bawder's bull and his broom-bright, stamping ground of hills to the jungle, where boys cut supple-jack switches, and the girls laughed and screamed as the tiny thorns of bushlawyer tugged their filament hair. Beyond grew nothing but stunted crab-apple trees, adorned in autumn with rosy O's of fruit; then, after bare hills, bush again, reputedly so thick that you had to slash your way with a knife. But the boys and girls didn't get so far. They stopped half-way, and the higher slopes dipped aloof into sunset.

All the girls had boys. Carly's was Trevor Sinjohn, a white-faced, black-browed chunk of clerical meat-to-be. He had fascination, the fascination of pale catlike eyes and an immense, obdurate selfishness. He would never do anything much, or try to; but all the time, seated in his little engine-house of flesh, he would be Trevor Sinjohn, clever Trevor, who saw everything, and didn't get hurt. The Bawder boy, a blundering, uncouth earnestness with a shiny face, was deeply in love with Carly, and had fought Trevor Sinjohn three times. But it wouldn't have helped him, even if he hadn't invariably been licked. His red face, so often plummy with black eyes or bleeding nose, made Carly uncomfortable. She touched the keys delicately. It was Trevor whom she loved, Trevor . . .

Eliza, though not quite thirteen when she came to Laloma, had her choice of three boys, one almost an idiot. She chose the grocer's boy, who could get plenty of sweets, and was very energetic in writing him notes:

Dear Jimmie,
You had better look out for Johnnie Tyler, he is mad over me, and will do you an injury.

There were laws. Your boy never kissed you, except in kissing-games (Trevor had kissed Carly). Relations were virginal until somewhere between sixteen and twenty years old. Sometimes then the girls developed babies, and the boys, after frantic wriggling with parsons and parents, married them at five months, both rather red-eyed. They rented little houses. Once the baby was in its perambulator, and could be tickled under the chin and praised, they were quite forgiven.

John was jealous of youth. Dark good looks, flannel bags, young girls with provocative breasts and sweet limbs beneath their limp voile frocks, lay back in limbo, sacrificed to strange urban gods, who asked him hoarsely, 'Coming along to the meeting tonight, Comrade?' Sometimes, not offensively, only just consciously, he tried to touch the girls' smooth arms, or to engage them in talk; but all the time he felt that they were laughing at him. Sacrificed, sacrificed. . . .

Sometimes the young laughter, the young puppy voices around the drawing-room piano, were unbearable. Then he shambled to the door, his brain torn with the agony of desiring to strike, desiring not to strike. The sunny ribbons, the pink lollipop faces, the suggestion of unfledged, unscorched devil, laughed at him and defied him.

'You're staying bloody late tonight aren't you?'

After a while the young men stopped coming, and the Hannays were a sort of subcutaneous irritation in the district, like jiggers. Augusta had to buy Trevor Sinjohn's attention for Carly with extra good suppers and flattery. And she didn't like Trevor, or countenance his family. John was dragging her pride low, watching her crawl so that Carly might flower into happiness.

He would give his soul to be transformed; at one stroke, to change all the hate into unity and love. Wasn't he a Socialist? But the miracle never came, he couldn't deviate from his path by one hairbreadth. He read long into the nights, Marx fused in a cloud of tobacco smoke with the memories of older, bitterly beautiful civilizations; slave-civilizations, their long-stemmed flowers blowing graciously over the sticky morass that fed their carrion roots. His daughter Eliza gave him a portrait of the Egyptian queen Nefertiti, and often he stared at the delicate little high-bred face, the slender eyebrows like wings, the lips which a thousand centuries could not stale to desire. 'Das Kapital' and that . . .

Outside Laloma, he did better with politics. Verbally he never won an argument, his temper was too heady, but he was no fool, and ten times as well read as the average professional politician. Carl Withers, who now ran a little journal called *Stingaree*, besides the second-hand bookshop, invited him to write articles. He called the series 'Mohammed to the Mountain', and often laboured over them all night, filling the blue room with rank tobacco-fumes and drinking endless cups of stewed black tea. Eliza read the articles, and said, with her young condescension, that they were not at all bad. He valued even the chips of her praise; she had a mind.

It was about that time that he began an odd habit; little in the telling.

'Come along to the pitchers tonight, Sandra?'

'Pictures, Daddy.'

'Pitchers, that's what I said. Come on down to the Gigantic, I believe it's a pretty good pitcher.'

'Not pitchers, pictures.'

'Pitchers. Pitchers. Then how do you pronounce it? You're all too bloody superior for me.'

'Don't argue, Sandra.' (From Augusta.) 'Can't you see that he's only doing it?' But Sandra ended in stamping furies, her velvet blue eyes swamped with tears. They were poor, they weren't allowed to talk to tram conductors because tram conductors gave cheek; she wanted the Hannays to be somebody, and she didn't know what, or whom. Then John said 'Pitchers.' The whole thing was a trap, a life-trap.

It went on, creeping into all the tested words, all the things stringently taught them as 'manners', holding them aloof from the weltering mass of old sad men who blew their noses on the backs of their hands and scattered their H's. Always, when Sandra stamped her foot, John replied with obstinate meekness, 'That's what I said, didn't I?'

The Water Babies, The Heroes, Tanglewood Tales; Gerard climbing up the tree, with the she-bear after him; Beatrix Esmond looking coldly down the staircase, her satin gown spread wide like a purple wine-stain; 'O Rome, my country!' 'It seemed an unspeakably dirty trick,' thought Eliza, 'to go back on that, on the one given thing. Without drink, without drugs, without robbing a till or running away with a woman, to go gently on the beach.'

But there was his trend, understood by none of them; to get into the masses who have no consolation but life and death, no refinements or artifices thrust between themselves and the blind things they would face. *Joy in facing, naked, such an enemy.* Obstinately, always by a wrong means, John was seeking to rejoin the whole.

All the time, even in the heat of combat, his eyes prickled with over-sensitive tears, his mouth, under the little brown moustache, twitched on the verge of the old smile. He couldn't understand why he was shouting, what it was all about. Wasn't he John, who had put coats over their beds in winter nights, and on Guy Fawkes' Day turned off the lights in the kitchen at Calver Street, and described great beautiful arcs of blue, mauve and crimson flame with Roman matches? But his façade of sham violence crashed against Augusta's genuine toughness of spiritual fibre. It was impossible to wound her on the surface, light wound for light kiss. She had no surface, she was all quite true.

Carly's Johannesburg gentleman turned out oddly for John, who invented him one night when they were quarrelling.

'Go back to Johannesburg,' he roared at Augusta. 'Go back to Johannesburg. Go back to your bloody *gentleman.*' On 'gentleman' the door crashed.

Carly had never quite got over her yearning for sworded aristocrats with laughing eyes, light manners, and town and country houses. (One reason for loving Trevor Sinjohn was that properly his name should be spelt 'St John', and his black brows and cat eyes were aristocratic.) The more John raved about the gentleman in Johannesburg the more Carly cottoned to him. He wore gold lace, she thought, and a red horse rubbed against his hand . . . but she didn't want any part in that, she was scared of horses.

She was by far the gentlest of the Hannays; a little owl with round, childlike face and clear grey eyes. Beside her, Eliza, all ragged, pine-needle hair and brown eyes, looked foxy. One night, following on an instalment of the Johannesburg gentleman serial, she looked up at John and said quietly, 'You're not my father.'

John's mouth dropped open. Augusta gave a little, wounded cry.

'No,' said Carly, with a glance, all affection and tender understanding, at her mother. '*He* is.' The Johannesburg gentleman thenceafter was Carly's story, and she stuck to him. John, after phases of rage, amusement and shame, did the most characteristic thing: he adopted Carly's legend, she was no daughter of his. She and her mother could go back to the bloody Johannesburg gentleman.

Between quarrels, he went about with tears in his eyes, declaring that Carly was the only decent one among his children. But Carly was not to be drawn. Her Johannesburg gentleman gave her a curious exemption from family troubles. 'I'm not yours,' she reminded John gravely; and he left her alone.

Sometimes Eliza wished she had thought of it first. But at the back of her mind there was still a cubbyhole in which her father's image was far clearer than those of the beautiful young men in flannel bags. She felt, 'You couldn't get much but babies out of them,' and despised Carly's adoration of Trevor Sinjohn. Daddy, at least, read books. The grocer boy and spotty Johnny Tyler didn't really count. Mr Duncan, like Calver Street, was an occasional and obscure memory, though sometimes she wanted to run and run back, and see his cross Scotch face behind the desk.

Before they came to Laloma, Mr Duncan and Daddy had quarrelled terribly; Daddy's fault, of course, Augusta said his filthy jealousy was to blame. He hadn't sent Eliza a word of congratulation when she won her scholarship, though she had worked mostly to please him; and when Mr Bellew pinned a silver dux medal on her front, and pointed out her name, first in gold letters on the new school's roll of honour, Mr Duncan wasn't there. Augusta said it was John's doing, and Eliza supposed she should have hated him.

She loved him; only, as he lay smoking pipes of fierce tobacco, drinking tea, reading the white lacy beauty of the antique world in an atmosphere which sweated like an Eskimo's igloo, she could picture him quite clearly, the pillows doubled back under his head, and she didn't want him to touch her.

It was a noisy house — old house creak-and-crack, with rats romping in the cellar and behind the walls. You could hear every little thing that happened, hear what people said, almost hear their hearts beat. Twelve stairs climbed between Eliza's little green room and John's blue one. If he had asked her, she would have replied, 'Yes, Daddy, I do love you. I'm not sure if it's best, it's such a different way from loving Mother. But I don't want you to kiss me.'

Augusta could be surprising, too. Once she was ironing starched things in the kitchen, while Eliza read out a poem from an old magazine, 'The Triad':

> But while I feel your kisses on my mouth,
> And while your live hair clings about my hand,
> I would not give this evil love of mine
> For all the freedom in the world.

'Yes,' said Augusta. 'Yes, that's what real love is like.' Then her right hand took up water from a china basin, and shook out drops on the starched collar. The starch hissed as she pressed down the iron, turning it into a gloss like cream velvet. Eliza stared at her. She didn't seem at all different — red hair, worn face, square-shouldered spare body — and yet she had said that about evil love. They had never known their mother, she thought, in the positive . . . the way she would be if she really loved someone: only in the negative, the way she acted and looked and talked if she didn't love a man. Of course, she was positive with her children — Carly, Eliza, Sandra, Kitch — but that was another thing; asking little bodies, asking minds, which often had to be put off. She was too *busy*, where the children were concerned, for any of them to stand apart and say, 'This is exactly how my mother loves me.' It all came in the form of groceries and little frocks run up on the hand-machine, and what you mustn't say or let people say to you if you're to pass muster among decent folk.

The bloody Johannesburg gentleman: John had invented him, Eliza was as certain of her mother's respectability as she was of the kitchen floorboards under her feet. But suppose, just as a dream, he had existed, still existed, and a whole intrinsic world around his face? Ah, in that world, a red-haired strong woman could drop her ironing, let the starch-water fall with a blue crash to the kitchen floor, and run and run and run . . .

The first time John brought home one of his *objets d'art*, Augusta simply couldn't believe her eyes or ears; not that the latter were at first affronted, for Olaf was one of our Dumb Brethren, and hardly opened his mouth except to shovel in great masses of pink rabbit stew. He had no top front teeth, and you could see a long way down his gullet and throat. Also Olaf had hair, like an old-fashioned English sheepdog, but less meek; a straggling moustache on which gravy had made a delicate dew, fierce little darker spikes in his ears and nostrils, and on his chest (visible through an open blue shirt) a thick dark pelt, which curled.

John, plainly in love, hung about the back of Olaf's chair, begging him to have some more pudding. When the pudding gave out, Olaf sighed, unbuckled his belt over his stomach, stretched his legs, and lit up. Augusta, her lips a thin red line, like British soldiers in romantic verse, rose to bring the tea, slamming open a window as she passed Olaf's pipe. John, pathetically anxious that the Hannays should pass muster with his darling giant, plunged into proletarian literature.

'London's *People of the Abyss* — great stuff in it, but with half his soul, Jack London was the journalist. He had his sovereign ready, he could climb out when he pleased. That's the trouble with his work. It's sincere as far as it goes — power, insight, but always the bus-fare home. He wasn't really involved. It's another thing when a man writes from his leg-rope.'

'Oy,' agreed Olaf. Augusta handed him tea, and he greeted her as a mother of the Gracchi.

'Ship, Oy ban choock her oop.'

'What's that?'

John explained about the cruel capitalist sea-captains.

'It'd make your hair stand on end, 'Gusta, if you knew what's going on aboard some of these little cargo boats.'

'I've no doubt,' said Augusta, setting down each cup with a firm little ring. 'What was your grievance, Mr . . . er . . . Olaf?'

'Food,' said Olaf. 'She ban crawl.' He poured his tea into his saucer and blew on it. Kitch said, 'Oo — we're not allowed—' but Olaf didn't notice.

'Oy tell Cook,' he continued tenderly. 'She can — himself.' Augusta made a sound like a tyre-tube pierced by a hatpin, and John slid swiftly into Jack London's *The Iron Heel*. Afterwards Carly played accompaniments, and Olaf bellowed from his stomach. Kitch, his holland smock stained with porridge and the day's travail, trotted beaming after them. 'Fwog,' he said, when Olaf had finished. 'Fwog.'

There was a kitchen war about Olaf's bed for the night. Eliza and Sandra heard their parents at it.

'You're not going to let that great brute sleep in your bed. He might have a disease.'

'He can have a shake-down under the house.'

'Prowling about in the cellars, and with not a safe lock on the windows, thanks to your laziness. It's a pity you can't think of your own daughters.'

John's remark about his own daughters was rather like Olaf's about the cook.

'Who paid for the beds, anyhow? Who owns this bloody house?'

'The Government, and by the rate you're going they'll still own it after you're dead and buried. And who's been your unpaid slave for twenty years? Who's wasted a lifetime cooking for you, bringing up your children?'

Sandra whispered, 'The Johannesburg gentleman comes next. It's a pity Carly isn't here, it perks her up.'

When Carly's black shoe was tired of pressing on the soft pedal, Olaf told stories about Sweden. But Augusta was victor in the kitchen war. John lent Olaf ten shillings, the giant said good-night, and was never seen again. Eliza and Sandra hadn't expected him back.

'I liked about when he was in the north of Sweden, and the captain turned him off with a kick on his pants, and it was below zero, and he went to sleep against the cow and would have frozen to death if the old woman hadn't come out with a lantern and said, "My poor boy, what are you doing here?" And where they all got into the one bed together, the old woman and her husband and Olaf and her son, and the bed shut into the wall like a cupboard. Carly, wouldn't it be fun to sleep four in a bed, shut up into the wall? I wonder if you'd sleep standing on your head? All the blood would run down . . .'

'Horrid,' said Carly. 'They might all snore, and you couldn't turn over.'

'He had nice eyes — blue, like a baby's,' said Eliza.

'Eliza always likes men,' said Sandra. 'But he won't ever come back. He blew on his tea, and he swore frightfully.'

'It wouldn't have mattered if it had been D, or even B. Mother doesn't like it, but she can put up with it. But not if it's F.'

Olaf was the first. The next was a rather nice, much less hairy little man called Harry, who kept a fruit-stall. His politics weren't very conspicuous. He hoped there would be a Labour Government one day, much as a patient snail may hope for the abolition of thrushes. But when John slanged the bloody capitalists, Harry said, 'Ah, poor old Billy

Massey.' The King of England was the Poor Old King, England was the Poor Old Motherland, the Germans, though a shrapnel-chip had stiffened his left arm in a crook at the elbow, were Poor Old Jerry. The leader of the New Zealand Labour Party was Poor Old Harry Holland, and Eliza was sure that if Daddy started on atheism instead of politics, God would be Poor Old God.

Then Harry brought a bride to call. When they had gone, she complaining shrilly of the ache Laloma's hill had produced inside her narrow patent leather shoes, Augusta collapsed in a chair.

'How could he? However could he? A vixen like that, a cheap, flaunting hussy.'

'Oh, my dear 'Gusta, how could he not?' asked John.

'In front of your own children—'

'When people get big in front like that, they have babies soon,' Carly explained. Kitch stuffed a sack under his jersey, and ran about, calling that he was going to have a baby. Carly stopped him.

'Don't be silly. You can't, it's only girls.'

'Why can't I?'

'Because.'

'I'll ask Mum-mum,' Kitch threatened. Carly's white, worried look claimed her little face.

'We aren't supposed to talk about it. A girl at college did, and Miss Verriam nearly expelled her, for spoiling our childhood. Please don't tell Mother, Kitch.'

'Tell-pie-tit, his tongue will be slit,' sang Sandra. She was still a baby as to her pale gold ringlets, which never grew up; but she was leggy and thin, and her Scandinavian blue eyes could be very determined. Kitch took notice of her. Eliza said, 'Come along and I'll tell you my poem about the goblins in the hedge again,' and Kitch trotted after her, quite enchanted. Alone in the world of men, he loved Eliza's poems.

Joseph, a fireman from a boat, was John's next prize; a whipcord, black-eyed little rat of an Irishman, with the shoulder muscles of a bull, and a heart full of the awe, wonder and glory of Joseph. He trolled *Two Eyes of Grey* in a fine baritone, staring boldly at Carly; but as Carly's reaction was to seize her white sewing and flee into her bedroom, Joseph turned to Eliza. Once or twice they went walking over the hills. Every night, Eliza undressed before the mirror in her little green room, and looked closely to see if her waist had grown any smaller; she longed for Augusta's unattainable eighteen inches, and liked Joseph because he could lift her over high barbed-wire fences on the hillside, as if she were a doll. He asked her to marry him, qualifying it, 'as soon as I get me divorce.' He added, 'You can trust old Joseph, kiddie,' and told her a long story about his wife on their wedding eve.

'She asks me to get into bed with her, and I says, "To-morrow night, anything you say goes, but not to-night, see? For I couldn't trust meself, Elsie, and that's a fact." So she says, "Won't you, to please me, Joseph? Won't you, now?" And I says, "I don't know what you mean, Elsie, but I'm going now," and with that I took me hat and walked out. A fine-looking woman she was, too, but with one of her eyes a bit crossed-like. . . .'

Joseph cooked his goose by dramatizing in Augusta's hearing. He was up in the sheets, the fell first mate stood directly below. . . .

'So I thought, "Got you where I want you now, you bastard" — saving your presence, Mrs Hannay — and with that I let fly with me spike, and missed braining him by an inch. But I took a chip off his fat ear.'

'That would have been murder. Deliberate, cold-blooded murder of one of your officers.'

Eliza, seeing her mother's face, thought, 'Good-bye, Joseph,' for like Balaam's Ass, so far would Augusta go, and then she stuck.

For a week or two, Joseph wrote her little letters beginning, 'Dear Freckles.' Augusta confiscated and burned them. Eliza raged and threatened to run away, not because Joseph stirred her, but because Augusta couldn't be got to see that the notes were 'my letters', territory not to be trampled on. Of complete integrity herself, Augusta was too strong, too overwhelming to let other people keep their dignity. She hit out with the hairbrush, and wouldn't understand that it was not just a smack, but a blow at one's new, quivering, desolate pride. She read letters, and quoted them in family council. She said things out loud — not hysterical lies, like John's, but hard, true things that she had picked up in moments of weakness. There was nothing to do but to shut one's eyes, blindly to strike back. But to hurt Augusta badly was almost intolerable, for if she ever cried at all, it came so hard.

Sandra and Eliza decided that Joseph, though in one way a point of honour, wasn't worth fighting for.

'You wouldn't know what to do with him if you got him,' Sandra said. 'He's pretty awful. There was something funny about that tattooed mermaid on his arm.'

Elderberries and wild honeysuckle, tangling all the way down to flat

Okori Road, which led to the College. Eliza called College 'Little Ease', after reading in an old book of a dungeon where you couldn't properly sit down, lie, or stand up. She was swotting now for her senior scholarship. When she got the junior one, nobody had seemed excited. Augusta took it in an 'Of course you did' way, though only Eliza and God knew how weak her mathematics were, now Mr Duncan had gone. And John, who was going through a Scarlet Woman phase, said that she had the eyes of a harlot.

On the dusty elderberry bushes cream flakes of blossom appeared; then the wine-coloured berries, in huge clusters. The boys said you could make crimson dye of them. Crimson . . . lovely word. The starlings and wax-eyes throve here, honeysuckle with its trailing branches sweetened the wild roads. There was a native tree, its red berries slit with a fleshy black pupil; they called it 'the red eye tree.' Sometimes you could find four-leaved clovers here; only among the kind that have ruby pips splashed on their leaves.

In the other direction, over the hills, lay the bush, its smell an aggregate of rotting leaves, mould, golden-brown water, sunlight and earth venturing into leafy decay. Karaka berries, purple, fell and rotted to nothing if the birds didn't find them. No stream ran clear. The sunlight mottled it with gliding fins, amber, and wild mint stood in it knee-deep, cattle used it and the spoil from the old cemetery ran down in wet weather: but the golden-brown maintained its thready way, and heaped around the cold flesh of trout. Boy Scouts caught the trout and wrapped them in handkerchiefs, stuffed them into their shirts so that the Ranger would not see. But Boy Scouts don't know everything, though it is they who make the thin piercing blue of campfire-smoke in the bush.

The bush loves Eliza, wants her. Beyond the first slopes and the crab-apples, you have to slash your way with knives. 'I'll run away,' she thought, 'I'll run away, live with the bush and never be turned out. It wants me, if nobody else does. Its berries will fall deep on to the soil, my soil, and the fantails come in surprised graceful arcs straight at me, and when they have found a twig behind my eyes they will sit there, preening themselves.

'It's funny that the natural sounds never wound, never irritate. I never lose my temper and pray, "Oh, God, don't let them," when it's streams and birds, and yet they are quite rowdy. But I feel as if they will take me, hide me, cover me up; and I never feel that about people.'

Carly sang in St Kevin's choir except when Mr Priestly was absent, and she had to be organist. Then the organ droned so loud (adenoids of thick red plush and the fuzz of years) that you could only see her opening and shutting her mouth. Sandra in church looked like an angel (she was ten now) but she had to be kept away from the Schmidts, who sold the Hannays Laloma, and who also attended St Kevin's. The moment they entered the church, she started an audible mutter: 'Meanies, meanies, mean old Schmidts.' The Schmidts, before leaving, had rooted out the dear little lily-of-the-valley, its blooms like seedpearls on its dark green leaves. Because of that, the Hannay children had never quite felt that Laloma was delivered over to them as promised. 'Meanies. Mean old Schmidts.'

Eliza wore a starched confirmation veil. When the Bishop lays his hands on your head, Something Wonderful will happen to you. . . .

It might have been anything, from a beloved white dove circling the altar to the gift of healing; the mad, glorious delight of being able to dangle serpents by their tails, or make the little girl Burke's tubercular hip suddenly round out again, so that she wouldn't lurch. She was nice — fourteen, apple-cheeked, with a square-set, stolid determination that, over all things else, it was her duty to get a boy. But you knew at once that while she lurched so, she never would. She couldn't see herself sideways on.

But when the Bishop laid his hands on Eliza's head, nothing happened at all, though other people, with other touches, had made her tremble, if they couldn't give her the gift of healing. After ordinary church service at St Kevin's, she could now remain and sip at the communion chalice, filled with brackish watered claret. It advanced along a row of kneeling people, and as each drank, the Vicar with a lace kerchief wiped the spot. Old Miss Tudor really needed a moustache cup, and nearly always she knelt next to Eliza. Her kneejoints crackled getting up; you could see tiny reddish beads of claret in her moustache.

> And, with the dawn, those angel faces smile,
> Which I have loved, long since, and lost awhile.

The strong voices, some tuneless, some thin like worn sixpences, rang on the rafters; beautiful because they were fused and unselfconscious, fused in an old song whose pattern was rubbed off long ago. The clothes of the congregation were dark, their shoulders ox-patient. Heads bowed or lifted, at the Vicar's command. A steam of breath frosted the windows;

the laborious, sighing wheezes of old Miss Tudor, the closed faces of middle age, mixed with the pink-and-white of little boys drugged by the air to lethargy.

A long time ago they had lost their angel faces, clear-minted with individuality and beloved significance. Now they huddled close, waiting.

O God, you pass your level sword of light very cleanly through the one stained-glass window they could afford. But wouldn't it be better to smash the roof and all the glass, saying, 'What a fug?' I would like You to be cold as frost and gay as fire: and yet, You know, the very type and image of them.

Meaningless, sad, constipated goodness . . . its Heaven is so worthless beside its earth. A revival would be horrible . . . treating God like a gigolo. Religion which is an emotional dilation, which finds outlet by puffing out its cheeks, is always at the critical moment going to play into the dirtiest hands available. Real religion is clear-cut, black and white; philosophy and magic. Philosophy for living, magic that man's stave shall blossom. I can't imagine the one without the other.

Which of us, by taking thought, can add one cubit to his stature? But don't You see, the way we live, everything, punishment, reward, system, all dwarf the stature — contraction, not expansion? Isn't man like a clenched fist, cramped, that of its own agonized irritability must hit out, probably at the wrong thing? You were a carpenter's boy, loving the smooth feel of some crude plane against wood. Didn't You feel better when the movement of hand and chisel fitted in with the soothing movement of Everything? Aren't the grained atoms the real morning stars, singing together? Listen, I will tell You. When we bought Laloma, my father got a carpenter's tool-set and also things for mending our boots. But he never planes wood now, and the greenhide slabs he plasters on our shoes, just anyhow, are so clumsy and thick that we cry if we have to wear them. It's because his heart is contracted, not his hands.

'Eliza, don't drop that collection bag.'

Thirty or more pieces of silver. Augusta's face is tired out. She has listened to every word of the service. Softly she shakes Kitch by the shoulders. His boy head is down on his coat. She frowns at Eliza, on principle.

There is a guard between the two, civil, military and religious. Above all, a guard of eunuchs.

CHAPTER EIGHT

Little Ease

I'M not afraid of those girls. I despise them, they are so ordinary.

Then why are your eyes watering, Cry-baby-cry. . . .

I didn't think it would be so big, or so lonely: so many girls in navy blue gym frocks, their thick hair plaited, bobbed, or tied behind with plain black ribbon. Mother won't let me cut mine; it won't plait, and it's so curly that, when it is tied, it stands out in a red bush. School regulation costume: navy serge gym costume, with plain white blouse, black girdle, black woollen stockings, black heelless sandshoes, Chisholm House tie; black band with college colours about your hat, which is in winter a straw cady, making a thick red furrow on your forehead; in summer — much better — a panama.

Some of the IIIA girls are very tall and sophisticated. They have been a year in the form already. Common sense tells that they are the slow ones, the left-overs, but it's hard not to be impressed by them. They know their way about, Christine calls to Fifi, 'Here, I've kept our desk,' and gives a scathing glance at any little cuckoo who flutters near.

If you have the slightest symptoms of a figure above your waist, the gym frock makes you look like a navy-blue barrel.

'Can't you climb up the ropes hand over hand? Can't you do somersaults from the horizontal bar? At our school, we always had gym. Watch Simone Purcell, she's *good.*'

'That's not bad, Eliza. Oh, did you hurt yourself? Didn't she come down hard on her head?'

'Girls, atten-*shun.*'

'That's old Griffin. You don't have to take much notice of her. Betty Peters is her favourite. I'd rather die than be a favourite, wouldn't you? Miss Griffin's got a young man. He can't be very particular, she must be old as the hills. She's always thinking of him, you watch the way she sits with her mouth pursed up. She writes letters to him behind her exercise book, when she's supposed to be correcting our work. One day Fifi Longford picked up a sheet of letter she had written, and it began "Sam, darling." Sam, darling! Fifi handed it back before all the girls. She was nearly bursting. I'll bet Miss Griffin must be forty. I'd rather die, wouldn't you?'

Dismembered pieces of buttercup: light, cold voice. Girls, this is the

92

calyx . . . this is the corona . . . here are the stamens. . . . If you hold a buttercup under your chin and it makes a shine like painted metal, you steal butter; but they don't say that. All the King's horses and all the King's men will never put dismembered buttercup together again.

Two rolls of pink crinkly paper have vanished from the classroom. Miss Adderley wanted them to make paper roses for the school bazaar. When she can't find them anywhere, she stalks out, two bright spots of displeasure on her cheekbones, to report the loss to Miss Verriam, the head mistress. The girls chatter volubly. Of course, old Mrs Macarthy, the caretaker's wife, must have moved them by accident.

A voice, flickering cold as a sword, whips out of its scabbard.

'Why don't you ask Eliza Hannay where they are? She's sitting right next to the windowledge where Miss Adderley left them.'

Of all the aviary voices, not one is chattering. Why don't you ask Eliza Hannay? There is a spot of ink right in front of her blouse, and her hair sticks out behind. The bush smells purple and golden-brown. They have put high wire-netting over these classroom windows, so that you can't look out. I was dux of my school, but the girls from Oddipore are all scattered, like the frail little pink and indigo blobs of jelly washed up at Island Bay after a big storm. What on earth would I do with two rolls of pink crinkly paper? At St Monica's church socials they always had it, festooned in streamers across the roof, pink lattice work and dusty roses over the stalls. Two iced buns and a glass of weak pink lemonade. Carly went as Cinderella, in a pink sateen frock and a white apron; her little Cinderella slipper was tied to her waistband, and her long hair touched her waist. Sandra was a forget-me-not. . . . Mother nearly worked her eyes out scalloping the blue satin petals, and I was Union Jack, though I didn't much want to be. I recited, and that girl with the red hair danced. She looked like wavering smoke. Anyhow, Calver Street was next door to a slum. I hate this clean place, the too many voices, too many bodies: too large. But I'm not going to cry.

'You needn't have made Eliza cry, Simone Purcell. You might just as easily have taken the crinkly paper yourself.'

'She's a baby. Fancy snivelling over a joke.'

'Well, you've no right to say she's a thief. If that's your idea of a joke, you might as well keep quiet.'

'Let her alone. Simone's only showing off.'

A queer face, Simone's. The forehead is bumpy, like a young boy's, and beneath very black brows stare out pale-green eyes, leopard eyes. They have a slightly vacant, wandering look, and are not quite straight. She has just missed a squint. Her hair is fine, perfectly straight, neither gold nor Saxon tow-colour, but fine gilt. Her lower lip thrusts out, sullen, and her hands are ugly, the blunt, ineffectual hands of somebody who should have been an artist, and can't. Always those blunt fingers are scribbling things on paper, nymphs almost lovely, but preposterously lean and long, profiles of hideous Austrian-looking wenches, all nether lip and top eyelash. And they aren't any good. The neat little unimaginative drawings of Fifi Longford come off, Simone's don't. Her body, in its shabby clothes, is lithe and slender.

Simone Purcell, I am going to make you sit up and take notice. Simone, why did you say I took the pink crinkly paper, when you knew I didn't, and you could just as easily have picked on anyone else? Because you knew I'd cry? But I'm not soft all the way through. . . . Or because the others hadn't interested you?

I can hit back. I can say clever things quickly, without stopping to think. At the end of a month, the girls laugh, and say, 'Eliza Hannay is rotten at games, but she *is* witty.' 'Look at the doorstep sandwiches her mother cuts her for lunch,' pipes little brown Alice Fagan. And when I am beaten, in a class debate, Fifi Longford, one of the big, handsome left-overs served up cold from last year's IIIA, says under her breath, 'Serve you right, Miss Eliza Hannay.' They're hostile, but they had three pretty good speakers against me, and mine were duds . . . poor little Kattie Bryce will giggle. Simone and I together could wipe the floor with them.

I hate Simone Purcell; and I can make her look round whenever I like. You don't say in your head, 'Simone, look at me — Simone, look at me'; that's a dud way. You just look at the back of her head, and make all the thoughts go bobbing out of your mind, like corks on a slack tide. The most absurd words and ideas go bobbing past. Then she looks. . . . When Miss Adderley or Miss Codrington says something funny without meaning to, she looks of her own accord, and poor old Coddie throats, 'Girls, I will *not* have undercurrents of understanding in my classes.' Simone's laughter comes up in little bubbles behind the pale-green iris. We know we'll never forget the phrase, 'undercurrents of understanding'.

But we are enemies. Our looks cross like daggers. I am only waiting my chance. Only her eyes are like grass with the sun on it. . . .

From the big hall where prayers are said every morning, and lessons read out of the Old Testament, rusty as if with dried blood, a wooden staircase mounts up beneath a wall hung with deep-coloured prints. Every

stair is slightly crooked and hollowed, where the feet of girls and girls and
girls, some of them wearing the great mushroom hats and muslin blouses
of the nineties, ran up and down. They used to play croquet and archery,
and this school was then an establishment for young ladies, with no
scholarship or Government subsidy brats. Somehow I love those wooden
hollows, inside me; but I will not tell. There is a dusty museum upstairs,
and the long, stained rooms are labelled 'Chemical Laboratory', 'Botany',
'Home Science'. But we never do anything by wholes, it is all
dismembered, like the buttercup, and nobody has the energy to stick it
together again. It comes as a little clean thrill, a shock of surprise, when
your mind makes even the most trifling discovery for itself, puts two silly
little bits of picture-puzzle together. I was thrilled when I discovered that
matter has the property of contraction and expansion — and yet, look
how easy. We were young and keen when we came here, we had passed
our examinations well. Now they get out their textbooks, and slap bits
and pieces into us. Things equal to the same thing are equal to one
another. Common are to either sex, artifex and opifex. Nobody ever says,
'You are learning this *because*,' and gives a reason. It's all cold, like jellied
sauce set around a dismal pudding. Only sometimes things explain
themselves — poetry, English, French. And then they dare, they dare, to
laugh at William Morris, and Miss Hebron simpers too. Not worth
learning. I translated for myself—

> Les sanglots longs
> Des violons
> De l'automne —
>
> 'Autumn's violins
> In lengthened sobbing
> Wound my heart with restless
> Dullness of their throbbing,'

   but nothing in English could be as lovely as the sound of 'les sanglots
longs'.
   At the bottom of the garden are two great oak trees, their leaves a
green murmuring summer. You can eat your lunch alone or in groups,
though if you sit alone you look left out. The girls get up lazily and play
croquet, or bump the seesaw against the ground, but the real sports play
basketball and cricket. Once Cassie James sliced a cricket ball right over
the high tin wall and into the street. She is ugly, stupid, and so round-

shouldered that she is almost hunchbacked, but the college is proud of her, as of some terrible hunting trophy, a pair of elk's horns brought home from the mountains.

Eliza on the basketball court faces the enemy. Run — dodge — splodge. 'Pass, can't you, pass.' As the hard leather smacks her palms, a sudden acute pain runs up the little finger Sandra once broke. When the whistle blows, her finger is beautifully swollen, and the ache red-hot.

'Back to your places, girls. Pass, there, pass.'

At half-time Eliza goes up to the nut-cheeked young sports mistress, whose bosom and sturdy haunches look absurd in just the same navy-blue gym. frock as that worn by the girls.

'Please, Miss Jamieson, I'm afraid I've broken my finger.'

Miss Jamieson starts to say, 'Nonsense.' Then she changes her tune.

'Cold water, bandages and a sling. Run inside, and Miss Hebron will fix it up for you. You've sprained it, anyhow.'

The finger is not broken, but dislocated; and, blessed sequel, it pops out again at the first impact of the leather. 'You'll be no good for basketball,' says Miss Jamieson, sourly. 'How are you going to fill in your spare time?'

'I'm on the Library Committee, Miss Jamieson' — but at sight of the young mistress's face, Eliza hastily added, 'and I'll learn to swim, and walk a lot, and play croquet, and perhaps next term my finger will be all right.'

And I love climbing the hills, especially when they're grey, and the two old oaks down at the bottom of the garden, and writing poetry, and the hollows in the stairs, and the colours in the Wars of the Roses prints — you know, the ones in the outside hall. And I like English sometimes, and French, but I've read to the end of the book while they're still on Chapter Two, and it's so dull sitting about. And I *hate* mathematics — to listen gives me a sick feeling in my spine, like cramp; and I read Tacitus from a crib, one of my father's books, because it's so interesting, and better to get the whole sense than blundering on from phrase to phrase, like caterpillars in a nightmare. And Miss Farquhar was not right in her translation about getting vermin and diseases from swine. But I love 'And the pearls there are darker than the pearls of other seas,' that's Tacitus, and 'Nox atra, qui abstulit colorem res,' that's in Virgil. Can't you see it? 'Black night, that steals away the hues of earth.' And you've got a skeleton monkey upstairs in the little museum. I like that too, I don't know why, except that skeletons look so clean and wise. I love Rostand's *Chanticleer* in the library, and so does Simone Purcell, the girl with the green eyes, whom I hate. You think she's a good sport because sometimes she can throw a goal at basketball, but you wait, Miss Jamieson — she's as bad as me, if not worse. And, Miss Jamieson, I hate the wire-netting over the windows, and the way the girls laugh about poetry, and the size of them massed together, because the navy-blue costume makes us look as if we were all bits of the same substance, overflowed into different vats. And I hate Miss Verriam, because she's a snob. But she's like my Aunt Bernardine. It's not our fault she had to take State School girls instead of remaining an academy for mushroom hats with respectable pinheads under them. Oh, and I do conversational French because Madame Renault is like a damson — there's a little dark bloom on her skin, and her lips are velvety. And I don't carry Miss Cairn's books to be a favourite, but because I am rather sorry for her. She means well and looks silly, doesn't she?

'Try bandaging with iodine,' advised Miss Jamieson. She was rather a nice girl, but too hearty, and her eyes popped.

A little while after, Eliza had her chance with her darling enemy, Simone. Simone slipped and fell on the basketball court, tearing one knee right out of her stocking. Her cheeks turned wild rose, her green eyes looked bewildered, then filled. Eliza suspected that the Purcells, like the Hannays, hadn't much money. Simone's clothes were almost worse than hers. Afterwards in the classroom, Miss Hebron asked Simone a question which anyone could have answered. She stood up; the leopard eyes looked about her in a hunted way, then she stammered, burst into tears.

'Sit down, Simone. Don't be such a child.'

'Coals of fire,' thought Eliza. She stood up.

'Please, Miss Hebron, Simone isn't a child.'

'Eliza Hannay, sit down at once.'

'Please, she isn't. Simone fell and hurt herself. She hit her head on the asphalt, I saw her. She has the most terrible headache, and she didn't want to tell anyone.'

'Oh.' A long pause. 'Well, in that case you'd better take Simone's terrible headache home, Eliza, since you're so concerned.' Miss Hebron was being sarcastic, but it didn't matter.

'Thank you, Miss Hebron.'

Outside, Simone, still crying, said, 'Liar. Dirty little liar.'

'If you howl any more, people in the street will think you've just come back from a funeral, or been expelled,' Eliza advised dispassionately. The hills were quite near, delicate hard grey. At one place a quarry made a high scar, hacked out of the grass. Eliza thought, 'Wherever she goes, I'm going too.' Water splashed down the misty threads. Simone climbed and climbed, as if she could never get tired. There was a glint of berry-red in the grass, and Eliza picked up a necklace of red beads strung on tarnished silver. She felt disappointed that somebody else had been there before, but the beads were pretty. The rocks were now like living things, animals with flat, out-thrust faces. They rattled and slithered underfoot, and suddenly Eliza's stomach felt sick. She heard her voice, too high, saying what her mind ordered it not to say.

'I can't climb up there. I'm not going any farther.'

Simone climbed on. Eliza scrambled ineffectually at a rock-face, got on a ledge six feet up, looked, and was not quite sure if she could get up or down.

'That's right, cry. You hate me, don't you?'

'I don't hate you, I despise you.' But to despise anyone, clinging straddled against a rock-face like a baboon, only a ridiculous little drop of six feet below, was just talk. And beyond that, she didn't hate Simone any longer, didn't despise her. The shadows of clouds moved mighty over the rocks and grass, and they weren't tainted by Simone's presence there. Trees had been planted farther along, little pines thrusting their nuggety brown-flowered heads into the arc of the air. They lay beneath them and laughed, sliding the pine-needles between their fingers. Eliza gave Simone the red beads on the tarnished necklace.

Next day in class Simone told it all, imitating Eliza on the rock-face. 'I d-don't h-hate you, I d-despise you.' One of the big girls said crushingly, 'Don't tell tales out of school.' Eliza didn't greatly care: Simone was hers. In a strange way, it was pleasant to look up in dream, look up the ridiculous inaccessible rock-face and see her friend's face above.

'Mother, I'm in IVA this year.'

'Of course you are.'

Eliza's name wasn't in the senior scholarship list, but there was an Elsie Hannay. 'It's a misprint. Of course you won your scholarship,' said Augusta firmly, and the gods obeyed her. Of course it was Eliza. . . .

'Mother. I'm in VA this year.'

'Of course you are.'

Carly, who was a year ahead in time, was among the B girls. But she didn't mind. She said, 'I know I'm not clever,' and didn't want to be. Carly hadn't to sit for matriculation, which would have frightened her out of her life. The ugly red mark scored by the school hat across her forehead made her look like a worried marmoset. She was dying to throw it away, to put on soft, floppy hats and dresses right down to the ground, dresses of flowered voile and organdie. While you were in school uniform you must never be seen talking to a boy, not even your own brother, but Trevor Sinjohn still took Carly walking over the hills every week-end, and she went up to the Sinjohn's house on Sundays to help with the cooking. Mrs Sinjohn, a tiny woman with swollen varicose veins, said Carly was a dear, good girl, a true daughter.

When Eliza was nearly fifteen, she thought she was in love with Trevor Sinjohn too, and wrote verses about him:

I bring thee passion-flowers of my dreams —

Trevor never knew. The grey hills, the oldness and dirtiness of the cemetery, leaned through the windows of her little room, leaned on her heavily. There was a clay road slanting up between far rows of pines, and the dying sun dwelt on it. She thought if she could one day walk up it alone she would be happy. At other times she cried: 'I'll run away. I'll run away and live in the bush.'

Augusta provoked her, and Eliza told her, 'I do love Trevor Sinjohn, so there.' 'You must be mad. You ought to be ashamed of yourself,' retorted Augusta. She was growing heavily middle-aged, her face in the light of the little green room was hard and uncompromising. She distrusted Eliza, and for a moment thought, 'Better she had never been born.' To take Carly's boy away, even to look sideways at him, would have been the unforgivable sin. But she need not have worried. After Eliza had thought of Trevor's cat eyes for a month, and written him several ardent poems, she forgot him.

It was Simone who understood, in her off-hand way — sometimes striking out, sometimes as good a friend as the black pine-tops. Augusta called Simone 'that little harlot,' because she put on lipstick; and because Augusta had intercepted a letter in which Simone said that they would have lovers when they were grown up, but not too many babies.

'Girls, atten-shun, Right wheel. Forward march. Touch your toes. Swing the trunk from the hips. Keep your abdomens in and your chests out. Stand at ease. Atten-shun.'

Part of the college grounds lay unfrequented, an elderly cottage and garden purchased but never occupied. Simone and Eliza could talk there, or Eliza could write.

'Smoke, Eliza Jane Maria?'

'No, thank you.'

Simone lit her cigarette. The advertisements called it Con Amore — 'scented with amber, tipped with rose-leaves.' That was why she smoked it.

'Let's see what you're writing, Liz.'

'It's no good, and a crib from Masefield's "West Wind".'

'It would be. Everybody cribs.'

She read it out, her lazy voice giving the crib something of grace.

> It's a far way to England
> O'er the dolphin-backs of foam,
> So far the wandering swallow
> Half dreads that journey home;
> Yet a patient star, that loveth
> England of all lands best,
> Shines on those weary pinions
> And guides them to their rest.
>
> There are greener fields in England
> Than the meadows of the sea,
> And the laughing daisies whiter
> In English pasture be
> Than starlight, spume or spindrift
> In all those tossing miles—
> And sorceress-white, the hawthorn
> Glimmers by English stiles.
>
> There are white cliffs of England
> Where the sounding breakers speak,
> And he who never knew them
> Has yet his home to seek;
> O Roman, Dane and Norman
> Would mock this vanquished land,
> Till her laughing beauty led them
> Like children, by the hand.
>
> There are green lawns in England,
> Broidered by flowers as gay
> As ancient missals painted
> By white hands fled away;
> And a King's cloak of twilight

And a minstrel's cloak of rain
Shall robe your dreams in silver,
Shall veil the scars of pain.

'Why pain, Eliza? Why England?' Light fell through the close-petalled snowball flowers, making little golden points in her eyes, that were green as the elfin things Eliza loved best. She said, 'You're rather a silly baby, Eliza Hannay. Don't you like it here?'

'I love it. But don't you think we live half our lives in England, anyhow? I was thinking — there can't have been anything quite like this since the Roman colonists settled in Britain: not the hanging on with one hand, and the other hand full of seas. Wouldn't we be different there, more ourselves? Come too, Simone.'

'Not to England.'

'We belong there, don't we? I suppose it's the bluebells. None of us has ever been, for three generations, except my father at the war, and that didn't count; he's never happy anywhere except in books. But mother has her white house like a Greek cross, just outside the New Forest; and I like the godwits.'

'The godwits don't go anywhere near England. They fly to Siberia.'

'Not in my story.'

'I don't believe in romantic bluebells.' She rolled over, lithe as a leopardess. 'Tell you what: I'm partly Hun myself.'

Mr Vaughan and Belgian sausage. The idea of your children calling Carly the Kaiser, Mrs Vaughan, the very idea. The cap fits nearer home. . . .

'Did you hate the war, Simone?'

'Not especially. I'm going to marry a pacifist. Not for sentimental reasons, but because I don't see the point of being smashed up. I like my happiness smooth, smooth as ice-cream. My father's English, his mother is French. It's mother who has the Teuton blood, and she's a seraph.'

'Does it make any difference?'

'It gives me stolidity. Mixtures are either unemotional or explosive, and I'm all against emotion. I won't get sloppy. So I won't pick bluebells with you, Eliza. If you like, we'll go to Paris.'

'What's the good of Paris?'

'Bright lights and beautiful young men. I want to dance.'

Eliza said, 'I'd like to dance,' and knew as she said it that she never would; not as the reed dances, or the smoke.

'Your soul would like to dance, Eliza Hannay. But your boots are too heavy.'

Never argue with her when she's brutal. Shopping in Wellington, though, trailing up dingy streets, past the plots of grass where pigeons preen emerald breast-feathers. Dragging, a dead weight, behind the others. 'Eliza, you can't be tired already.' And Eliza always was. I want so much to be alive, alive as a poised wave, she thought, and it drains out of me. When you say, 'I'm tired,' people don't understand, and if you say you're sick, it's lead-swinging. But to be alive, to drink in airs and colours through your very skin. . . .

'I'll go with you to England, Eliza Jane. If you like we'll buy a caravan, then you won't be tired.' Simone, always Simone understood. When she was gone, Eliza tore another sheet out of her exercise book, and tried to write her down: not Simone in the navy-blue gym costume, Simone in her proper colour, green like chalcedony.

> Back sped her yellow hair against the dusk,
> Back fled her dark-green hood:
> Oh, dark as holly, round about the face
> Where ice too soon was brittle; wise too soon
> November eyes, beneath an April moon.

She crumpled the paper, with a sigh of impatience. November . . . snow . . . ice . . . holly . . . robins in the snow . . . springtime, the only pretty ring-time. . . . None of it happened, had ever happened to your sight, hearing or taste, and yet everything else was unreal, because you had been weaned on it. The Antipodeans did truly walk on their damfool heads.

Simone's people (a retired cavalry officer, floridly handsome, bad-tempered, mentally always in the act either of toasting the ladies, God bless them, or damning the women, God blast them; a thin, terribly tired, humorous mother in unvarying shabby black) moved from their town house out to Black Valley, twenty miles away and real country. The Hutt slid against it. Wild gorse flared on its hills, turnips wrangled with the knotty furrows, a brown stream ran through the farmyard, full of stumps and prickles. Eliza thought the Purcells' new house wonderful. Hadn't it got a pink slate roof, instead of red tin?

'Now you'll be able to ride,' said Simone, her eyes brilliant. Later she called, 'Fool — you'll come off,' as the thick-bellied roan pounded his heels into muck. The agony of sitting a trotting horse bore a rather interesting likeness to the agony of mathematics. Both started a sick little pain in the spine, spread till every cranny of one's being was filled. Eliza could bear the roan better if he galloped, even though she broke her neck for it. 'You look like a sack of beans,' shouted Simone, thrusting alongside on grey Jeremy. She was beautiful herself — her cheeks whipped, slender shabby body erect. Fine, fine . . . like a snake or a leopardess, admirable beasts. Augusta said, 'She tries to look like a Badwoman. But of course, she squints.' Badwoman was said all of a piece, with the accent on the first syllable.

'You're doing fine, kiddie,' said George Brennard, the Purcells' next-door neighbour, who had come over to help them settle in, and was a little in love with Simone. George had limpid brown eyes and a shock of silvery hair, and was always being wounded at the pertinacity with which female things allowed themselves to be hurt, like moths sizzling into candle-flames. A sparrow cheeping in distracted circles around her tumbled nest was an event for him, a crisis of pain in his mind. He made the worst farmer in the world. If he had had his way, nobody would have suffered; there was hardly any woman whom he did not love and admire. He had no discrimination, mental or physical. Eliza's brown mane, her breasts under the ugly navy serge, were as beautiful to him as Simone's whipcord; neither was any better, or sadder, than a brood of new chicks, yellow life-dust suddenly formed and scuttling round the lamp of the incubator. George kept an opium pipe on his mantelshelf. It was only a curio, but sometimes he thought he would go to one of the Chinese in Haining Street . . . and then dream, and dream, and forget the world.

'Anyhow,' said Eliza, 'I didn't come off.' It was true, but only just. Grace, poise, were the things the wet boughs had, and the hills, for all their titanic heaviness, and Simone riding between them, her bright cheeks dangerous. Either you are born with these things, or born heavy-handed, empty-handed. Then (for you may not surrender) you must learn to act.

They were alone on the uplands of the Black Valley, Simone and Eliza and a black spaniel named Fool. Although they were fond of George, they were glad he had gone, for they wanted to talk, and a male thing impeded them. Soggy paddock broke into quivering emerald of reed-covered quicksands. Then came a brief, strange paradise of native trees, rimu and wild honeysuckle, bark ragged-red. The leaves of native birch made a bronze mist in the air. One tree looped a huge arm over the path. Catching it, you could swing out and out, body a pendulum.

'Look at me, Simone. Not so bad?'

'Are you afraid of wild bulls, Eliza?'

'Why?'

'Garston's bull is loose in this bush. George Brennard says Garston ought to be gaoled for letting it go wild. It's killed three people already.'

'Yes, I'm afraid, as much as ever you like. I can't run as hard as you, and what's more, you know it,' said Eliza's coiled-up demon. But her voice stayed self-possessed.

'I shall lie down quietly and say I'm dead. If it's a noble animal, it will leave me alone. Only the *canaille* touch corpses.'

Simone laughed, silly as the girls at College, who think 'Eliza Hannay is witty.' Easy to pull the wool over almost anyone's eyes. . . . Moss cushions squelched with bright dew under their feet, sometimes spurting up in a bright, tall jet. Out of the manuka bushes, whose grey presence now took command of the whole world, shutting out sky and valley and the ridge behind, were shaken great globules of rain, and millions of grey moths, as fine as silver powder. They fell into the girls' hair and beat on their eyes, they were part of their skin, part of the thought one thinks and leaves behind, only to find it waiting at the very end of the trail. The black dog wriggled and panted as big drops hit his curly pelt. There were myrtle berries, red as the bead necklace Eliza had given Simone, and a green and grey life of small spiders and insects went on behind the hanging strips of bark, between the slender, ragged trunks.

Presently Simone said, 'Aren't you tired?'

'No. Are you?'

'All right. There are wild pigs over these hills. Ever seen one?'

'Only at the Zoo. A dirty old devil, with yellow dribble on his tusks.'

'They're much wilder here.' Simone's hat was cocked over one eye, her hair fell in wet gilt strands. The bright golden moss had gone, leaving bald earth. Leaves, leaves — a million to every bush, pointed and grey, little flint arrows. The dusty bodies of moths were an excrement from the manuka, one grew tired of brushing them away.

Tired of everything but going on, wet through, enclosed in the grey shell of the moment; because, no matter how often one discovers that this is the Glory Hole, always one feels, 'Perhaps this time it won't be.'

They weren't properly lost, though the rain had come on and drawn darkness down in its fine bow-strings. Simone knew the way down, but wasn't quite sure whether in darkness they would strike the quicksands, and be drowned.

'Father will roar,' she said unemotionally. 'He bullies mother. Fool, my lad, go and tell mother we're all right.' The spaniel wriggled his wet little body at her shoes, abject. He wanted to be picked up and carried. He wanted the sensations of a blazing log fire, steaming him, then baking his coat into a hard curly mat, but he couldn't remember where these things had been, or what made their glow. The girls kept moving, very cold, a little frightened, a little silly. Tree-stumps came jaggedly out of the dark and bruised them. Once they heard a crashing in the undergrowth. 'Wild pig,' said Simone.

Red lanterns, ladybirds, skirted the edge of the quicksands. 'Oh God,' said Simone, 'it's a search party. Can't you die, Eliza? Father might forgive a corpse.'

Eliza tripped over a stump. She wasn't hurt, but when Simone cried, 'Did you fall? Are you all right?' she didn't answer. Cold wet, cold wet . . . She shut her eyes, and the spaniel, moaning, came and lay beside her, its fat little body palpitating. Simone found her, and said in a slightly awe-struck voice, 'Have you fainted, Eliza?' Eliza let her head fall back. She remembered reading in a book how a woman pretending to be asleep was found out because she looked too ornamental, and decided on an open mouth. The search party crawled up the hill.

'Eliza's hurt. I think she's unconscious.'

Mr Purcell said, 'Where's the damn' brandy?' and somebody answered that Harris had got it. Harris was down at the slip-fence. George Brennard and Mr Purcell formed an arm-chair and carried Eliza, who let herself lie limp; once they slipped and dropped her into a pit at least eight feet deep, and Mr Purcell sprawled on top of her, exclaiming, 'Christ, God, Jesus. Mind the hole, Brennard. Bring that bloody lantern.' 'Now I really *am* hurt,' she thought, but said nothing. On the edge of the manuka they struck Harris and the brandy — horrid, sputter-making stuff, pouring fire down the chest. She opened her eyes and saw Simone, wet-haired as Fool, and Mr Brennard in the act of being fond of her. 'A little Briton,' he said, patting Simone's shoulder, 'game as a regular little Briton.'

Mr Purcell said curtly, 'Where's this girl's frock?' Simone said, 'Inside her bloomers,' and hauled it out. They had both tucked in their skirts when the manuka first brushed them with its heavy wet, but of course Simone wouldn't be caught. George Brennard turned his face away, distressed. Seeing a girl in her bloomers was nearly as bad for him as seeing her assaulted. He felt grieved for Eliza.

Mrs Purcell, standing at the door, said, 'Get them both into the bathroom,' and her troops, steaming and sweating, disappeared with the brandy-bottle. Her worn, pale face stayed expressionless as she peeled off their wet rags, but somehow Eliza felt it was time to recover consciousness. 'Get into the bath,' said Mrs Purcell. Then she shut the door and left them. The girls slid down into the great bath of smoking champagne-coloured water. It was silk, golden silk. Eliza let her hair slip under, and it came up streaming dark. . . .

'Was it an adventure, Simone?'

'Don't talk rubbish. You made it up.'

'It happened, anyhow. And you were scared.'

'Anyone 'ud be scared, with you pretending you were dead.'

'If I hadn't pretended, your father would have gone off pop, you said so yourself.'

'You needn't pretend it was that, little heroine. . . . Can't you hear George Brennard saying to his friends, "And that poor little Miss Hannay was — er — er — rather lightly clad?" '

'Anyhow, George called you a little Briton. I may be Anglophile, but I don't believe I'd care to be called a little Briton. Would you like to see the bruises your father made when he trod on me? I believe it was an adventure.'

'Oh, shut up.' Mrs Purcell trudged silently back with warm towels. Then they lay in a high-ceilinged room, where on the wall hung a picture of red Saint Bernard dogs snuffling at footprints in the snow. So different from Fool. The circle of pines outside moaned like the rising sea. Millions of moths, millions of little arrowed leaves, sharpened behind shut eyes to hunt somebody down on the far side of the black ranges. If we had stayed there and been lost, what could have happened? Nothing, except to be dead and clean, among the great sluggard roots of the trees. One could do worse. . . . Simone's shoulder was like ivory under her shabby silk nightgown. The Purcells had a little more money than the Hannays, but they had put it all into Black Valley land and a car for Mr Purcell.

In the morning, life was too busy for anyone to bother them. Mrs Purcell cooked porridge and flat, anæmic girdle scones, and Mr Purcell said loudly over his newspaper that Eliza was a fine woman — a fine woman.

'He likes 'em with bloomers and busts,' murmured Simone. They wandered about, watching day-old chicks fuzzle out of the incubator. Eliza loved the sweet muck smell of the place, the sharp-edged flaring Black

Valley hills. Mr Purcell drove them down to the station for Eliza's train, and they sang, 'Come back to Erin, mavourneen, mavourneen.'

At Laloma, all the old coinage was wearing thin. The talking-games had stopped long ago, when Eliza got her green room and was labelled 'studious'. Instead of being bunched together, as at Calver Street, the children seemed now to be strung out, with leagues of difference between them. Augusta still quarrelled endlessly with John. Once, when he had had a Christian Science fit, she almost decided to encourage him; but she found out that a woman lent him the Christian Science books, and couldn't resist chipping him about 'that fat Mrs Carradick'. Then Mrs Carradick wanted John to please Mary Baker Eddy's ghost by giving up tobacco, and gratefully he went back to being an atheist.

Carly was equal parts of 'I'm not clever,' Trevor Sinjohn, and love for Augusta. She still looked like a little girl. Sandra was much the prettiest, with pale, clustering bee-curls and blue eyes. Next year she was going to Chisholm, but she wasn't a scholarship certainty, like Eliza. Eliza thought Sandra was nearly imaginative, but not quite; and because of the not quite, she was becoming hard, practical, a stickler for everyday things. They all hated Simone Purcell, even John, who suspected that the pale-green eyes laughed at him. When they said she was a Badwoman, Eliza rushed to the defence; she didn't really care whether Simone was bad or good, but she knew that the Hannays were wrong. Simone's devil was lost, like the artistry of her blunted fingers. She should have been bad, perhaps, bad and queenly. She was only a little laugh, hopeless, and lost in the darkness. Little grey goddess.

Kitch still loved poems about the brown men with bandy legs who live in coprosma roots. Sometimes they took him mushrooming, finding white buttons and large tasty brown ones, propagated under gorse-bushes in ancient cow-droppings. Kitch trotted along, like a sack of potatoes unreasonably given action and a mind of its own. Now and again he plumped down, Buddha-like, and they knew he either wanted to be carried the rest of the way, or else was putting things into his mouth. When Sandra scolded, he would smile beautifully, opening his mouth just enough to whisper, 'Mush'oom.'

'It's a toadstool. It's a Devil's Stink Egg. You'll turn black in the face and die.' Unmoved, Kitch smiled on, till Sandra and Eliza turned him upside down and shook his prey out of his mouth.

Those long hills were very ridgy. From their summer grass, larks and sparrows blew out, light as chaff. Blue-gums, slim ships' mast trees with sickle leaves, were planted on the harbour side, far down lay white roads and the Gardens, old three-decker houses with red tin roofs. Then, misted in vague creeping blues that sometimes went to jewel colours, the city spread out, searching after its seas. It found them in most different places — sometimes intercepted by suburbs, sometimes in scalloped bays, or running lean and very much alive, a questing beast, up channels between hill and hill. Always there was that blue shout of surprise. Then the waves tossed white aigrets into the air and started laughing, like big kids of chieftains that would eat you if you couldn't first make them grin. But once they began to be merry, they kept on, having nothing else on their mind but killing a ship now and then; or rippling in long, pliant dazzle-ropes, between the meshes of silently swooping nets.

The land was living, like the sea. A land's always alive while it can grow hair, and this place sent up scrub and trees, gorse and bracken, long grasses that wear slippery in summer when feet run over them. Hedgehogs slid out, like hair too, beards off the chins of spiky old customers, philosophy out walking, ready for a dig at anyone. Beyond Thorndon, black and slatternly, the city was guarded by the full monster strength of a range lying with its head on its blunt paws. It was quick soil, ready. The whole earth was filled with the potency of moving again if it liked, of feeling all contacts strongly through its veins and marrow. The children who ran across it were moving inside its movement, little kites on a string controlled by its big will.

Simone left Little Ease a year earlier than Eliza, when they were both in VA; and though Eliza afterwards hauled herself through matriculation, and realized that her mathematics were impossible, the faint box walks of her sciences falling into disrepair, the whole was flat and stagnant. 'I can work,' she discovered, 'if there's somebody I love to work for, or looking on. But not unless.' From room to room they slid. They could have the leg of frog for science, the half of a nasal accent for French, Bowdlerism for literature. But they never glimpsed the whole of anything. Afterwards, walking rapidly to assignations with Simone in Highland Park, Eliza felt her dead mind come alive, receiving whole the fierce little pink trumpet of a flower, every face of the dozen listless deadbeats slumped together on a seat outside Parliament Buildings. Of those she could think, 'I will remember them for ever.'

To counteract Simone, she tried bringing other girls to Laloma. Little Kattie Bryce adored her, in a pink and stolid way, but when she came she always ate herself sick, and afterwards, out on the hills, came a dreadful halt, while Kattie, her eyes dark with misery and shame, held her stomach and murmured, 'I do feel so bad.' Then she lay where she had fallen, and gave up everything except the ghost.

In their final year, the girls had lessons in ballroom dancing, a tiny grey china cat of a mistress supervising the efforts of a veritable dancing master. One-two-three-turn. One-two-three-glide. One-two-three-hop. One Saturday evening, each fortnight, the classes were mixed. Boys from the Menton Boys' School attended, perfectly at home. But the tall blades of the Sixth never asked for dances unless you belonged to a select little coterie: Eulalie, Marian, Beth, Joan Roberts, Ursula . . .

Little Kattie Bryce, nervously smoothing out the folds of her navy-blue foulard, which bears a white pattern like enraged comets and bicycle-tyres: 'Eliza, do I look all right? My nose isn't shiny?' But nobody asks Kattie to dance.

The Maori boy says enigmatically, 'Good floor, isn't it?' or 'Jolly music, don't you think?' as if he revealed dark secrets. All the time, his veiled golden eyes are quite abstracted, thinking of something as personal, safe and private as a cat's ideas. Eric Chisholm has come to the dance in his slippers. Everybody sniggers, but he forgets; his father is very poor, and he wants to be a famous conchologist. Nobody understands, but he explains with pallid vehemence, 'Shells — shells — things you pick up on seashores.' He comes to the dances because his mother insists that he ought to make good connections, and that dancing is a social grace. But as if these flamboyant girls had the pearly lustre, the spiral secrets of shells.

Destiny waltz. One-two-three-dip . . . 'But come, Beloved, come, it is the dawn of love, the world is at our feet, the moon of gold above. . . .'

I am dancing with Dal Saunders. He is one of the big, laughing boys, and the older girls sniff, and say meaningly, 'I wouldn't sit out with *him*,' which means they would, like a shot, if he asked them: or else they already have. Kattie's face is a pink blur against the wall. If you're a wallflower, it doesn't feel so bad if you smile and shut your eyes, let the dark music go gliding through you. But you needn't be. It's Kattie's mother's fault. All those white things looping up her frock like cobras. . . .

The Boys' School has a fire escape. Sometimes they use it if they stay out late at nights. They all tell this story, daringly, wittily, as if each were the only one to whom it had ever happened. At the end of a perfect night, you have it off by heart.

Kattie Bryce and the Maori boy: those two are fated, the others will be all right. You can see the shadow dark against the walls, thrown in heavy relief behind their heads. It moves as they move. And it came true. The Maori boy was knocked down by a tram, and had a funeral *cortège* nearly a mile long. Kattie Bryce was engaged to a returned soldier who, at the last moment, drowned himself and left a note for the coroner about shell-shock.

Menton Sports Day. Eliza was wearing black silk gloves, a black hat, a white frock trimmed with flounces of the black-and-white lace Grandmother-in-China sent the Hannays years ago — almost her last present; she didn't seem to bother after the war. Even Simone opened her eyes wide and said, 'It can't be Eliza — it's too smart.' Little glove-buttons, jet-black, like the ones Augusta had on her sage-green delaine frock.

Kattie Bryce brought up her brother. 'I say, won't you have an ice-cream?' They sauntered across the green, clinging to Stephen's arms. Such a lovely day for the Sports. Of course the grass has been rolled a dozen times, but last night they shaved the banks as well, and the smell of short moist grasses, bruised daisy-stems, was still on the air. Boys ran along a sand-patch, flung back their chins, showed their teeth in agony or derision, and hurled themselves at the high-jump bar. Ominous quiver of the bar . . . oh, unfair that it should be so light. That little boy, bending nearly double as he runs . . . he simply must clear it. And he does. A roar goes up from the young white-flannelled lions. Bryce says proudly, 'That's Potter. It's a record for the High.'

Heads back, elbows tucked in, knees moving in a high piston gait that would be ridiculous if it hadn't the sheer grace and power of speed, the long-distance runners sheer round the bend. 'Oh, go it, Haig. Kick it in, can't you, Haig.' Haig, dropping in one long slither on the right side of the tape, sits there, his ribs rising and falling. 'Good old Haig,' chants Stephen. Kattie's face is like a bright berry, for she is the simple sort, who'd as lief share success as steal it. Anything nice that happens to anyone, any vicarious triumph is good enough for Kattie: if she can just touch the arm of the winner and not be snubbed.

'Phillips — Custance — may I introduce a couple of friends, Miss Hannay?' Stephen simply must break away to congratulate Good Old Haig. Sauntering through the grounds towards the college, Kattie and Phillips fall behind. Half-way up the staircase, Custance quickly kisses Eliza.

'You look so pretty under that floppy hat. You're not annoyed, are you?' Eliza isn't annoyed, only a little disappointed. It is the first time since

growing up that she has been kissed, and she'd have preferred it to be like
—

The Glory Hole again. But then she thinks of a couple of lines to fit
Custance, with his long flannelled legs and his cool lips, and likes him
again.

> He trod the ling like a buck in spring,
> And he looked like a lance in rest.

Custance says he will see her at the Sports Ball and wants all the
waltzes. So he is gone, like the shadow of a bronze boy falling cool across
clean turf, clean sunlight. All the boys are the same. The great lawn is
sundial for their young bodies, and they don't know it. Eliza is happy.

Simone, walking home, asks, 'Who was the youth?' Her voice is a
needle unpicking the thread. It doesn't matter; it wasn't a wonderful bit
of sewing, anyhow. Cool turf, that was what mattered, cool turf.

Breaking-up day at Chisholm School, the very last. There was a play,
in French, so that the parents could see they were getting their money's
worth, and Eliza was the witch. 'So she won't need any makeup,'
commented Miss Hebron; but Eliza liked witch parts.

Lorna Calmont was the Princess. She had fat, limp plaits of golden
hair, well past her waist. Sleep for a hundred years . . . sleep for a hundred
years. . . . No, that's too good to waste on you. I'd rather have it for myself.
There were real spinning-wheels on the stage, and dragons of real incense
wreathed up, tenuous, chasing and swallowing one another's blue tails.

> La fileuse, que rien ne presse,
> Travaille en chantant —

People's faces in the audience were featureless pink eggs, but Lorna's,
as she closed her eyes for the sleep of a hundred years, was very white. The
Prince came on, wearing staled crimson velvet, Eliza and her spinners
were driven away.

'Thank goodness, that's over. Oh, how my head aches. I'll never act
with your horrible incense again, Eliza Hannay; it's all your fault.'

'Of course it is. But it wasn't the incense. I was willing you to go to
sleep for a hundred years. I nearly got you, too; then I changed my mind.'

The Prince, Vashti Greene, said: 'Don't listen to her, Lorna. She's
mad.'

Between items, school prizes were distributed. Miss Verriam handed Eliza the Book of Job and a Tennyson whose red bookmark lay against:

> Move forward, working out the beast,
> And let the ape and tiger die.

For a moment she wondered if Miss Verriam had done it on purpose, in which case her respect for Miss Verriam would have gone up by leaps and bounds. Then she decided that her head mistress hadn't enough intelligence.

From the wings she watched a girl she had never met dancing an idyll called 'The Spirit of the Wine'. How on earth had it got on the programme? By accident. . . . The girl's hair was perfectly white, and came down in a harsh square-cut shock on her shoulders. Her feet were naked, and made no sound as she moved over the stage. She wore a wine-coloured tunic, which did not hide the thick white limbs, the in-cut jewelled shoulders, that spoke of power.

The young girl raised her arms. Light as a dream, her body drifted backwards, her long steely hands supplicated the air, then linked above her head. Her body thought for her, there was not an instant's pause between flex and flex. She bent from the waist, effortless, until the inverted cup of her face touched the dust. The wine-coloured gauze moved very slightly, a sigh or a mist on the air. Long beams of light were wedded to her. She lay still, not stirring her white hair or her narrow hands. The flower was broken in its ecstasy. Eliza did not want to see it mended again, used as a trivial bouquet for sniffing and congratulations.

That, that is what we are: not this other, that you would make us. That, and after that, the worst you can say of us — why not? Dance once, and then begone.

CHAPTER NINE

Reflections in the Water

A SPECIAL Day's Bay voice, hard and authoritative like a chunk of brown wood, shouts from the lower deck, 'Stand away from that rope. Stand clear, now, stand clear of that ro-o-ope. You up there, catch a-hold of that ro-o-ope.' The coil whizzes, the eager little boy on the wharf catches it and drops its noose cleanly over the stanchion. For a moment his heart knocks against the frail cage of his ribs, with fear that he might have missed, that perhaps this time the rope won't stand the strain. Every fibre in the hemp creaks, then stiffens. The little boy suddenly sees his own face in the bearded sailor visage peering up at him, sees his own head under the peaked cap. He is the *Cobar's* captain. At first this intoxicates him and fetches a long whoop out of his chest. Then he remembers his new dignity, and saunters away down the wharf, looking askance at the loungers who thread the water with fine needles, the silvery bodies of minnows used for snapper-bait. The Dago, a glum youth with brows like iron bars, is the only one who has caught any snapper. As soon as he pulls them up, he beats their heads against the stanchion, and there they lie, their red mouths bloodied and helplessly wide open, their wet silver porridged with dust. The little boy, passing with whistling mouth, does not mind, but automatically he rejects the Dago from his crew.

Quivering like a wary animal, the *Cobar* swings inwards, and Augusta says, 'Kitch, hold tight to the seat, darling. Eliza, mind you don't drop the cups out of that billy.' They hit the wharf with a bump, the piles recoil, and the *Cobar's* siren screams, 'We're here, we're here.'

Picnickers crowd the gangway, while the sailors sing-song, 'Stand clear, now, stand clear. One at a time, please, lady.' Tall, bare-headed boys, with their girls in organdie frocks and brimmy hats, middle-aged men in flannels, their stomach sagging pear-shaped, small girls who have knelt up on the hard seats so that their bare knees show a red crisscross like the pattern of waffle irons, crowd forward. The little girls are pleased at having crossed the harbour in the *Cobar*, known in Wellington as 'The Holy Roller'. 'Oo, didn't she roll, Em'ly?' they pipe. 'Oo, didn't you feel sick?' Their mothers, like large, patient black beetles, but with red or parchment faces, scream, 'Davie, you come here this minute, d'you hear me or not? Hold on to Mum, lovie, or you'll get trod on. Don't you push behind — what's all your hurry and shove for? Can't you see I got a kid

113

in me arms? The very idea. . . . Bill, don't you dare forget that lunch basket and me good kitchen knives.' They form into a solid wedge, one flesh, shuffling along the gangway an inch at a time, buttocks and things neatly curved into breasts and things; suddenly developing legs again as they jump down at the far end. On the wharf young people in frocks or flannels crisp-white as daisies wave their racquets and call impatiently, 'Oh, hullo, Pete . . . Hullo, Glad . . .'

Between the *Cobar* and the wharf the water is marled, pale and transparent, full of thready green veins like those in jade. Eliza feels if she could once get the look and feel of those waves absolutely right, in a poem or a picture, everything would be well with her soul, and she wouldn't need, every fortnight or so, to grovel for It to come back again — the uncontrollable, incompassable power. But it's no good, her poems are rotten and she can't paint at all, not even so well as little Kattie Bryce, who takes lessons and paints horrible native birds and sprays of kowhai on black velvet cushion covers. She sighs, and is prodded in the ribs by her father. On the far side of the wharf a notice says, 'Danger! Twelve Feet Deep'. Boys with dark gold bodies, wearing only Vs, jump on the stanchions, steady themselves, then plunge down like gannets. In a minute their dark heads bob up, they shake water and laughter out of their eyes, ears and noses, swimming leisurely overarm to the wharf steps.

Eliza can't dive, but she belongs to the sea. Day's Bay sand is smooth and warm, honeycombed with tiny airholes in which hide the blue crabs. Sandra is the only one who claims to have been bitten. Somehow she attracts the hostilities of nature. She comes in, her blue eyes swimming. 'Look, a bee stung me on the leg.' 'Wilson's foxie snapped at me, it nearly broke the skin.' Carly is afraid of the water, and won't go in. She will sit on the beach with Trevor Sinjohn, the chunk of white clerical meat, who is now officially her boy, though he hasn't given her an engagement ring — too stingy. Carly is eighteen and a half, and wears home-made frocks of voile, down to her size 3 shoes. Her engagement with Trevor Sinjohn is called 'an understanding', on the grounds that they are too young to be formally engaged, and every week-end she helps old Mrs Sinjohn, the tiny, sad mouse who says, 'Carly is such a sweet girl.'

At home in the evenings, Carly sews for her glory box, though by day she works in an office. Doilies, table-centres, nightgown-tops with patterns of lilac and violets, camisoles, are born and folded away like papery flowers. She does her brown hair in two puffs, drawn over her forehead. She has lovely eyes, grey to witch-hazel, but in spite of these and her tiny hands and feet, she thinks herself plain. 'If only I hadn't such a big mouth,' she mourns.

Trevor squires her off the boat, with the slim indifference which is his weapon and Carly's wound. He can always hurt her now, merely by not being there, by not smiling out of his bright, rather haggard eyes. Especially Trevor can hurt Carly on the bloody fields of her only public life, the church dances and socials, where the Maxina, the Valeta, and the waltz alternate with musical games, in which everybody prances round the hall, singing:

> A-hunting we will go,
> A-hunting we will go,
> We'll catch a little fox
> And put him in a box,
> And a-hunting we will go.

Open mouths baying. . . . All he has to do is not to ask her, 'May I have the pleasure?' He needn't even dance with another girl, he can drift outside, to smoke and talk with the big boys crowding the stairway. Other boys leave her alone, because tacitly she is Trevor's. Carly is the little fox. She sits in her primrose *crêpe de Chine*, feels its petals wilt softly and damply against her breasts, her thighs, all the soft, vulnerable parts of her that she would so gladly do without. She feels her mouth stretching wider and wider across her face, as if it must crack, like a clown's. Sometimes old Tim O'Keefe, smelling slightly of alcohol, his boiled shirtfront creaking, one stud undone, steps up to her like a gander. He dances well, but with a sort of rhythmic hop. One-two-three, *one*-two-three, One . . . two . . . three. . . . Carly, floating in his arms, smiles her darkened smile at the dancers, at the stairs, at the two old spinsters, Miss Blair and Little Miss Blair. The fat one has the reproachful, aqueous eyes of a frog. They look out of the trap at Carly, who is soft enough also to be trapped, whose wounded love is bleeding on the air, bleeding in the cloakroom that smells of Three Flowers powder and lavatory, bleeding through the thick blue smoke puffed by the louts. 'What a sweet girl Carly Hannay is, and so obliging.' Anything they can do to make Carly like themselves, shining church brasses, breaking off the tall stems of lilies to fit the altar vases, that surely they will do. The dead are anxious for company, so also are the living dead. Carly doesn't know this, but Eliza does, and would at times as soon take a sock at a ghost as not. Eliza is not a sweet girl.

But Carly at Day's Bay is another person, she has the field clear and sunlit. Trevor is there, swinging a billy packed with sandwiches, looking down at her with his bright haggard eyes, half schoolboy, half faun. He has brought a camera, and presently they will be snapped together among the sandhills, Carly so absurd in her long voile and perching hat that a decade later people would shriek with laughter at her: so soft, so radiant in happiness that the same hard decade might crawl on its marrowbones after her, asking, 'Carly, dear, how did you do it? However did you manage to love like that?' Trevor gives her his arm as they cross the road. Her day is made, her little face, looking back, is an enchanted face. Augusta suddenly loses her grip of vertical worry-wrinkles and set lips. 'Come along, John, let's get the hot water for tea, then we can settle.' John shambles in her wake, like a very thin, very patchy brown bear.

The macrocarpas have dipped the tips of their plumes in white dust, but their higher fronds are velvety, turning where the light catches them to the golden-green of old plush whose pile is worn. Behind lies a small brown artificial lake, with swans sailing, their breasts only slightly soiled from the mud of their nests, their black bills snapping for bits of bread. Once there was a Day's Bay Wonderland Exhibition, and the derelict water-chute still stands, from which flat-bottomed pontoons used to bounce out on the lake. Farther along is a closed stucco shell, adorned with a laughing, moth-eaten tiger and labelled, 'The Whispering Gallery'. In the pines rises a double-storied bandstand, its stairway blocked up because it is rotting and dangerous. Eliza can think of nothing but the Whispering Gallery as she helps Sandra to fill the billies with boiling water, 3d. a can, and trudges up behind the pond to the bush.

When they have passed the mamuk' tree-fern which grows right in the middle of the path, they know that the Day's Bay fetish has been properly observed. The fern is like a Siamese King's green umbrella or a curly throne. Sandra says, 'Wouldn't it be lovely to sit plump in the middle?' They pass the enormous rabbit hole, large as a cave, and catch up with their parents. John says, 'You can't get the tea-things down there, it's as damp as muck,' and Augusta retorts, 'Oh, don't be such a boob,' and sets foot on the scramble-trail into the gully, where there are many ferns and skeleton leaves, a brown stream, and nothing to sit on but overcoats. If other picnickers are in the gully, the Hannays scowl and move on. But most people prefer to lie on the beach, turning on their gramophones and slowly cooking themselves the colour of raw steak.

Trevor and Carly lay the cloth. There are egg sandwiches, ham is too dear. Everyone hopes the sausage-rolls will go round twice; they should, for this is Eliza's sixteenth birthday. Carly, Sandra and Kitch all have winter birthdays, but Eliza's is a January day, and always Augusta pronounces, 'We'd better go to old Day's Bay, it's so sheltered there.'

After lunch Trevor rinses the cups in the stream, despite John's protest, 'Dogs may have been drinking there.' Augusta says, 'You children go and get your dip, then we can go for a walk. No, Carly, I'm quite all right. Well, go with the others, even if you won't go in. You're a silly about the water. Trevor, you're in charge.' John lights his pipe and takes out *The Martyrdom of Man*. He would like to splash in the sea, to shake the drops off shoulders and hair, a happy wet dog, but he doesn't quite dare. He is afraid and envious of the young. So he growls a little in his throat, and is left in the glade with Augusta and Kitch, the lissom sunlight slipping down through the boughs on each, and on the queer, lonely kingdom of sticks and stones, new ferns and last year's broken bottles.

The men's dressing-shed is much bigger than the women's, and of stone, not tin. Under the women's roof, the room divides into wet-floored sandy cubicles, in most of which there are cobwebs. Carly whispers 'Don't stare,' to Sandra, because a woman in the cubicle opposite has her clothes off, and shows not only rolls and rolls of apologetic pink flesh, but patches of dark, frizzy hair. The Hannays undress discreetly, keeping on their vests until the last possible moment. Eliza thinks how queer it is that suddenly the smoothness of skin should be interrupted by funny little curly beards, and how awful she felt when she first noticed that Carly had broken out in this way. But everybody's doing it, even Simone, who uses a razor on her underarms because the smell of depilatories in the bathroom makes her father so furious that he threatens to thrash her.

Her feet are bare, the sandgrains have an odd, brusque feel. A girl races in from the sea and splashes under a streaming tap, until her eyes, hair and mouth are one gasp of water. Then she slings her bathing suit into a cubicle and stands naked. She looks as if a sea-tree had just prodded her. Carly whispers, 'Roll your stockings in your bloomers and hide them under the seat. A girl last week lost simply everything, and had to go home in her togs.'

The sand is mounded with bodies, flabby white, brown, crayfish. They stare a little, mostly quite peaceful, like seals. Dear little sun-babies stagger about with buckets and spades, sitting down suddenly and coming up with sand pasted over their blue rompers. Carly sits down in water just waist-deep, and won't go any farther. Her legs wash in and out with the tide. Trevor, without a glance, flashes past and sheathes himself in waves, swimming overarm to the raft. Eliza can't do that, but she lies flat, turning over like a porpoise, thinking, 'Oh, I'm so happy. Take me away with you.' The marled waves laugh and run faster. Sandra puffs laboriously on red water-wings, her eyes screwed shut, her arms like two broomsticks. A foxie runs in and dog-paddles madly after a stick, then runs out again, feeling very efficient, all his black beauty-spots showing through his short coat. Eliza thinks suddenly, 'There might be a shark'; the wharf steps are thick with old, cutty barnacles. She starts to shiver, and runs out, passing Carly, who is still sliding her legs in and out with the drift of the waves.

The others are tired and want to sleep in the bush. A party quite near has a gramophone, American honey-funny dropping through the tree-ferns.

> Carl me back, parl o' mine, let me dream once again,
> Carl me back to your heart, parl o' mine . . .

Carly clicks the camera shutter. Trevor flings back his faun head, posing; he takes a goodish snap.

'Come along, Eliza, you and I will go for a walk together.'

Augusta and Eliza take the up-path, past tree-boles and hollow stumps to rocks set in the rapids beneath a waterfall. There is kidney fern, sprayed dark pads, and Augusta steals a root, but they come up against high barbed wire, keeping them from sight of the fall, the white bridal veil misty over some unseen slide of rocks. Because it is shut off, it becomes fairylike.

'Ach — everywhere in this country, barbed wire. You never hear a New Zealander laugh, you never hear a New Zealander cheer, except over their filthy racing and their filthy football. Give me my dear old kookaburras.'

A few yards down the trail, she is wishing the barbed-wire fence back again, slabs of it. Two lovers are lying in the fern, the man covering all of the girl except fragments of crumpled white dress, filaments of bright hair caught in the moss over which the fantails make their delicate starred footprints. Over the lovers a wild myrtle peppers the air with little red berries, and under their pressed hands the earth is golden-brown. Eliza almost treads on them but they take no notice.

'And only man is vile,' says Augusta, hurrying down the path. But Eliza hadn't seen anything vile, only a man lying over a girl and a green-and-bronze mist of leaves above their heads. A bellbird strikes, like a peculiarly sweet-toned little clock, and they are out in open, sunlit road, the only big residential one in Day's Bay. Its old houses comfort Augusta with their lazy serenity. A hedge is very bright blue, and she stops, saying suspiciously, 'Plumbago. . . . I didn't know they could grow plumbago in this country.'

Then there are great masses of hydrangeas, rose, cobalt and snowy, inside colours of a glacier; disorderly with the rich and perfect disorder of the cultivated thing that knows how to let itself go. Old houses. Augusta stops.

'This is where I'd like to live, you know.'

'There'd be bellbirds in the early mornings.'

'Somewhere like this, or in England, in my old white house like a Greek cross. I always had two blue vases, one very tall, one squat, for the primroses and little things.'

In a bank of clover, leaves splashed with the ruby pips that sometimes mean a four-leaf, Eliza hunts till she finds several, and gives them to her mother.

'Perhaps they'll bring you the trip to England. This is the loveliest birthday I ever had.'

'Is it really?' The guard was down between them. Then Augusta said, 'Man, woman and child; man, woman and child.' She said it standing in the silent street, with the four-leaved clovers pinned to her fuzzy astrakhan stole, and the old houses dazed with peace and the coming of sunset, behind their hedges of bright plumbago and the tumult of hydrangeas. Nothing was sharp on the air at all, except the faraway grey ecstasy of the hills, that climbed above the bush and beyond their limitations; (great roaring billows splashed their far side, on a beach where Maoris speared fish by torchlight); and the smell of macrocarpa, and in a tennis court the hard, clean ping of the balls, as young men and girls cut clean across the nets. Every now and again, their voices came like a shower of fountain-drops, and were gone. This youth and lithe sharpness of movement were all around her, and her own life and that of her forbears passed out of her in words as dark as blood, and stained the dust round her feet.

'Man, woman and child; man, woman and child.' They smiled at one another, and went back to the others. John had been left with his book, and the children had gone to play rounders on the flat in front of the Whispering Gallery. Trevor had the bat, and Carly threw underarms up to him, sloppy shots; he couldn't miss making the full circuit every time, though Sandra and Kitch fielded well, Sandra a golden-haired giraffe, Kitch a stolid little brown idol. Trevor ran hard and cleanly, but as he came into the base he smiled and said, 'Kid's patball.' He was attractive, in his pasty way, but by no means Carly's Johannesburg gentleman.

When the *Cobar* slid out, everybody sang, boys and girls lying in one another's arms, and the middle-aged, and the squawking brats who, having sunburned their noses, were now trying to drown themselves from the lower decks, in waters that flamed and faded, waters grey like the wings of a moth, but with a so much colder sheen. They touched Rona Bay in the dark, bumping a wharf lit with lanterns: and the passengers they took on, and the gruff unseens shouting good-bye, were people they had known never and yet always, people coming from a secret town on their tide. Eliza thought one day she would write its saga, write how the shags bob their black necks and come up again, glossy and insolent, and over the horizon lies a milky smoke, a diamond sparkle of towers. She made the first line.

> Out of the Tower of Babel I save the one word 'Greeting'.

The boatload sang:

> Nights are growing very lonely, days are very long,
> I'm a-growing weary only list'ning for your song,

and that Maori thing, that took the voices into its refrain so softly. 'Hine, e Hine.' 'Maiden, O maiden. . . .' Wipe that out, she thought, wipe that song off the face of the waters, if you can.

CHAPTER TEN

Timothy

TIMOTHY-getting-out-through-a-hole-in-our-back-fence.

Afterwards Eliza tried hard to re-create the first chapter of Timothy, but only the drawing-room's stiff, robustious life, filled to overflowing with hard shiny pot-plants, the piano, Carly's snapshot album, the big dark picture of Bonny Prince Charlie and his two Scottish lairds, the brass irons in the fender, came out clear. Blurred, ill-focused little figures sat on the sham leather chairs, making faint remarks at one another. 'Won't you have some more cushions, Mr Cardew?' and 'I'd sooner have men who work on the roads than men who work in offices.' That was from Eliza, to please John, who struck in heavily. 'Ah, she's right, she's right. If I had my time over again, I'd see them all damned before I'd lick the clerk's platter of leavings.'

When Augusta told Eliza that she was to waste her Sunday afternoon meeting Timothy Cardew, she was indignant.

'Who and what is Timothy Cardew?'

'One of your father's Bolshevist horrors, I expect.' Augusta helped with the top back buttons of the Indian Squaw dress, its green flannel slashed into fringes at neck and hem. 'They work together. Your father says he writes poetry. You know what he is for picking them up.'

'But, Mother, Simone and I were going eeling in the Hutt this afternoon.'

Injudicious: Augusta and Simone didn't mix. 'Stay home and do as your father asks you, for once,' Augusta commanded; then, rather abstrusely, 'Since he works in the office, he won't have vermin. It'll be in the mind, then.' Eliza went into the drawing-room and strummed the keyboard of the piano — tra-la-la, *Melodie d' Amour* — seeing Hutt River pools blackish-silver, old tarnished coins. Stumps under the surface, and prickles, and Simone sitting with her knees drawn up . . . the only person worth fighting with. 'Curse poets. The good ones are all dead. This will be an ape.'

Timothy-getting-out-through-a-hole-in-our-back-fence. The hole was under the ngaio tree, much too squeezed to fit his shoulders, and he looked up and laughed, backing ungracefully into the empty section whence the Hannay cats came marching home, their fur a mass of bidi-bidi, and sat madly scratching their tummies on the settee. The snap came clear there. His eyes were bright green, much darker than Simone's, not vacant, not at all thwarted. He said, 'I'm going to run now,' and did — as abnormal as if he had sprouted wings and disappeared flashing over the house-tops, but a trick of which Timothy never broke himself. In argument, in sorrow, in passionate love-scenes (Timothy made passionate love-scenes, in dead earnest, but always with the proviso that some other time he was going to kiss some other girl), the thought slid into his mind: 'Now I'm going to run. Oh, by Peter and Michael, now I'm going to run.' If you were a good comrade, even if he felt sorry for you and wanted you to see the light, he grabbed your wrist, and before you knew it your feet were pounding turf or pavement, whichever came nearest. You sobbed and struggled, but Timothy never pulled up until your heart had long since escaped from your ribs, and the gorse-bushes, the tufty grass, the houses with red caps on crooked, were a jolted rhythm of sheer insanity. Then he dropped down, laughing, and pulled you down beside him, starting to kiss you with quick, hard kisses, themselves rather like pebbles or pieces of turf. Hedgehogs came tumbling out of the yellow grass, with their funny little cold noses and shrivelled paws, and Timothy watched, pointing them like a setter as the grass-heads swayed. When he had them, he made them uncurl, and tickled their underneaths. 'Soft-belly, soft-belly. . . . These are our mascots, aren't they, Eliza? These are our special beasts.'

Timothy, when he had covered in a few strides the empty section, getting the ends of his grey trousers matted with bidi-bidi, stopped for a moment and looked down. Streets and houses made vague explanatory gestures between the bare golden drops and the bays, but the sea had no need to explain itself.

He laughed, and out of three old tiled houses beside the Botanical Gardens chose the centre one, against whose garret windows the sunset was heliographing in fierce flashes, long and short, short, two longs and a short. In this house he installed Eliza, and told her to cook a rabbit for supper. Then he suspected that she couldn't cook, and reminded himself that he liked live rabbits, and was now a vegetarian, A.D.G.B.S. So leaving the fleshpots, he led her to the bookshelf, and was upset to find that she hadn't read Maurice Hewlett's *The Forest Lovers*, or Stephen Phillips' *Marpessa*. 'But, my dear child —' 'Rostand's *Chanticleer* is beautiful too,' she excused herself. He laughed, thinking her childish, and would have taken her upstairs to bed; but loving Eliza brought back other women to his mind — Damaris Gayte, whose forty-year-old wisdom and coiled black hair made him think of a steel river; Lucy, whom he had hurt so much that seeing her face made him actually cry, tears like red-hot needles pricking his eyeballs. If Lucy had had a baby, he would have married her — he thought he would marry any girl who was going to have a baby of his — but he was glad she hadn't. Living with a girl whose face made his eyes prickle would have been too much discomfort. He swerved back to Eliza, and thought that after all, though childish, she was interested in books as well as in being a girl, and he had never met one of the type before. He wouldn't ever take her up to bed in the red-tiled house, he would teach her Nietzsche when she was a little older, and keep her white, for an ideal.

A little wind came and caught him a soft, weightless blow under the chin, like a spaniel trying to attract notice with its begging paw. He forgot women, and with the spaniel at heel plunged down into the valley, which was now misted over, a large basin of curdled, crinkled milk, sapphire at the edges. From a road on which he met no one and smelt nothing but wild honeysuckle, he broke into Tinakori Road, which ran past the Gardens into the city; a road obviously of the horse-drawn age, though beetle trams crawled along its midriff. Its three-decker houses, crooked and out of drawing, leaned weighted with fantastic shadows, weighted with humanity. Against lighted windows Timothy saw hands and heads moving, sometimes ponderous, sometimes shrivelled like crazy leaves. A girl plunged into a pianoforte solo, spraying the notes laboriously behind her. Her lampshade was red. Timothy listened, then walked swiftly on, lifting the roofs off, smiling, loving the inextricable intimacies of a city at night, just as he loved the bidi-bidis on his only good pair of trousers. At the Dog's Hospital he had once helped the vet to confine a Pomeranian, and was amazed at the tininess of the wet rat puppies, their blind heads breaking out of the silken bag. He wondered how the Pom was getting on; he would have liked to pat her head, saying gently, 'Hullo, old girl . . . hullo, old girl,' just as he had before the vet poured chloroform above her aristocratic nostrils.

In a waiting-shed he saw a blurred and shapeless figure sitting, an old tramp. Timothy adopted what he hoped was the tramp slouch, and sat down. Easy to get into conversation by offering a fill of tobacco, and he loved the seared face and horny eyes lit up by the match, but he was disappointed when the tramp called him 'Sir', instead of 'Digger' or 'Mate'. In his dreams, Timothy was the complete godwit, always boarding ships for London, working his passage among the roaring black-and-gold

gizzards of furnaces, men jagged as tree-stumps in the dead landscape of
Hell. When he landed, he wasted no time on white cliffs at Dover, but
made straight for the city, touching with gentle hands and thought all
the lives huddled up, lying about on park benches. It was as if he knew
for certain that among all the oysters named Dud was the pearl named
Of Great Price. But the others he loved also, because they were Duds,
because they hadn't any pearls. Another warm throb of affection went
through him, as he remembered Eliza had said she liked best men who
worked on the roads, not in offices. She was right. . . .

He walked into a second-hand bookshop kept by a little twisty Jew, a
devil of a Jew, with a drip under his nose. (Pearl of Great Price?) Here he
bought her London's *Martin Eden,* and on the flyleaf scrawled, 'In this
see ourselves, but with the discipline of creation.' He underlined
'discipline of creation', yet was less sure what it meant after he had
dropped the package into a pillar-box than before. As he swung along,
the idea came back to him: creation in the artistic sense, powerfully
diverted from the body. It seemed tragic to him that at twenty he hadn't
created anything worth while; though he liked 'Song Soul', his clay bust
of a woman with head thrown back in an ecstasy of singing. Clay was his
second string, and he handled it much better than verse. But it crumbled
under his fingers, irritating and brittle, while the line lasted.

Are the crippled children, then, the sick thoughts of God?

He was right under the oblong shadow of the match-factory, a thin
lemon rind of moon hanging on its shoulder. It chilled his blood a little.
The wailing of a Chinese fiddle squalled down the streets, which farther
along offered up stench, as if a main had broken. But it was only the
smell of life, where garbage-cans, tomcats, listless Hindoos sleeping in
ragged rooms, are all details. A girl of perhaps ten, thin-legged, hopped
by like a sparrow, keeping pace with a great hulk whose shoulders were
so hunched that she was midway between giantess and dwarf. Her
menacing voice said, 'And I says to him, that's no bloody good to me,
see? And either you'll do as I says, or I'll bust your bloody face open.' The
little girl giggled, a shrill fountain of laughter in the dusk. There was a
white women's street in the Asiatic quarter. Fat voices spewed out of
doorways.

"Ow about a —, boy?' He couldn't go in, he was too much afraid, not
only of disease and of the prickly heat called shame, but afraid that they

might laugh at him, the great horse-laugh of the body for the other body that had tangled itself up with a mind. Yet he was good to look at, proud. One day in London or Liverpool, he'd try it. Right down into the gullet of darkness, like the King's diver in the poem:

And the youth from the waves shall return never more.

Two cadgers whined for the price of a meal. Timothy felt his panache come back. They were old and seedy, Cockneys with broken teeth. He linked arms with them. 'Come along to the pie-cart, boys.'

Timothy as John's domestic pet lasted about a week. Then Eliza had a note from him, a funny little note, hurt and incoherent. He was going away from Wellington, without another visit to Laloma; 'Your father says — of course, he's perfectly right.'

They were all at table, John buried behind his newspaper.

'You couldn't have said things to make Timothy feel like that. You couldn't have.' (One keeps saying, 'You couldn't,' meaning, 'You did — you have.')

'Can't have him turning your head, my girl.'

'You brought him here, you forced me to meet him. You've insulted a guest, you've more than insulted me. I'll never forgive you.'

Augusta said, 'Your father's pleasure is hurting his own flesh and blood.' Timothy had impressed her.

John began to shout. Unconvincing; he was just jealous of any man who touched any of these women he didn't want. By and by, he'd be equally jealous of Kitch. Eliza went out, down past the cellar, where once Kitch had got stuck in the awful Spider Place; down the steps, away along the bush road. Something rather comic in sizzling off like a charred moth, but heading for black dark instead of the lamp. Phosphorus slid between the old graves, there was a mist with a hurt childish face, a crying face. In the one lonely farmhouse, spellbound within its circle of macrocarpas, lived an old couple, both blind. All they wanted was somebody, once a month, to read aloud their letters from their son, who had gone to Canada.

Not to be able to see. Not to be able to touch.

The dreadful lesson of humility; take what you are given, it isn't permissible to ask for more. Of course you can *get* — manœuvre, cheat, play your hand — but that's a different matter. The salt is gone. It was a long time since she had loved anyone, except Simone: not since Mr Duncan, and that was before the war. Trevor Sinjohn didn't count. . . .

Phantoms, or our own face on the gloom,
For love of love, or for heart's loneliness.

Timothy, what was Timothy? Less bright green eyes, less the delicate
stalk and catkin of the sea-grass pencilling his face with its line of shadow,
less a voice musing in the shelter of the great green waves past the Red
Rocks, than the infinite endurance of a moment: while he was there, time
and the world stretched out and out, you could hardly hear the little foam
that burst around their edges. Standing with her hands pressed against her
throat, she accepted fact. 'I love Timothy. I must love him, because my
throat is hurting me.'

Being in love was a sort of tapu state, full of constraints and
superstitions, not quite real. It had to be kept away from the world. When
she had finished walking to the bush in the daytimes, she continued in
dream; especially towards the pool. There was a dark trail, forgotten all
about, and a stream came with edgings of fine malachite ferns, and beds
of tall nettles stung the hands in white blisters. Purple berries lay fallen,
rich as damsons, but not so big, and good only for the fantails and that
black and white gust of feathers — ah, so tiny — called Love's Messenger
in the Maori. But the real place was the pool itself, nearly six feet deep,
and with a huge round boulder in the middle, where she could sit. The
stream came down in a waterfall, and broom tilted over it, petal on petal
of eager gold, rafts on the water; but with summer came the musketry of
bursting pods.

Eliza wouldn't take Simone to the pool. She told her about Timothy,
but lamely: 'Grey tweed sports coat, green eyes, little freckles, tall, cleft in
the chin, fair.' Simone said cleft in the chin meant a flirt. She was hard
then, nearly seventeen, hard and rather fierce. She rode well, but swished
Grey Jeremy so irritatingly that once he threw her and broke her arm. She
had numerous love-affairs, so openly that Augusta, who did not forbid her
the house because then Eliza would be always about with her outside, used
her most scriptural language about her. But what Augusta didn't know
was that Simone's idea of a love affair was dancing all night with the same
hypnotized youth, then laughing him out of countenance if he tried to
kiss her. She wore little shoes shot with opalescence, always a size too
small. To go to dances, she had to stay with a maiden aunt up on the
Wellington hills, and the boy who saw her home had no catch, for all her
bright-green eyes and his bright-green hopes. Her feet hurt her too much.
She was always dying to meet somebody who would remove her shoes and

her intelligence, but never did. Her fastidiousness was quick as a cat's.

With Eliza she let go. They had quarrelled and blundered their way into friendship, she met sentimentality half-way, as Eliza met her hardness. In the manuka she burned with a restless, silvery fire, and every line of her was cup and curve, like those nymphs she had tried to draw. Simone was her own one and only successful nymph. They made a special god for wet black nights, Little God Pot, the brother of Pan. Simone said she was going to marry, and marry well. Mostly Eliza argued against matrimony, and to fame via London and unlimited poems: for even if Timothy came back, she did not believe that he would marry her.

Simone said, 'I could take almost any man in the world away from you'; the cold voice in Eliza's brain cried, 'Yes.' The Hannays didn't seem precisely lucky in love; they were too soft and too hard, too intelligent, and such bloody fools, besides being matter out of place. Aloud, she said, 'Your youths always seem a pretty scratch lot to me. And if you want to know, Walter Lestrange is extremely affectionate when your back's turned. He even tries to flirt with Sandra. He'll get himself a scratched face yet.' Simone didn't want Walter, but she'd mind — hurt in her pride, seeing in Sandra a new competitor. She would hate Sandra, prize Walter a little bit more, and have something to take her mind off Timothy. Cover and double cover. . . . Becoming a woman, that's it; partly the noble art of defence, partly passivity.

Sometimes for days at a time she hardly knew Timothy existed. Then a sudden pain shot through to the surface, she wanted to strike out blindly at anyone, heard her voice saying hard, unreal things, or talking aloud as she walked alone. It would be good to break, to stop talking.

She had sunstroke, after letting an artist, the queerest little brown patch of a woman, sketch her on a grilling beach. It was no compliment to her shape, Mrs Macey only wanted a flesh-coloured blob in the foreground. What she really enjoyed painting was spiders, and she kept them in bottles at her studio. But the Academy refused to hang her insects, and in desperation she had turned to painting blue flapjacks of sea, yellow flapjacks of sand, titled, 'The Bay'; like all the other accredited New Zealand artists. When she had earned enough by the sale of 'The Bay', she was going after a wolf spider. Eliza liked her, though Mrs Macey always made her imagine many legs on the back of her neck.

Relief to sink down, to be quite ill and lie flat in the little green room, never moving a hand, like somebody who will not stir again. Relief, cool darkness and no voices.

At the end of Eliza's sunstroke, John came into her room with an enormous letter in a blue envelope.

'That's from young Cardew,' he said, and tramped out again.

CHAPTER ELEVEN

Broken Trees

TIMOTHY, straddling the big pohutukawa root thrust out from the cliff, flashed his cleaver through manuka and tough scrub that had to be hacked away where the tunnel was going through. Each time the blade swept, three-foot white arc, it carried his whole force with it, and his mind sang 'One-two, one-two,' like a kid going up and down in a swing. Cut manuka, bleeding sap, fell in piles to make a green mattress twenty feet below, its clean wounds staining the air with pungence. Gripping the root with his knees, Timothy swung round to see Birkett ten yards on his right, Martinovitch on his left. Sweat rolled down the Dalmatian's matted chest. Martinovitch came from the gum fields, and worked as if God were in him. The two men, and others out of sight, sat in slung board seats, and thought Timothy a fool to work unroped; but he found pleasure in knowing that he might break his neck if he were clumsy, or with a wrong shy of the cleaver might take an arm or leg off, clean as a whistle.

The world behind and beneath was all green, clear, sharp-edged, impaling on little stakes a pale bubble sky. It brought tears to his eyes, it was so raw and zestful of conquest, springing up slopes, ringing the few old trees left broken on the ridge. This was burnt-off country, black-and-green on top, blue papa underneath, too poor for the grass to be more than a bristling crop. Raupo, the nearest station, was one of those little shows where you never see anything but a red tin shed, a tank, and a train gulping down water, her steam ghostly, her passengers, drugged with sleep and their own vapours, staring out of the window like doped flies. None of them ever got off at Raupo, but sometimes Timothy thought one should — a good man gone wrong, worth pulling into the bracken.

People, white and native, lived in the landscape, though you didn't see them. A bawling sheep or goat, a ribby cow eating its living somehow among the manuka, were the only signs of tenancy except on Saturday nights, when a shed a mile from the station was unlocked, and the pictures flickered on. It was Maori country, which meant no licensed hotels, but plenty of sly grog — the good stuff down to de-rail, denatured alcohol and meths. The only common ground besides the pictures was the post office (rumoured to house a new girl, a goodlooker) and a shack store kept by a tight-lipped Ulsterman who did more with sly grog than with his groceries. The linesmen lived in tents, with a board cookhouse. Timothy had been there six months, and liked the life.

He turned from fledged grass back to cliff-face, and worked for half an hour, sun grilling him through his cotton singlet. When the Boss called, 'Smoke-oh,' the men scrambled down like baboons, sprawling themselves out on the thin, tender grass, their muscles relaxed, their throats scalded by the black tea stewed up every few hours. Timothy pulled a wad of paper out of his pocket, and began to scribble. Birkett called, 'Hey, what're you making, Sonny Boy?'

'Writing to my girl.'

'Christ. Fancy turning in a smoke for a bint. What's her name?'

'Eliza.'

'Christ. That's the hell of a name. Not too much my fancy. I like sumpin a bit flossy — Rosie, or June, or Vi'let. Bit o' the hot?'

'Not much. This one's my proper girl. She's only sixteen and a bit.'

'Christ. Well, young or old, my old woman or the next, it's all the same in the finish. A tart's a tart.'

Birkett's broken nose, his short jockey legs and frizzed chest smudged the clear green of the young grass. It was wrong to spoil colour.

'That's a foul way to talk about women, Birkett.'

'Oh, come off, lad. Bint's a bint, isn't she? I wisht you'd a known what I'd a known —'

'And I wish you hadn't known what you say you've known. Only a lying, foul-minded swine like you would have made it up, anyway, if he'd never been off his mother's back door. That's life for you, Birkett — dog-brag.'

'Them's harsh words, laddies,' said One-Armed Dutton, rolling his long body between them. Birkett wiped his mouth.

'Christ — getting cocky, aren't you, Sonny Boy?'

'Better than get just plain stinking, like you.'

'Well, this to your tart,' said Birkett, and spat. 'All right, come on,' said Timothy, suddenly happy again and losing all his dislike of Birkett.

The men formed a ring, Dutton on a stump as time-keeper. Larry Kirst said, 'Sock 'im in the brisket, Kid, 'e's all wind downstairs,' and Timothy nodded. He stepped into the ring, liking Birkett's square chest, his short arms jolting back, swinging out again like flails. But the ex-soldier was slow and out of condition. When he landed a jab it was like iron, making Timothy's breath stop. It was easier and safer to play with him, step back like a cat, then barely tap nose or mouth. Shadow-boxing made Birkett mad, and he hurled himself like a wild boar against the stump where Timothy should have been, jagging a long rent in his slacks. 'That nearly done 'im, where girls was concerned,' remarked Larry's unfeeling voice. Birkett pasted hard on Timothy's ribs. Timothy countered downwards, reaching the solar plexus, and Birkett, gasping, sat down on the grass, shaking his dogged head from side to side as if he had water in his ears.

'Had 'nuff?' asked the Boss, puffing up blue rings. Timothy, panting but not really winded, thought of the doped faces in trains; no air, no bracken, no love-your-enemy, no working or living in rhythm, poor cows. He caught Birkett by the shoulder.

'Spell-oh, Boss. We're going to drown our troubles.'

'Whaddya mean?'

Timothy gripped Birkett's arm. 'Come along. Run. Run.'

'Oh, Boss,' whined Birkett, 'will ya clean off this mess?' But the Boss only grinned, and Timothy, handcuffing Birkett's wrist with his fingers, tugged him across the gully to the black swimming-pool.

'Strip, will you?'

'I'll see you . . .'

'Oh, no, you won't. This isn't Cairo. Will you strip, or will I beat you to a sheet of tin? I'm going to wash some of the dirt off you. Not without dust and heat . . . there's too much dust and heat on your grubby body, Birkett.'

Timothy grinned. Birkett, saying, 'You're either mad or else sissy,' eased his sore body out of his clothes. They hit the water in two white splashes. Timothy stood neck-deep, pouring it over his head.

'Oh, man, isn't it glorious? Doesn't it sting?'

'Oh, man, don't you sound like one of them creeping things from the Y.M.C.A.?' Birkett's stubby body, blunt face became friendly, like a gnarled potato offering its flower. 'See here, kid, I don't bear no malice. You get wise to yourself. Don't go flossing around girls, they'll do you in. They hang about, see? And the so-called nice ones is the worst. They're the same when it comes to brass tacks, but they looks different, so you've got to behave nice and not make 'em cry. That's rot-gut, that is. If you'd a known what I'd a known.'

'My girl's not like that.'

'The soldier's dream,' said Birkett. 'Virgins in Egypt, which wasn't also a bit of clinging vine.'

'You're right.' Timothy poured the water from his cupped hands, baptizing himself at the shrine of some ancient derisive Maori god.

'You're right, Birkett, and I'm right, and my girl's right, and most of all, God's right. Listen: I've just thought of a new definition of God.'

'You *wot?*'

'Don't look so shocked. I ask you to tax your imagination to the extent of endeavouring to conceive such an entity as this. Take every good impulse that has ever stirred you from the depths of your own heart, and that residual modicum of good that you feel is always present, and can't get out: add to this the feeling that the thought of your mother gives you, and the similar thoughts and feelings of everyone in the world, and the love of a little child, and all the beauty that Art ever called into being: collect this into one big space, add something that will contain and transcend the whole, and there you have what I think God is.'

'Speaking of mothers,' said Birkett, 'strickly between ourselves, I'm a bastard.'

'We're all bastards. We're the illegitimate sons of God out of vanity.'

'Oh, I give up,' said Birkett hopelessly. 'Now God's a womanizer too.'

They scrubbed themselves dry of the peaty water with handfuls of grass and rush. Birkett thought, 'There's always something funny about chaps with them very white skins. Either they're bloody killers, or else they go out like a glim.' They strolled back to camp, and Timothy caught a Maori pony to go down for the mail. When he got to the post office, he found that the yarn about a beautiful new girl was gospel, and fell in love with her on the spot. He had already been there with the Raupo schoolma'am, but the water was very cold, deep and wet, so he fell out again. This girl — Shelagh — had blue eyes, golden-brown hair, and white teeth all her own. Timothy dated her for the pictures that night — it was a Saturday — and jogged slowly back, reading his letters as he went. Damaris Gayte's made his blood run cold. It wasn't so much what she wrote, but a steely exasperation, a steely longing between the lines. Eliza's, twenty pages on blue paper to match his own, was a different story. He laughed over it, and made a memo to write to her, 'You're the one little glowing spot in my heart.'

Landing back at the tents, he was chipped by the boys, who wanted to know why he had to shave himself in the afternoon, and were divided between envy and amusement when they found he had already dated up the new postmistress. They had supper — bacon and eggs, beans, huge flat scones fried in pig-fat and served sizzling hot, black tea — and when somebody spilled milk on the table, the Boss lifted up the camp mascot, a tabby cat, and told her to lap while the lapping was good. She mewed and drank thirstily, her body pulled out of shape by a batch of kittens, just about due. She was a draggled thing, with beautiful furtive eyes of amber. Timothy was nice to her, caressing her throat until she relaxed, and came softly butting her head against his legs, jumping into his lap, shining on him from huge glow-worm eyes.

After supper he added collar and tie to his suit, brushed back his hair, and sat down by candlelight to write the first few pages of his letter to Eliza. Twice or thrice in the week he wrote to her, enormous letters. It was a relief to talk, to get away with somebody young and far-off, interested in books and poems, half-fledged theories, in anything but the hard acceptances of this man's kingdom. Before more than half a dozen moths had time to crisp in the candle-flame, Birkett put his head round the flap, saying, 'If you want to catch that bint while she's still piping hot, you'd better hurry.'

The men watched him ride away.

'Too many skirts,' said the Boss, removing his pipe from his mouth.

'Too much potry and God, if y'ask me,' responded another. But Birkett, his eyes beautiful as the cat's in his ugly face, said, 'Ar, you leave the kid alone. Too young, that's all the trouble is with him. He'll grow up.' 'Oh,' said the Boss, 'like that, is it?' Everyone felt this was a final comment, and settled down to show-poker.

When the flickering screen at the pictures showed love-embraces, the Maoris, who had ridden in from twenty miles around, squealed 'Kapai, Kapai.' and made plopping noises, sucking their lips in and out. An enormous Maori, his stomach bagged in his puce jersey, put his hand on Shelagh's knee. Timothy, hearing her little startled, 'Oh,' in the darkness, picked the hand up and neatly dropped it back where it belonged. Sometimes incidents of the kind started a free-for-all, but the Maori merely grunted, sagging back in his seat. When the serial began, the Maoris got really excited, and shrieked and moaned as the Iron Claw set fire to the building with the white heroine on the roof. Shelagh whispered, 'Oo — don't they smell fishy? Is it mussels?'

'Partly. Partly it's just Maori. You'll get used to it.'

She said, 'In a way, I like it,' looking up at him with a round white sixpence of a face whose only clear features were its big eyes, like the cat's. Women did like this country. It gave them enough trouble and hard work to beat their brains out, and brains — half-brains — were what ailed most of them.

On the way home, with Shelagh behind him, the horse's hoofs trotting softly through swishing bracken, Timothy felt a sudden tense desire to make love to the postmistress. He had known all along that this would happen, but now, ardently, he wanted it to happen of itself, because Shelagh said so. An edging of new moon on the fern made the hillside a place of rime and shadows, moth-like and faintly sinister. Each stalk of grass was alive to its delicate tip, the bracken spat out little witch-words in its dry cracking. Shelagh tightened her arms around his waist, let herself go heavy and limp. He halted the horse, and for a while they lay in the fern together. The crumbling soil with its mat of growth-fibres, its sooty black of old burn, was lovely to touch; lovely Shelagh's body, its skin warm and beating. When he looked again at her face in the vague moonlight, he saw that she had been crying a little. The tears were beautiful too, like the tracks of wet silver a snail makes on a dark leaf.

'Little girl . . . little girl . . .'

She said inconsequently, 'I must look a sight, I don't know what came over me. I was lonely, I guess. It's that big out here, and the old broken trees look that funny. It looks as if somebody had died here. I had a baby once, Tim. You won't tell any of the other boys, will you? I don't mind telling you, because you're a gentleman. You wouldn't let anything like that happen to me again, would you Tim?' He kissed her eyes. 'Of course not, dear.' Then, 'What happened to the baby? Did it die?'

'No, I boarded it out. I used to go and see it a lot, but what's the use? The woman was an old cat to me, and when they grow up they don't like you any the better for it.'

Queer, the premonitory pang that sometimes shot into his mind, the absurd thought, not to be exorcised until he had said it aloud. That lifted the tapu.

'Somehow I don't think I'll ever have a son.'

Shelagh said indifferently, 'Oh, go on,' but he could see she didn't care; that a man should actually *want* children was incredible to her. He was sorry for her, as for a little grey moth in a web, or the draggled she-cat at camp. Sorry no less because she lay in the shadowy grasses, as easily picked as a stalk of bracken, and comforted now; and her tale was so little, unless the flame came down from Heaven which makes it magically more. With the loss of desire, he had lost Shelagh, lost everything except a shadowy girl who was tired and opened her mouth in a little yawn, longing for sleep. Timothy shivered for Shelagh, as well as for himself. Oh, the dividing loneliness of life. She was contented. Back in the saddle she swayed softly and drunkenly. She said good night at the door of the shack behind the post office, her mouth passive as a child's. The bitter lines of Iris Tree came into Timothy's mind:

> It yet is something to have cheated God
> And bored the Devil, with so easy prey. . . .

Half-way back to camp, he dismounted by an old paddock that had been an orchard once, but had failed for want of deep soil, deeply rooted hopes. He dropped rein over a paling, jumped the fence, and started to hunt for windfalls for the boys. Suddenly a deep sigh in the apple-thickets froze his blood. He felt his hair rise, and taking tight grip of his courage kicked out into the bushes, routing out not a ghost, but a scoffing herd of Maori pigs, preposterous lean-snouted Calibans of the moonshine. Timothy laughed and laughed; then, a little shaky, stroked his horse's blaze, and told it to stay cropping where it was. He ran the rest of the way to camp . . . his panacea for everything, flinging himself into the wind, making rhythmic contact between the soles of his feet and the hard earth. The stars blazed bitterly white. Birkett came in when the others had doused their lights, and tried making up to Timothy. Timothy refused, but not ungraciously.

'It's not that I don't see what you mean. But I've got a girl.'

'Christ,' said Birkett, 'she must be some girl, all right. Take my word for it, Sonny Boy, you'll be sick of girls before you're through.' He said this not bitterly but sadly; his ugly veteran's face had all the pain of living, in the candle-light his middle-aged wrinkles showed up like trenches, and the dead lay unburied. Then he blew out his candle and went away.

Much later, Timothy awakened from a dream, a vague, rambling, nightmarish dream; the worst of it was that he couldn't tell wherein the terror lay, and yet it still pressed down on him, breathing heavily, blackly. He could only repeat to himself softly, 'It's terrible. I'm lost. It's terrible. I'm lost.' His fingers found the matchbox. The sparkle showed nothing but black and grey, the land of broken trees. He saw Eliza's letter lying where he had thrown it, put it into the pocket of his pyjama coat, lay down again and went off to sleep, quite happily, having circumvented whatever threat was in the air. Outside the trees glistened skeleton white, a ghostly army. It needed only one trumpet note to bring their silent company together, ready to march down for an inexorable revenge on the men who had murdered them, and left their broken bodies standing, a mock for sun and moon.

CHAPTER TWELVE

Business Girls

SIMONE said, 'You look the complete dairymaid,' and it was true, because of Little Miss Blair's frocks, against which even Carly revolted, sobbing, 'She makes me stick out all round, and I don't.' 'Look how those girls have stood by their poor old father,' said Augusta stubbornly. The Blair girls would never see forty again, but they were prominent in church circles, and their lonely respectability had won Augusta's heart. That was all very well: but as Carly pointed out, you could tell Little Miss Blair and tell her, while she knelt on the hearth-rug with a mouthful of pins, taking measurements and tacking up seams, and always she would assure you that she quite understood. Then, the moment you had gone, Miss Blair Proper would put on her spectacles, and say to her younger sister, 'Now, Clemency, no nonsense.' God had given women certain geographical features, but St Paul had the last word, and the result was always the same old sack-race silhouette. Sandra said, 'Well, Carly's blue makes her look as if she's going to have a baby any minute, and I don't see that that's so very respectable,' and got her ears boxed.

Simone's dark red lipstick in its gold case was called Coralie. 'She would,' said Augusta. Only a little more beauty, a little fining of blunted hands and prettying up of full, scornful mouth, and Simone would have been the picture of a French marquise. But somehow it was right that her beauty should be broken, flawed opal like the rest of her. She worked in a frock-shop, drawing designs. Sometimes Augusta said, 'I call her a very ordinary little thing, and she squints'; sometimes, 'Well, if she doesn't get a man in that rig, she never will.'

Queer; getting a man was almost equally important to Augusta and to Simone, though at bottom neither of them cared a rap for men as such. In practice, Augusta hated matrimony, and Simone would much sooner have been an artist, if her fingers had been differently shapen, her ambition just a little more straitly winged. Or if she wanted a man at all, he was a dream, an elaborate mechanical toy, old school of faun, plus Oscar Wilde conversation, plus beautiful dancing pumps that circled for ever and ever, plus some form of heroism or distinction that wouldn't be too uncomfortable — a leper island doctor, for instance, would be right out of it — plus — oh, what the devil? Heaven and Hell, black night melting into a face. Most women never grow up, the others are born that way. No, it's ourselves we reach out for, Eliza thought, our own undiscovered selves.

Nevertheless for Augusta and Simone, when a man, almost any man, said 'Will you marry me?' — even if he were so abject that you turned him down without a second thought — it meant you had not lived in vain. And always you allowed it to leak out that he had proposed to you.

This made Timothy's letters extremely awkward. He wrote three times in the week — oftener than Trevor Sinjohn cared to stroll down the road, and re-establish the fact that he was still Carly's boy — but although he said over and over again that he loved Eliza, sometimes in words which could very nearly be hung up to dry as a proposal, on the next page he thought nothing of mentioning that he had just fallen in love with somebody. Eliza knew them all — Damaris Gayte's profile, Lucy's soft, hurt face, this new creature with the blue eyes and the teeth. It wasn't that Timothy bragged — he understood that relations between men and women are far more often defeats than conquests — but it didn't occur to him that you were supposed to love one person at a time, and that done well.

Eliza herself wouldn't have cared, except for loneliness. She wondered if the Hannay generations had introduced somewhat a touch of the tarbrush, for her mind took to polygamy like a duck to water. So long as he loves me best, I don't see that the others need be embarrassing. . . . But Simone asked, 'Has your Timothy proposed?' and Augusta, who wouldn't directly ask, was worse. She would adore Timothy if he married Eliza; if he wouldn't she would hate him all the more for being charming. In family council, her tongue would flay little bits from Timothy . . . and from Eliza.

Timothy just doesn't know, she thought, he doesn't realize how naked we are until some man clothes us with his honourable intentions. Ugh. . . . Lovely to inherit things, of superb right: hateful to hang about, like a freckled charity child at a bun-fight. Simone, looking into the cloakroom mirror at whatever dance it was, touched with the slim pencil lashes already dark around her green eyes, and said, 'Almost anyone would fall in love with me sooner than with you. Your Timothy comes from the country, doesn't he?'

Why should I be manœuvred into hating you because you're beautiful — when all the time, at the back of my mind, I don't? Separate and apart, your cold green eyes, lakes with the dusk thick around them. Because of that, I could forgive you anything. More than that, I could become disembodied, stand apart, only wish you to continue ever as you are, in this gentle evening light.

Once she left Simone standing alone on the crowded pavement. I'll never go back, said the cold voice, I'm better off without her. She rode up and down in the diminutive cable-tram, plunging through tunnels and past bright toy gardens. The driver was a one-legged man, his face calm as Pluto's. All day tunnel and sky slid over him. In the evening the tunnels went topaz, the open spaces cool black, scented by flowers. Lights gave themselves to the air, like sparkling lovely women with wreaths pinned in their breasts. He had nothing to do but push a lever up and down, smiling vaguely at the passengers. This left him with a face emptily serene, like a god's.

Bright toy gardens, the wild unbounded sun of a marigold, concentric rings of orange light, cool dark inside the tunnels. (You could make me happy for ever, and yet it is more important, somehow, that I should belong to you than that you should belong to me. Possession is nine points of the law, but whose law? Not any law I wouldn't take up and smash against these sliding tunnel walls.) It is not fitting that Simone and I should quarrel over a lust for possessions. My hands are full of grey tunnel and blue sky, like big, strange birds, tumbled out of an airy nest, screeching and gawky. How do you like my eaglets, Simone?

The patch of grass outside the Ladies' Rest Room was black-dotted with people, boys and girls eating their papered lunches, tired women suckling babies whose heads looked too big. One man, a shy fellow with a shiny black coat, had the pigeons so tame that they perched on his head and shoulders, big murmuring puffs of opal. He was bald except for a dark little ring of hair, and scurf lay on his coat-collar. He laughed shyly, inviting people to admire his gleaming pigeons and ignore his shabby self.

The tea-room Simone liked was full of dud antiques, Ali Baba jars smeared sticky crimson, two shell-parrots tittering, engrossed in a pygmy idyll. Women's voices loomed immense over their cage.

'Oh, look, Betty, do look. He's kissing her, the dear little fellow. We must get a pair, aren't they too sweet? Do you think the pale-blue are prettier than the green?'

A last shot, the old picture-show everyone called the Fleahouse. Simone was sitting near the front, her short-sighted eyes peering up at some film negroes. One negro's white lips were pasted right across his face. He rolled up his eyes and capered. Simone had to wear glasses at the pictures, and sit almost against the tired mechanical pinging of the unseen theatre pianist, who dreamed from one pre-war melody to another. She seemed immensely pathetic. The grey and blue birds flew out from Eliza's hands into the stagnant air.

'It's an unbearable picture. Let's go.'

'Oh, it's you.'

At the top of the Gardens, the quiet manuka place where sunlight stroked the seamed old face of the world, she was so much more Simone: a girl in a green and golden shellcase, deciding that women are inevitably licked, that somehow, magically, she wouldn't be. She would win — but she hadn't the faintest idea what she wanted to win.

'What's the good of love without marriage?'

'What's the good of marriage without love?'

'You're a fool. You'll only get cheap.'

'A thing given can't be cheap. In the meantime, you might as well be nice.'

'You ask for it, you're a soft. One can't help teasing you.'

Picnicking children, carrying their lunches in paper bags, clattered by on the paths. They were not to go too far, not down through the trees to the swings, because there they might meet a man. They were ordinary children, with sunburnt tow hair and little socks slipping in wrinkles about their ankles. But they looked beautiful and strange, like wild ponies. Their shrill conversation drifted up from their own world.

'You're always tryin' to be the Boss.'

'Shut up. Look in the bushes — there. I seen a fantail.'

Their faces, upturned, saw also the grown-ups, the two fantastically dressed creatures with silk stockings and hats, lying side by side in the brown grass. The grown-ups smiled at them, but the children's leader marched on, bouncing her black hat-elastic under her chin. There was no admission into their intimate and delicate companionship.

.   .   .   .   .

When Eliza was seventeen, enterprise and scraps of rhyme got her a job, a spidery, likeable job at thirty shillings a week, scribbling notes for a little paper on Woman (of whom she knew nothing she would have told). The job gave her new standing. Augusta, always scrupulously fair where money was concerned, wouldn't take a penny for the first year. Ninepence a day for lunch at Gamble and Creed's, the rest for tram-fares, books and clothes. No more Little Miss Blair. Ready-mades glossy-new from the shops, and little hats that turned perkily up or solemnly down, the only known styles of the day. Augusta was pleased, yet with the pleasure mingled a strange disappointment. Thirty shillings a week — good. But somehow, out of the clouds, there should have been another way — a brilliant scholarship, a clear-cut genius for something more profitable than eternally scribbling poems and crying over them.

Poetry and boys and Simone Purcell — that little harlot. Augusta used scriptural words quite clearly and frankly in her household, without going to the ends of their implications. Simone was a little harlot because she used lipstick, had once written a letter saying 'Lovers, but not too many babies'; because the whole purpose of her defiant gold and green was to be admired by many and married by one, probably a catch; because she was better-looking than Augusta's own children — except Sandra, perhaps — and Augusta wouldn't trust her an inch.

Eliza sat on a stool in a little dungeon, razoring from foreign exchanges anything that might be taken as a hot tip for women (generally assumed to be darker than Erebus in matters of cleaning their pores, curing their children of spots, keeping their man). She read the sex blackmail of a thousand advertisements — even your best friends won't tell you. Why is Jim interested in other women? I wouldn't care to dance with *him* again, pink toothbrush, one in every five has it. Samples will be posted in plain wrapper. I was a wallflower, too. Do you know that serious diseases can result from this simple neglect? Communicate Dr Smith, Box 19937. Men — do you want women to look at you in the street? In ten days I increased my chest measurement. . . .

Leeches for suckers. Americans and the imitators of the Americans, shouting, fawning, cajoling, lying, demanding money with threats; selling by print everything from toothpaste to abortion: fastening always on the lonely people, the little duds, the shy ones, who believed what they were told, and were afraid in their tragic hearts of being left out. And if you could invent an advertising slogan for the further intimidation of these people, it was worth real money. Spectacled Yanks would buy it, and offer better wages than you could get in newspaper offices. You could sit working in offices whose internal walls were all glass, so that the Boss could tell at a glance who was loafing on the job. There would be printed cards about the sacredness of your work. You could put money by. . . .

And die at forty, with your belly ripped open to get the cancer out. Not much.

Timothy wrote, 'I wish to God I could make my living as a writer,' and even Simone respected Eliza's job. Eliza loved it. People all around her, mostly Queer Mossies, rustled and slithered in and out of rabbit-hutches, stealing one another's electric light bulbs, and complaining bitterly about the sub-editors. Life in the office was dingy but warm, little embers pressed down in the bowl of a meerschaum pipe.

She picked up its thread again in Gamble and Creed's, where everyone ate hurriedly in a good smell of coffee and a bad one of stinking rubber-lined mackintoshes. 'Brahn sandwidges, Miss. Here, Miss, there's no mustard in these sandwiches. Get a move on, Miss, I've got to be getting out.'

Choleric little faces, they had; queer, bonded race, so helpless and yet so powerful. Women, a minority, sat alone, reading books propped up against the drip-nosed nickel teapots. It was interesting to watch them come in. They always looked about for a table where there was nobody, crossed the whole length of the room to find one — as if a ghost occupied the seat opposite. They were all business girls. Many kept sentimental trysts with themselves, pinning bunches of daphne or heavy-fragrant brown boronia on their costumes. The men fraternized, talking shop. Flying particles of it came over — stock exchange, politics, smut, all on a harder, crisper plane than feminine talk, though you could spot a goodly percentage of bores. It wasn't that the men weren't ignorant, but they had the courage of their gutturals. It was evident at once that they had a life apart from the women. The women — they had the toy boxes called their homes, the rag dolls called their babies; or the business ones had a room ('the flat'), with a pink lampshade and an imitation bit of Lalique. The value of men to women was plain in everything they did; even among these close-faced women, who watched unobstrusively as a cat watches. The value of women to men was debatable. If women weren't there, Eliza had a feeling the men would continue to talk shop for about ten years before they noticed anything. Then, presumably, they would want some fresh tea . . . or to reproduce their kind. Unless they had killed one another off in their wars.

And for both, when they were old, there was the last sexless companionship, a possibility of being people instead of men and women. But for most, since they had got so thoroughly into the man-and-woman habit, existed only patience, a withdrawing into the frail, battered shell of the body. Little black people living in old, ramshackle huts, by the green edges of an imperious sea. One has a lump of ambergris on his mantelshelf, one has only a Maori weatherglass, the bubble of air cut out in its leathery case from the strands of bull kelp. A little beauty, a little wisdom.

Eliza wanted none of it. Only the rafters of pinewoods over her head, and Timothy, his sandshoes slipping on the warm russet needles, his eyes full of little prickles of light. She would have liked to make a song at the top of the pine-slopes; but if she died going up, and was marked with a cairn of stones, soon scattered, it didn't matter.

Her immediate masters at the office, Mr Dill and Mr Lennox, said, 'Don't dream, Ginger.' They weren't Queer Mossies. Mr Dill was little and quizzical, Mr Lennox large, mild and plaintive, and they both stared down on her like dogs humouring a kitten.

Timothy wrote from Raupo. He was coming down, he said, Eliza could expect him any day.

CHAPTER THIRTEEN

Road Roundabout

TIMOTHY fully intended to catch the train at Raupo. But the mists were so fine, the milky gossamer denied to all heat. Pools of mist lay knee-deep on the valleys, and into them the cows waded, discovering there some immense, mild satisfaction which made them sink prostrate, only their slow eyes and grazing jaws in motion. The valley looked like a white mirage. Timothy laughed, and tried to halloo the dream-cows into action, but they gazed through and over him, Poppaeas in the milk-bath, too torpid to consider men at all.

Every stem of grass, pink where it caught the turn of light, was a wire threading tourmaline beads, some as small as dust, the big ones ready to break and run down like tears. A spider shambled out of his trap-door. Over the few paling fences hung the Maoris' bundles of tow, cut when the flax was stiff and green, bleaching now to biscuit-colour. From a shack doorway old Kahu, her breasts immense under a bright orange jersey, gave him 'Tena koe.' She wore a man's plug hat, and had had children by so many whites that they all looked alike to her, big kids.

Timothy hesitated; suddenly and strongly, he didn't want to board his train, which was already in the station. The string of sheep-trucks packed with bodies like dirty fawn rugs, bodies alive and bleating until they reached the slaughter-yards and were reduced to a black jelly of blood, joints on iron hooks, raw hides and a stink of fertilizer, decided him. Beneath his belt he swerved back to Shaw and vegetarianism.

He passed the station and struck north. High drifts of aniseed-smelling fennel companioned him. The hills were bare except in gullies still rife with bush, disappointing unless one stared at it long enough for its tangled sinews and strange body to take shape. Knolls planted with circlets of pines or English trees always meant a homestead, built in the rectangular mode of the commonplace which ran through the whole of the country's architecture. Red tin roof, wooden walls, a tank, sometimes a rusty watermill. At one of these square-jowled little places, he drank raw milk, watched by the golden eyes of a collie, and the black ones of a woman whose husband was out turning the cows into paddock. Suddenly she pressed her hard lips against Timothy's.

'I hate him, see? With him, it's all just habit, regular as clockwork.' She put her hand to her throat, staring in angry defiance at her landscape,

143

where a few high-headed old cabbage palms lifted their thick cream bushels of flowers, looking peculiarly untamed in this air, which carried no dust to clog them. Under her apron her breasts were firm as winter pears. She said without any sort of importuning or apology, 'He'll be gone an hour, see?' and Timothy said quickly, 'All right.' The little bed-chamber looked extraordinarily pathetic, lifelike but not alive; it had a flowery paper and clean sticks of furniture, but a heavy, misshapen hand was over it all. The farmwife clung to Timothy, saying, 'I hope I have a baby of you. Oh, I do hope that.' Looking at the discolorations under her eyes and chin, dark patches which meant that her youth was just taking grief to itself, he could not voice his old haunting superstition, 'I don't think I'll ever have a son.' Instead, he thought only of the farmwife, until he was shaken by a kind of ecstasy which made the room's shadow, the pear-brown face and throat seem very lovely and confused. She looked at him with luminous eyes. Already in the chambers of her mind she was transmuting him into memory, a secret from which she could defy her husband. A sunbeam played rippling white on the door, and he noticed how modest the farmwife was, drawing the quilt up while she straightened her clothing. When he was going, she said, 'You'll be wanting your hat, young man,' and laughed at him. 'I wouldn't mind staying with you for keeps, Mother,' he said. As he went out by the front door, whose broken glass was stopped up with paper, he could hear the thin rhythmic clanking of pails, and wondered if another Timothy would hear it some morning, see against solid weight of sky the fantastic gestures of the cabbage-palms. He didn't feel any compunction at the idea; it was good country to be born in, and if that wife had a son, she'd fight for him like a tigress.

Birds broke away from under his feet, scuttling quail, skylarks from England, then the hedge-birds, living on berries and the sweet hard hearts of the palms. In the swamp bits, where the water was steel around quivering green isles of flax, pukeko stalked, old Red-Nose-Hiding-In-The-Raupo, plumage indigo, bill scarlet. All the time Timothy's feet were touching what he liked best, earth stripped of pavement. Smooth curves of hill passed in and out of him; sometimes he felt a violent desire to go back to the farmwife and try her again with a fiercer argument, sometimes there was nothing in his face but sheets of marsh water glittering, plumes of toi-toi, the little hills colliding at the back of his mind.

In ten days he had reached his father's house, and found it unchanged, the macrocarpas drawing their big sleepy circles around it, its old people moving through the dream — his father, who loved Dickens so much, and used to cry over *Little Dorrit,* his mother light as a feather and crinkled up in sweetness, but stone deaf. He could swing her up and play with her like a doll, but it seemed strange that she would never hear him now if he cried out in the night.

This old place, a very early farmhouse, oppressed Timothy and yet endeared itself to him by the hum of its quietude. He wrote to Eliza of the bees making summer in the macrocarpas; that reminded him that he should have been in Wellington, taking Eliza over the hills, perhaps asking her to marry him. He started with his formula, 'I'd marry her if she were going to have a baby,' then reminded himself that he was keeping Eliza white for an ideal, so there was no chance of a baby. Her ghost made him restless. Always woman comes with an importuning face. . . . He wished she could play a good hard game of tennis, and laugh as she knocked the ball back across the nets.

His brother Laurie, who had been his hero for strength and lack of bodily fear, seemed now to have grown into the rooting and quietude of the place. Men as trees walking, men as trees forgetting to walk. . . . The dusty mobs of sheep were his inheritance, the great bull tossing his sullen head in the pastures, and all things crying quick and clean inside the drawn circle of the macrocarpas. When Timothy said he had a girl, Laurie put down his newspaper and said, not boastingly, but as he might speak of beehives or ewes, 'Well, I've got the pick of the place. Some of them aren't bad.'

'I might marry her,' said Timothy. Laurie looked at him with his faintly mocking smile.

'Marriage? That's bad, boy, and you so young.'

'A man has to settle down some time. How else did all this grow? Our mother came here by bullock-wagon, when she was eighteen.'

'Sure.'

'All girls aren't alike. And I want a family.'

'I had a girl three years back, but there wasn't anything said about marriage. Come to Auckland for a good time first. We'll go to the Military Ball. I haven't seen a dance in months, outside of the local hops, and they're rough as bags.' He got up, flexing his arms before the crackled mirror that was painted with a swan. He didn't seem the same Laurie who had dragged Timothy home on the plough, over acres of black new-turned soil, with the horses blowing blue from their big nostrils, and the smell of gorse warmer than its colour. He took things very easily, smiling out of amber eyes. Somehow he made Timothy think of the mirage-cows in the bath of milk at Raupo. Easily Laurie might have been their bull, their king. Even the thickness of his neck had in it the calm satisfaction of a pride and force that have never been successfully challenged.

There was a patch of white clay down by a stream. Timothy went out and flung himself down among the gorse-roots. He puddled the clay, then, when it was soft and pliable, started working on it, making a figurine six inches high. Her smooth round limbs drew out of the shapelessness, then her body, and the taut muscles of the throat. He wanted her to be strong in throat and chin, an answer to his brother's strength. But when he had got her so far, the tiny arms would take no attitude but that of beseeching. All the women's faces that had looked up at him demanded her face; not one of them but asked. He stroked the dim clay tresses, modelled the forehead boldly, turned her chin from oval to the shape of Britomart's shield. It was no use; she wouldn't stand alone, his clay woman. Her lips were too sensitive, even the reserve of the calmly moulded lids in the little caverns beneath her brows spoke of hunger pressed down and running over. Everything about her told unfair fight. He had made her strong, given her good limbs and shoulders and forehead, but only to lose. 'God went wrong somewhere,' he said, and dropped his clay woman into the muddied pool beneath the gorse-bushes. The moment she had gone, he wished her back again, but the yellow waters had washed her into mud. Green beetles thudded softly about him as he went back to the farmhouse.

They went to Auckland on Laurie's motor-cycle, Timothy riding pillion, wildly excited so long as the rushing air parted against his face. Laurie had a captaincy in the military reserves, and danced in uniform. Timothy found himself slowly circling the corners of the ballroom with a red-haired girl in his arms; slowly, a little vapidly, exploring the walks of a garden where lilies floated, pearl as the Taj Mahal. The red girl's mouth was discontented, heavily painted. She said, 'What a crowd of oafs. God save the King, rule Britannia, and climb with spurs up your partner's underwear. Old General Tysnoe and the jellies. They wobble, and he glares. Or is it the other way about? Honestly, can you think of anything more inane?'

'Don't you like soldiers?'

'When you're dying for me, you're too lovely. In time of peace, oh, my God.'

'Were you always so *blasé?*'

'From my mother's womb, I think. They sent me to Europe last year. They wanted me to marry, but I didn't see anything. Now the world looks so small. Do you care for vice?'

'I don't believe I've ever really tried it.'

'I think I'll go in for it; die at thirty-five, with an epitaph in scarlet letters. They could use neon lighting.'

After he had kissed the red girl, Timothy thought possibly that was more inane than the dancing; she hadn't the lonely craving of poor little Shelagh, or the honest, angry desires of the farmwife, only a sickly slim body that had to be pepped up before it could enjoy, and then wailed that it hadn't enjoyed, after all. Only a recognition of sex as one way out of things likely to tax the imagination. No guts. A moment before, she had been hard and taut. Now she was limp — her answer to everything. If it were a law of nature, Timothy didn't like it. He stared at the pearl lilies, and didn't like those, either. He would have enjoyed swishing their heads off, as he used to cut off the dark heads of soldier-grass when he was a child. Laurie came out of the ballroom, with a small, scrupulous cough, though really he was quite indifferent to the red girl's feelings, and she to his. He said to Timothy, 'The Murchisons are taking us on to Anakawa.'

'What's Anakawa?' asked the red girl. Laurie smiled at her.

'A cave. Haunt, perhaps, of the ancient caveman. Want to come along?'

Timothy could feel the cord of her listless desire straining away from him and towards Laurie. He opened his arms and let her go. Just because Laurie was older, had serene yellow eyes. She was wasting her time: Laurie wouldn't waste his.

In the evening of the next day they were camped at Anakawa with the Murchisons, a family of the ex-squattocracy, the two women brown and able with conversation, the men rather apt to dwell on the subject of rabbits, but very dependable when it came to getting the big, burly buffalo bullocks, their only means of transportation, down the cliff-face. Outside the cave's mouth dropped the myriad-stamened flowers of the pohutukawa, crimson and live coral. Beyond that, beyond shore, a vast surf repeated shingly roars for all eternity, rushing up the sand with pebbles and swirling driftwood in its throat, to spew them out high on the beach.

The Murchisons, having bathed in very proper neck-to-knee costumes, baked mussels in the ashes, turned on a portable gramophone, and lay down to dream. They had christened Anakawa 'the cave of a thousand faces'. Timothy tried mentally to outline each face, dark and clear, mostly wicked, as behoved a place where the white man disputed occupancy with the thundering surf, and with bleached Maori skulls trundled into the darker passages long ago.

He could not sleep. At midnight he slipped out past the smouldering fire of driftwood, and stood watching a silver and ebony sea. Great fans of foam opened on its bosom. It was more than a challenge, it was a warning. He walked down the sands, and threw off his clothing at the edge of the surf. Naked and in the sea, he felt his feet swept from under him. Currents pulled him, like the lingering hands of very cold, very powerful people. The Maoris had tales of devils with great houses under the sea, houses whose every chink was stopped up against the light. The thousand faces of Anakawa danced, and his head went under. Suddenly he felt a grasp stronger than the water-grasp, and cried out. But it was Laurie, who towed him into a lagoon where a creek forked out from the breakers. They floated quietly for a moment, near shores where mangroves thrust up their air-breathing suckers through the mud, trying to be trees instead of phantasmagoria. Laurie said, 'That was a silly thing to do.'

'I don't know. I'm not happy.'

'Then get along out and go to Wellington.'

'You mean, go and see my girl?'

'Sure. If you want anything off'n a girl — looks, brains, or just to put your finger on the spot and know that what you want isn't there — you'd better go ahead. Only I thought you wouldn't be such a young fool. I thought you might be wanting a good time. We could have stopped up here and played round a bit.'

'What about the Murchisons?'

'Leave them to me. I can keep them entertained. You're only my fool of a kid brother. Anyhow, I'll tell them you've got a girl. They'll roar with laughter.'

Timothy said, 'You're the missing link, Laurie. I've read about you in books.' Laurie continued to float, belly to moonlight, and Timothy ran up to dress in the orbit of firelight. He didn't wake the Murchisons. They were Laurie's, they and the portable gramophone. By luck, he got a lift from the cliff-top, after only three hours on the track — a three hours during which he had seen a whole world fallen and ruined and wrecked, lying in opalescent stillness, its craftiness gone, nothing left of it but the inhuman. Over it burned great sheets of dew, like crackling glass.

A traveller who claimed to have been the first man to fly Cook Straits plied him all night in the train with whisky and conversation. He had been shooting, and carried a dead golden pheasant between his knees.

Half-way to Wellington, he passed the pheasant to Timothy, so that he could stretch his legs and concentrate on unscrewing the flask. The world turned into a dingy dream, studded with small inverted bowls of light along the roof of the carriage. Timothy never quite lost consciousness. When the hills and thin trees outside the window were blue with dawn, he heard himself repeating, 'Yes, I will, old chap, by God I will. Never dreamed of the possibilities.'

The traveller wrung his hand.

'Tha'sh right. Good boy. The moment you got into the carriage, I said to myself, "Speed and class. That boy's got speed and class. The others — jush look at them. You trust yourself to little Horace." ' He laid one finger against his nose, and winked, but just before the express drew into its final station disappeared into a lavatory, never to return. Timothy at first failed to miss him, watching the train plunge down like a black eel in a falcon's jaws, out of the last tunnel, into the bright sea-blue and little filthy black houses of Thorndon. At last he got out of the train, very stiff, and asked a porter if he had seen a man answering to the traveller's description. The porter replied stolidly, 'Can't say, sir, I'm sure. Must 'a' got out the other side.'

'Well, he was drunk,' said Timothy, 'and we're in on a deal, but I can't call to mind what it was.'

'Sorry, sir. You'd better go along to Enquiries and Complaints. I've got to get on with my work.'

The gnome set his shoulders to trundling. After a moment's thought Timothy decided that he did not want the traveller, and didn't care about their deal. But he was still holding a dead pheasant, its wrinkled claws tied by a piece of string. He tried to deposit it on a seat, but an old hunched gentleman sneezed over his moustaches, and stared fiercely at him. The pheasant had burnished wattles and breast, proud flashes of gold and jewel-green. Its wrinkled lids were closed in profound contempt, the scorn of a dead Pharaoh. Muttering, 'Blasted bird,' Timothy walked out of the station; just beyond the row of gesticulating taxi-drivers he met Eliza. She wore a little brown hat with an orange feather, and he thought, 'She's put her hair up, and it makes all the difference. She looks like a woman now. How tall she has grown — I thought she was rather a dumpy little thing.' Eliza said uncertainly, 'Oh, hullo, Timothy — am I late?' He replied, 'No, we're just in,' before he remembered that he had not wired to her, and she had no means of suspecting that he would be on this particular train. Then why was she there? Like the disappearance of the commercial traveller, it didn't seem to matter much. This whisky had left him dazed. They began to walk slowly up the road together. Timothy carried the pheasant dangling, and its haughty tail swept the dust.

'How did you know I was coming?'

'I didn't. I like meeting trains and boats — but not when they're going away, that leaves me too envious.'

A possible use for the pheasant occurred to Timothy, though he could not look at it.

'I brought this down for your mother. Do you think she'd like to cook it?'

A little pattern of repulsion formed in the pupils of her eyes, clear as the circle-patterns on the bird's tail.

'I suppose so. But we've never had pheasant. Don't you have to hang it till it's high, or something? I think it's too pretty to eat.'

'I've been thinking that all along,' said Timothy, with relief, 'I feel like the Ancient Mariner. A traveller gave it to me, and I couldn't find him again. What shall I do with it? I can't stand those confounded eyelids.'

'We could drop it in the grass,' said Eliza. Timothy let the bird fall, its brown-and-gold feathers sprouting out of the dusty wayside grass, and Eliza picked two white daisies, which she dropped on its breast.

'I don't want to go straight to your house, Eliza. My head's going round. Where can I sit still and look at you? Can you talk?'

'Not very much. There's the old closed cemetery at Boulton Street, nobody goes there now. Isn't it lucky that you came on a Saturday? I'd have had to go to the office. It's nice in the cemetery. There's a little chapel with broken windows. Sometimes I have my lunch there.'

He said, 'Aminee the Ghoul ate her rice grain by grain, and then went off to the cemeteries for dinner *à la carte*.' Two old men strayed about among the graves, their hooks swishing down piles of pale-rooted grass, which made the air very sweet. The place had been closed for so long that nobody put mourning wreaths or flowers in jam-tins at the feet of the graves, many of which were mossy wood, their inscriptions indecipherable, the remains of scrolls or Roman lettering showing beneath their beards. A tombstone marked with two tiny marble coffins, like pointed Chinese slippers, said, 'Twins Taken.' Farther along, thirteen of a family had died in an early-days epidemic of diphtheria, and their tombstones lessened in size down to Amelia's, whose marble door would barely have let a rabbit through. Arms of wild-rose, streaked irises, great masses of red-flowering weed, grew about. Timothy asked, 'What's the red stuff?'

'Kiss-me-quick.'

'I will that.' She could feel the little bones in her body making themselves smaller, drawing close together. She thought, 'Now I'm happy,' with a desperate sense of imminence. Sun floated over the graves, grass-scent on the air, and Timothy made her bones small and afraid. Through the ash-leaves the light was queer and laughingly freckled, little sweet cowslip moles of light.

'I promised myself solemnly I'd never make love to you.'

'Did you really? Why not?'

'Because I wish you could play tennis. I wish you were a strapping, sporting girl.'

'Don't you like my frock, Timothy?'

'It's too heavy. I like anything that fits you.'

(Oh, God . . . oh, Little Miss Blair. . . .)

Timothy, staring at Eliza, said softly, ' "Our unwalled loves thin out on the empty air . . ." '

'That's Rupert Brooke.'

'Yes. Do you know Rupert?'

'Of course. I think I like, "The stars, a jolly company" best.'

'Rupert's almost my hero, or he was while I still had heroes. One person whom the world loved, just before the light went out.'

Eliza said, 'I'm glad he died while he was still a boy.' As she sat with her skirts spread out in the grassy sunlight, Timothy liked her again in the centre of his heart. He said, 'One day I'll introduce you to Nietzsche.'

'Why not now?'

'He has a cutting edge.'

'Yes,' thought Eliza, 'you think I'm soft, and yes, I am.' A tree with sharp edges, a bluegum, all little sickles, cut into the wind and the pale flesh of the light, a few feet above their heads. Timothy pulled down a cluster of the dancing leaves, and with a half-shy, half-taunting smile slipped them down the front of Eliza's Little Miss Blair frock.

'Keep them to-night, and dream about them. Do you dream?'

'Waking and sleeping.' They went out of the cemetery. The chapel with broken blue windows had been long since strawed and bespattered by the starlings, who dashed in, thudded about in panic, and presented only the drops of blood from their torn breasts as communion wine. There was nobody to see that their wings were not purely black, but shot through with green and violet, especially violet. And cobwebs were spun silvery across the jagged windows. Eliza looked up at them helplessly. She would have liked to leave Timothy, to go into the chapel by herself and pray for good luck. But the windows were broken, the mouldering door was shut and locked.

CHAPTER FOURTEEN

In Your Stupidity

WE can't possibly have made a good impression: Zoo, and none of the animals in pairs.

Timothy ran away from Damaris Gayte's house to come to me, to spend his twenty-first birthday under this roof. It was nice of mother to give up her room. She wouldn't for anyone but Timothy. He showed Damaris that awful snapshot of me, and she said, 'She looks the typical young enthusiast. You'd better not encourage her, or when you take your leave you'll find her waiting down at the station with her little bundle.'

Forty years old, with coiled black hair and wonderful strong profile. At forty you ought to have a cutting edge.

Timothy's asleep, she thought, turned over in bed so that when he wakes up he'll see the morning hills, and that cemetery. I wish people wouldn't put up dirty broken marble teeth to the memory of their loved ones. Timothy, Timothy . . . funny name, like something in a nursery rhyme. If he made the slightest movement, even if he were lying awake, I'd know it. But I can send out all my own thought, until it's great sheets of moving colour, blue fans in the air, and it never touches him; not strongly enough to wake him up. Perhaps it makes him dream.

This is what they call asking for it. Nothing else needs to. Dusty moth rains into moonlit flower, his eyes are rubies and his antennæ finest fawn silk. And the shooting star, ablaze from head to foot, leaps into a jet-black sea to quench his thirst, while on a marble floor the dolphins roll around him in soft amaze.

She pulled a coat over her nightgown, and went upstairs. Her father was still moving about in the kitchen, with small weary noises, not larger than a badger would make in its earthen house. He was sitting at the table, in front of him a book which he wasn't reading, and the smoke from his pipe carved for itself a still blue way in the atmosphere, before it turned wispy and faded out in strings of grotesque, bobbling dragons. His eyes were bloodshot-tired.

'Hullo, Dad.'

He thought she had come about the tea or the electric light, and glared suspiciously.

'What are you doing? What do you want?'

'Can't sleep. Any tea in the pot?'

He drained a few cold yellow drops.

'I'll put the kettle on again, but shut that door, and for Christ's sake don't wake your mother.'

He made the tea, and came back to stare at Eliza. He remembered her when she was a baby; she had pretty little ears, and once, valiantly, had climbed up and clouted him over the head with her hobby-horse, for pretending to be drunk and frightening 'Gusta. But long since she had been lost, and had no part in that rich inward life where he strode along the pavements, declaiming speeches, interjecting from the gallery at the House, doubling up his big fists under the noses of the flunkeys who ran to throw him out. In this world, he rose easily from being Tom McGrath's confidant and sympathizer — Tom was his Union Secretary — to saving Tom from mistakes, warning him against pimps, exposing the white-livered curs who were plotting behind his back, sneaks trying to split the Union and crawl to the bosses. He could see the appreciation warm in Tom McGrath's eyes, Tom's hand reached out 'If it hadn't been for you, Hannay, Christ knows what would have happened to-night. Oh, yes, the cows were trying to put one over, all right. Now, you and I . . .'

He saw Tom involved in a street accident, down under the wheels of a car driven by one of the bosses. He heard the hard shout wrenched out of the belly of the crowd — 'Look out!' — and sprang forward to save Tom. Sometimes, among screaming brakes and grinding wheels, he was there just in time, and yanked Tom back to safety, shaking his fist at the white flabby moon-face behind the wheel. Sometimes he died for Tom, and was buried, and the men at the office came soberly to his funeral. Sometimes, however, he failed to save Tom, and made one of the pall-bearers, and afterwards people said curiously, 'That's Hannay, who was such a pal of McGrath's.' And a change then, a dark, tall, resolute change had come into his life.

Suddenly through the haze John could see his daughter's feet. They were bare. 'You'll catch cold,' he said. 'Better put these on.' He kicked off his slippers, revealing a mighty corn on the third left toe. It gave him pain, but satisfaction as well. Having a corn made him more working-class, and drew him into the round lantern-beam of Tom McGrath's approval. 'I'm rough,' he thought. 'Those that don't like me can lump me. Not one of your bloody gentlemen.' Eliza slid her cold feet into his slippers.

'Smelly,' she said, in a matter-of-fact voice. 'You're late up, too.' He began to complain softly.

'I can't sleep. I get shooting pains here, right through the temples. It's like a knife. I can tell you, sometimes it's red-hot. No wonder, working ten hours a day by electric light, and then coming home to be growled at by your mother. Mind you, your mother's a good woman — a very good woman.'

'Of course she is.' The ghost of Carly's Johannesburg gentleman twirled his pepper-grey moustache huffily, and stalked out of sight. 'Anyhow, you're no pacifist on the home front yourself.'

'Who would be, slaving his guts out and getting nothing for it? I'm not so young as I was.'

'Why don't you try something else?'

The forlorn eyes of somebody who, having made his bed full of iron lumps and hummocks, is constrained to lie on it because he is afraid of finding No Room at the Inn.

'Your mother wouldn't hear of it.'

'What would you like to be, Dad?'

'I should have been an engineer. Once Bert Quigley and I were going to chuck the job and start an antique shop together, but your mother—' 'He's an awful little rat. He would have sloped with the cashbox. But an antique shop wouldn't have been a bad idea for you.' Profile of Nefertiti the Queen, looking down calm and bitter-sweet over John's shoulder. 'Dad, why don't you run away?'

'I can't leave you children.'

'I don't see why not, if you don't like us. We're nearly grown up, except Kitch. If you like the wharfies and hate clerks, why don't you go for your life and be a wharfie? You're only young once. See Timbuctoo and die.'

Eliza, too, was seeing visions. She watched a beaked ship, black and rusty-red, and stowed away somewhere in the creaking inward parts, her father, who wore a black jersey and a criminal-looking cap; whitefaced, but mysteriously himself again. Staring over the side of the ship, watching the holes vomit white water. . . . A sailor fishing for snapper chucked a lump of fat pork overside, and the gulls screamed as if the tops of their heads must come off. The ship quivered. Her father, drawing in his head like a winkle retreating to safety, looked his last at the gorse on the port hills.

'I did it, Mother. I persuaded Dad to desert us.'

('Father,' said George Washington, 'I cannot tell a lie. I cut down your cherry-tree with my little hatchet.')

He shook his head.

'I can't make you out at all. You'd better go to bed before you catch cold. You'll wake up your mother, and there'll be another row. You'll get consumption, that's what you'll do, hanging about with next to nothing on.'

'I wonder if you know a poem — I can't remember who wrote it, or what its name was. The first line is:

I cannot sleep — the night is hot and empty,

and then,

> Outside, the small cicadas,
> Complaining of their passions, weak and shrill;
> Oh, from what whips! oh, from what secret scourgings,
> All Nature's children bend beneath her will!'[1]

John had never heard of the poem; it woke in him not the faintest spark of curiosity. 'You'd better go to bed,' he repeated.

'What do you think of Timothy, Dad?'

He had forgotten all about the beautiful young man. He said, 'Timothy? Timothy? Oh, young Cardew. . . . He's all right, I suppose. Like all the other young fellows — head full of pleasure, women and racing. They make me sick.'

'I think he's the perfectly natural man.'

'Don't make yourself cheap running after him, that's all.' Eliza's father sounded mechanical and dead tired; he was longing to be left alone with Tom McGrath. She rose, saying, 'Here are your slippers,' and kicked them off. A moment later she put her head round the door again.

'Good night, Dad.'

'Good night,' he answered, and went out to the scullery, to kindle again the surprised crocus of gas-flame under the kettle. A little clock in Eliza's heart ticked, 'Old, old, old, old'; but only for a short time, and then she slept.

Timothy wakened very early, aroused by a thrush which shuffled its stout body among the coprosmas, ate itself into the gripes, and then whined outside his window-pane. He lay in his strange bed, beautifully warm. A sunbeam went white ripple-ripple on the syrup-coloured door panels, and he recognized it. He had seen that sunbeam, none other, when he was a boy of six, sick with diphtheria. He lay in bed then, waiting for the doctor to come and give him antitoxin, and it was such a fine day outside, and his throat hurt. His mother wept bitterly when the doctor produced the needle. 'Oh, Doctor, that great thing for his poor little body! Oh, why couldn't it have been me, instead of my baby?'

'I'm twenty-one,' he thought, suddenly wide awake. 'Golly, Damaris will be wild.' He wasn't sorry for Damaris yet. She was like a toothache; she would, and she wouldn't, and of late was always working up scenes, drinking Eisel and eating crocodiles. Then she turned off the lights and played Rachmaninoff's *Prelude*, a performance which had once made his blood run beautifully cold, but which now left him uninterested, though the gleam of her thick wrists raised in darkness, striking at the piano-keys like angry cobras, still impressed him as majestic.

He put her aside. He was in Eliza's house, Eliza was just over the corridor. He had said good night, liking her eyes so well that almost he postponed saying good night indefinitely; but he could hear all the Hannays did and said upstairs, and supposed that they also weren't deaf. He liked their tribe. 'Mother could be a Tartar,' he thought, 'but that's as it should be.'

He got out of bed, did exercises until he was sick of Bernarr McFadden's young men, and putting on his rainbow dressing-gown, crossed the corridor, to tap on Eliza's door. Since she didn't answer, he opened it in obedience to a command from the genii of the air, and went in. She was asleep, her hair dishevelled. It was a nice little room, simple and green, full of indiscriminate drawings, and very well-meaning books. She wouldn't wake up while he stood smiling at her, so he knelt down and started to kiss her face and arms. That awakened her, and she said in a muffled voice, 'Who is it?'

'Tarquinius Superbus. Have you ever been kissed there?'

Eliza sat up, rubbing her shoulder. 'That's mine when you've finished with it,' she said, like a schoolboy. 'Your chin's scrubby, Timothy. You can't have shaved.'

'Do you mind? May I come in and talk it over?'

'Not in these, Tarquin. You'll wake mother in a minute.'

'Would mother care?'

'Ask her. She thinks bedrooms are unchastity, while as for beds . . .'

'But we could explain.'

'Let well alone,' said Eliza, with a firmness surprising to herself. 'Who gave you the dreadful rainbow?'

'Damaris. It's the most beautiful of my dressing-gowns. Do you mind?'

'Oh, I forgot. I forgot all about it. I never wished you many happy returns, and I didn't know it was your birthday till last night, so I haven't a present for you. It seems very niggardly.'

Timothy said, 'Come for a run with me now. Birthday treat. Hurry and get your clothes on, and don't put up your hair. I like it down. If you're ready in five minutes, I'll forgive you everything.'

'Then go away.' Timothy turned his back and screened his eyes.

'I don't look. I never look when women are dressing, it's too disappointing. One — two — three — twenty — how slow you are! Shall I help with the hooks? Get a move on, Boy.'

'Ready.'

'Very apt,' said Timothy. 'I like the little pansy-coloured thing. What do you call it?'

'It's a smoking-jacket. Don't you wear anything yourself?'

'Much better not. Naked, we absorb the actinic rays . . .'

'Remember mother, and dress,' said Eliza. His voice slid over from the room across the passage.

'Where shall we tell them we've gone? I know — we went gathering mushrooms for your mother's breakfast. We knew how she liked mushrooms.'

'Only they're months out of season.'

'Then we went gathering nuts and may. That was it, nuts and may.'

'Hurry, idiot,' said Eliza, and they slipped out of the front door, through the little morass of bright bowing flowers, silken tents encamped in the wind. 'Poor mother,' said Eliza. 'Nothing grows properly here, what with the clay soil and the northerlies.' In her heart she thought, 'I'm perfectly happy. Perhaps this will be the happiest day of my life.'

They were on the bush road, curved like a bow; half-way, they turned and struck up over the hills, into a clear crest of morning sultried with yellow gorse. Little breakwind pines grew along the hilltops, their thick yellowish-green pollen flying up in clouds if an arm shook them or a foot unsettled the close grass beneath them. Timothy walked barefoot, his shoes slung round his neck. 'I get all the virtue from the ground,' he explained, and persuaded Eliza to try it. But she was a tenderfoot, and limped pitiably until he laughed, and catching her up in his arms carried her a few yards.

'Put me down, put me down,' she called. A pine-branch struck Timothy softly across the face, like a lady with a green glove, and he dropped Eliza, but held her close for a moment. Then he released her, with a little laugh. There were prickles of gilt light in his eyes. 'Heavy lot,' he said.

'Where are we going?'

'To a hole in the ground, a quarry. I nearly broke my neck there once, running in a thick mist. You'd never have met me. I threw stones down, and it sounded most uncanny, rattle and splash.'

They found the quarry, slant-edged, with a bright cut of furze bushes, all in blossom on a hillside which but for the occasional burrowing of rabbits and the patches of dried dung dropped by wandering cattle might never have been touched at all; a curve lifted out of the world, into space. But the quarry was deep and desolate, and a sickly smell streaked up. Not far away stood the shell of a deserted farmhouse, all its windows smashed, staring and blinded. 'Somebody died there,' whispered Eliza. They looked at one another like guilty children. Then Timothy said, 'Yes, it was a cow, and there are the old girl's bones,' pointing to remains in a quarry. They both laughed. 'But I liked the pine trees better,' said Eliza.

'I know another place. Give me your hand, Boy.'

'Oh, I can't,' she thought, a few moments later, 'I can't keep this up. Tim, let me go, you're hurting, Tim; I've got a stitch in my side.' But she was too breathless to get the words out until he had pulled up by the stile, and then it was too late. Timothy swung her over into a world of unkempt ribbon grass and neglected trees, natives treading on the gnarled roots of exotics.

'This was a garden once. Now it has run wild, beautifully wild. Isn't it lovely? Doesn't it smell of leaves and freshness and dew, all cleanly things? Look, here's a crab-apple, but the wasps have been at it. I'd like to make a clay statuette of you — Girl with Crab-Apple. Kneel down, and tilt your chin. No, come farther along; there's a pool I want you to see.'

'I can see smoke. Isn't there a cottage somewhere?'

'Only the caretaker's. He's very old and Scotch, and he calls the plants by their Latin names. If you're a good girl I'll introduce you, and he'll give you damper scones cooked in a camp oven. Women can't cook.'

The pool was brown and stagnant, the irises around it still tightly furled, their purple hard in spikes; but the feel of the roughened turf, delicately harsh, and the streaks of green and yellow in patterns of osier leaves, were ease enough. They drew aside into the ways of the trees. Long ago, somebody had kept bees, and the white hives stood there, half-decaying but full of their people, black bodies and thin wings clotted against combs oozing dark gold honey. The bees had taken to the treetops for a living, bringing home the essence of manuka and rata, native honeys mixed with the sweet they sucked from the veins of cold pink belladonna lilies, standing in surprised colonies on the edge of the pool. When Eliza saw them she could only say, 'Wild pink lilies,' and draw her hand across her eyes, as if she half-wanted to shut out the sight of them. And she did, for there is something dangerous in such a perfection, and the cold statelihood of nature's things, reverted to their types, seemed to her best left alone. But she had no more than a moment to think of anything, for the sunbeams shot blanching through the boughs, riding little cock-horses of supplejack and lancewood, and Timothy's eyes had the gilt prickles in them as he pulled her down, murmuring, 'Sit there. The light comes through the branches.' He picked up her hair and smothered it over her face, one strand after another; then pressed her back to the ground, so that she could feel the brittle bits of twig and old leaves tangled, and raised her hands to comb them out. Timothy caught her hands and put them aside.

'Leave it. That is how I love your hair.'

He put his arms around her, and Eliza felt her bones making themselves small and light, shrinking away like little slaves that cannot intrude into a scene written all for softness. A fantail ran out, starclawed on the wet earth; saw them, gave a peep of distress and warning to his mate, and flew off among the bushes, waggling his black-and-grey fan.

Everything I knew in darkness, but wrongly, foolishly, painfully . . . all the broken pieces of love I ever threw over my shoulder or dropped into the rubbish-heap . . . are somehow gathered into the one place. I know. . . .

She said the last two words aloud, 'I know.' Timothy looked at her.

'What do you know?'

She felt as though the sunlight had drugged her beyond answering. It hung in long dazzling ropes, pliant snakes dazzling from the trees, dropping their gold liquid heads into the grass, forking their golden tongues. She repeated, 'I know.'

Suddenly Timothy kissed her on the mouth, and said, 'I'm going now.'

She did not think she had heard him aright, not when without a word he rose from the brown-and-green earth, not when she heard him running, a sound dulled instantly on the turf leading back to the stile. He was gone, but that was a flat contradiction of what all the rest said, the thin glazed wings of the bees, the colonies of the belladonna lilies, the birds that presently came out and spoke loudly, intimately, over her head. For a long time she was sure Timothy was still there, or would come back in a moment; and when she sat up, at first she could only notice things which had no connection with herself, and might have been seen, impartially, by an old man or an idiot in any part of the world. They weren't hers, though they clung to her sight and touch. One of the bee-hives was defaced by a scummy green moss, and the wood was full of skeleton leaves, flowers too, which had parted with their picture-writing of colour for this more delicate calligraphy, crabbed and brittle. Her fingers crushed a cluster of these fleshless things, and she thought, 'It's a whole head of hydrangeas, every petal reduced to bone, not a single one missing. Flower-bones. I've never seen anything like it before. If I were still at school, it would be worth taking to the museum.'

Her throat hurt her, but she could not cry. Now the pink lilies looked too remote. A judgment had been passed on them, sentencing them all to exile in this beautiful wild loneliness, where no one saw or gathered but the bees. But the spikes of iris were too hard. She broke off one stalk, but when the white sap oozed, as if trying to staunch the wound with a cobweb of its own making, she slid it down into the brown edge of the pool, and left it standing there. Presently she said, 'My hair . . . my hair . . .' and started to comb out fragments of leaf and stick. Then she walked up the turf pathway. A bend of the track brought her in sight of the caretaker's cottage and its plume of smoke. An old collie dog lay there in the sunshine, and rhubarb spread great branches of red behind him. He barked as she approached, but when he came up, pointing about with his narrow golden-brown head, she saw that his eyes were opaque with pearly cataract. He was blind, and had no idea who passed over the stile.

When the Hannays were all at the breakfast-table, Carly ready for work, Sandra in the navy-blue gym costume which Eliza had worn a year ago, she said, 'Timothy had to go and get his books. I walked with him part of the way.'

'Fine time of the morning for it,' said her mother. 'Hurry now, and eat.' The room smelt of frying, comfortable, warm, rather dirty, with the dirtiness of appetite's arrogance when you are sick, and everybody else clashes things across the table.

'Don't you let him go making a fool of you, my girl,' said her mother. John came out, his clothes half-fastened, and stood blinking in the light.

'I can't find those damned and blasted braces. I can't put a thing down in this house without somebody—'

'Go and look for your braces in the top drawer, the proper place for them. You can't leave your litter about all over the house. And don't come out like that before your own daughters.'

Behold the days of man are like unto the grass of the field, which today is . . .

Sweet creatures, humans; pink lilies sighing out their souls in exile, because nobody stands over them talking bacon and braces. And they think I want marriage first: Timothy, Timothy, fool, how can you think I want this?

'The wonder to me is that you've got a job at all, if you sit about mooning in your office as you do at home.'

'I don't want my job. I'm sick of it. I'd just as soon let it rip.'

Carly said, 'That's wicked. There are hundreds of girls who'd do anything for a good job.'

'Then let them. I don't see why people should have daughters if they don't want to keep them.'

'A nice temper your Timothy Cardew's left you in this morning, I must say. I thought he looked too good to be true. If that's the effect he has on your ambition, the less you see of him the better. And the sooner your father forbids him the house again, the more trouble he'll spare himself and everyone else.'

Eliza thought, 'Now I can slam the door. Now it's just a family row — something to shout about.'

'Shut up about my job. I'll live my life in my own way, and if you interfere with me, I'll clear out.'

Pink lilies, pink lilies, pink lilies . . . mornings are something to run through like mad, like a sped arrow from a bow; so that you won't miss your tram.

When next she saw Timothy, only a few hours later, for he turned up at supper quite unperturbed, with a book of Bernard Shaw's for her to study, she was surprised at the ease with which she could keep the little coloured balls of conversation bouncing over the table. Verbal ping-pong. . . . The Hannays were all good at it, except John, who was too grandiloquent, and roared if he thought his children were making fun of him. Everybody joined in, few points missed, no quarter given or taken. John, with invincible valour, always stuck to the wrong side of the argument. Even Timothy was against him, laughingly, with a friendly, look-here-old-chap manner. John would like that about as much as arsenic. Old Chap eventually went off growling to his room. Augusta did the ironing, and Eliza had the drawing-room for entertaining Timothy

— the inalienable privilege of any female Hannay with a youth in tow. She played *Moonmoths* on the piano; the sweet, sticky little driblets of music ebbed between her fingers. She had put perfume on her reddish bush of hair, and to Timothy she seemed childish. A full moon beat with chilly outspread wings on the windows, but nobody let it in.

'I think you all treat your father rather disrespectfully.'

'Tum-te-tum, tum-te-tum. . . . Isn't this a juicy thing. I suppose we do. He asks for it.'

'After all, he's your father.'

'Sometimes he says not. Anyhow, we understand one another, better than anybody outside.'

'Am I an outsider?'

'You're certainly not a Hannay. Thank your stars for it.'

'This morning I didn't feel much of a stranger. I had to run away from you. Do you know why?'

'Not particularly.'

'I was afraid I might make love to you.'

'Wouldn't that have been dreadful? Poor Tim. . . . Did you go straight to Damaris and confess? And did she say, "Hold your nose and swallow down the brimstone neat, my lad, there's nothing else for it when it's spring again"?'

'Do you really think I'd do that?'

'Why not? It wasn't important, and you looked so funny, running away.'

'You sound experienced.'

'Oh, I've known heaps of men. Dad fishes them up from the vasty deeps, you know — some of them would make you laugh, real old toughs. The others come from the office.'

'Were you ever in love, Eliza?'

'Off and on, nearly always. It's temperament. If you like I'll play you *Spring Song*. I fumble a bar or two, but it goes well with love.'

'What do you think of love?'

'Much more important to be friends.'

'It's half life,' said Timothy. 'It's a sweet white poison. It's Hell and it's Heaven.' The room was too shadowy for Eliza to see his face, but his head was bent down, and she wanted to cry, 'No, no, it's only pink lilies in a lonely garden.' But that would be to give the show away, and she struck out the bars of *Spring Song*, softly and dimly.

'I like it,' said Timothy, like a child. They heard the gate-latch click.

'Carly,' said Eliza. A man's low voice murmured, down by the coprosmas. 'And Trevor Sinjohn, Carly's young man.'

'Is he pleasant?'

'He's a louse.'

'What I like about your opinions is that they're definite,' said Timothy. Carly came in, her little penny-round face full and blind with moonlight, as if she walked in her sleep. When she saw them, she smiled and said, 'Hullo,' gently; but the daze didn't go out of her eyes. Sometimes the boys took their girls up on the hills, in such evenings, to little hollows in the grasses, where hedgehogs moved about and they could watch the harbour lights, and feel the delicate, brittle chill of the air, a touch to be shut out by their nearness to one another. But when it came starlight, it was time for the respectable ones to go home, and nobody could say Carly wasn't respectable.

'Let's go outside,' said Timothy. The silver had escaped from Carly's eyes and into his heart. When he had Eliza out in the little blowing garden, he slipped an arm around her waist, and they started to walk quietly down the path, down the half-dozen ungainly steps, up into the silvery darkness. Eliza thought, 'Once for the day should be enough; don't be a fool, a mad fool.' Timothy, if he thought at all, said nothing, until full under the round white disc of a street-lamp he stopped and turned her face upwards. Then he kissed her again and again, with quiet lips that were almost cold, still lips bent down in a dream.

'I swore this morning I'd never do that again.'

'Why not? Why not?'

'Because it isn't right. You're so young. I do love you, as much as I can love any girl.'

'But that isn't very much? Well, I don't know that love can be measured by quantities.'

'I have to go to London, you see. I want to study, to travel and live. I'd give anything even to live as you do, by writing. I think creative work is the way of the soul. I can't see why you don't work at it harder, having the chance.'

'Other things to do.'

'It's just the tiger-vitality lacking, isn't it? And the incentive. But I've got to prowl over Europe, and sleep out with fuzzy tramps, and steal turnips, and live as Jack London lived. If I don't do that, I might as well not have been born.'

'I can come too.'

'You can't, a woman couldn't.'

'I'm not a woman; not for ordinary purposes.'

Timothy laughed; 'Can you turn your hair up under a cap?'

'I can do anything.'

'Then I'll take you. You can be my cabin-boy, and steal turnips for me. Look down there, past the bluegums. I always loved this place. The lights in the water whisper "London," to me, and I hold my breath.'

'The trees are very dark. I love the smell of bluegums, next best to pines, I think. The old pines are best, they are so friendly. You're the complete godwit, aren't you, Timothy?'

'What do you mean?'

'The one who has to fly north, whether he wants to or not. But I understand, I've been one myself, and sometimes still am. What can I be to you, Timothy?'

He said, 'Mistress,' lightly, daringly and proudly, his face tilted back in the vague light; as if there were something of special glamour about the word, not obloquy. For a moment Eliza felt sorrow for her mother. 'Now is the moment,' she thought, 'when according to everybody I have to keep my head and play my cards right. But I don't play at cards.'

'I could make you happy, Eliza, quite easily. I'm always making women and girls happy. But with you, I don't want to be the complete hedonist. I want to make you think.'

'Thinking won't get you far.'

'You're a sensualist, aren't you, Eliza?'

'Yes. I like the pine-needles underneath my hands, too. And lots of things. But I don't think I can be your mistress. Supposing there were a baby?'

'Then I'd —' He was going to say 'marry you,' and stopped himself. 'I'd take you away and live with you. I wouldn't leave you.'

'Because you've got to go to London, travel and study?'

'Yes.'

'Sensualists . . . Aren't you fond of Rupert Brooke's "Blanket's rough kiss . . . cool comfort of the sheets. . . ." Remember?'

'That's all right. It's another one of his that makes me think of you. I don't know if I can remember it. Yes, I can:

> 'In your stupidity I found
> The sweet hush after a sweet sound,
> And when you spoke, it seemed to me

Infinitely and like a sea
About the slight world you had known
Your vast incertitude was thrown.'[2]

'I'm not so very stupid, Timothy. Only young, and rather inarticulate.'

'There's a lovely stupidity. But some day I'll have to kill you, you know. The Emperor always does. For being unfaithful . . . will you ever look at another man? Or for coming in at the wrong time. . . .'

'Now's the time, too,' she thought, 'when I ought to laugh out loud and sweep it all away with my hands. If I go on, whatever happens I'll have to pay for it. He'll go away to places and leave me. He'll make love to people, and I'll pretend I don't care, and begin to mind when I stop being a novelty. I'll introduce him to Simone, and he'll make love to her, and the only comfort I'll have is the cold, grubby comfort of knowing he'll walk out on her. He won't understand, he'll make love seem servile, he'll accept all the price-tickets — you're cheap, you haven't any pride, no self-respecting woman would do as you're doing, so on and so forth. If he goes now, right away, it'll hurt for a while and then somebody else will come.'

'Take me to England with you, Timothy. Promise me.'

'I promise.' The moon made two little silver pennies and placed them on his eyelids, so that his face had a deathly look, its mouth and nostrils soft slants of darkness. Above in an intricate pattern of curves the bluegum leaves moved faintly, their sickles shearing the wind. The full moon put off her robes, and moved across the harbour. The night and all things in it stared and breathed, conscious only of silver.

'We must go home,' said Timothy, 'mother will be worried.' His smile had a sudden boy-sweetness. He was part of the nature world which gave no quarter, but he was twenty-one, and Eliza's mother, whom he liked, mustn't be worried.

They shook the leaves off. On the way down the hill they met a hedgehog, and Timothy carried him to their gate, arguing that he had no right to be abroad without a tail-light. In the garden he told it, 'Oh, go peddle your papers,' and the hedgehog dug its nose into darkness and scuttled, freezing every few inches into a most noticeable ball of prickles, which it thought exactly like a stone or a little thorn-bush. Bawder's cart went rumbling by, Bawder's red lantern shone on the driver's seat, as he cracked a slow whip over his sway-backed nag. Timothy wasn't sleeping at the house of Hannay. He was away again, most probably to Damaris

Gayte's house. The last Eliza heard of him wasn't any word at all, but a whistle, like a blackbird startled untimely beneath the hedge.

CHAPTER FIFTEEN

The Sparrows When They Fall

THE voice having authority said, 'You'll have to get her out of that bed. I want it for an appendix.'

The little voice, 'She only came in this afternoon, Sister. Doctor ordered an injection.'

'I can't help that, this is an abdominal bed. She'll have to go on one of the shake-downs. What do they expect, if they send me more than the ward can hold?'

At first the words were cut adrift from meaning; but when four nurses were standing, one at each corner of the bed, everything became clear and terrifying.

'Don't move me again — don't move me again.'

'Nurse, take the edge of that drawsheet. That's right. Steady, now.'

'Please, Sister, don't move me. Please.'

'You're in a special surgical bed for abdominal cases. It's needed at once, so you have to be moved.'

'Then they shouldn't have put me here, after that ambulance. It isn't fair.'

'Lift. That's right.'

The crying that is like tearing apart of muscle from flesh: fairness, right and wrong, no longer count. In the surgical ward there are three laws. Somebody is going to die, somebody is going to be hurt, keep the counterpanes straight and the lockers tidy. The Sister's tongue rates the little pink probationer nurses unsparingly. Most of them are nice girls, eighteen or nineteen, drifted into pink uniforms and the big, rules-ridden hostel, the lark of living together under stern laws which make them cry when they are carpeted in Matron's office, giggle when they are in their dormitories, the prolongation of their schooldays. They thought there would be more romantic doctors and fewer dressings. A few had Florence Nightingale visions. These the Sisters weeded out in their first year. That variety of spaghetti saviour had nervous breakdowns by the wayside. The efficient, cool-lipped little smarty, who could come away from her second major operation and eat a hearty dinner, was the stuff for the overcrowded hospital's game of battledore and shuttlecock.

Somebody is going to die. . . . Somebody is going to be hurt. . . . Keep the counterpanes straight and the lockers tidy. Badgering the pink uniforms about Law Three kept their minds off Laws One and Two. 'Nurse, *look* at those beds.' 'Nurse, I thought I told you that the patients are not allowed to keep fruit in their lockers. If this happens again, you go up before Matron.' The little pink uniforms, threatened with their super-spider, buzzed about yanking brown-paper bags from the lockers, and asking the patients, 'Have you got your own eggs? You've got to have them marked if you want an egg for breakfast.'

'Straighten that drawsheet. That's right. Now you can settle down and go to sleep.'

Easier said than done: easiest of all, lying on the shake-down with the harsh red light of the surgical ward pricking between stiff eyelids, to sob and sob, knowing all the time that the best are those who bear pain quietly. The bed on the right holds the flat, pale shape of a girl with peritonitis. No sound comes from her lips, only the oval of her face can be seen directly beneath a red lamp, and her arms lie so very flat, palms upspread, as if death already rested on them, an immense, obdurate weight. Presently the Spanish house-surgeon, gowned in white, comes through the surgical ward. He is beautiful because he moves slowly instead of clattering and rushing. From many of the beds come, 'Good evening, Doctor,' 'Good evening, Doctor.' He speaks to each. Sister complains because an old lady's shoulder splint sticks out over her locker.

'It looks so untidy, Doctor.'

'Never you mind about your lockers. Attend to the comfort of my patients.'

He is on our side, against the bustle and slamming, against being hurt. He stops and looks down. He isn't at all handsome, rather like one of the sad, wizen-faced Captain monkeys at the Zoo. They were called Captain monkeys after old Captain Puckle, who seemed to us to have the same kind of face. They used to run up and down the bars, like Captain Puckle climbing to his crow's nest, and they had little old agitated faces.

'Where's her card?'

'It hasn't been made out, Doctor. She wasn't admitted till late this afternoon.'

'Shouldn't be on that shakedown. Well, kiddie, how does it feel?'

'Oh, Doctor, it hurts.'

'Give her a sixth, Sister.' He moves away, white-gowned through red shadows. Presently a senior probationer comes back, a Scotch-looking little nurse in blue. Pros. wear pink, senior pros. pale blue, Sisters indigo, the Matron white with red and silver nursing medals.

Scottie dabs on iodine. 'This is going to prick a little.'

'I don't mind. It'll make me go to sleep. I want to go to sleep.' The syringe jabs down, almost at once the strong pulsing of relief begins, spreading in dull gold waves all over the body; full tide, quiet tide. As pain leaves not a cranny of flesh or spirit untouched, so the golden peace, exhausting but beautiful, conquers everything that lies in its path. It is like lying under a huge golden-flowered tree, whose perfume is too heavy for anything but dreams. It makes the eyelids very heavy, fills the eyes with slow tears.

'Don't go away yet, Nurse.'

'You're a fractured hip and internal, aren't you?' It sounds funny, but obediently Eliza answers 'yes.'

'How did it happen?'

'I fell down a bank, getting away from a runaway car. It didn't hurt much, till I was in the ambulance. Then I thought I'd die. I prayed to be dead.'

'Your people live near?'

'Up on the hills. Mummy came in the ambulance.' (That was wrong; ages ago, Augusta had said, 'Don't call me Mummy, I've told you that till I'm tired of it. Call me Mother.')

'How old are you?'

'Eighteen.'

'Rotten luck. Never mind. Feel sleepy yet?'

'Don't go away. Yes, Nurse, I'm going to sleep. I like you but I don't like the other nurse.'

'That's Sister. She's quite all right, but the ward is far too full. We're crowded out everywhere. In the diphtheria ward, the beds were so close together that the nurses had to crawl over them.'

'I hate her, she's cruel. But I like the doctor, and I like you. Your hair looks misty.'

Soft laugh through the red darkness. 'Cupboard love.'

'I'm going to sleep, don't go away. It's funny, I just thought of something ages ago. It was a little marble tablet, with a mother-of-pearl parrot on it. It came from under the Taj Mahal. My grandmother sent it. It was broken at one end, and I had it in a collection of curios the year before we left Calver Street. Mother lent me her Indian shawl to take up to school with them. I wonder what happened to it?'

'If you shut your eyes, you'll be asleep.'

'I can stand some kinds of pain, but not if it keeps on throbbing. There was a picture of Joan of Arc — I wrote a poem —'

'Go to sleep.' Little far voice, at the end of a round tunnel of blackness. Joan with dark hair cut straight across her shoulders, leaning forward, her face quite eager. . . .

Cupboard love. Not to be hurt, not to die. To Eliza the first seemed inestimably more than the second; but the strangest, weariest old voices, like flakes coming down from some queer grey snowstorm up in the sky, begged for life from, or tilted beds asking help of, anyone — 'Nursie dear, Doctor dear, oh, dear God, dear Holy Mother of Jasus.' From the tone of their crying, monotonous and sad, you could tell they had no real belief. 'Don't let me die — don't let me die,' all on the one note through a summer afternoon.

'Ah pore thing — she's got six childring, and she takes it crool hard leaving them behind.' But she left them, whilst others, dried leaves out of the whirlwind of death, escaped and lay on long cane couches, or wandered about the slippery polished ward, their hair lacklustre, their eyes large and vague in sallow faces. And others again demanded death, demanded him imperiously with cries whose agonized strength showed that he would be long in coming.

'She's got cancer. Every time they move her, she screams like that, and she's kept it up for the past six weeks. Crool hard, I call it.'

Doctor is the one who gives me morphine. Give her a sixth, Sister — or if it's very bad, Give her a half, Sister. The nurses are the ones who'll move me if I don't look out. Scottie is the best. The roughest in the ward is a tall, red-headed girl who says threateningly, 'Oh, so I can't, can't I?' if you protest against being moved. But she can be conciliated by tinpot comic rhymes about the other nurses and the house-surgeons, especially Dr Trovey, who makes toffee in his room after hours. Nurse Jamieson, the fat one with greasy little curls under her cap, is the one who tells what the patients have wrong with them: and little Minna Craig, who hasn't much wrong but a poisoned toe and an undernourished wisp of a body, hops about between bed and bed, distributing and picking up grains of news.

'She's at the change, and she jumped out of the upstairs window and broke her leg. They're taking her off to the asylum to-morrow.' Shrieks, white-hot, pouring out of the little room off the ward. 'She thinks the black devils are after her, and the nurses are laughing. There's three of them in there, laughing at her.'

'It's crool to laugh at her, the pore thing.'

Nothing left, apart from the tyranny of one's own body, but a light, vague, battening curiosity, a sense of being linked together as girls at a school are linked, and endless gossip. The stomach-pump clanks and gurgles at night. Next day a young woman in a flannel dressing-gown walks about, sullen and brooding, one black bruise from eyebrow to breast. 'Her old man knocked her about, so she went and swallowed lysol, but they pumped her out all right, and she's going home to-day.' Straight black hair, falling from the forehead of a girl in the coarse flannel nightshirt of the hospital, the kind you wear if you have nothing of your own. 'Well, I must say, really. They're keeping all her things apart, cups and everything. Do you know what that means? She's got a disease, and they've brought her in here to have the baby took away. I had two operations for that myself, but mine was different, it was because I had T.B. A shame, I call it, putting her in with decent married women and young single girls.'

Dark faces, dark sullen faces, their silence remembered for ever. Nobody spoke to the girl in the flannel nightshirt, one of us might have done. . . . And the little sparrow gossips. 'Two years since I had me radium in, and now the doctor says I've got to be opened again. Life's a business, isn't it?'

Kathleen with the tawny lion's mane around her white cameo of a face, her eyes grey, her mouth lovely. 'Appendicitis — not her. Don't you have anything to do with her, my dear, she's no better than a street-woman. I'm warning you because you're a young single girl. She's been in here before, she has.' But Kathleen sat on the side of Eliza's bed and talked. Once she was a waitress; there was a baby, and now she was here. 'Just appendicitis,' she said, shaking back the lion's mane.

'I can't stand any more. I can't stand any more.' The doctor's voice said gravely, 'No, I don't suppose you can.' Eliza thought, trembling, 'That's why I like the doctors, because they don't laugh at pain. If they did, when they're making their living by it, I'd want the earth to open with a crack of thunder under their feet, and swallow them up.' The old rhyme out of 'Robin Hood' danced in her mind:

> To take from the rich, and give to the poor —
> And so God aid me, in His power.

Screens were drawn around the new girl's bed, nothing was allowed out but her high moaning. Presently, when the doctor had gone away, enamel basins slammed and nurses scurried. 'Nurse, Nurse, look at this floor.' Minna Craig whispered, 'It's blood. It's soaked right through the mattress and made a pool on the floor. Sister's not half wild.' The new girl's voice had grown dreamy and mechanical, she had nearly forgotten what she wanted to say.

'Doctor, I can't . . . oh, Doctor, dear, I can't . . .' Screens closed right round her bed, wings folding, hard white wings of death.

'That's what you get for messing about with married men, me dear.'

'Yes,' thought Eliza, 'And Arthur Waley wrote in his translation of the little Chinese poem,

> How sad it is to be a woman,
> Nothing on earth is held so cheap.

The kind and the lovely . . . the kind and the lovely . . . their faces drift back through the twilight. Men, you have sentinelled your doors with them. It is a false judgment, the judgment you passed on them, and false the sentence of pain, and the base metal with which they were paid for living. But this is true. Their arms were white, their heavy hair fell back, wet as sickness had made it wet, their grey eyes kept a secret, and in twilight their mouths were kind. They did not remember to blame or to condemn you; if they spoke of you at all, it was quietly, with the old words of love. They were a flower that has spread itself too wide, and a moth that could not hate the flame. Grave-eyed, they were garlanded; brave-winged, they flew on into dust.

There was something here about a bone that wouldn't set. The little old man who presided over the fizzling golden X-rays wouldn't have Eliza moved. Twice the big machine lumbered round to the side of her bed, and stood over her behind the screens. We're going to put you under. . . . Breathe deep, old girl, move your little finger if you can still hear me. She's off, Sister. The rush of protest, the cry impossible to utter: 'No, no, I'm not off yet. Don't touch me yet, Doctor.' Then nothing but wet blackness, and running, running along an endless stretch of sands.

Presently Eliza's bed, with an iron cradle over it, was wheeled out to the balcony, which ran round a little square courtyard infinitely more pleasant than the redlit ward. The dank fountain never played, but its basin made a splash-bath for the sparrows and the silk-hat raiders, four glossy starlings living on the slanted roof of the ward opposite. Soon she had the sparrows trained to sit on the cradle, asking for crumbs every noon and five o'clock. How do they *know* what time it is? But punctual to the moment, they always do know. At five, when the thick cups of tea, lumps of bread, plates of fish, tripe or rabbit were handed around, out of the sky came whirring dusty grey and chestnut wings, the dress of the gamins. The starlings waited in the courtyard; when a sparrow hopped off with a large-sized crumb, they waylaid him, bullied him, pecked him, grabbed his crumb and sent him off with a flea in his ear, like big townies attacking a schoolboy outside a tuckshop.

Biddy Kissin, with a tubercular spine and two white shells of plaster of paris, above and beneath her, lay in the right-hand bed and knitted. Her fair plaits hung against a plump, rosy face, which always wrinkled into discontent when her husband came. Biddy couldn't be sure that he had remained faithful, and he wasn't telling; she bombarded him with questions, appeals and threats, while he sat beside her, the paper bag of oranges dandled on his knee. All his infidelities, if they existed, stayed behind his hard-shell little face. When he had gone, Biddy was always in tears. 'What I've got to put up with. Little a girl knows until she's married. Oh, I'm that unhappy. Didn't I bear his children for him? And me lying here, and him up to I don't know what. . . .'

In the left-hand bed Rangi, the Maori girl, lay watching until the nurses were out of the way. Then she slipped her thin legs from under the bedclothes. 'Now don't — somebody ought to stop her. Rangi, you get back to bed.' But Rangi, never seeming to hear Biddy Kissin, smiled her fixed little smile and reached out for the balcony rail. She didn't know much English, and had forgotten what she did know since the big tubercular abscess broke out on her hip. She smiled vaguely at everyone, her eyes liquid brown as a deer's, her skin brown-eggshell-smooth. Holding first to the galvanized iron bedrail, she jerked a step forward, then stood wavering. Her smile was still fixed. She half lurched, half fell to the balcony, caught the rail, and started to drag herself along a little at a time, teaching herself to walk again. On Sundays her husband came, a thin Maori boy in a scarlet jersey cap, and they talked together low-voiced in their own tongue, as if they were meditating escape. Perhaps Rangi really did want to run away with him. When he had gone, she lay back, brown and smiling, her great eyes closed. She was eighteen, the same age as Eliza. Presently she was taken away, and died in the hospital for consumptives. Maoris are very much afraid of white hospitals and white medicine, and like best to die in their own way outside.

Twice a week the outer world drifted in, admitted by ticket, a little frightened, a little muddled; Augusta with new-laid eggs and Fiji oranges,

John with books, Carly with pink and lavender bed-caps, all satin streamers, lace hearts and tiny flowers. You were supposed to wear them pinned on your hair. Eliza knew Carly had taken them out of her glory-box, where she was keeping things for Trevor Sinjohn; starting with the vogue for Richelieu work, which was in when she was still at College, passing through lazy-daisy and cross-stitch to eyelet-holes, which were popular now. Sandra, tall, awkward and pretty, a golden giraffe, bit her tongue for shyness. She was having a stormy passage at school, if you spoke to her suddenly her blue eyes swam with tears. Once — queer once — she said, 'Don't you think all the trouble began when we left off playing games after dark?' One Hannay didn't need to ask another, 'What trouble?' Lost, in a wilderness of brick and mortar, rules and regulations, love and hate; instead of the thicket where there were supplejack bows, and streams with eels and wild mint.

Simone came once, with a tall, fair, square-shouldered boy, Toby Brian. She wore a fur coat — Eliza knew Augusta would explode about that when she had gone, and want to know how Simone got the money — and chattered and laughed a great deal. 'Darling, how pretty you look — all pink in the face, and with those enormous eyes. Being ill does suit you. I think I'll have to try it, I'm so battered.' But at the end of the visit, she bent down and whispered, 'I'm not coming again, what's the use?' Her green eyes had the old blinded look. Eliza nodded. She didn't want her lovely free ones in the hospital ward — not Timothy or Simone.

Timothy had gone away again to Auckland, before she had had the accident, and she only thought sharply of him once: when a surgeon, half-joking, asked her if she wouldn't rather have her leg cut off. Timothy running in the pinewoods, under the green rafters. Timothy, wait for me, I've got my leg cut off. She said, 'No, no,' and the doctor laughed. 'It's all right. I was only joking.'

On the balcony she began writing a novel, an overgrown fairytale about a little boy who fell off the earth and went wandering through space. She could see thickets and campfires for him, but the plot tailed off, and writing against the iron cradle made her tired. Mostly she lay quiet, or clicked together the big wooden knitting needles Carly had brought her, with mauve-pearl wool to make a wrap. The wrap never got done. . . . Days were much better than the nights, when the red light pricked through the windows, and always somebody came moaning or retching out from the anaesthetics, and it was impossible to get morphine, she had had far too much, and was better now. Biddy Kissin lay a white restless mountain in her bed, a tap dripped, a little piercing pinprick that went cleanly into the brain. She had dreams in which she was always running, taking high fences and rocks with great, easy leaps, Jack-the-Ripper leaps, which yet left a dream-feeling of dreadful effort. Then terror came in. Lions and tigers were after her, and she had to stop and persuade them, with long, plausible arguments, not to tear her to pieces. Sometimes she simply hid from them, once or twice she triumphed over them and they let her ride on their backs, but the feeling of effort and fear was never gone.

The nurse most unpopular with Sister, a tall, angular girl who had put on the pink uniform far too late in life, came and sat on her bed. 'We both do our best, Eliza.' Her eyes were always red-rimmed with weeping, her cap bedraggled. She had bad dreams too, dreams of laying out bodies. They were so bad, the things they had died of so appalling, that if she didn't tell them she thought she would go mad. Often she heard a loud, insistent ringing in her ears.

'I'll give your back a rub with meths. I'm not supposed to, after tea, and I'll get into trouble if I'm caught. But why shouldn't I, if it makes you comfortable? I'm not such a bad nurse to you, am I, Eliza?'

'I think you're a very good nurse, far better than the Sister.'

It wasn't even true. Red-eyed kindliness didn't go for much, rush and bustle got there, and were quite human so long as you didn't cross their path, deface their polished floors, their polished rules. Like little old Mrs Calgary, who would spit. At times you could hear her muttering, 'I'm not goin' to spit on the floor, I'm not goin' to spit on the floor, that's a dirty trick, that is, spittin' on the floor, oh, dear Lord Jasus, don't let me spit on the floor.'

At Laloma, Augusta and John were trying something difficult; they had to have their say; and simultaneously, they must keep their shipwrecked barque from going to pieces altogether.

'You lost your promotion. With your daughter as sick as she is, perhaps a helpless cripple for life, you had to play the fool and lose your promotion.'

'Because I didn't crawl. . . . Get out of here, and leave me. I've had enough. Go and live with your crawlers.'

The little articles, 'Mohammed to the Mountain,' in the magazine which some had considered Red: John had always been immensely proud of them. Years after it was due, after younger men had been passed over his head, promotion was gazetted; a tidy little job, the charge of the clerical staff in a branch firm, and no backblocks concern, either. His new job was well away, in a town where his position would be quite respectable. He had thought, once or twice, of buying a cheap car. As soon as Eliza could be moved, Laloma was going up for sale.

And then, at the office, John argued with the wrong man. There was a word and a blow, and in the little inner office where things were decided, copies of *Stingaree* were spread out on a desk.

'You lost your promotion. You had to skite about your politics, and lose your promotion.'

Looking backwards, John could see himself in his first youth. No money, not much of an education, but his father by then was established at a place that counted; a tall, well-moustached, grave-eyed old soldier, sufficiently dignified to pass at a glance for the real and not the self-made article. His little Frenchy mother laughed, waved fluttering brown hands, and kept parroquets in a long wired balcony. After the Boer War . . . there were thirteen of us who held a bridge that had to be held, nine were potted, and that's where I got this little bit of tinware on my chest . . . at least he wasn't bad-looking, not a complete fool. Confusedly he stared at the gap between, and couldn't quite understand it.

'Because I wouldn't crawl to them. That's it.'

He was rash enough to fight the little notice that cancelled his promotion. Then they hit him, hit him from all sides at once. Men who had worked beside him for years played sweet with the Bosses. They said straight out, 'If you get on the wrong side of Shenstone, you're done.'

Unfit; they stung him with words, safe in their cover of money and smooth white flesh. He had a wife and four children, one of them in hospital, and the bills mounting up. He had to stay on and be grateful, while the young passed over and over his dusty head, laughing at him.

'That word job,' he thought, 'there's something queer even in the sound of it. Take the things it rhymes with — nob, rob, slob, shut your gob, the Bosses are coming. It hasn't anything to do with work. The cockies work harder at their farms. It means — oh, God, what does it mean? See the white collar round your neck instead of the serf's ring. See yourself getting softer and softer, whining-soft, at a hard life; for that's what it is, a hard, base life, a deprived life.'

Augusta, looking forward, saw nothing for herself. She saw Carly, Eliza, Sandra and Kitch — what the strong, contemptuous honesty of her brothers, the Mallee Giants, would have called, 'Neither fish nor flesh, nor good red herring.' She hadn't brought them up for the butcher, the baker, the candlestick-maker. But no money, no poise, no key to her white house like a Greek cross, her two blue vases sitting on the mantelshelf, the tall one stork-necked, filled perhaps with irises, the squat one bubbling over with the manifold primroses she had never seen.

If they had been characterless she would have had more faith in their destiny. The straws ride easy. But Carly had the soft and delicate force of unasking love. Eliza — ever since she had made up her mind that Timothy Cardew wasn't the marrying kind, she had thought, 'Better dead,' and now there was this smash; Sandra needed comfortable things, laughter and pretty frocks and girl friends, to round off the edges of her shyness; Kitch was still her little boy, passionately in earnest over model aeroplanes, generally quiet and good. But when his time came he'd present his bill, the bill you get twenty years after the gasping agony of giving another individual life.

Through the windows of her drawing-room the soft full light burst down on the hills, gilding the cleft between the pine trees, and the farther, barren peaks which lifted grey as rosemary above the last of the bush. Everything in this drawing-room, and the other five rooms of the house, she had managed somehow to buy out of the housekeeping money — never more than £4 a week, at first £1/19/-, a man and two children to keep on it; the piano, of course, that came from Rufus's money, and Eliza's illness would eat up the rest. But the big picture of Bonnie Prince Charlie, she had lugged that home under her arm from an auction sale. Half the time she hadn't had the money for tram-fares, and she could see herself now, scarlet-faced, sweating under the bands of her black straw hats, toiling up the hills like a beast of burden. And not just furniture. Good food for them, though she remembered sitting at table with one egg, and that wasn't for her, though Sandra was coming. And when they were little, her children's frocks were always the prettiest and best, though now her sight blurred behind her spectacles, and the old sewing-machine broke the thread so often that using it taxed her patience.

Still the hills drew back her glance. She thought, 'I wish I'd gone all round them when I came here first. Now it's too late.'

All her life from girlhood, she understood now, had never been lived at all, unless a woman is nothing but the machinery for producing and manipulating her children. In England the white house stood empty somewhere, the little clenched fists of bracken thrusting up beside its paths, its windows like golden blinded eyes. In a room, the soft drawing crackle of the log fire was the only sound breaking the stillness: as she listened, a log crashed, and the yellow embers heaped up. The scent of hyacinths thickened in the air like cream.

Drudging in little houses, bringing up children, heckling John to make him what he wasn't, and didn't want to be — that wasn't life.

'Days should speak,' said the Book of Job. In soft reverent music, in a bird's voice calling and the unheard sound of a primrose's pink stem parting the moss, her days should have spoken; but not in this huddle, the crude complacent gabble of a place where everyone was on the make.

A summer fly buzzed, and fell brown dead against the inside of the windows. She had no part nor lot in the grey hills, whose flanks melted into one another as if Maori gods lay asleep, promiscuous in one another's arms after the belly-loading of some immense, noble banquet. But she didn't hate them. Her eyes felt dim, her mind heavy, unable to take in with youth's elasticity the span of skies and the ragged grey saplings of clouds. She wished it were not so; she wished she had tramped round their edges years ago, instead of huddling into the auction sales. It was all she could do now for the hills.

CHAPTER SIXTEEN

Barbarian for Caesar

THE boy next in line whispered, 'I say, I don't half like this.' Immediately Timothy felt better, and when a piece of coal rapped him on the cheek, he was almost his own man again. 'They've got a hope,' he said cheerfully.

'But what say they turn nasty?' Timothy laughed. Yet the hard disconcerted pose of the striking seamen, their mouths that didn't open except to spit, stuck in his mind. They were so exactly the men he had cultivated in life and in books, the men of whom he had hotly declaimed, 'They're right, the rest of you are fools.' And in the linesmen's camp they had taken him in and treated him, with a bit of banter, as one of themselves.

Now he was helping to break their strike; they sat on wharf-edges, or stood about, black lumber against the tin sheds where grain was sacked, and the newspapers over half a world were screaming about them, because this war had spread wherever ships jutted out their funnels and rolled their black-and-rust bellies. They made him feel, without speaking, that *Martin Eden* had been a pose, a sham. They looked fools and skulkers, they hadn't a word to say for themselves beyond the 'Yah — scab!' of the street bully, but they were bigger than Timothy, much bigger than Timothy's little adventure.

A white gob of spittle landed direct at his feet. All the way down the wharf, against red sheds, silent men stood and spat. The drooping lily to the rear of Timothy kept up his heart. When somebody's afraid, when you feel a man or an event may actually turn and strike you with a lion's paw, you can keep your head up, under its new peaked cap, keep from turning to the silent ones and saying, 'I say, this is why I did it. I don't want your wages, if I knew where to send them I'd shove them straight back into your Union funds, and good luck to you, but it's like this. You won't go with your ships, and somebody must — a chance that may never come again. Well, I've got to be a poet and a sculptor — just as important as your being a seaman and a striker — and I've grabbed this while it was going.'

For two pins, for a single, half-baked reproachful speech from one of the seedy dock lawyers who every now and again jumped on the stanchions to rally the spirits of the men, Timothy would have dropped his adventure for their adventure, the bigger adventure of sticking things

180

out. But nobody spoke to him, except in white gobs of spittle. He shuffled forward, wanting the newness to wear off his cheap jersey and white cap, for a little while to be part of the ship, as much as her iron rust-streaks and fishwife gulls were part of her. A banjo twanged down from the fo'c'sle, the ship's cat, indifferent and bedraggled, stalked abroad. She knew that the *Ionica* was sailing, and this strike broken. 'Hurry, Sister,' he advised the boy in front. Then his feet were on the gang-plank, touching the little irregular steps.

Only the lanky tin sheds had reality, only the faces. Perhaps things didn't swoop into change. But the change was there, straight ahead by stars' compass: Tropic of Capricorn, Equator, Tropic of Cancer, calms, pearly nautilus, flying fish, Suez, coffee faces, harim, great torpid heat, the Bay of Biscay, the white cliffs of Dover.

He was crowded against the *Ionica's* lower deckrail, the banjo still mourned, and with a single bright-edged shirring of the green waters in between, the faces became impalpable: the great dream, the England dream, became solid and true. He could have laughed, and turned to anyone there. 'Well, I've made a break.' But he had no one to talk to, beyond the drooping lily, who seemed to find some forlorn comfort in Timothy's back.

In a south place where he had stayed, only one peak remained eternally capped by the snows. White in summer its lustre streamed, and the darker denuded foothills edged up to it, shouldering against its implacable dignity. And from his boyhood Timothy had called the white mountain Caesar, and the darker hills were the dark chieftains of Gaul, Britain and Sparta, bringing their tribute of windy odours. Caesar was London.

A barbarian I come to you, O Caesar, smelling of gorse and the rank fleece of sheep, able to tell you of a red-flowering tree in my own land, of winds stalking in the flax like the great lost bird, the moa, and of a green weapon-stone whose cold touch is more beautiful than the kiss of a woman. Like the plumes of black impis, the six-foot toi-toi feathers dip and skim beneath the wind. With my own hands I have rounded out the belly of a boat, clinker-built, and straightened her keel so that she rode like a tern on the waves. I have broken sharp oysters from the rocks, and burned strange woods in my campfire. Yet thin grass stooping among the starlight was more than all these. I have picked up ambergris washed from the mighty feeding-grounds of the sperm whale, south of Solander Islands, and found minute rubies in the far north; and I know the story of the lost cinnabar mine, and the sulphur island where men are afraid. I have left the prints of my bare feet on a beach of glittering iron-sand. If I come before you now, Caesar, and roll these discoloured pearls out of the piece of beaten flax in which they are wrapped, will you not look up, satiate though you are? I have been afraid, and made others afraid, and I know the beach of azure blue shells. I have seen strange things, and I am not yet twenty-three. I have been told, Caesar, that you have a shortage of young barbarians lately. . . .

A taxi-driver who had dropped his fare at the passengers' gang-way looked up at the strike-breakers. Timothy beckoned him.

'Take a wire to the Post Office for a bob?'

'Righto.'

Timothy scribbled: 'Off on the great adventure. Will come back to you. Aroha nui,' and signed it. Very carefully he wrote Eliza's name and address on the back, and handed it down to the driver.

'You won't forget to send it? It's important.'

'Naw. The Post Office is along me way.'

The man drove off. Suddenly and quite desperately, Timothy wanted to get off this lumbering ship; not only the strikers, he thought, but Eliza, Damaris Gayte, poor little old Lucy, that green-eyed girl who was Eliza's prickly friend. Once he had written her a poem, and if he hadn't got out of town that might have gone further.

Of late Eliza had been stowed away in the back of his mind. She was ill, in hospital, writing letters of thin cheerfulness, out of his reach unless he had gone down to Wellington and played district visitor — and that he wouldn't want to do. He was sorry, he wrote that he was sorry; but pain, sickness, were a kind of separate little Hell, inaccessible unless one pretended. Something in Augusta Hannay's face cut into him like a knife. Best to pretend things were right, unless suddenly they *were* right, and you all sat back, with the picnic-cloth spread white in the centre of the group, and laughed and laughed.

At a dozen places in the assembling group he could see Eliza's face, beneath the little brown hat with the orange feather. Her frocks were always clumsy, and he said, 'Why can't you wear things that show you as you are?' Then she looked at him. She was at an uncomfortable stage; neither child nor woman, neither go-as-you-please insouciant, or cool little rectory piece. She would find her feet, and follow . . . limping. Impossibly melodramatic: in six months he'd be back, crowned and bronzed with adventure. A woman, aiming wildly, threw a bob of paper ribbon at his chest. He caught it, and the slim pink unrolled between them. Then a heavy-moustached man impatiently elbowed it aside, and walked hunched along the wharf, a taggle of pink against his coat.

Water churned white around the tail of the ship, her voice became an eager, throbbing, monotone. The gang-planks seesawed gracefully into the air. Somebody pushed Timothy's shoulder.

'Get below, you. Had enough of an airing, ain't you?'

He went down to the stokehold, clinging like a monkey to little iron ladders. Below dwelt roar, burst and clang; the door of a furnace swung open, and with a searing crackle white-hot flame rushed out. Timothy saw lifted up a seamed devil's face; the flames made a phœnix nest of its tattered hair.

'And 'oo the 'ell's this pup? Oh, Christ, with a cargo of scabbies and infants wet from their muvver's milk, what I'm going to 'ave to put up with, and grin, and look as if I liked it. Oh, Christ, get that shovel, carn't yer?'

Timothy laughed. For a moment he held with his crooked fingers to the rungs of the last little iron ladder, then dropped down into Hell's teeth. He was going to like this voyage, this little dandy, Martin Eden voyage. 'I've made the break,' rang the final coin of his thought, triumphantly, 'I've made the big break.'

Kitch, bare-footed in spite of his awful cold, came running along the sands to the rock where Eliza sat, shouting at the top of his voice, 'You've got a tely-gram. You've got a tely-gram.' Little Mr Dill, her office chief, had lent Augusta a cottage for Eliza's convalescence, which was kind of him, but Kitch had to come too: and his cold, combined with his adenoids, made him snore so loudly across the passage at night that she cried hysterically, saying she hated Kitch, she couldn't bear him.

The sun was very hot. While she sat with her back pressed against the sugarloaf rock, she felt no pain at all, only a supreme disinclination to move. It seemed interesting to shuffle the fine gold grains of sand through her fingers, then to lie back and stare at them. Seagulls bobbed and shone about the waves. Kitch was building a moat round his sandcastle, which had a seaweed flag on top. He was very painstaking, but the sea ran into his moat, frizzed, and was mysteriously swallowed up. His nose was pink, his naked legs scarlet.

Eliza read the telegram, and lay back watching the seagulls. Bob . . . flash . . . scream. It didn't make so much difference. Timothy had grown dim, anyway, in that place where you died and suffered, begged and prayed for morphine. No, you can't have any more, you've had far too much morphine already. Morphine was inestimably more than Timothy. Timothy hadn't been there on the first day when she walked: and all the blood rushed down into her leg, and she screamed, and a little pink nurse, who didn't understand, laughed out loud. Timothy hadn't said 'Steady as she goes' when she first moved her crutches, like two long dead branches, over an endless slippery floor, and wondered why, why people insist on having nice polished floors in hospitals. Timothy never sat beside her in tramcars, when rather deaf old ladies said in piercing voices that everyone could hear, 'Have you hurt your foot, my dear? I ask because a cousin of mine had a bad leg, and she got the most wonderful results from rubbing in Goanna Oil.'

She wished she could feel quite light again. She'd go dancing with Simone, who loved her, in spite of having leopard eyes. They'd dance in the funny little hall at Black Valley, and the sweating farm-boys would like Eliza best because Simone scared them ('That apricot does suit you. Being ill has done your complexion the best turn of its life.' Never a word, never an indication, that seen sideways on she looked queerly stiff.) Afterwards they'd compare notes and laugh and laugh, sitting in willow arms jagged through with black and silver moonlight. And if they bathed naked, the water would be very cold, dirty brown, full of prickles and laughter and eels.

Only he mustn't ever come back again, that would be unbearable. The race is to the swift, the battle to the strong, and Timothy has gone to England. Let them have it, but keep what else you've got. The Kingdom of the Defeated: you can't get in there on a reporter's ticket.

Kitch whirred his model aeroplane along the sands. It actually rose three inches, rose and hovered; but then a black root of seaweed caught it.

'Timothy, darling . . . oh, Timothy, the godwits.'

Kitch came up and dug his spade into the sand. 'Did you see by bodel blane fly?' he asked, through his pink nose. 'She went grand, Elize. You're grying. You're a silly chump for grying. What're you grying for, Eliza?'

'Everybody goes away but us. The godwits.'

'Look, a bosquito's stung me sobthing awful. I shouldn't wonder if I got boisoned. Stop grying, Elize. Eliza, look ad by bachine.'

'Eliza, didn't I tell you not to let Kitch get his trousers wet? Just look at him. He'll have pneumonia. Really, you can't be left to do the simplest little thing. You may have been ill, but that's no reason you shouldn't treat other people with ordinary, decent consideration. You know what

Kitch is when he gets cold properly.'

'Leave me alone. Leave me alone. I don't want to talk to any of you.'

'Something in that telegram, I suppose. Or else you're making a fuss again. I should think you'd have more pride. Plenty have to put up with worse.'

'Leave me alone. Leave me alone.'

Kitch felt slightly embarrassed, slightly injured. He thought of his model aeroplane; it was a beauty, its wings gauzy blue as a dragonfly's, and he had made it at least partly to amuse Eliza, because she had been ill. Now she wouldn't notice. He took it in one hand, and skimmed it along in short, grazing flights to the sugarloaf rock. There its aquiline nose jagged on pebbles, and he found that he had damaged it. He climbed up the sugarloaf, a short black-shadowed figure silhouetted against the pale sky, and returning with his injured feelings and broken aeroplane into his little boy's kingdom called hoarsely, 'Mad old Eliza — mad old Elize. Mad old Eliza, grying 'cos she got a tely-gram.'

CHAPTER SEVENTEEN

The Kind Green Arm

THEY lay under the lacebark trees, on the shabby kapok mattresses with which they had lined the bottom of the lorry. Little cool flowers broke off, white scales of blossom, and crumbled down on their sunburnt faces. A boy named Borden sat up, mixing a salad which he called 'Cooled Off'; it had passion-fruit, crème-de-menthe and crayfish.

'It tastes lovely, but we'll all be dead,' murmured little Annie Carr, in a sleepy, happy voice. They pulled their handkerchiefs over their faces, and wanted to go to sleep in the lacebark-mottled sun, the squinting green picnic sun. Jim Braythwaite lay next to her, and she hoped he wouldn't get up and go away: but, as she might have known, he said to the stranger, 'Come for a walk,' and Annie between her lashes watched them scramble up from among the quiet mounds of bodies.

Really the purple mountains were extraordinary. Somebody had scissored them out of painted cardboard, all except one higher peak, covered with snow, and like a white glistening cow turning its udder to the sky, feeding the clouds, which took on palpable substance as they sucked. The lake water at their feet was flat and still, lipping thinly through reeds, each of which stood out separate, brittle as glass. A bird in the reed-beds scuttled and cried, midges danced in a spire of air, which meant full sunlight for to-morrow. Eliza thought quietly, 'Yes, I'm happy here, quite happy. And I feel so well.' She said, 'I heard there were deer in among the lacebarks. I'd love to see one.'

But no large mournful shape stood pushing its hairy cheeks and distressed eyes through the branches, and they went on to a sticky place, half morass, where Jim Braythwaite carried her over. On the other side was a deserted farmhouse with lemon trees standing behind it. The thick golden-green curve of the macrocarpa hedge, breaking now into high scented feathers, was an accomplishment in itself. It was a protective arm, a kind green arm, crooked around the fallen little place that people once living here had made. Eliza thought, 'If the man once here never did anything else in his life than make that hedge, still his time wasn't wasted.' The rest of the garden was freckled and dew-splashed in high green ruin. She stood crumpling the pale crinkled lemon leaves between her fingers; their scent crept into the skin of her palms.

'Isn't it lovely? Who lived in that old house? Isn't it ghostly, the way

186

the old pink roses shudder and fall to bits, as if a hand had touched them?' She looked at Jim's face, which for once was not smiling and not ugly. She could not tell what he was thinking. It seemed his bitter drained mouth did the thinking for him, and behind his dark eyes nothing lived at all. She shivered a little, for he was more ghostly than the breaking roses, and to stand in a dying garden with the swarthy ghost of a man, watching for whatever animated him to come back behind his eyes, was going deeper below the surface of things than Eliza liked. She could not be sure if she admired or hated his darkness. It was like a black cup; the sweet air and the sunshine were poured into it, and — and died. Yet he wasn't old, he couldn't have been more than thirty-five or thirty-seven.

Jim said, as if he read her thoughts, 'So you really think you like us here?' He smiled down from his thin height of six feet and an inch. She hesitated. 'Yes; I think I do. I like the climate, and the smell of sulphur. It's so seldom Hell gives warning, but here it's frank, don't you think? Even your flowers are hellish—pantomime-devil flowers. They stick up red wands and blue daggers out of the white dust.'

'And the people?'

'Oh, it's all cut-throat bridge, isn't it? With the exception of one or two who seem to have got here by accident, like that girl Carr. I liked her. The rest are exactly like their country. At any moment, you feel they're going to do something excitable. Anyhow they're not dingy.'

'And I?'

'You're most terribly obliging. *Preux chevalier*, or have I got my French lesson mixed up again?' (From Mrs Ancell, when the death-watch beetle of a headache ticked again behind her forehead, 'Jim, darling, do get my aspirin'; from Cecily Wetherby at the races, 'Jim, darling, this is a sure one, you'll come in on it, won't you?' From all the other little emaciated maidens, little stout widowettes, petitions and requests; and Jim attended to them all like a robot; yet he was just too tall, just too dark and grinning, to be lapdog.)

'Then, on the whole, you'll stay and register approval?'

'Oh, I'll stay: to the end of this month, anyhow. I like the climate, and I like my dress with the large cherry flowers. Only one thing . . .'

'Why don't you say what it is? We'll attend to it.'

'The circus. I do so wish the circus hadn't come to town. The moment I saw the tents tethered, down at that little green place, I started telling myself that it didn't matter; and I know perfectly well that it does.'

'We've struck a complex,' said Jim. 'Like an iceberg, when everything looked such lovely plain sailing. This circus hasn't got anything more than a starved-looking yellow menagerie which hopes you'll feed it peanuts, and a few monkeys combing fleas, and my drunken pal Bristol Joe, who is *not* this world's greatest trapeze artist. Then aren't you going to give them their miserable shilling, and come along and suck ices with the rest of us to-night? Or are you one of those creepy humanitarians — want to let all the animals out of their cages?'

'No, I'm afraid it's exactly the other way about. You see, Jim, nobody would ever guess it who looked at me now — sturdy wench — but once I was desperately ill, and the roaring of lions and tigers got into my dreams. I had some remarkable arguments with them. It went away, but if I'm anywhere near a zoo or a circus, back it comes, and then I want to do idiotic things. Or else pack up and run.'

'Idiotic things, such as what?'

'Oh, scream and scream, you know. Not a bit of the boy Daniel.'

'We can't have you running and screaming because of a couple of moth-eaten old lions. And does the complex only operate at night?'

'Yes. If I wake up in the dark and hear them.'

'Then if you wake up, my room's only across the corridor. You could come in and have a spot.'

Eliza said, 'Or you could come into my room.' Immediately she felt, 'Just what the pantomime-devil flowers ordered.'

'I could,' said Jim. Then he did another thing she hadn't expected of him. He said softly, 'Once in a blue moon, I get a funny dream myself, you know. Houses falling into one another, slap-bang, like a pack of cards, and then dust coming up in huge billows. And I don't like it at all.'

'When did it start?'

'I was seventeen when I got into the very tail-end of the war — just the dying flip. And at one place there was some very heavy bombardment going on in a street. Funny.'

Eliza said, 'Yes, funny'; because the desperate things that happen, the monopolizing tragedies and grievances, are funny; man-eating jokes. The cold arc of the lake cut across their sight as they walked back. There were three lakes in this chain—silver, green and blue. You could stand on a knoll of little height but thick bush, and have those three colours, uncompromising in their difference from one another, cut into you. The green lake was loveliest, perhaps, a naiad with a heartless face, her hair rippling out towards her shores, where nobody lived and nothing moved except the shirring of bird wings, or the hoofs of red deer set down stamping in thick mud. Their feet stumbled over knots of couch grass as they walked. They met a limping black cocker spaniel, a mere baby, with a broken paw and eyes like topaz. The farmhand said he was to be drowned, for a nuisance. Jim bought him for five shillings, picked him up and comforted him, pressing the little black quaking body against his tweed coat. Eliza thought, 'Yes — he could be gentle.' They got to the picnic-place, and the girl Annie, with a restless, sun-scarlet face, ran to meet them. 'Oh, here you are at last!' They all sang songs driving back on the lorry. Jim had a fine voice. 'But he doesn't quite pull it off,' thought Eliza. 'None of my friends do, and none of them will be satisfied with anything less.'

Black silk for night, blue silk for day, red silk over the light in Jim Braythwaite's room. The impacts of roses and sunsets on the eyes, the cold little elfin scatter of fountain-drops, perfume a fine silk touch, were parts of the new life on which she could rely. No agony in them, no lying awake and thinking. In the cherry-coloured dress with the vast vague flowers, she looked so well that she told herself, 'Nobody would ever know I've been broken and put together again.' Of Jim Braythwaite she wasn't so sure. She thought, walking in the gardens, how mad it would be to scribble on a postcard, 'Having a lover isn't much to write home about,' and send it off to Timothy. She had burned Timothy's two letters from London, because in both he had said that he was coming back to her, and that was more than she could bear. Now she could only remember a phrase from one of them. 'London is wonderful — oh, the smoke, and sun just a copper-red ball!' Well, somewhere in that old phœnix nest, Timothy either blazed or wilted, according to his luck. In her two hard years, her two hard-working years, when for months she had dragged herself about on crutches, and made money just the same, she had never heard any more of Timothy. At this date, she didn't especially want to: only, how strange it would be, to see him come running round the over-smooth edge of the bed that thrust up fiery daemonic flower-spikes, wands and daggers! How childish he seemed, against Jim's dark pit of a face, where all the sunshine had long since gone into coal. The sleek arcs of fountain-drops broke, and drops leapt big as frogs into a basin, to be lost on the lily-pads and the calm scarlet water-flowers, very wide open.

No, really, Timothy, having Jim Braythwaite as my lover hasn't made any difference. Like the Bishop and the confirmation service — but you wouldn't remember that. They all said, 'Something wonderful will happen to you,' and I went about in a state of excitement for days, but nothing did. I guess I just don't react to revolutions. . . .

Or they should be different; like a secret smile, like a secret dream in the night.

Jim went out to work daily from his summer cottage, and Eliza went over and tidied up his things. That gave her more pleasure than anything else left in this hot place. The house waited, passive, helpless and mysterious, like an old wooden child, and the curly piano lid in the drawing-room hid a forest of slender green melodies. She could open the lid and make them climb up, forests too brittle and magical to last when another person knocked on the door. Not that she was anything of a musician; but the slumbrous dream in the piano woke and answered her dream. She liked picking the flowers in the little garden, wavering poppy-stalks with heavy heads, cool sweet peas and the fragile misty gypsophilas. No fierce colours here. . . . Jim laughed at the fetish she made of his house. It contained in its bedroom the whole of his unwritten history — the ostentatious gold-lettered dressing-case Cecily Wetherby had given him, the shagreen-covered brushes, the dressing-gowns, *La Vie Parisienne*. She liked to put each back exactly where she found it. In Jim's life she had no part nor lot. Only, after dusk, like two absent-minded strangers, they met again, and their quick, careless love affair, begun and ended on a laugh, went on. It wasn't that there seemed nothing to make him memorable. His thin mouth, the swiftness of the sting he could dart into talk, his dark eyes, seemed to her as attractive in a midnight way as Timothy. She herself didn't look ugly. She was white and red, red of the cherry frocks, white of the languid pallor dealt out by the sun which burdened the flowers with too much colour. But it was as if they had resolved to be nothing more than surface: two shapes lounging, walking, gesticulating, serving out cool salad and drinks with olives, suddenly close together, in the shadow play of a Harlequinade. She liked him best when he sang with Annie Carr. His voice wasn't so very good, the girl's a mezzo that had become entangled with soprano aspirations, but there was something childish and touching about their limned profiles. The voice of Annie was heavy with her little-complaining love for Jim.

Oh, my cinnamon tree! my cinnamon tree!

'Yes,' thought Eliza, 'I like them together. Poor children, poor dear children. If he were wise he'd marry her, but I'm afraid he's learned too much, in that scrappy way.'

Cecily Wetherby came to the races, and Jim trotted obediently at her heels, her thin black dog; Cecily was very rich. Appropriately they said, 'She's rolling,' for she did, rolls and rolls of fat pink above and beneath her corsets, showing through the thin embroidered clothes she insisted on wearing. Cecily's little parasol, mauve faille, sprouted above her head like an astonishing flower from a pot. Her body was tight curves, and a round little frizzled head sat up, surprised, on top. In the sunshine streams of perspiration ran down her face, clogging the streaked pink powder. But for all her awfulness, she was so good-natured, such an amiable, shrewd, easy-laughing bundle, that nobody could dislike her. 'Jim — Jim darling, you'll go on this, won't you? It's a good thing.' And who paid, if the good thing refused to show its paces? Cecily's thin black dog liked money.

While the races were on, Eliza explored alone in the sun. The soil was white with pumice dust, nothing grew in it but ti-tree and the blazing foreign flowers . . . the little, bright, astounding gardens, blistered with colours, sweating flowers. Once, climbing a hill, she twisted her ankle, and heard behind her a liquid exclamation of distress. A big Maori woman ran up, and put a hand under her elbow, murmuring sympathy like a pouter pigeon. She wore a kilted cotton skirt and a red blouse which made the day seem even hotter. Her bare feet happily trod the stony, blazing skin of the soil. Her skin was golden-brown, like the smoked shark she ate at feasts, but when Eliza looked at her eyes, they seemed so lovely as not to be human at all. Liquid, dark and bright, the eyes of a fairy-tale bird, they looked out with detachment from her brown face, bagging into heavy seams. Her soft voice coaxed the stumbling pakeha to a seat. Then she brought milk in a dirty cup. Eliza sat watching a row of bronze boys, the little ones quite naked, diving from a bridge into a hot creek for the pennies flung to them by tourists, whose faces were the faces of kind horses. Down went the brown pennies, cutting holes in a so clear, so green water that you could see the sand beneath. Down swallow-dived the scrawny naked boys, coming up with coins in their teeth, striking back their little shoulders bravely. The women of the place looked shapeless and too thickly clothed; their thick lips smiled, showing very bad teeth, the golden great-headed babies dangled in shawls on their backs. The sun had brought out scrambling children like flies on a dung-heap. Some of their faces were scarred and pitted, some of them coughed.

But her eyes were like the eyes of the bird in Olive Schreiner's fairy-tale, the beautiful dark bird that cried, 'Immortality — immortality', bringing sorrow to human hearts. Which is the Maori race? Or a little bit of both, I suppose. . . .

At Jim's cottage one day a woman knocked on the door. Eliza opened it with a broom in her hands. The woman was tired from travelling, middle-aged, pleasant-faced.

'But he's out, I'm afraid. Is there any message I could write down for him?'

'Oh, no.' The woman hesitated, then smiled shyly. 'Are you his wife?'

'No, no. I just come over sometimes and tidy up. I'm a stranger here, you see, on holiday, and this gives me a little to do.' Then, as the woman's look did not run away and hold a little scandal-colloquy behind her eyes, Eliza asked, 'Won't you let me get you some tea?'

'Well, really. . . . If you're quite sure it won't be too much bother . . .'

'Do, please, come in. It's coolest in this room. The old jasmine is very pretty, but it makes the dining-room stuffy.' There were mother-of-pearl papers and dark woods behind the tired woman's head, and in the safe tomatoes and lettuce leaf, still curly. Eliza cut the bread very thin. When she had carried the tray, the tired woman laughed and talked; her eyes grew brighter, in a sudden intimacy out of nowhere. At last she got up, shaking her dusty skirts.

'This has been so delightful. I feel now that I can bear to go on. It's the heat, isn't it?'

She was gone away out of the gate covered with jasmine. Eliza thought, 'I only know her name, and that doesn't matter, but I believe that's why married women can put up with staying in their houses. Playing host and guest, serving things cool. . . .' For a moment she wished she had been born in the Japanese country, where women are taught for years the arts of flower-arrangement, and wear their hair in huge black shiny buns, taking hours to compose. Then she waved her hands impatiently at the sunset, which stood like a row of solemn flamingos all along the west. 'Oh, no, no. One would get first bored, then frowzy, then secretly insane. It's only my loneliness.'

Loosen, tighten, break. A queer little thread, never quite meant to hold, was coming to an end. Jim and Eliza had reached the place where they had to go on — closer, more understanding — or go apart. The cottage Eliza saw in clearer light than Jim. A willow bough scraped affably against its roof as she swept the floors, outside the jasmine made a mass of dark leafage and little white stars. She felt heavy sick and hot; her food tasted of the sulphur that lay always in the air. The green days, green and crystal days under running feet, seemed as clean as they were far away. To feel cool again, one would have to strip off the whole casing of flesh and of thoughts.

She was never going back to the cottage any more. Its piano, its flowers and its shagreen cases, which now seemed faintly sly, could take care of themselves. On the last night she stayed at the boarding-house, Jim came over from the cottage and slept in the next room. He did not speak to her, even look at her, but his door stood wide open as she passed, so that she saw him sitting, his back towards her. Light made a little round sail of the water carafe, pinned on it the ruby moth of lamplight. His hair was cut short, she could see nothing else but his hands, strong, ugly, and spread out before him on the table.

He looked like somebody lost, lost in an immense jungle. The lamplight reached down long red stalks that grew all about him. He was frightened by a dream of falling houses and dust billowed out by earth's great sigh, she by the lions and tigers. But the lions and tigers were far away now, stale and unreal. Truer was the great golden-green curve of that hedge by the lakeside, the kind green arm. That had been a thing well done. Lemon leaves smell lovely after rain. The fragile misty gypsophilas are withering now in your vases where I put them, Jim. I liked you best when you were singing with Annie Carr. You should marry her, but I'm afraid you won't. *Auf Wiedersehen*; but not even that out loud, or the whole thing will start again, and I want to get away, I want to get away. I feel sick, and I'm going to work all this off. I'm going to work so hard that you wouldn't believe it was I. . . .

In the night, the wind rose, and the open door of Jim's room banged once or twice. At about four o'clock he got up quietly and closed it. A long while afterwards, Eliza wondered how two people so utterly alone could have taken the trouble to hurt one another.

CHAPTER EIGHTEEN

Farewell and Adieu

'You don't want to marry me, do you?'

'I came down here with a perfectly open mind.'

'But you don't want to. Well, you haven't got to. Listen. I'm going away to Sydney. Nobody need know. I haven't told. I've got my passage money, but not much else. I'm afraid you'll have to help.'

'Of course I'll help. But what about the baby?'

'You'll have to marry me if it lives — if I live. Somehow I don't think I will.'

'Don't talk like that.'

'Do you mind promising — if that happens?'

'Of course I promise.'

'I do wish the waitresses wouldn't clatter so. I suppose they can't help it, poor little devils. I've often thought, of all beastly jobs a waitress's is about the worst. This seems such a funny place to talk.'

'Best place; we're two in a crowd here. Look, will this be enough to go on with, for the time being? I'll send you more later.'

'Money changes hands. . . . It looks too much. I hate having to take it. Poor Jim: you made a rotten bargain.'

'Sydney's a big place. Do you have to go so far away?'

'Yes, I must.' Anything to get away from eyes.

'You're very young to go all alone.'

'Can't be helped, can it? I'll be all right.'

'How do you feel?'

'A bit sick. All right, really. I fainted the night before I brought you down — fainted in the tramcar. It was the first time ever in my life — the weirdest sensation. You get cold in the middle of your forehead, and your arms won't lift up. Don't they make a noise? This is a horrible place — chattering, chattering, like an aviary.'

'Have you told anyone at all?'

'Only Simone Purcell. She knows — but not your name.'

'Girl friends aren't usually discreet.'

'Simone's all right.'

'Won't you eat something?'

'No, thank you. Jim — '

'What?'

'I'm sorry if I seem chilly about it. I did love somebody once, frightfully. This is just like a dream. I was trying to get over the other, and I couldn't. Perhaps you were, too. It's no use our getting married unless we can't help it. It wouldn't work, would it?'

'I suppose not. I came down here — '

'With a perfectly open mind. I know. And not wanting me. Unless I can't help it, you're not going to have me, either. But you do understand, don't you?'

'Of course.'

'Then all we've got to do is to stick together and stand firm. If I die and the baby shouldn't, you promise you'll have it for your son? You do promise, don't you? I'd leave your letters with Simone. . . .'

'You wouldn't need to. I promise.'

'Then that's all, isn't it?'

'Just about all, except that I'm sorry, too. Where shall I write to you?'

'Oh, care G.P.O. I'll be Mrs White. Nice and contradictory. Mother would say Mrs Unmitigated Scarlet.'

'Very well, Mrs White. Do you want me to stay down until you've sailed? I had to make rather a rush trip of this, and some of them will be wondering.'

'No. I'd much rather you didn't.'

'Then this is *auf Wiedersehen*.'

'Yes. I thought that about you before, the last night at the boarding-house, but you see, it didn't happen so. You've got tears in your eyes, Jim. Is it the first time this has ever happened to you?'

'Yes. Is it the first time with you?'

'You ought to know that.'

'I do. Then *auf Wiedersehen*, and good luck. Don't forget to cable me if you're in any sort of hole.'

'I'll be all right. If they only wouldn't clatter the dishes. Good-bye and good luck, Jim.'

'I suppose you hope you'll never see me again?'

'It just happened like this, didn't it? Neither of us could help it — much. We're so nearly in the same box. Good luck.'

At the last moment, Simone came down to the wharf. Toby Brian was with her — fair-haired, good-humoured, obstinate in a bulldoggy sort of way; a bodyguard for Simone against Simone. Her eyes were very bright, her hair, against the fur coat which had cost her a year's skimping, looked finer, cleaner gilt than ever, almost as fine as it was before Simone had it cut short and waved. Simone sat on the bunk.

'Darling, you've got a cabin all to yourself. Monarch of all you survey.'

'It is nice, isn't it? Look at my little green portholes.'

'Write darling. These are for you. Miniatures.' She fled, and was standing beside Toby Brian, waving and waving from the wharf. The Hannays were there, a forlorn little row. Eliza knew that Augusta's shoes were hurting her, but that she had put on her best because Eliza's going to Sydney, where she might really strike it rich, was a kind of festive event; and John, uneasy, worried, thin in his shabby suit, was muttering under his breath, 'I can't understand her — can't understand her at all. Why can't she stay home and behave, like any other girl?' Blue streamer broke, rose streamer held. Long green seam of water, lapping, widening. Not since the war, when the troopships sailed camouflaged. The wharfies were nice, they gave us half-crowns for the Copper Trail. Sandra sang *Three Cheers for the Red, White, and Blue*, but I kissed my wharfie.

Little round New Zealand, blue and brown, with bright unfinished samplers of gorse. Eliza opened Simone's parcel to see the miniatures. She expected Simone had painted something funny, a souvenir. But the miniatures were quilted blue baby shoes, embroidered with cherry blossom. She looked at them blankly, then put her head down into the crack between the flawless narrow pillows. Timothy darling . . . you fool, stop crying, do you hear me, stop crying. . . . Timothy, come back quickly, come back.

CHAPTER NINETEEN

Alien Corn

DARK city of dreams, almost purple in the early morning when the ship docks; palm trees rising up like the frigid stalks of fountains, and houses down to the water's edge; no wildness, no great bare tawny patches or hills like the flukes of sea-monsters. Houses and purple dark, curious faces crowding through long arcades. From the first Eliza was frightened of the wheeled traffic, especially of the great horse-lorries lumbering down to the wharves and the markets. Horses are such kind old dears, this world's innocents; but the steady stream, wheel rumbling after wheel, unbroken and unbreakable, challenged her with a strength she had no mind to resist. You could stand on a kerbstone, muttering. (She had noticed old leaf-like people doing that.) Your voice grew shriller and angrier, as you realized that neither the line of lorries nor the wand of your fear would break, that there was nobody to hold up a magic hand and say 'Halt,' even to sympathize with you in your confusion. Crossing a Sydney street was an orgy of cowardice; exhaustion, when you reached the safety of the far side.

Dimly she realized, 'I wouldn't feel like this if I weren't ill.' But at hand there was no relief except the bright flagrant colours of the flowers, lovely Australian colours, piled high on handcarts and barrows, which were owned by little grotesque men, one-armed, one-legged, nobbly as gnomes, tending their sixpenny bunches in Martin Place. Iceland poppies were in, millions of gay pink and orange flags. After those the boronia and the redolent native roses, young redgum-tips from the mountains, shiny as new spider-webs. Flannel flowers came next, white with green tips, and on the first of September the wattle, masses and masses of fluffy chicken-gold balls.

Eliza said to her landlady, Ena Burns, 'I'm going to have a baby, and I'm not married.' She hadn't intended to, but as Ena stood watching her unpack, there was a pale insatiable hunger for knowledge in her face which drew out facts like a magnet. Ena didn't mind. She murmured, 'Men are dirty brutes. They oughta leave decent girls alone.' Eliza folded away her clothes in the chest of drawers. The big, dank room looked out on a perfectly flat little street, running along from nowhere to nowhere. The name of the suburb was pretty — Surry Hills. Eliza's taxi-driver was a pirate, and demanded ten and sixpence for bringing her from the docks, but she was afraid to quarrel with him, and paid over. She had worked out the strength of the money Jim gave her; it came to nearly £2 a week, if he sent some more later for the nursing-home and the doctor. She paid Ena thirty shillings in advance, and decided soon to go out shopping and buy things for her baby — lovely things, lace and hailstone muslin and little absurd caps. Since Simone had given her the miniatures, the baby didn't seem quite such a fantastic dream. She didn't love him — she loved nobody except Timothy and Simone, and, with a faraway dulled love, the lost people of the house at Calver Street. But she could think of her baby as an individual, very small and dark, with a white face and Jim's eyes. No children ran along outside her window, but men passed, dark and shapeless, their bodies exactly level with the edge of the Venetian blind. On the air was a heaviness of white dust. She closed her window, but dust seemed to live in the air.

When she went down the steps to the kitchen, Ena's husband, called Bill, her old father and a little girl of seven were seated at table waiting for her. She could see from their looks that Ena had told them why she was here. Bill lifted a sweat-red, shy, honest face, crowned with curly hair like a dog's, saying, 'Pleased t' meet you. Sit down.' Old Mr Simons had roughed it in his day, and bore the trade-marks. He had lost an arm and a leg, his skin was bright yellow, and a Chinese moustache straggled white against it. When he moved about the kitchen, he stuck the stump of his leg through the crutch-handle, and hopped, a ragged trouser-end flapping. You could see where his stump ended and nothing began. He was shrill and querulous. 'Let's have tea, Ena, can't yer? Gitting late, it is that, and I want me tea.' The little girl, with a quaintly Japanese face under short-cut bright yellow hair, sidled up to Eliza. 'My name's Polly. Tell us a story. Tell Polly a story.' Then another child crawled out from under the table. Its face was very dirty, and as it stood smiling uncertainly, its white legs wobbled. There was a sixpenny coloured ball in its hand; to tell its age, from its preternaturally aged face, was impossible. Polly ran up to it and hit it to get the coloured ball. 'That's the kid next door,' she explained. 'We've got to mind him 'cos his mummy's sick. He's only not crying because you're here. He always cries if I punch him. Give me your ball.' She hit the dirty child again, and he suddenly found his voice. 'She hit me on my cut,' he shrieked, 'she hit me on my cut.' Polly said, 'Well, give us your ball,' and the dirty child sobbed. A Rosella parrot, dainty red and grey, laughed in its cage. 'Have some frankfurts,' said Ena, stringing bright scarlet, scalding little sausages out of the pot. They all ate frankfurts and pickles, bread and cheese. A whippet bitch edged under the table and crowded their knees, quivering with its sensitive, half aristocratic, half mongrel head against Bill's knees. 'Good dog,' said Eliza politely, and the thin liver-coloured dog cowered. Bill's face brightened. 'We're going to run her soon. Aren't we, girlie? Who's a lick of greased lightning?' Ena said, 'You and your dogs!' Her flat voice held the perfection of scorn.

After supper Polly showed Eliza the backyard. It had been bricked, but the bricks were falling apart, and a horse lived there, shoving its white inexplicable face over a box. Where it stamped, the earth was greasy with manure. The little boy from next door wobbled out and stood smiling, but Polly ran and smacked him. 'You get along inside, we don't want you here.' There were fowls and a scraggly cat. Eliza told Polly the story of the three bears. She was bright-eyed, but liked the same thing over and over. 'Tell us again, tell us again,' she shrilled. Then suddenly she burst into shrieks of laughter, and ran inside the house. A little later, from her bedroom window, Eliza watched Polly in the street. She had the little boy from next door by the fist, and was showing him, quite carefully, how to play hopscotch.

The bathroom was up a flight of rickety stairs, and the water had to be carried in basins. 'It was full of coal when we came here,' said Ena. Ena and Bill's bedroom was beyond it, and Polly's cot stood now in the same room, while the old man slept on a couch in the kitchen. 'It don't matter about Polly. She's only a little 'un, and we had to put her there now we've got a boarder,' Ena said.

The bright insatiable hunger in her eyes was not easily appeased. She was a sallow wisp, her neck swollen with goitre, flat strands of lustreless brown hair parted round her face. Two of her babies had died, and she had a miss last year. 'It's the milk,' she said, without resentment. 'And that hospital's something cruel. Tessie was a dear little thing, but her bowels didn't act. And when they'd got us to put her in there, they kept us sitting and sitting outside, and all the time she was dying, black in the face. The other one, Gert, died of the croup. You don't need to go into that hospital to have yours, if you don't want to. You could have it here. I had all mine on the couch downstairs. Mrs Molloy is a wonder at it. But the trouble with her is, she drinks a lot.'

'Didn't you have any chloroform?'

'I held on to a towel. The last baby caught somehow, and we was two nights waiting, and Mrs Molloy making cups of tea, and cups of tea, and reading the cards to try and cheer me up. That hurt something awful. If you like I'll help you do your shopping for the baby.'

'I wish you would. That would be very kind of you, I don't know the names of the shops.'

'Oh, it's nice to get out a bit, isn't it? Shopping's a bit of fun. We can go to Dyers', they've got the time-payment.'

'What's time-payment?'

'You put a bit down, and get the things when you want them. It's no use your getting a lot of baby-clothes you mightn't need, is it?'

She had said it herself, Eliza remembered: I won't live, or else the baby won't live, so you haven't got to marry me. But something in her cried out against Ena, fierce and angry. She silenced it. Ena was only being sensible.

'I'm very tired, Mrs Burns. I think I'll go to bed.'

Is it like this? Funny little streets running nowhere, like those sentences in conversation that you never remember, and horse manure on the broken bricks, holding on to the towel, and dust, and dust?

Courage is a beautiful sleek horse, she thought, a thoroughbred, with its eyes blazing and the wind tapering round its ardent flanks. It is sensitive and swift, nerved for the one crucial thing. I haven't got that. Only the slow, plodding mule-gait: and I give in often, and cry for help, but when help doesn't come, I can manage, as a rule.

It is light very early in the Sydney mornings, not with a clear, sharp burst of light but with a humid grey veil. At noon the torpor is intolerable. The moist colours of the fruit reach their peak of incandescent brightness; then they bloat, like dead things, and commence to rot.

Ena Burns and Eliza went shopping at Dyers'. Ena's light eyes were hungry as they roved over the soft crumply baby-things. It wasn't that she had another coming, even that she thought of childbearing except as one of the inevitable, irritating punctuations which break the long sentence of life. But the cold little red-haired creature beside her, not showing it yet, only a bit pale and dreamy about the eyes, picked up things that crumpled light and sweet as flowers, and said, 'I'll have this,' 'I'll take that,' for all the world as if she were a duchess. Her clothes were good, too — a narrow dark green frock that wouldn't look so comfortable on her inside two months, a prancy little hat of leather. She wasn't like some, crying their eyes out with the shame of it. You could see she didn't like the idea of Mrs Molloy, who had been good enough to bring Polly into the world, and Gert, and little, darling Tessie, the one that Ena had loved best of the lot.

Thin blue dirty milk in the cans . . . summer sickness, she'd better go into the hospital, Mrs Burns. Nonsense, we'll have her right as a trivet in no time. No, you must wait, Mrs Burns, Doctor is on his rounds. I'm sorry, Mrs Burns, there was nothing we could do. Oh, no. . . . None of that for green-and-leather; a decent hospital, and a doctor with chloroform in case her high-and-mightiness might have to find out a little of what real life is like; and these white baby-things that crinkled up — all for being no good. Yet Ena didn't want green-and-leather to stop buying. The mere sight of the things being folded away, their swish against the crackling brown paper, gave her pleasure. She would have liked to go on and on, buying the store out. Afterwards they went downstairs and ate at the cafeteria; at least, green-and-leather looked sick and said it was a little too hot for her to eat, and Ena stolidly ate her way through from pie and Worcester sauce to peche Melba, for which green-and-leather couldn't do anything less than pay.

Within a fortnight, Ena started taking the starch out of green-and-leather. To her own surprise, she found it was quite easy. She could go to lengths she wouldn't have believed. Starch on top, softy underneath. She asked Eliza to give her a hand about the house in the mornings, watched for a few days, then pulled on her scarlet beret, went out, and got herself a job at the shoe-factory. She said to Bill, 'Mrs White *said* she don't mind helping, Bill,' and Bill agreed that the extra bit of money would go handy. He was embarrassed, his big red-brown hands caressing the whippet bitch beneath the table. When women wanted to fight, his motto was, leave them in the ring and let them go to it. Nothing was ever said, but by the way his wife handed green-and-leather her food at table, he knew there was a war on. Ena took peculiar pleasure in leaving her bedroom for Eliza to fix, the double bed hot and tousled. She was weak in her kidneys since little Tessie had come and gone again. If Eliza left anything undone, Ena moved about with a tight, shut mouth, but Polly came sidling up. 'Mummy says you didn't shake the mattresses proper this morning.' The summer swelled like a great red child in the belly of a sky, and the house became filled with whirring flies. Sometimes they caught in cobwebs, and their death-agonies . . . whirr, whirr, whirrr . . . made Eliza sick. It was like having your brain drilled through. 'We'll soon fix them,' said Ena, and came home with long spirals of dark-brown fly-paper, which swung directly over the table as she layed out the unchanging frankfurts. On them the brown flies stuck and buzzed; if you listened to them long enough, their buzz was the scream of maddened horses, of every scrap of life trying to break free from death. Ena watched and smiled. Bill's big disconsolate hands cosseted the whippet bitch, and the old man shunted himself about the kitchen, his stump sticking through his crutch. Sometimes Polly came edging up, lonely little yellow-haired elf-child. 'Tell us a story. Tell Polly a story. Tell Polly again.' Sometimes she ran lithely out into the yard of broken bricks or the flat street, and the yells of the little boy next door came down. 'She's hitting my cut. She's hitting my cut.'

You were never clean, Eliza thought, until you'd got away from that house where the flies buzzed. Green, the stalky withered green of a Sydney park, was quite a long way off, but she got there, and sat on a bench sewing. The baby-coat, made like a midshipman's jacket, was so ridiculous that she knew at once it could never be worn, but she did not throw it away. One night, coming in, she turned on the kitchen light. The walls were covered with great black crawling things. They had wings, they might fly on you. . . . She shrieked, her hands brushing ineffectually at her dress, and Bill came running down the stairs. Bill was a Samaritan. 'Fuss over a few roaches,' grunted Ena, sleepily irritable. She was tired after her day at the shoe-factory, but besides her pay got all her shoes dirt cheap, red sandals, white canvas shoes for summer.

Thunder and lightning. Great cold blue flashes, perfectly silent across the sky, followed by the splitting peals. The sky was a blue flame-flower, you could burn in it, freeze in it. Great drops fell down, like marbles. You could hear their roundness break. Ena came in and slammed the bedroom window down.

It was a nightmare, but it had the saving grace of almost complete unreality: to be all the time in a daze, heavy and stupid, too heavy to save yourself. But the milk-floats were the trouble, jarring over the rough broken streets from dawn till about six. At nights Timothy came back in a ship, not to Sydney, to Wellington. There were the bluegums, gleaming and steadfast, there the wavering columns of light in the harbour water. The ship's cabin had the old furze smell of his tweed coat, the one coat Eliza had ever seen him wear. There was no quarrel between them, though everything was known: only the quick, ecstatic flinging back into old companionship, old laughing love. But somehow they were never able to land, though they could see the streets steep in front of them, black and silver, wet with moonlight as with heavy scouring rain.

A man in a café stabs another man through the cheek with his fork. Funny to see. Another man speaks in the pictures, follows, only a little drunk. Somebody to talk to, perhaps. Why is it that one being a man, one being a woman who is going to have a baby, matters? I'd talk to almost anyone, gladly, but you can see what an impossible position. . . . Vaguely she turned and wandered up the street, followed by the drunken man's 'Gor bless you. Gor bless you, lady.'

Another man said that. The doctor to whom she went when she wanted to feel a little less ill. He scowled at first, his face pursed up. 'I don't do that sort of thing myself. But I'll give you a letter. . . .'

'Oh, that isn't what I meant at all. It's only that I felt so sick, and I didn't know what to do about it. I want the baby.'

The doctor said, 'You *want* the baby?' His tired face stared down for a moment. Then he scribbled out a prescription. 'God bless you, my dear. God bless you.'

Ena had told her about the street called Abortionists' Row. It looked quite respectable from the outside. She went there now, and walked down it in the slow drizzle of rain, thinking about the doctor and the baby. That she had said, 'I want the baby,' even accidentally, made a difference. A little hard knot of defiance formed in her throat. The shabby old red houses looked out through their bleared eyes, but they weren't everything. Beyond loomed the night, lace-edged with foam at Coogee and Manly, filled with just that crisp black blowing softness which had been all wonder a little time ago. It hasn't changed at all, she thought, it's only myself. It's one of those dreams when you come on wearing no knickers, or something like that, and are terrified out of your wits in case all the staring eyes concentrate upon you. But, Lord, you wake up. I'm going to wake up.

She walked on through the full maze of the little boxed streets, whose nonentity became sinister when one had passed twenty of the same shape and size. Gramophone music lurched out between the long beaded fringes which covered the doors. But in some streets, silence hung like a thick cloud, and all the street-lamps were smashed. There were Dalmatian cafés, and straggle-lettered notices said 'Good beds 1/6.' One man spoke; then, grinning with his broken teeth, he said, 'Aw, you needn't try to kid me, girlie.' Of the men she did not feel at all afraid. The women, sullen at the street corners, were more ominous. As they moved, the great full breasts under their sleazy jumpers swung like udders, their sullen faces and feet might tread the world down. But more than that was the voiceless, lightless cry of the streets, and its words were, 'I kill.' What brutal hand pressed them down? What stirred the filth into the blue thin milk, so that little Tessie died; and made the women these heavy things, and the men scuttling crabs under the vast stone of darkness? There was something to be done. As from a cellar the lean white tentacles of a plant reach up for chlorophyll, so all this world brutally demanded light. And it was right. It was right that a million should suffer, if they were irrelevant to that climbing purpose.

She was looking for the smell of the gorse. Dark nights in New Zealand, she reminded herself, always mean the smell of the gorse. She did not find it, but came out at last on a sea place, cliffs cracking immense over the pearl and ebony fans of the waves, which spread and dissolved far below. For a moment, hearing the sonorous voices of eddies in unseen caverns, she thought, 'I'll throw myself over, that's what I'll do,' and the purpose seemed sane and beautiful, the calmest thing left in life. But a stray cat sleeked against her legs, and she spoke to it gently. Its little singing-box expanded inside its chest. It was so pleased to be alive, alive and in conversation.

She knew it was a lie that she hated life: a lie that she hated the streets, and Bill, and Ena, and Polly. They were right, they were the resistless ones. . . . Only in this life at least, the barrier between them was too high to be broken down. The dark grew up in little thornbushes, its cold black winds jagged her cheeks and fingers. The cat purred and arched, flinging himself, in a crescendo of little growling noises, against her knees.

CHAPTER TWENTY

Thorny Mauds

WHEN Kay, undressing, stretched up her arms, her skin was clear honey-brown, and the white silk she wore crisped softly against it, like foam on sand. She despised girls who didn't wear white underneath. She was coolness on the eyes, because she always looked so fresh. Her hair was a shiny black shingle that might have been varnished on her round head, her brown eyes soft enough to be Maori eyes, but livelier — old sherry, not treacle. The American sailor boy said of her, in his long drawl, 'Say, you're just like them little leaves when they come out — not the green ones, the little pink ones.' People were always falling in love with Kay, desperately and inconclusively. She called them Jimmie and Johnno and Hugo-Love, and gave them toehold on her sunny raft.

'Did I hurt you much? I didn't mean to barge into you like that. I'm always barging.' Then Kay's open sunny face changed; Eliza felt herself draw up, tight and hard, inside her green gown. 'She knows,' reported the hard, tight self, 'I can't wear this dress any more. I must be getting conspicuous.'

Rightly, then, her self should have taken her by the shoulders, swung her round and marched her off. But instead of this, Kay and herself were walking along together, talking; and Kay said, 'You're going to have a baby, aren't you? I'm a nurse. . . . Oh, *that's* nothing.' And she told several stories about girls who had illegitimate babies. Their babies were always the prettiest and smartest. 'Because they're the little wild roses,' said Kay. They bought some Thorny Mauds from a fruit barrow, tiny green-cased mandarins, thirty for sixpence, full of sweetness inside their vivid shells. They went to the Haymarkets, where every nationality sold every product. Chinese held by the legs squawking poultry, and sold viridian blocks of ice-cream. Kay crunched three between her strong white teeth. 'Nothing makes me sick. But maybe you'd better not.' They bought sixpenny bunches of native roses, hot pink, and tucked them in their gowns. One shop had in its windows a wonderful raffle trousseau, value 400 guineas, a dozen of everything, all in *crêpe de Chine* and lace. They took raffle tickets. 'But look at me,' protested Eliza, half-laughing, half-crying. 'That won't last for keeps,' said Kay, 'you can't tell me, I'm a trained nurse.'

They were in the Peking Café, and blue paper birds, like creatures on

205

the painted lanterns sent long ago by Grandmother-in-China, soared out on threshing streamers, softly hitting outstretched palms. Then the smell of coffee made a broad brown river, all down a street where little shops ground it piercingly new in their mills. As they walked side by side, Eliza talked in a high self-pitying voice about Ena and the roaches and making the slovenly warm beds, which made her feel sick. Kay said, 'But don't you pay?'

'Of course I do, thirty shillings a week. But I said I'd help, or she said it, and then this happened.'

'Then why don't you clear out? Sydney's a big enough place, goodness knows.' Kay stopped, and said accusingly, 'You're afraid of them.' Her eyes were two little brown gardens. Eliza cried, 'Stop, Kay — you don't understand. It's not ordinary being afraid — it wouldn't be much use if I were, everything's happened, and I can't get worse hurt than I am. But everything seems unreal, don't you see? My hands and feet don't feel as if they belong to me, they're so funny and far away. If I put out the light at night, it's like a thick blanket crushing down on me, I can feel it lying over me. I can't be bothered fighting them when I feel like that.'

Kay said, 'You ought to move away from there.' There was a hole in the flimsy golden sunshine, through it she could melt away as easily as she had come; she stood on the Sydney pavement, brown and lithe, and behind her shoulders the Gardens sloped down, two rows of dirty plaster casts, cut grass, then the sea.

Eliza said, 'All right, Kay. I'll move. I'll start looking for a new place to-morrow.' As soon as she had said it, she was real again, and knew that she could actually move. Life was a queer music, shot through with many colours. Kay said, 'Let's walk down Greek Street. I think it's rather romantic, all those funny dago shops.' Eliza's problem being cleared up, Kay herself became faintly sad, after the fashion of one young girl with another, when their story is not stale between them. She talked in her clear, full voice of a married man she had loved once. And he had gone away, leaving a great bunch of red canna lilies outside her door, and she was always thinking he might come back again. But meanwhile there were Jimmie and Johnno and Hugo-Love, and they all proposed.

Polly sat battering the lid of a tobacco tin against the bricks in the backyard. She sang to herself as she played, a little shrill war-chant. Her streaky yellow hair flew back from her Mongolian face. Ena came in when Eliza had nearly finished packing. The clean white things she had bought for her baby spread over her hands. Ena's sallow little face, with the heavy goitre underneath, fell into its lines of sullenness. She said, 'Well, you didn't seem to make yourself at home, Mrs White.'

'Your father was horrible to me. And you knew.'

'I think Dad was quite right,' said Ena. But it didn't matter what she said, there was a taxi outside, and Eliza could say, 'We're all square about money, aren't we?' Only, far beyond them, far out of their individual reach, the fight went on, the fight of the dying slum plants for their sunlight, the antagonism of the dying slum plants for anything that got in their way. In the long run, it had to be Ena who won: not because she was worth more, but because her hair was lustreless under the wet red streak of her tam-o'-shanter, and because she held on to a towel when her babies came. But for the moment Ena's victory hung suspended. Eliza went out from the little house, and saw in the strips of brick and mud big sunflowers, heavy-headed like the little boy from next door. They nodded their thick brown and clarified gold in gardens Eliza would never see again. As the taxi jerked, she thought of one line Rainer Maria Rilke had written, and it said everything for them, though they would neither hear nor care:

Children and cherry trees are always ailing.

She went first to a high, cold, central hostelry, many stories high, and lined with blue-and-white tiles. It had lovely bright bath-taps, nickel bright as silver. Months since she had swum in a really clean, really hot bath. She liked fingering the clean taps. Mostly she lived on Thorny Maud mandarins, but the sickness had gone away from her now, and she could go down into the underground cafés for a sixpenny hot meal each day. One place, run by two old Scotchwomen, was small and friendly. Eliza told them that her husband was away living in Melbourne, and they laughed, the kind, matey laugh of respectable women joking another into their circle. 'You'll have something to take home to him, won't you, dear?' After that, while she was hunting for lodgings, she nearly always had dinner at the Edinburgh.

She no longer hated Sydney: only sometimes the noise, sometimes the growing heat. But she had to be desperately careful about the next lodgings, because some of the little houses were vacuums, ready to suck in and swallow anyone strange, either for the money or for the sake of someone to talk to. The women were liked caged animals: no, worse, liked domesticated animals, all stare, and readiness either to scratch, or to be friendly once their curiosity was appeased. They saw she was going to have a baby, and they told her, leaning on their brooms, how their own were born and died. She walked along their streets, where the old flaky stucco was the same colour as the sunshine, and an Old Men's Home had the extraordinarily peaceful name, 'Sunset.' But she supposed, watching the old boys potter about in their garden of blind roses, that this too was Have, like most official things. At last she found a room in Stanmore, where the woman was taken up in her own daughter, seventeen and too pretty, and where nothing intruded but the blare of a radio through the wall. Kay came and celebrated, on new-ground coffee, strawberries and asparagus; they lay in their white knickers on the bed, trying to keep cool, and Kay told about her patients who had proposed, and the one who threw the flat-iron instead. But for most of the time, Kay would be out of town. She was qualified to take private cases, and went anywhere.

Under the huge Moreton Bay fig trees in Centennial Park, grass tangled in green undersea forests, stealthily cool. Boys and girls riding on ponies made upright shadows across the asphalt that divided the two seas of grass, the last edging out towards a pond. Wild duck with pointed wings rose into the air, and flapped crying into the sky's greater mere. The liquid grass made its touch against hands and face, like old jade. The boys and girls were beautiful, with their brisk whipped faces and good hands carelessly on their bridle-reins. They did not ride fast, any more than a bird sings fast, but they urged their mounts into the cool of the morning, leaning forward slightly against the wind. Eliza sat watching them, or sometimes read Nietzsche and Melville, and odd scrappy books of poems picked up at the great Library where they would give you books as if you were a Prince, almost without asking who you were or whether you would really return them. While the grass touched her, her body seemed to live a rested life of its own, not disconnected from earth's vitality. But while her mind touched Nietzsche's book, a stinging clear exaltation ran into her, and she knew what it was Timothy had found lacking in her. Flavourless and cold, the minds that had never been touched by this writer who bore a sword and a burning brand. Then Melville's strange book, *Mardi*, ran by in a cool stream. A little unknown poet, Rachael Anne Taylor, said:

> Sleep, sweet, sleep —
> The gods of beauty seek in the spring
> From out of the world's white flowering
> Some delicate thing to keep.

She looked out with cool eyes across the ponds, and an old solemn couple, wandering by like two grotesque black ants, came and talked to her about the life beyond. 'Sister,' they called her. They were spiritualists who had lost an only daughter, and were perfectly convinced that by rapping and the pale light of séances, this missing ant would make herself manifest to them. They shook hands warmly with Eliza when they left. 'Dear Sister,' they said, 'Dear Sister.' And a leaf's weight shore through its stalk, like the thin neck of a young girl, and dropped into her lap. She walked past the lotus pool to Palm Drive, where at night the cars' lights were golden frightening dragons. Confusedly she thought, 'I'll not forget any of it.' The heaviness of her body was momentarily a sweet heaviness, and this grassy place its consummation.

Eliza was a sick restlessness, awake in the night, thinking, 'Cars, cars, cars. Radios. Why don't they turn off their radio. Bloody devils, I'd like them to be dead, I'd like to kill them. Why can't they turn off their cars and their radios?'

White face, black hair in small ringlets. Like the dream, but too white. Yet not cold to touch.

'Make me go to sleep, please. Make me go to sleep.'

You shall be betrayed again and again, on a lonely field, and your seed shall perish, or be taken from you. And always you are host to your own enemy — fear, pain, love, mortality.

It is easy to love the little dead. They make no heaviness, they are not a load to carry about. Yes, but the face which has never lived, only been seen for a moment, makes its own demand of a love that can never be wholly selfish. It is so lonely, so lonely.

The jacarandas are a far, pale mist, evening's colour drenching the leafless limbs of trees. Little buds nuzzle on the grey bark of those trees not yet in bloom, others still hold the lingering greenish colour of the sap. The coral trees prick up their scarlet ears. Lie so, relaxed and light, not in the labour-room but in a big old room upstairs, the first quiet room in the world. No more pain, but morphine. Go to sleep. That woman wrote:

> Sleep, sweet, sleep —
> The gods of beauty seek in the spring
> From out of the world's white flowering
> Some delicate thing to keep.

But the wrong one slept. Timothy would have been sorry, he wanted a baby, he would always have wanted my baby. He would have picked up my baby and carried him under the green rafters, running with long strides.

The morning after her baby was born dead, Eliza, still heavily drugged, recognized in her mind an old companion. She felt neither happy nor unhappy, merely still, as the nurse moved about the room. When she was alone, words ran in her mind, measured themselves, a steady chain of which no link was weak enough to break. Long ago, she had called the power 'it'. It was years since her poems had fallen into a foolish little rubble of shards and ashes, schoolgirl sentimentality. This was different. It was the old power back; but with a stronger face, an estranged face, it sat down in the house of her mind.

On the afternoon of the seventh day Ena Burns came. She entered in a little rush, her sallow cheeks reddening like the old tam-o'-shanter.

'Oh, Mrs White, I've been that upset about you.'

'She'll go away soon,' thought Eliza, lying flat and quiet, answering back when Ena wanted to be answered back. At last Ena did rise to go. She got as far as the door, came back, shook hands again, then hung about, uncertain. At last, her eyes over-bright, she spoke out.

'You'll give me something to remember you by, Mrs White?'

'Whatever you like.'

'His little clo'es. Since you wouldn't be needing them, I thought perhaps you'd give me his little clo'es. Even if it was only the shawl. . . .'

'Yes, yes. Of course you can have them.' Make your voice flat and quiet, quiet as your body.

CHAPTER TWENTY-ONE

No More of Me You Knew

IN the Blue Mountains the wildflowers pressed their millions of faces, all one peering eye, up through milky heat-haze and against the wide blue of the sky. There were other blues beneath, colours shredding into folds and folds, torn mists, nymph-like water-hues in the weeping Valley of the Waters, where through and under the creeping tears that seared the rock-walls, tiny green ferns trembled, each frond a precarious balance for a troy weight of dew. The ant chimneys, tall and very quaint, stood among the redgums; funny little beasts lived here in the mountains, Kay kept pointing them out as they folded up or ran by. That was a goanna, doesn't it look proud, the way it walks with its head and tail in the air? That was a wallaby, like a little old man.

You stood on a peak, a flat spur of rock running out into the void, with your thin light body propped up by the winds, which streamed imperiously, almost visible in their long robes, down and up the gullies. The screech of falling rock came up, and the rattle of the hard waters. All the time, somebody kept saying, 'Isn't this lovely? Oh, boy, isn't this air glorious?' and you said 'Yes, it's very beautiful, Yes it's glorious.' Better to lie still at night between the two reds of moon and smouldering campfire. The world was loud with insects, and at dawn you could see the ground under the blankets exuding streams of red ants; life marching on, a harsh colour, but seemingly not at all impatient or angry.

Sometimes Eliza wished the clay soil could make itself less red. Three bluegums in the cemetery, faceless white daisies; and she had forgotten, utterly forgotten what the cemetery's name was; only that you crossed a bridge over blue water to get to it, and Kay, pointing, said there were oysters down there. Lot 125, Section 4. She remembered that perfectly, and the old man who had given her a lift to the next station in his gig when she missed the last train, but she didn't like to ask the cemetery's name, because Kay would think her absurd. She thought, 'He's little and lost and hasn't got an identity, only a face, and I'm almost the only one who saw it. Not that I asked much for him.' At other times, she put it out of her mind. Best not to think of it, to be a body balancing on a clifftop, no longer at all ungainly or needing to be hidden away: to say quickly the light, bantering things required by Kay's brown young men. The myriads of soft flannel flowers crowded out space, and everlastings with their

211

paper hearts fringed in prickly petals, ruby and umber. Dead flowers, you could only last by being dead. The air was cool here, a fragrant stinging coolness in which the upreaching heat of summer was dissolved. At night they sang in the campfire's circle, then crawled under their blankets, complaining a little about the soldier ants and the hardness of the ground. There was nothing else, it was a hiatus in time and space, and in the mornings the squatting backs of the boys looked like those of brown savages, as they brewed the first coffee.

At one rock water came widely down in lace flounces. As you watched, these turned to stalactites, moving with a slow hypnotic movement that sent the green and blue world, cut from its moorings, steadily sliding up and up. In a while this movement was inverted, and the pointed branches of water-trees led the sight downwards, a thin spume of snow on their heavy fir-like green. Your body became a mere shelter for your mind, which watched, in detachment, all this written in water. Images came and went easily, like frost changing shape on a window-pane.

I want to go home. I want to go home.

Kay said, 'But, honey, you can't want to go back to that man, he's just a yellow dog. He didn't even write to you, and you might have been alive or dead.'

'But he was so exactly like the baby. Even its hands. I feel I've got to talk about it, don't you see? It's not himself, it's the baby.'

The brown boys got out of the car on the way home, to fetch them huge cones piled with ice-cream. But all the way was blowing with dust, billows of it, flying into eyes and hair and heart. You did nothing but sit patiently between them. Kay was a little worried, a little angry because she was anxious. But I'm not ill, darling Kay. Truly I'm all right. And I'll write to you, every week. Oh, I hate saying good-bye.

Kay was gone, and the ship pitched its squat length heavily along grey sea. From the bathroom portholes Eliza could see little circumferences of grey, heaving and flecked with white. They looked very cold. Suddenly in her body something seemed to break. She stood still, then steadied herself towards a basin, and watched the blood stream down. She felt not sick but dumb, like a beast that has been hit with a mallet and does not know how to cry out before it dies. But her body wouldn't die, her hands still mechanically gripped the silver-plated rails. Presently that was done, and she got herself back to the cabin, afraid to speak a word to anyone. The woman in the top berth looked at her with tired, resentful eyes. The rhythm of the boat was very monotonous . . . throb, throb, throb, heavy and plaintive, like the march of the red ants. All endeavour could be made to fit that octave.

Over in Sydney, she thought, at this time of the year all the gardens would be parched and brown, and I'd be lying with nothing on, probably in a cold bath that would feel hot and sticky, wondering how on earth I'd ever get cool again. Here the Christmas lilies, wet with the rain that fell the day of her coming back, were broad white cups, their gold stamens sticking up, nearly drowned. She thought, 'How thirsty they'd be in Sydney now, how terribly thirsty.'

She had no right in the world to come here, to be sitting in a hotel bedroom listening to this one man talk. For it had been perfectly understood between them, Eliza had said it herself — if my baby dies, you won't have to marry me, you needn't ever hear of me again. Dark eyes, dark hair, dark square-cut hands. Jim was saying, 'I'm a married man.' She moved her head from side to side. 'That nice girl? Annie Carr?'

'It was Mrs Wetherby.'

'But she's quite old — how could you have done it, Jim? She's quite old, quite old.' Jim's face was angry, and she said, 'You must have married before I was out of the hospital.' It was all unfair, uselessly unfair. You let the dead bury their dead; only, the labour of heaving their soil upwards, single-handed, without a week's delay, because they have to be out of sight this very minute. And she couldn't remember the name of the cemetery. She cried out, and Jim said in a voice which was quiet, yet twisted like his old bitter look, 'You can't stay here. I'm taking you home.'

'Then does your wife know?'

'Yes. I had to tell her.' Jim put his arm through Eliza's, and led her carefully down the hotel stairs. They were out in the dark streets, and he said again, 'I had to tell her, you see.' She did not listen. She walked by means of putting one foot in front of the other foot, until they were at the gate of a house, and Jim called out to its lighted doorway.

It was her twenty-first birthday, and Cecily was giving her a birthday tea; not anyone else, of course, just their three selves. After they had talked a little, and Eliza had promised not to cry any more or to tell anyone about the baby, they were perfectly reconciled. There was an iced cake, cut open darkly rich to show cherries and walnuts. Eliza said, 'I never had any birthday party before, because my birthday is in the summer. We always picnicked at Day's Bay. And I was always promised a special one for my twenty-first; I'm twenty-one to-day.' But while they smiled at her, wise and consoling, the table and the iced birthday cake went into a throbbing brownish-red colour which seemed to come from her forehead. She stood up and fell. She felt Jim help her up, towards the bedroom. 'It doesn't matter,' she said, polite through the scum of brownish colours, 'I think to-morrow I'd better go straight away. Straight down to Wellington.' She knew they would both be pleased at that, and in the morning Cecily was so kind, so heartily kind. Two young men were to drive Eliza part of the way, to the railway junction. 'It won't do to have you looking like a little ghost,' she said. 'A girl can't ever let her face go to wrack and ruin.' She dusted sweet-scented powder over Eliza's face. 'Now just a *touch* of colour. There, doesn't that make all the difference?' The painted face looked out with thick indifference from the mirror, it was like one of Carly's dolls, but sleepier. Jim waited outside by the hedge to say good-bye. He didn't say anything except again, '*Auf Wiedersehen*'. He broke off a piece of the dark velvety-red geranium growing in the hedge, and put it in the pocket of Eliza's coat. His mouth smiled uncertainly. There, he's gone, she thought, he's gone, and I didn't love him, I hadn't any right at all in that place. Now I've got to forget all about it. The car broke down on a white-blistered road between two gullies of fern, and the two boys were unhappy at keeping her so long in the sunshine. But she smiled at them and joked, sitting erect.

They said, 'You're a sport,' and the car limped at last into a garage. While they drank lemonade there, she could see great grey rats running along the rafters, looking down with beady eyes.

'I won't go on to-night,' she told them presently, 'I'll stop here at this hotel. It looks quite comfy, and it won't be so tiring as going straight through in the one day.' The boys waved good-bye, and she turned back to the hotel, through whose bedroom windows showed the sliding green of river enamelled with willow-leaves. When she had unpacked her night-things and tidied her hair, she went out to find a chemist's shop. The first chemist was curtly positive in his refusal to give her anything that would make her go into a sound sleep. But the second one sold her a dozen packages of a white fine-crystalled powder, and another one gave her tablets. By that time, there were no shops left to try in the little street. She took the powders and the tablets in her bedroom, all together, drinking the hot staled water out of the hotel carafe to wash them down. They tasted bitter. She lay down, watching the river slide by. Just before sleep had taken possession of the thin populous world of dreams there was a knock on her door. She stood upright, crossed the room and opened it. A man was in the hall, his face contorted in one of the queer apologetic smiles which sometimes people wear when they are lonely and ashamed. She remembered having seen him in the hotel lobby. He said something about having a talk, and smiled again. Eliza pushed the door to, and drove in the bolt. Sick things, mortally wounded things, they leave a trail of weakness on the air, and you follow. But I'm dying now, and there you can't follow me. The ringing of bells was very heavy in her ears as she walked again to the bed.

I can't be really alive, she thought, it's a dream. But the willow leaves shirred their pale brightness against her window, and in the river the gleams of sunlight caught and dinted like swooping dragonflies. Then she didn't know quite where to go, what to do. She dressed and walked through the town, and parts of it closed misty behind her, like the cemetery which held Lot 125, Section 4. She was in a green hot place, sitting by the lake's edge and watching. There was nothing else to do. She ate nothing, but thirst came, and presently she bought from a woman with a little sweet-stall a poisonously green bottle of soft drink. It was called Green Water. Its colour and acrid taste mixed with the river sliding under her hotel bedroom, the man who had pushed against her door, and the cold undine lake where once she had stood with Jim, looking down. I can't go back there, she thought; I must catch the train to-night. But she had no idea of really getting to Wellington, really trying to be alive. She wondered if the chemists would give her any more tablets or powders. Out of town, she found another little shop, and bought there all she could get. She didn't know the names of any drugs, except morphine, and that, she knew, she couldn't possibly get. Mention it, and they'd stare her out of the shop. She said, 'Something to make me go to sleep, please,' and the little sharp-faced man said this ought to fix it, he knew what insomnia was.

The train was in the station. Somehow it seemed the best idea to take the powders, and stand on one of the little black jolting platforms. When the train curled round the first rough bend, your drugged body would be jolted off, and everybody would say, 'How sad — an accident.' But she took the powders too soon. She saw the train standing in the station, knew as clearly as she had ever known anything in her life that she must walk quietly across the platform and board it. There was nothing more to be done, only that easy step. But everything went black dark, darkest dark.

She wakened in a little lighted room. Against her skin she could feel the prickling harshness of canvas, her arms were strapped close to her sides. But her hands were free, and quietly she began to unfasten the straps. A weary-looking girl in a nurse's cap nodded there, inhuman in the naked light. She roused suddenly, and called out. Then a young white-gowned man came in, and stood at the head of her bed; his hard voice said, 'Well, young lady, where's the baby?'

Eliza said coldly, 'My son is dead.' Then it was black dark again, an escape, for that white-lit room, the easy curl of the doctor's lip as he stared down and said where's the baby, were a rape not of the body but of the soul.

The doctor next day was uneasy, jocosely polite. 'Well, you gave us a scare that time. But there's somebody waiting to see you. We found two letters in your purse.'

When the strange young man entered the room, Eliza could not understand why they had ever let him in. He was nobody she knew. Yet vaguely, like words out of a broken sentence, the old answer to a riddle she had forgotten, he commended himself to her. He sat with his hat twirling between his knees, his fair thick hair brushed back, and said, 'I'm very sorry that you've been ill.'

'I've forgotten so many things; it's silly, isn't it? I'd be scared to let anyone know how much I've forgotten. But I can't . . .'

'I'm Laurence Cardew,' said the fair young man, 'Timothy's brother. It was his letter in your purse, you see. Miss Hannay, I don't know how to tell you . . .' Go on talking, go on twirling your hat and talking.

'Is Timothy home yet? Or has he married and settled down in England? We were great friends, Mr Cardew.'

Laurence said, in quick, agitated jerks of speech, 'He was always fond of you, far fonder than he'd ever admit, even to himself. About two days after he took ill, he got delirious, so there weren't any messages. It's a horrible thing, a hateful thing. I can hardly believe it even now.'

'You mean that Timothy is dead, too?'

'Three months after he landed in England. He had pneumonia and bronchitis. You know, that chest of his was always weak. He wrote home saying he'd struck a good job, and he sounded so happy, and then . . .'

'But he really did die? Where did he die?'

'I shouldn't have told you. They said you were all right now. He died in Birmingham. He'd just gone there.'

'He went to England, and he died in Birmingham. I wonder if there was anyone there who knew him?' Laurence sat twirling his hat, and Nurse opened the door.

'There's another visitor for you.'

'Well, old dear,' said Augusta. Her face looked seamed and ashen-grey, she was wearing the horrible fabric gloves that burst their seams, or came undone at their tops. She smiled and said, 'Well, old dear.' Eliza kissed her on the cheek. But there wasn't any place on earth where you could lie still as long as you liked, whether you took tablets or not. No place on earth except Birmingham.

CHAPTER TWENTY-TWO

Carly

CARLY never looked now at her glory-box, but it was neither destroyed nor taken away, and she never wore any of the soft folded things which she had embroidered with such patience that they seemed like parts of herself — green, primrose and pale blue *crêpe de Chine* appendages, with Richelieu work, wreaths of lazy-daisies or cross-stitch designs. Several Christmases ago, everybody had stopped giving her cups and saucers, *crêpe de Chine* odds and ends, 'for your box, Carly'; everybody except a few of her girl friends, who had gone away to live in other places, and didn't know that Trevor's 'understanding' with Carly was over and done with.

She pressed her forehead against her bedroom window, wrinkling it till she looked like a marmoset. At the moment she was thinking not of Trevor, but of Kirsty Blake. Kirsty was her best girl friend, tall and thoughtful (though capable of a good laugh) and rather religious, in a scared way; very much under her mother's thumb. Often Kirsty and she had talked about going into an Anglican Sisterhood together.

Kirsty was out there, directly opposite, beyond the mist which hung grey and strange over the cemetery. Carly had a snapshot in her album showing all the wreaths propped up, and neatly labelled, 'Kirsty's grave.' Dead-and-buried. It had all become quite normal. Death was queer until people started to hop round taking measurements — so much for a nice concrete railing, so much for a nice wreath from the office, so much for a nice china wreath under glass, so much for a nice In Memoriam, to be kept up every year in the evening paper. Poor old Kirsty, people said: Do you remember how she used to — and then, suddenly, you don't remember, neither the favourite colour nor the favourite kind of sundae, nor the screamingly funny thing Kirsty came out with at the staff picnic. The face, like the little yellow O of light at the end of a tunnel, slips quite away.

Three tragic things, thought Carly; they say things always happen in threes. Trevor; then Kirsty; and then Eliza. At the thought of Eliza, the little curtain dropped down over her mind, as it had at school when any of the other children mentioned something that Augusta would think dreadful. Children who talk about such things, said Augusta, are horrible children, you must never play with them. You can't touch pitch and not be defiled.

Your sister has been ill and had a nervous breakdown. That was all. Now Eliza was away down in the South Island, getting less terribly, leaf-like thin, less vague about the eyes. She wasn't often talked about, but Carly knew her mother worried. John — except for the fact that one of his daughters had been ill, and he was sorry for her, Carly didn't think Eliza entered his mind once a month. Almost instantly he had retreated into his world of books, which grew and grew about him until squares and oblongs in brown-paper covers had completely conquered his little blue bedroom. And the others were young: Augusta knew, Carly guessed and wouldn't let herself look the guess straight in the eye, nobody else even questioned.

She hoped desperately that Eliza wouldn't come back and live in the house — live under this roof; this although, when Eliza had been so terribly ill, it was Carly who took her the only things she would eat, those Peek Frean animal biscuits. That Simone girl, whom they had always disliked, was in the room, but when Carly put the tin of biscuits into Eliza's hands, she sat up all of a sudden, and said smiling, 'Hullo, Carly — hullo, Simone.' And the Simone girl said, 'Darling, how beautifully white and clear your skin's gone — now you only need to lose those last few freckles from your nose, and you'll be quite good-looking.' Cat, Carly thought, green-eyed cat. Afterwards she had learned that the Simone girl had pleurisy quite badly when she came up on the train to see Eliza, and was sick for weeks, so it must have been brave of her. Just the same, Carly couldn't stand her. Kirsty's grave eyes, smiling somewhere behind the china wreaths, comforted her from the thought of girls with green eyes, who suddenly struck out, or just stared! Whom she did not understand.

Not here, not to be a mystery under this roof, and one that in time their mother couldn't help jabbing with her tongue. That would be awful. But one day, Carly thought, something might just come to pass, and you could *run* back into waiting, desolate love, into the empty playroom at Calver Street, with the packing-case doll's-house standing in the middle of the Chinese matting. Perhaps not until you were dead, like Kirsty, tall Kirsty with the glowing eyes. In life it was by no means safe to talk.

And now she had a hard thing to tell her mother. And in spite of Trevor Sinjohn and her many girl friends (Carly made girl friends easily, but they all got married and had babies), if it had fallen to her to say which one must die, Trevor, or any other of the Hannays, or her friends and their white woollen babies, she would unhesitatingly have saved Augusta and let the rest go.

She went out into the kitchen. Augusta was lying on the settee, with her feet up. She had fallen asleep over the evening paper, her mouth was just open, and she snored slightly, occasional, pathetic snores, ghosts of weariness. Her magnificent auburn hair was brindled, her body looked heavy and shapeless. Carly knew her mother had been through the change of life. That, and Eliza, and Dad's not keeping his promotion. The many queer, potentially dangerous things that happened to the body and mind of a woman, even if she stayed always respectable!

Augusta awoke wearily. 'Eh? Eh? What is it?' The kitchen was nearly dark. Carly slipped down to her old Kaffir squat beside the settee.

'Mum, I've got something to tell you.'

'Eh? Eh?' Then into Augusta's heavy body came back the spirit of dignity and command which made her Carly's wonderful mother. She said quite gently, 'You've something to tell me? What is it, child?'

'Mum, I've given up my job at the office. I've given in my notice.' Carly's body stiffened, waiting for Augusta to grow angry. Augusta sat up.

'You've *what*? Three pounds a week. You must be mad, Carly. Unless — it's not Trevor again?'

'Oh, *Mum*. No, it's nothing to do with him. I'm not going to marry, ever, you know that. It's something quite different.'

Augusta's voice became small, almost inaudible. She asked, 'Carly, you're not in any sort of trouble?' and Carly saw that her freckled hands were clutching the front of her dress.

'No, no. It's — ever since Kirsty died, I've been wanting to, Mother. When she was dying, she said the nurses were angels. It was almost the last thing she said to me. I wanted to be a nurse. I put my name down, months ago, but I didn't want to tell anyone until they'd accepted me.'

'Fifteen shillings a week, instead of three pounds — and you'll start among girls years younger than yourself, you're twenty-four. And how do you think you're going to stand up to operations — you, that went out and fainted in the wash-house when I had my toe lanced? I tell you, you're raving mad.'

'Not operations, Mum. I'm going to be a maternity nurse. I'm going into St Beth's.' Carly added, 'I like babies. I think I'd be quite a good nurse with babies.' For a moment they didn't speak. Carly's mind filled with a procession of white woollen babies. Oh, isn't he *darling*? The fingers, too teeny. Yes, Betty, of course I'll be godmother. Pink ribbons for a girl, blue for a boy. When they're born they weigh seven pounds and a bit. One candle on top of a white cake. Sweet talc powder smell — did they, then? Did they? Sally Meade suckling her baby girl, an operation which first made Carly feel shy, then developed into a lovely, laughing freedom, the very gayest thing she ever knew. Sally's baby was born five months after her marriage, but I didn't care, he's a little love. The man had married Sally, which made it all right.

Augusta, her voice harsh and heavy with pain, said, 'It won't be so easy as you think, my lady. I suppose you realize you'll have to sleep away from home?'

'I know. I hate that part of it. But I had to do it.' Looking down at the girl's head bowed in the dusk, Augusta both understood and failed to understand. Carly, the best of the bunch. . . . She still loved Eliza, in a dim way she even sympathized, and thought Eliza queerly beautiful — so long as Eliza and her secret weren't at home. As her child Eliza was lost and done with. The younger two were still her own, but unexplored yet; somehow another generation, remote and brittle. But her first child, the good, obedient one, who had done no more real wrong than if she had never left the cradle! A few childish fibs and tempers, a few tears; otherwise, Carly was her own still.

The first ten years of a girl's youth, she thought, the beautiful first ten years, that ought to be such fun, go on loving something in trousers. Mine did. There's no man so rotten he won't find some woman to coddle him. And after that, what's left? Physical and emotional wrecks, little ghosts.

'You don't know what you're doing, Carly. You're giving up a good job, three pounds a week. If you saved, you could be home to England. Why, when I was your age, and with no more education than a servant girl, I'd worked my way half round the world.' It was no use. Carly didn't want England, she wanted the nearest thing to the baby Trevor Sinjohn hadn't condescended to give her. Augusta's voice dragged, a child-bearing voice. Augusta's voice went with child, and the name of the child was resignation.

'Giving up a good job . . . jobs aren't so easy to get, when you're twenty-four.'

But Carly was winged, confident.

'I know I'll be happy, Mum. I'd love to nurse the babies.'

'First the babies have to get there,' grimly prophesied Augusta. But during the next fortnight Carly was happy. Her office gave her a lovely attaché-case, and she sat making caps and aprons, running them up on the old hand-machine, nearly past its time, which had made her first frocks. She tried them on before her mirror, humming:

Mid the war's great curse
Stands the Red Cross Nurse,
She's the rose of No Man's land,

one of the ballads still in vogue when the boys and girls used to group
singing around Laloma's piano. Augusta thought she looked still a child,
a brown-haired wisp of a creature who'd never get on. Carly in the nights,
a little scared, clenched her hands. Not a blank alley: not the dreadful,
dusty loneliness of going for ever into Mr Shorter's office, waiting, notebook in hand, while her dry voice rapped out answers to letters that
didn't matter, that became, if you looked at them in a certain light, quite,
quite insane. Now she would have to do with life, not with dust.

She went to St Beth's in a taxicab, waving wildly through the back
window. Augusta's thoughts ran about like mice as she padded around the
kitchen, getting ready a stew for John, Sandra and Kitch. A good job —
three pounds a week. She'll never stand up to it, poor little scrap. That
dirty swine. . . . Oh, if I'd only been a man, if your father had only
thrashed him. Lost your promotion, lost your promotion, lost your
promotion. You had to make a fool of yourself, showing the Bosses how
smart you were, and now look at you. Eliza — no. Not to be talked about.
She used to be such a dear little girl, always smiling. Jean Ingelow's poem:
'I had a nestful once of my own, ah, happy, happy I.' But you can't
encourage girls to hang about, they ought to be married. Tramwaymen,
road-workers. Tom, Dick and Harry. John, we're not going down to that
slum. You've dragged us here, but my children aren't going to that school.
At least he's a gentleman. Carly's Johannesburg gentleman. . . .

The steam of the stew became fragrant with onions, boiled tender, cut-
up bits of herbs, sage, sprinkled parsley and marjoram, which she had
grown herself. She did not dislike these things. The world was all right,
grubbing in the garden gave her a sort of freedom which made up for the
stiff crackle of her knee-joints when she rose. But it was when every
thought and feeling in your body became tied up with somebody else —
and it did, of course, however practical you tried to make yourself. Life
was a long waiting for the right dream, the right person, to come in at the
door. And that happened to be the Kingdom of Heaven.

Turning the gas low under the saucepan, Augusta went to the settee,
put her feet up and closed her eyes. Disked against the lids she saw
bracken, clear and brown, around the white house in England, the house
like a Greek cross. Winds ran nibbling at the fern, there was a great tree,

a copper beech. Her face relaxed in lines of weariness, her mouth opened a little. Sun came through the window, and spun a cobweb of red-gold over her old hair. To the alert yet drowsy things in her kitchen, the flames popping under the saucepan, the motes of dusty light, the three-years-old calendar with a blue-robed, non-Hebraic Madonna and Child, she was an old woman. They had known her for ages, they were safe in her hands. But it was not an old woman who lifted up her naked, enchanted face from the fern beneath the copper beech tree, whose leaves were still Jesus-mild with the newness of their sap, and had not yet hardened into rims of colour. Not an old woman, only a girl with red hair, teaching the copper beech tree its way into spring.

Carly didn't know where to put her hands, they felt so enormous. She clasped them behind her back, slipped them into the pockets of her apron, and still they moved about, twisting. A voice called, 'Nurse, Nurse,' and she looked with frightened eyes at the only other uniformed girl in the long shiny hall. A Sister in blue came running out.

'Nurse — Nurse Hannay; you're to go into the theatre at once.' She whisked away. Carly stood petrified.

'Hurry up, and don't drop anything.' The other girl's voice was friendly. Carly asked her, 'Will — will there be a baby?'

'Oh, no. An elephant. Go on, there's nothing to be scared of.'

She was standing alone; there were other figures, a probationer nurse, a Sister, and a woman with grossly congested body and face, but none of them seemed real at all. The Sister told her to do things, and she obeyed, with her mind ticking. 'You mustn't drop anything — mustn't drop anything.' The tick got larger and larger. The woman's knees sprawled out, and Carly focused her face, a blind, tormented face, torn in two every time it quacked. She thought, 'Oh, why ever don't they give her chloroform? Why don't they call the doctor?' But they worked on, like machines. Their uniform might have been white aluminium paint. Purple face, grotesque in white hard light, crying out inanely, 'Oh, I can't bear it. Nursie dear, Nursie dear, I can't bear it.' And having to, because there was no pity.

At last they funnelled chloroform over that gasping face, and the cries ceased. What went on didn't escape from the mechanical horror. 'Hold that — pass that towel, quick.' Things were thrust in and out of Carly's enormous hands. Carly was holding a baby, a new baby. Her mind ran back to Kitch, red and new in his cradle. She had seen him the first night, when Eliza and Sandra didn't even know; scarlet and puckered, but such a dear little boy, not like this. The Sister turned from the unconscious woman, stared at the baby. Her eyebrows frowned. Carly's voice came thin and weak, as if she were the patient.

'Is the baby all right?'

'Of course it isn't all right,' said the Sister impatiently. 'The mother's almost an idiot. What do they expect?' She went on working, in a pattern of scarlet and white. Carly said to the other nurse, 'Please take it — please take it.' She felt a desperate sickness rushing behind her chest, and called out loud. The Sister's voice pecked furiously at her. 'Nurse Hannay, stop that at once.' Carly lay on the floor.

'I can't help it,' she thought, getting into the taxicab next morning. 'I've failed, I'll never be any different, and I can't help it. I can't possibly stay there.' The monkey-lines of worry across her forehead and under her eyes were so deep and dark that she looked dirty. It seemed mad to her, horrible, that every single person in the world had been born.

A good many of them, said the Sister, are feeble-minded. Often their babies are illegitimate. And we don't call in the doctor unless it's absolutely necessary, or give them chloroform too early. It's better to leave it to Nature.

She got out of the cab a little way from Laloma, and wandered along by the side of the road. Broom-bushes touched her, and she saw how the dark pods, turning brown, were twisted and split to show neat little rows of seeds, ever so pretty. Fly far away. . . .

White woollen babies; some girls had them as early as sixteen. She herself, if Trevor Sinjohn hadn't broken off the understanding, might have had a baby by now. All her girl friends did. She accepted the position mutely; they were right, she was wrong. It was right to be hideously tortured, like that woman on the high flat bed, so that in a little while you can say, 'Oh, isn't he a duck? Look at the little creases on his wrists — that one means lots of money. Doesn't he look sweet, in his little blue bonnet?'

Not right, of course, for your baby to be like that one. Or dead, and unmentionable, into the bargain. Carly began to cry a little, slow, quiet tears for all the wrong babies in the world. And she hadn't the courage or the strength to help them, she could only stand there crying.

There's something wrong, she thought, with all our family. We take things too hard, and we're too ignorant. It's ignorant to love so much, and in this wasted way. And we fight, instead of trying to save one another. It didn't matter, it didn't matter, about Dad's losing his promotion. It didn't matter even about Eliza. . . . The cold steady tears were an exhaustion as well as a relief. She stood below the gates of Laloma, sunlight heaping on her hair like white ashes. She still had Augusta left. Augusta at first sight would be angry because Carly had given up her job, her good, safe job, and couldn't even keep this new one. She might have a dreadfully hard time finding another job. At twenty-four you have to work harder for it than at eighteen. You had to put on lipstick, and dazzle, and then . . .

Agnes down in the strong-room at Kirsty's first office, with Mr O'Keefe. You could hear from upstairs the girl's high, silly laugh, the man's voice low and urgent.

That woman on the high hard bed.

But I'll be quiet and do everything, she thought; mother really does love me and want me. She'll be wild, but that's only because she's afraid for us. In a while she'll get used to it, and I'll answer every advertisement, and go to shorthand classes at Tec.

Augusta opened the door. Carly barely heard her 'There — what did I tell you?' Through the rain of her tears she clutched at her mother. There was a tiny panic in her heart as she thought, 'Some day, mother might die. Then I'll be all alone.'

'Stop that crying. Pull yourself together. Do you want a doctor's bill, on top of everything else. Stop . . . poor old darling. . . .'

It won't be for a very long time that mother dies, thought Carly. Not for ages. Perhaps I'll be dead first; I might easily get run over. Kirsty died long before her mother.

She sobbed still, but she was content. All the love she had could be buried away in her mother, just as it was in Calver Street, before Kitch was there in his cradle. Augusta said, 'I'll put a match under the soup. You do look a drowned rat. It beats me how I came to have such children. I suppose you all take after your father.'

Carly's Johannesburg gentleman gave her one look, and disowned her. No, he said, I'm afraid not, Carlotta. You're too soft. I wouldn't be likely to have a softy for my daughter, would I now? Softness is far from aristocratic.

She didn't want him any more. She couldn't quite stop crying, but she was sure she'd be perfectly happy so long as she had her mother.

CHAPTER TWENTY-THREE

Absalom, My Son

JOHN kept his nose buried in *This Believing World* until a shop assistant started to hang about with that look of ratlike inquiry and disdain which preceded, 'Is there anything I can show you, sir?' Then he closed the book, with an ostentatious yawn, and strolled away to the Poetry Counter. (For years he had had *This Believing World* in brown-paper covers on his shelf, but looking at it gave him his pretext.)

At the Poetry Counter, which looked unbrushed and obscure, and bore no large excitable placards in modern type, he made a few passes over the Augustan Series, and a nice set of Browning in vermilion leather covers. Then, stealthily, he slipped his hand down to the lowest shelf, where humble little books lay tethered in elastic slip-bands like ladies' garters, old style, and drew one out. Its title was *Stranger Face*, and for the hundredth time he thought he had seldom seen a worse job of printing. Feeling the shop assistant's eye burn a little hole through his collar, he pretended to be glancing through the verses. When the coast was clear, he unfolded *Stranger Face* at its centre pages, and set it ostentatiously in the middle of the top shelf.

For a second he stood admiring his handiwork, then moved away; when he got as far as Travel and Biography, rage seized him as he saw the inquisitive assistant take down *Stranger Face* and thrust it out of sight in its garter. Half blind with temper and the cups of bad tea which were beginning to affect his sight, he lingered over Travel and Biography. Lowell Thomas — the world had come to a damned fine pass if it waited for Lowell Thomas to revolve it upon its axis. And this shop assistant! . . . Providentially, the inquisitive rat was summoned to another counter. John scurried back to Poetry, found *Stranger Face*, dusted it with clumsy gentleness, and set it back in star position. A hand touched him on the shoulder.

'That's not the first time I've caught you at it. What do you think you're coming at?'

For a moment the ghost of his father entered into John. He roared, and the shop assistant wilted. His face looked as funny as if against his will he had performed a double back somersault. 'What the devil do you mean?' added John. 'Do you take me for a pickpocket? The last time I come into your miserable establishment! . . .' (Bluff, for he never purchased at this otiose plate-glassed place, only at the second-hand shops.) The assistant felt better when Mr Hansen, his departmental manager, popped briskly out of Atmosphere.

Mr Hansen was brisk. 'What's all this? What's the trouble, sir? Simms, we can't have disturbances here. What have you been doing?'

'This man' — John glared, and Simms amended it to 'This gentleman. He keeps moving the books about, sir, on the Poetry Counter. He's done it at least half a dozen times, and when I put the books back in their proper order, he waits till my back's turned, then he deliberately interferes again.' Simms began to feel that he was wronged. His voice trembled with indignation and hurt pride. 'I ask you, sir, how I'm to keep stock of my own counters if I can't arrange the books without the public stepping in and interfering?'

'What does he interfere with?' Mr Hansen still believed, in a faded way, that the customer, even an escaping customer, is preferably right. 'This little thing, sir.' *Stranger Face*, paper-covered, dangled like a dead rat in Mr Simms's contemptuous paw. 'Right middle top, he puts it, and centre pages *full* spread, with Wordsworth on the one side and Tennyson on the other.'

'How can you expect to sell a book if you keep it under the counter, done up in a female's leg-band?' snarled John. Mr Hansen said gravely:

'This, sir, is a local production. I'm afraid local productions don't do us much good. The public won't look at them.' He swept wide, white hands, exonerating his shop, damning the public.

'Can't you tell poetry when you read it? Local production — you're a local shop, aren't you? You live by local custom, don't you? Then what do you mean, letting snippets like *him* look down their noses? I suppose a poet's a poet, even if born in this country or in the middle of the Sahara desert.'

'A very poor bit of book-production,' sighed Mr Hansen.

John said stubbornly, 'Well, read the verses, can't you? Surely if they're good, you can do something about it.'

'As it happens, sir, I have read this book. And my opinion is' (Mr Hansen's voice grew solemn, as if he were pronouncing on a vintage wine or a cigar) 'that in spite of its unfavourable appearance, these verses are very creditable. Very creditable indeed. But the misfortune is, there's no sale for a book of the type.'

'If there's no sale, can't you make one?'

'Well, sir, from the outside covers, it doesn't look *good* enough to recommend as a Christmas present. You know what I mean. There's nothing between the people who buy seven-and-sixpennies and the people who buy Christmas cards. Unless it's mottoes and little books of that sort.' (Mr Hansen indicated a dishevelled counter, whose Little Flowers and Bright Wayside Thoughts were systematically pawed over by unhappy fabric gloves looking for Something between ninepence and one-and-six, please . . . yes, just that sort of little thing. Oh, is the corner a little bit bent? Oh, I see, it's reduced.)

'The market is for cards and mottoes,' said Mr Hansen, sombrely. 'Look at the Augustan Series — beautiful little books, and yet I can't give them away. I estimate the entire poetry sales in this country as under three hundred, unless there's a made name or a very special appeal, and in the case of this little book, there is not. Of course, sir, you may tell me, when we get inside it's a different matter. But who gets inside? Who gets inside?'

Irrelevantly John thought of Jonah and the whale. He mumbled, 'Well, it's good poetry, that's all. I bought half a dozen copies myself; why shouldn't others do the same?' He turned his shabby back and walked away from them. His too-long navy coat made him look vaguely like somebody who has been kicked out of Holy Orders. The plate-glass door swung smoothly behind him. Mr Simms sniggered. Mr Hansen said a little severely, 'A customer's a customer, whatever his tastes. You may leave one copy out.'

'Top shelf, sir?'

'Certainly not. Second top shelf.' *Stranger Face* still dangled like a dead rat from Mr Simms's paw. It fell open as he moved it to second top shelf, and he beheld without seeing:

> She stands an instant in the sun
> Athwart her harsh land's red and green —
> Hands of a serf, and warrior eyes
> Of some flame-sceptred Irish queen.
>
> One moment, still. A little sob
> Shakes parted lips and straining breast,
> As if she hears the feet of those
> Who tread her own forsaken quest.
>
> As if she does not care that life
> Has reft the jewels from her hair —
> But grieves that menial needs and base
> Were those that left her palace bare.

Then, with a strange and iron hand,
Destiny reaches forth, and grips
The ruined cities in her eyes,
The bitter beauty of her lips.

Yes, thought John, shambling along the pavement, his thin unkempt hair giving him his usual wild look, probably Eliza's poems were good, since she said so; but he couldn't make head or tail of them himself. Poetry, like loving Peggy Lippincott all those years ago, was something that happened to you or it didn't, and it couldn't be helped.

Only Eliza should get a fair deal. Things shouldn't be so shabby. He remembered her as a plumpish little girl, declaiming Byron, without a thought in her head as to what that full-fledged poet had really meant. And yet . . .

There is none of Beauty's daughters
With a magic like to thee,
And like moonlight on the waters
Is thy sweet face to me. . . .

An ultra-sophisticated poet could write that, a child could understand it, or an ageing man, against whose ink-spotted shiny navy serge the Iceland poppies in men's flower-barrows cocked their impudent little snooks. There was a language, then, which all could speak. Poetry had something to do with it and the far lines of music, and the unspeakable patience of the grave; and even machines, when people extracted themselves from thinking whorishly of machines *as* machines, and thought of them as the consummation of many tall woods, the stroking of the gentle breasts of many harvests. So the poet and the iron age of to-day crept together — one to make the clamouring iron hands, one to teach the iron hands that, even yet, they were the thought and means of flesh.

Sometimes Eliza bobbed in, quick and laughing, and sat swinging her legs from the kitchen table, her new-cut hair red-curly in the electric light. She had written a book, so he could give her a little place for pride: but intimacy? Something had gone wrong ages ago, and he was too befogged ever to set it right. The walls of Laloma, the Abode of Love, creaked and groaned with too many suppressed complaints. They were *anguish*.

He was an atheist, and Eliza was a girl, not a boy. But standing in the streaming chill sunlight, white clear and radiant on the oval of his sharp argumentative head, the words of the old King were in his mind.

'O Absalom, my son, my son. Would God that I had died for thee, my son Absalom.'

CHAPTER TWENTY-FOUR

Various Goods

THEN, after all her lamentations, Mrs Sidebottom decided she would have a little fresh sole, or perhaps a couple; nothing else but one of those custards, and grate plenty of nutmeg over it, please; oh, and when you've done that, and counted out the linen, you might just run down the street and get the soles, Eliza, and order those cakes for to-morrow, and remember to tell him, this time the *cream must not be on the turn*. Last time, I was so ashamed when I saw the look on poor Mrs Raymond's face. And you'll be sure the soles are *nice* and *fresh?*

She lingered anxiously over the little fresh soles. Her digestion had failed her, and as she lay in bed, mounded with pillows, she spent a good deal of time thinking what she could and could not eat. Alchemist seldom searched for the Philosopher's Stone more vigorously than Mrs Sidebottom for the substances which would not upset her stomach, or give her heartburn afterwards. Rock-oysters with squeezed lemon, plain custards, drinks like barley water (which would be like a platonic marriage, Eliza thought), white meats, little fresh soles passed in procession before her faded blue eyes. She met them on bloody fields and, when routed, turned to her temporary maid with a quiet triumph.

'There, what did I tell you, Eliza? It's made me sick again.

'And Eliza,' added Mrs Sidebottom, a little fretfully, 'when you're changing the linen, do look and see if it has a pattern on it or not. I suppose you don't know that last week you put my husband to bed in my best damask tablecloths?'

'I'd rather like her,' thought Eliza, 'if I knew her in any other capacity but that of stomach and stomach-pump. Little fresh soles. Oh, blast her. What a hill.'

The wind flapped like a great slipshod kite clear over her head, the coloured town streamed out, triumphantly claret-roofed and brown-hilled. She bought the little fresh soles, told Huggins about the cream, smiled at a Hindoo boy in a fruiterer's because he was letting a dusty row of sparrows peck at his green peas, as if he were God Almighty and didn't care what helped itself, and was up the precipice again before she realized that she should have asked the little fresh fishmonger to skin and fillet the little fresh soles. She looked at their hides with distaste. Half an hour later, she was still tearing at them in the kitchen sink, while Mrs Sidebottom wailed, 'Eliza, haven't you got those soles on yet? Eliza, what are you doing?' Mr Sidebottom came in and said gravely, 'If you stood on the tails and pulled, the skin might come off. Like getting a very fat man out of his pants.' He took the knife and showed her how to fillet soles. His hair, pale frizzy yellow, stood straight up on end, his blue eyes were always twinkling.

Anyhow, thought Eliza, trudging down the hill again to catch the tram for her lodgings (she was the Sidebottoms' girl, clean, £1 a week and sleep out), I've earned enough to pay for my bridesmaid frock.

Mrs Sidebottom's stomach alone couldn't have done it. She wrote stories and articles, free-lanced, interviewed the slightly dim Hollywood stars that shot smoking through on their way back from making the First Great Australian Film, once even sold an advertising slogan. She had written her first book — poems — but, of course, that didn't pay. Quite the contrary, as the publishers reminded her, hopelessly, about once every three months.

Mrs Minnet, her landlady, had again taken off the electric light bulb and substituted a defective one. It wasn't that Mrs Minnet was either poor or needy, or didn't get her rent from Eliza, but she suspected her lodger of using the light, writing and reading till all hours, and the thought was a little iron claw in her heart. She sat up at nights, long, pale and strange in her nightgown, with the convex enlarged family photographs all around her, listening for the click of Eliza's lightswitch; failing to hear it, and thinking, with passionate resentment. 'She's still burning that light.' If Mrs Minnet were a millionaire, still the thought of light flooding her barren rooms after ten o'clock would have agonized her. But she didn't like to give Eliza notice, because the last young woman had had men in her bedroom, and the couple before that — such honest-looking people! — were unemployed, and left her with three months owing. Eliza called, 'Mrs Minnet — oh, Mrs Minnet. The light bulb's gone, I'm afraid I'll have to have another, please.'

'It was all right this morning,' sullenly lied Mrs Minnet.

'It's fused now, and the room's like Tut's tomb, and I've got to have light for my work. Sorry.'

'There's a candle in the stick,' said Mrs Minnet.

'No. A light bulb. I must have it, please.'

Hating all women, Mrs Minnet took the good electric light bulb out of the drawer where she had hidden it, and took it to Eliza's door. 'I can't get off to sleep when you put coals on the fire to all hours,' she said gloomily. She was a queer old figure, lean, horse-faced, capped both by night and by day, encased for ever in a flannel dressing-gown. People, like paintings, got fly-specked with time and weather.

Eliza took the bulb. 'Would you like an egg?' she asked. 'I forget how long I've had these, but if I don't use them soon they'll grow wings on me.'

Mrs Minnet accepted the egg. Getting it for nothing made a tiny glow of pleasure in her, but simultaneously she was angry. The waste . . . the wicked, wanton waste. . . .

Eliza grinned as her landlady went out. These small, wrathful encounters were in their way the spice of life.

Well for you if you can remain angry. Beyond anger there is another country.

Her bridesmaid frock of green panne velvet, with a great silver fleur-de-lis and flares of silver tissue, hung against the wall like the stiff ghost of a woman at a dance. Even in electric light the too-large room, islanded with old furniture, was uncanny. Frocks that year came four inches below the knee. Everybody wore flared skirts for evening, except the very thin, who swayed out at both sides in shepherdess panniers. Simone had a silver-panniered wedding gown, silver and rose. She had designed it herself, of course; a goose-girl princess frock.

Simone with the haunting green eyes, to whom the experiences and feelings of the body seemed to matter so little, the body itself so much. When she bought a trousseau hat, she didn't buy it for her face and hair alone. Before a full-length mirror, trembling with those delicate becoming lights they always string up in milliners', Simone's ankles, her stomach and hips, her slender shrugging shoulders, all had their word, arguing whether or not the new hat would do. The shop-assistants, to whom she was adorable, but from whom she never bought because of caprice, dark young Jewesses with down clinging on their upper lips, protested, 'Becoming, most becoming, Madam.' But if Simone's waistline said, 'No, we don't quite like ourselves,' the Jewesses might as well save their time. Older women tried to be sham-frank, managing. 'No, that one doesn't suit you — not your type a bit. But this one does. If you go through every shop in town, you won't find anything better.' They made their sham-frank faces downright and convincing, and it fell flatter than pancakes. On the other hand, they always parted with Simone perfectly good friends, whereas Eliza, who would be capable of buying an abominable hat in a moment of weak-minded sympathy, would be just as capable of flinging into a temper about all hats, all wearied shop-assistants.

All that beauty, eccentric like a dragonfly's: and now things are changing. Simone is getting married. Perhaps she'll have a baby, an enormously large family. Perhaps be frightened, perhaps horribly, aggressively confident, as some young women are when they're married. But I don't think so. Eliza tried to imagine Simone, but could only see her in a sweeping green hat with real ospreys. Then they had both ridden up in the little cable car, and sat in the Gardens among the thin ragged manuka, and talked until with a swish the drop-curtain of stars was right at their feet.

But she is marrying Toby, big and fair and curiously solid — character, I mean — who has a trick of getting his own way. He keeps a great deal in reserve. He is very obstinate and proud, and for two pins would keep all that shut up inside him to the day of his death. He likes to pretend that he is still a schoolboy, and plays absurd pranks. He has rather a good profile. Simone takes snapshots of it and shows them around.

She very nearly didn't marry Toby, didn't marry anyone. Till the last moment she was looking for her lost daemon, looking in dance-halls and books and black willow-crotches, looking beside the Hutt river, looking in her nymph drawings. Then, one evening, there was a haystack, and faint, mild, dreamy rain. Like Davies' 'A rainbow and a cuckoo, Lord.' Toby said, 'You're throwing away something very beautiful, Simone,' and Simone, my friend, turned and said, 'I'll marry you whenever you like.' Just that. Queer Toby, too. Queerest of all if Toby turned out to be the daemon. Inside marriage she'll have a new face, a stranger face. What could I have done, Simone? I had nothing at all but the grey ti-tree and the huge silvery globules of rain falling, hitting our faces. I never once saw her from her own side, I turned her into a fantasy. . . . So now my frock is green and silver, and I'll drink a little too much and break the awful solemnity by saying something ridiculous to make them laugh. Toby is taking her away into marriage, and then for a while into England. She's going to be a godwit.

Feet tramping by in the darkness. This is a flat, stiff little terrace, bristling with all the sins of ugliness. And they never kill Abel except legally, by the neck until he is dead. And somehow I like it. I have a mania for the flat, stiff places, the spawning-ground of life and its unwanted children. If ever the Star of Bethlehem shall arise, its unearthly clear jewel will mellow over such a place.

The passer-by whistles *La Paloma.* Dearer to me than my heart, you unknown, who pass and do not stop. I am tired, more than bodily tired. Where am I going? Into dreams, travel, fag-ends of love thrown down in gutters by those who did not want them, poetry, journalism, drink, drugs, the steep blue country of melancholy, where I have been before? Or down the road to the fishmonger's to buy Mrs Sidebottom's little fresh soles? It doesn't matter much.

She picked up the library volume of Rainer Maria Rilke's translated poems, flipped over the pages: there was the one she liked, beginning:

> That was the wonderful deep mine of souls

and,

> Already she was no more that fair woman
> Who often sounded in the poet's poems,
> No longer the broad couch's scented island,
> Nor yonder man's possession any more.
> She was already loosened like long hair,
> And given far and wide like falling rain,
> And dealt out, like a stock of various goods.
> She was already rooted. . . .

That's it, she thought, various goods. I am a stock now of various goods, some evil and some not, some merely sentimental. But more or less for everybody. I'll cling again to things and to people, quite insanely, hurt myself desperately for love of them, because that is my nature. But when I'm detached and cut down, when they turn and laugh in my face, I suppose I'll go on, vaguely interested in all of them. The little brawling workman, coming home in the tram with his belt of leather strapped about his middle, the belt he uses for thrashing his wife when he is drunk, escaped being Timothy Cardew by a series of miracles. And that both were flesh, not brick or stone, is really very strange.

> Out of the crowd, the faces blind and striving,
> Bent on their gains and bitter in their loss,
> Or arrowed through with rain, or fragmentary
> With wasted answers from a wasted Cross,
> O piercing look, all-seeing, compassionate!
> Find me and search . . . I move in darkness wholly . . .

But it must be the look reflected a little on all the faces, she thought. Oh, let it be strong on one face somewhere! Let it be strong and clear, because I have done so many foolish things, and it is not right to punish a person always with his follies.

She lifted the window. The thin distributed music of the rain broke itself into many slivers. Its voice was one and yet partial. The threads of light slipped down and down. She unlatched the door, and stepped quietly out, hoping Mrs Minnet would not hear her. A little way she walked in the rain, with slant beams of gold melting into the blackness of pavement under the street-lights. When she came to the bandstand at Oriental Bay, where great round lights glowed softly like melons, houseless men were sitting dejected, huddled there. The black sea rose and fell before them, and settled gulls no less ephemeral than the glimpses of lamplight-shattered foam. Light in little pieces, like a kiss from a laughing splendid woman unseen, came and dwelt on the faces of the men. They were old enough to be Eliza's father; few of them had shaved, their clothes were hopelessly battered, and their odd disjointed thoughts about their homes and life's work were the hermitages in which they dwelt. Yes, they looked holy and wise as ancient hermits, watching out to sea. Their faces had been battered into the sorrow and protest which are the next things to a petition for love. Presently one of them got up and slouched away home. Eliza walked on the opposite side of the road, for she did not want him to stop her or speak to her. But she heard his footsteps keeping pace with her own, quiet and dogged in the wet streets. When she had come to the doors of her lodging and stopped, his footsteps still went on. To capture them or set them back was more than a King's golden impatient armies might dare. They would go on for ever, and she stand on the pavement, smiling and listening.

A Note on the Text

The text of this edition was originally reset for the 1970 Auckland University Press/Oxford University Press edition from the first edition, published by Hurst and Blackett: London, 1938. Some misprints from the first edition were silently corrected: for example, in the Author's Foreword, 'Dead Men's Bread' in the first edition (7) was corrected to 'Dead Man's Bread' (1970, xx). Other errors were retained: for example, 'taffetas' (first edition 96), incorrectly retained in the 1970 edition (70), is corrected here to 'taffeta' (70); 'Bernarr McFadden's young men' (first edition, 202), retained in the 1970 edition (157), was altered, incorrectly, to 'Bernard McFadden's' in the 1993 edition; and is corrected here to 'Bernarr MacFadden's' (157).

The first edition Table of Contents listed the chapter numbers in roman numerals and this was altered in the 1970 edition to arabic numerals, which are retained here. The first edition Table of Contents also incorrectly gave the title of chapter ix as 'REFLECTIONS IN WATER' (on 149 the chapter title is 'REFLECTIONS IN THE WATER') and the correction in the 1970 edition is also retained here.

Several minor errors introduced in the 1970 edition have been corrected here. 'bird;' (1970, 23) is corrected to 'birds;' as in the first edition (37); 'Eliza always like men' (1970, 86) is corrected to 'likes men', as in the first edition (116); 'places, girl' (1970, 96) is corrected to 'places, girls', as in the first edition (128).

Notes

A note on the notes

The notes Gloria Rawlinson prepared for the Auckland University Press edition of the novel in 1970 have been retained here and their authorship indicated by [Rawlinson] at the end of the note.

A general note on Hyde's use of quotation

Robin Hyde's fondness for quoting verse from memory has led her into minor inaccuracies of punctuation and line arrangement as well as several misquotations, although in some instances she may have altered words to make the verse more apt. In any case her own text has been adhered to throughout the book. Where possible the correct versions, sources and authors are given below [Rawlinson].

p. xviii
the beautiful and intelligent who went away and died, in wars and otherwise, the beautiful and intelligent who went away and hopelessly failed
This passage echoes Edna St Vincent Millay's 'Dirge Without Music', which Hyde admired. The last verse of the poem reads:

> Down, down, down into the darkness of the grave
> Gently they go, the beautiful, the tender, the kind;
> Quietly they go, the intelligent, the witty, the brave.
> I know. But I do not approve. And I am not resigned.

Edna St. Vincent Millay, Collected Poems, ed. Norma Millay,1917;
rpt. Hamish Hamilton: London, 1956, 241.

p. xvii
Think not without a bitter price....
An earlier version of the 'Little Ease' chapter of the novel included the following:

> 'Think not without a bitter price
> These hills shall furrow to your plough.

And the other unfinished thing, scribbled and thrown way on the hilltops:

> For some were husbandmen, and brought me seed
> Of little foreign orchards, far away,
> And some their darker grapes, their poisoned mead
> Vialled in wrath....'

(Auckland University Library, AU-B12b, Folder 4(fragment 2) 120).

238

p. xxxiii
(Don't you remember? We call them Dead Man's Bread.)
'[Hyde] was aligning her project with that of her most significant predecessor, quoting as she did so Mansfield's well-known poem ['To L. H. B. (1894 – 1915)'] to her brother Leslie Beauchamp, killed near Armentières in 1915. It was this death that triggered 'Prelude', 'At The Bay', and 'The Doll's House', based on recollections of Wellington childhood and among Mansfield's most luminous New Zealand stories' (Michele Leggott, *The Victory Hymn 1935 –1995*, The Holloway Press: Auckland, 1995, 13).

p. 3
And she had diabolos
Diabolos are 'the game on two sticks': a double cone made to spin in the air by means of a string attached to two sticks held in the hand.

p. 4
stingarees
Alternative for 'stingray', especially *Trygon Centrura (Dasyatis centrurus)*. The Lyall Bay boys, possibly intending the word 'stinger', meant jellyfish, the popular name of various acalephs, medusas or sea-nettles, so named from their gelatinous structure. Later in the novel, John Hannay is invited to write socialistic articles for Carl Withers's 'little journal called *Stingaree*' (*Godwits*, 81) and is stung by losing his chances of promotion (*Godwits*, 177). Hyde's father wrote two articles for *Working Woman*.

p. 5
It was Bob Malley who owned the Glory Hole
A 'Glory hole' is a receptacle (as a drawer, room, etc.) in which things are heaped together without order or tidiness. It is also, in glassmaking, the peephole in the wall of a blast furnace, used to check the temperature. The first meaning suggests an imagistic structure to the story, juxtaposing apparently random or unlike things – so that they can radiate meaning into larger rhythms and patterns, as the second meaning suggests (the glassmaker's furnace is the place where a transformational fusion of materials occurs).

p. 9
she recited 'The Spanish Mother'
Recitation, learning and repeating narrative or dramatic passages by heart, was a popular pastime. Eliza's fondness for it here and elsewhere gets on her family's nerves – 'Eliza, don't recite while you are washing up the dishes' (*Godwits*, 42) – but it is also part of her apprenticeship to the poet's craft (as John and Eliza's shared appreciation of Byron's poems on pages 44 and 229 shows). Hyde herself took part in reciting competitions when she was a child, and her prodigious memory for quotation is evident throughout her work.

'The Spanish Mother' is a 96-line poem, written by Sir Francis Hastings Charles Doyle (1810–88), who was professor of poetry at Oxford and whose most notable work was a number of patriotic military ballads. This bloodthirsty poem is about a

woman who sacrifices the life of her child for her nationalist cause. Hyde's quotation
starts at line 33 and puts the first couplet of this quatrain with the last couplet from
five quatrains later (lines 55–56), then gives lines 59–60:

> The woman shaking off *his* blood, rose raven-haired and tall,
> And our stern glances quailed before one sterner far than all;
> 'Both food and wine,' she said, 'I have; I meant them for the dead,
> But ye are living still, and so let them be yours instead.' [lines 33–36]

> That woman's voice was heard at length, it broke the solemn spell,
> And human fear displacing awe upon our spirits fell –
> 'Ho! slayers of the sinewless, ho! tramplers of the weak!
> What! shrink ye from the ghastly meats and life-bought wine ye seek? – [53–56]

> 'Feed and begone, I wish to weep – I bring you out my store,
> Devour it – waste it all – and then, pass, and be seen no more –
> Poison! is that your craven fear?' she snatched the goblet up,
> And raised it to her queen-like head, as if to drain the cup – [57–60]

The poem appeared (probably among other such collections) in *The Sovereign
Reciter*, ed. A. H. Miles, Cassell and Co.: London, Paris, New York, Toronto and
Melbourne, 1908, 125–7.

p. 11
in the Toys Department at the D.I.C.
'D.I.C.' was the Direct Importing Company, a national chain of department stores.

p. 14
that blessed woman, Mary Baker Eddy!
'Mrs Mary Baker Glover Eddy (1821–1910) was the founder of Christian Science,
the doctrine of which she propounded in *Science and Health with Key to the Scriptures*
(1875); the Christian Science Association was formed the following year' (*The
Oxford Companion to English Literature*, ed. M. Drabble, OUP: Oxford, 1985, 306).

p. 19
Oddipore
Melrose, Newtown and Haining Street are all proper names; Oddipore is not, but
can be safely translated as Berhampore. [Rawlinson]

p. 24
Grandmother-Hannay-in-China
Hyde's own grandmother lived in India, rather than in China. Although Eliza's
grandmother-in-China is referred to a number of times elsewhere in the novel, there
is one place where an Indian connection occurs: 'It was a little marble tablet, with
a mother-of-pearl parrot on it. It came from under the Taj Mahal. My grandmother
sent it. It was broken at one end, and I had it in a collection of curios the year before
we left Calver Street. Mother lent me her Indian shawl to take up to school with
them.' (*Godwits*, 170).

p. 30
Drift, logs, drift, down the shining stream
Source not found.

batyushka gosudar
In Russian, 'batyushka' is father, 'gosudar' is sovereign or monarch.
The imperfectly recalled song is Eliza's nearest experience of the 'otherness' of Russia – containing Siberia, destination of the godwits – and she tries to occupy it imaginatively by thinking of Mr Duncan as 'batyushka gosudar'.

p. 32
Arbor Day
Arbor Day was first celebrated in Nebraska, USA in 1872. New Zealand's first Arbor Day planting was in Greytown in the Wairarapa on 3 July 1890. The first official celebration took place in Wellington in August 1892, with the planting of pohutukawa and Norfolk pines along Thorndon Esplanade.

Bird of my na-tive land, beau-tiful stranger
Source not found.

And the cabbage-palms and tree-ferns people grew in their backyards – like beasts in a zoo – looked cowed and sick
Hyde wrote elsewhere of the cabbage palm, in an article about travelling up the Wanganui River: 'A test of whether you know New Zealand or not is your knowledge of the cabbage palm. The stunted, sad, dingy little dwarf of suburban gardens – how plain it is, and how lifeless! But in the wilderness here, the palm takes back its old supremacy. Its slender height is as untamed as any tree in the world: and that rich perfume, ebbing and flowing on the winds of an evening.... It is a lonely fragrance for a lonely world. Something you should try to experience for yourself.' 'On The Road To Anywhere: Part 5, 'A Matter of Pipis and Kowhai'.'(*New Zealand Railways Magazine*, Vol. 11, January 1936, 37). By linking the cabbage-palm with the Silly Boy (*Godwits*, 36, 65) and other inhabitants of Calver Street (with its echo of Calvary), Hyde shows Eliza's sense that some choking and distorting force is at work in her world.
    See also 'The Houses II', from *Houses By The Sea*, 120-21:

> Now she has evening all her own; the hot
> Cream scent of cabbage palms, trying to flood out
> Like man's love, or the Blessed Sacrament:
> Sunset peaks over her, a copper tent,
> Wind like God's breath goes past her in a shout:
> Behind this street shine houses that are not,
> Playmates she loves, or loved: but then forgot.

Leggott links the motif of the cabbage palm in this 'untamed' state with other patterns and 'narratives of emergent female sexuality' in Hyde's writing ("Opening the Archive: Hyde, Duggan and the Persistence of Record', in *Opening the Book* (1995), 270-71).

p. 33

the godwits, who fly every year from the top part of the North Island
Hyde put some of her fascination with the godwits' flight into an article called 'The
Flying-off place: stuck on Ninety-Mile Beach', written in mid-1937, shortly after she
had completed *The Godwits Fly* and *The Book of Nadath* (which also uses the godwit
motif in the section called 'The Far Flyers'). The link made here with Maori belief
in a migratory journey from the physical to the spiritual realm provides another
level of resonance to her use of the godwit motif in *The Godwits Fly*: ' "Te-rerenga-
wairua." The flying-off place of the spirits. A young man in Whangaroa told me that
was its proper name – New Zealand's own Land's End, beyond Spirits Bay and
Hector Macquarie's funny little Pandora, beyond that bare country from which the
godwits make their yearly flight to Siberia. . . . By the way, the mana of Allan Bell
stands high among Maoris and others in the north. One man told me that if any
white man had ever seen the godwits fly, it was Allan Bell. Others have seen the
great gatherings of birds, and the frequent false starts, but Bell laid a regular plan of
campaign, and is said to have caught the godwits in the act. He died at Spirits Bay,
and, like the Maoris he loved, departed from Te-rerenga-wairua. It was explained to
me that the spirits wait until a great number of them are gathered together. Then
they travel along their last journey and make the plunge in company. And a female
taniwha is said to follow their footsteps, but whether she is there in a friendly
capacity, or waits like the monsters of an Egyptian stream, nobody seems to know'
(*New Zealand Railways Magazine* Vol. 12, September 1937, 43).

p. 41

who was an I.W.W. ('I won't work,' Augusta translated.)
Industrial Workers of the World. This international union movement was begun in
1905. Other well-known 'translations' or plays on the acronym included
'International wonder workers', 'I want whiskey' and – best known of all –
'Wobblies'.

those Waverley novels
Waverley was the first novel published by Sir Walter Scott (1771–1832).

p. 42

O Rome, my country, city of the soul,

> O Rome! my country! city of the soul!
> The orphans of the heart must turn to thee,
> Lone mother of dead empires! And control
> In their shut breasts their petty misery.
> (Canto the Fourth, LXXVIII)

> :dost thou flow
> Old Tiber! through a marble wilderness?
> Rise; with thy yellow waves, and mantle her distress!
> (Canto the Fourth, LXXIX)

From *Childe Harold's Pilgrimage*, Lord Byron [Rawlinson].

all cold and zamzoid
In his regular 'Language' column in the *NZ Listener*, Professor Ian Gordon reported having the word 'zamzoid' brought to his attention by an extramural student studying *The Godwits Fly* as a set book. He could find no explanation, he said, until he remembered ' the south-west country and Zummerzet. Thereafter it was easy. My English Dialect Dictionary swiftly produced an adjective *sam* meaning "half-heated" (of food) and an adjective *sammy* meaning "soft, clammy, sticky". I was clearly on the right track for those imperfectly washed forks. A further scan produced (in various phonetic spellings *samsawed, samsawdered, zamzawed, zam-zawey*) a clutch of examples of past-participle/adjectival forms all with the sense of "lukewarm" – used of food that has been cooked and then laid aside until it has begun to coagulate into a sticky mess.
  'This is obviously what was intended in that kitchen sink conversation written by Robin Hyde. Somewhere in her family English background there lurked an old south-west dialect word that sprang from the back of *her* mind as the right word for the occasion' (*NZ Listener*, 21 December 1985, 102).

p. 48
Oh, that's C. of E., same as us.
Church of England; Anglican.

p. 54
Eliza from the deckrail, or from the invisible funnel through which the yeasty bubbles are sucked up to God
'Wisdom in its solid form is incommunicable. Dissolve it, then, into streams, sieve it into the yeast of almost invisible air-bubbles, dancing between earth and sky' (*Check to Your King*, (1975), 186). The image of bubbles with similar metaphoric meaning occurs elsewhere in Hyde's writing and also in Stella Benson's *I Pose* (Hyde admired Benson's work and reviewed her short stories in the Christchurch *Press*, 12 December, 1936, 21).

p. 56
sometimes a tarantula gets into the house
Cousin Katrine's 'beady-eyed, foot-wide' spider would be a doubly surprising visitation, since the tarantula is not found in Australia. The large wolf-spider, *Lycosa tarantula*, is found in Southern Europe; the great hairy spiders of the genus *Mygale* are natives of the warmer parts of America.

p. 62
Their Aunt Bernardine was matron of the Agricultural College at the Yalla
Yallah College of Technical and Further Education is now part of the Illawarra Institute of TAFE in New South Wales.

p. 68
Lord Kitchener is drowned
Horatio Herbert Kitchener, Earl (1850–1916), figurehead of British Imperial power, had a distinguished military career, becoming chief-of-staff to Lord Roberts in the

Boer War of 1899, and succeeding him as commander-in-chief. He became War Secretary in 1914. In 1916 he sailed on a mission to Russia on the cruiser *Hampshire*, which struck a mine on 5 June and sank; his body was never recovered.

p. 71
Hush thee to sleep, O gentle babe of mine,
Although no other copy seems to be extant this is one of Robin Hyde's earliest poems, written when about ten years old, and titled *A Soldier's Babe*. [Rawlinson] The Challis collection has a letter containing MS of the poem. The letter (one page, incomplete) is a copy typed by Lyn Challis of a letter to Hyde's grandmother Augusta Butler, 15 Oct 1916.

p. 74
even after he caught the influenza himself
A worldwide influenza epidemic reached New Zealand in September 1918, near the end of the First World War. Almost 7000 people died in the three months that the epidemic was at its height. The 'spraying machine' mentioned on this page was a controversial mass preventative treatment. It involved having people directly inhale a spray mist of zinc sulphate or, as here, formalin (Formic aldehyde): the strong disinfectant may have damaged the mucus membrane it was intended to protect and so made people more susceptible to infection.

and Augusta, who was a V.A.D.
Volunteer Ambulance Driver. Volunteers, especially ex-nurses, were called upon to assist in the national emergency.

Toy Town is covered up with weeds
There are several versions of a toy town poem by Hyde (AU 374.1, 2, 3) but it doesn't have this line. A 'Troy-Town' can also be a maze, labyrinth or bower, rather than the Homeric Troy.

In a letter to Schroder, Hyde wrote that she had been offered a room to rent in Oriental Bay in Wellington, which appealed: 'because of those lights in the harbour waters. They waver down from the ships, scarlet and green, and I love to pretend that they are the ruby and emerald columns of drowned Atlantis. Don't you like the Atlantis poem?

> 'In many a marble chamber room
> The Atlanteans wandered there —
> The paleness of their faces was
> Like ivory, so pale they were.'

So I'm going to have a harbour view if I have to climb five flights of stairs and roost under a chimney-pot before I get it' (ATL Schroder MS Papers 280: 29, 1 Sept 1928). (The letter is also transcribed in Lisa Docherty's PhD thesis '"Do I speak well?"A Selection of Letters by Robin Hyde 1927–1939, Auckland University 2001). The Oriental Bay lights also figure in the ending of *The Godwits Fly* and may have resonated for Hyde in this imagined glimpse of a marvellous 'other' or submerged world.

p. 75
the music was far too large for them. It seemed to swell out of the ground, out of a
magically opened doorway in the hillside
Another account of this mysterious earth-generated sound, marking 'the real end of
the war' occurs in a number of places in Hyde's writing, including her 1934
autobiography, an unpublished short story called 'Black Forest' (Challis collection)
and the 1935 poem 'Rain in the Night':

> Speak for me, rain in the night. I have said overmuch,
> And of trivial things;
> Surely there must be a city of silence for such
> As are humble with grasses and wings,
> And who never walk in the crowd, without that backward-turning
> Glance which should spell the love of man, if only
> The heart of man were not a strange thing and a lonely,
> A banked fire slowly burning.
>
> Listen, for this is the truth. Once on a thyme-steeped hill
> There was a harp, and wild music. No harpist was there.
> I had come upon God's minstrelsy unaware,
> Therefore with blind hands I fumble the chords of beauty, until
> Their meaning shall ripple clear;
> Rain in the night — torrents of amber, of crystal and blue —
> You are the harp-strings, you.
> Speak for me, rain in the night; it is sweet to lie still.
>
> *Persephone In Winter*, 99.

p. 76
State Advance mortgage
The State Advances Corporation provided low-cost government-backed loans to
returned servicemen for capital investment in farms and homes.

p. 82
Joy in facing, naked, such an enemy
In the First Version of the novel, Eliza became involved in spiritualism, and the
activities of a spiritualist called 'Shadow'/John Calladyne. This dimension was
removed from the novel when it was redrafted, but elements of Shadow's story were
absorbed into the portrait of John Hannay. 'All that is valuable in [spiritualism] is
there for any man, *who can have the courage to stand naked in the stinging swarms of
realities and not merely ignore them, but never to know that they are there*' (First Version,
AU-B12b, fragment 3, 287).

p. 84
an old magazine, 'The Triad'
'In the 1922 days stuff you remembered was going into Triad pages, some haunting
poems, prose that had an edge like a scimitar. A man called Baeyertz was running

the show' (*Journalese*, 21). The magazine was published in Australia; though there was also a Dunedin periodical of the same name.

p. 85
London's People of the Abyss [*and*] . . . The Iron Heel
Jack (John) Griffith (1876–1916) wrote under the name Jack London. He was a socialist who attacked capitalism and exploitation with great vigour. *The People of the Abyss* (1903) is 'an emotive documentary based on some weeks spent in the slums of London's East End'; *The Iron Heel* (1908) is 'a novel about the class struggle, which prophesies a Fascist revolution'; the semi-autobiographical *Martin Eden* (1909) describes the struggles of a sailor and labourer to acquire education and to become a writer, only to become disillusioned and drown himself on the way to the South Seas. (*The Oxford Companion to Literature* (1985), 583).

p. 88
for like Balaam's Ass, so far would Augusta go
Numbers 22: 21–34.

down to flat Okori Road, which led to the College
Iris Wilkinson attended Wellington Girls' College; accessible from hilly Northland Road where the family lived via the (relatively flat) Tinakori Road.

p. 90
And, with the dawn, those angel faces smile
> And with the morn those angel faces smile
> Which I have loved long since, and lost awhile.
>> From 'Lead, Kindly Light, amid the encircling gloom',
>> by Cardinal Newman. *Hymns Ancient and Modern*, 298.

p. 95
Les sanglots longs
> Les sanglots longs
> Des violons
> De l'automne
> Blessent mon coeur.
>> From *Chanson D'Automne*, Paul Verlaine [Rawlinson].

p. 96
And the pearls there are darker than the pearls of other seas
The quotation from Tacitus is taken from Chapter Twelve of the *Vita Agricola*. In that chapter Tacitus comments on the way in which the disunity between the various British tribes has been a major factor in the Romans' favour in their wars of conquest: 'Once they owed obedience to kings; now they are distracted between the warring factions of rival chiefs. Indeed nothing has helped us more in fighting against their very powerful nations than their inability to co-operate. It is but seldom that two or three states unite to repel a common danger; thus, fighting in separate groups, all are conquered.' (Tacitus, *The Agricola and the Germania*, trans.

and introd. H. Mattingly; trans. revised S. A. Handford, Penguin: Harmondsworth, 1948, 62). This passage shows that Hyde intended the reference to underline the novel's critique of an education system, and a social condition, which exhibited a debilitating preference for division over integration. 'But we never do anything by wholes, it is all dismembered, like the buttercup, and nobody has the energy to stick it together again', Eliza says (*Godwits*, 95). The linkage to a colonial mentality is made in another way when Eliza says: 'I was thinking – there can't have been anything quite like this since the Roman colonists settled in Britain; not the hanging on with one hand, and the other hand full of seas'(*Godwits*, 101).

Nox atra, qui abstulit colorem res
The Aeneid VI, 272. Guided by the Sibyl, Aeneas enters the fearsome cavern which leads to the Underworld: 'They were walking in the darkness, with the shadows round them and night's loneliness above them, through Pluto's substanceless Empire, and past its homes where there is no life within; as men walk through a wood under a fitful moon's ungenerous light when Jupiter has hidden the sky in shade and a black night has stolen the colour from the world. In front of the very Entrance Hall, in the very jaws of Hades, Grief and Resentful Care have laid their beds. Shapes terrible of aspect have their dwelling there, pallid Diseases, Old Age forlorn, Fear, Hunger, the Counsellor of Evil, ugly Poverty, Death, and Pain. And the iron chambers of the Furies are there, and Strife the insane, with a bloody ribbon binding her snaky hair' (W.F. Jackson Knight, trans. and introd. *Virgil: The Aeneid*, Penguin: Harmondsworth, 1956, 155).

The reference implies that Eliza too is passing among the 'people that sat in darkness' (see note to page 235 below) in the hinterlands of Hell. Like Aeneas, she will win knowledge not normally given to humankind from her own dark journey ahead.

This passage in Book VI of *The Aeneid* is preceded by Aeneas finding the golden bough which he must give as an offering to Persephone/Proserpine, queen of the underworld, in order to make the journey. Hyde knew Sir James G. Frazer's *The Golden Bough: a Study in Magic and Religion*, which investigated the psychological forces at work in the mythic patterns surrounding the golden bough. She was also interested in Jungian and Freudian analyses of such patterns. Frazer begins and ends his work by locating the sacred grove of Diana Nemorensis above the woodland lake of Nemi, called 'Diana's Mirror'; and it is very likely that Hyde's repeated use of the motif of 'reflections in the water' carries an echo of this lake and its mythic significance (see note to page 113 below).

p. 99
I bring thee passion-flowers of my dreams
From a poem of which several versions exist ('Slave Song', 'Slave Girl', 'Slave Love'), written by Hyde aged about 15. Published in the *New Zealand Times*, 4 November 1922 as 'Slave Song' (identified by Leggott).
Part of the college grounds lay unfrequented
Elements of this passage also occur in an unpublished short story called 'Scented Verbena' (Challis collection).

p. 100
'It's a far way to England'
A handwritten copy of this poem by Robin Hyde gives the title as 'That Journey Home'. It was written some years before the novel but date of composition is uncertain. [Rawlinson]

p. 102
Back sped her yellow hair against the dusk
This has not been identified amongst Hyde's poems.

p. 111
He trod the ling like a buck in spring, and he looked like a lance at rest.
From the 'Ballad of East and West', Rudyard Kipling. [Rawlinson]

There was a play, in French,
In 1933 Robin Hyde wrote an undated letter to Mr. J. H. E. Schroder in which she mentions that she once played 'the Bad Fairy's part in a little French play, "La Belle au Bois Dormant"'. The play was most probably a dramatised version of Perrault's fairytale of that title (The Sleeping Beauty). [Rawlinson]

p. 112
Move forward, working out the beast,
>   Move upward, working out the beast,
>   And let the ape and tiger die.
>   (CXVII)
>   From 'In Memoriam', Alfred, Lord Tennyson. [Rawlinson]

p. 113
Reflections in the Water
The title of Chapter Five of the First Version (about falling in love with Timothy, not the Day's Bay picnic described here) is 'Reflets dans l'Eau' (Challis collection). There are strong thematic and verbal echoes in the First Version passage of a short story also called 'Reflections in the Water', published in the *Otago Witness*, 24 October 1928, 80.

A special Day's Bay voice
Day's Bay is across Wellington Harbour from the city, and was mainly accessible by ferry. An entrepreneur, J. H. Williams, had purchased land in the bay and developed it as a pleasure park which soon became a popular excursion for Wellingtonians. Williams also established the Steam Ferry Company to transport visitors across the harbour. By the time in which the novel is set (1922), the park was past its heyday. The amusement park constructions had fallen into disrepair (see *Godwits*, 116: 'the derelict water-chute still stands, from which flat-bottomed pontoons used to bounce out on the lake. Further along is a closed stucco shell . . . In the pines rises a double-storied bandstand, its stairway blocked up'). The area had been taken over in 1913, somewhat reluctantly, by the Wellington City Council, and was renamed Williams

Park after Williams's death in 1915. Day's Bay had also been subdivided for property development since about 1905 and the ferry service became more of a commuter service during the week (David Johnson, *Wellington Harbour*, Wellington Maritime Museum Trust: Wellington, 1996, 245–8).

He is the Cobar's *captain*
The steamer *Cobar* joined the harbour ferry fleet in 1906. In 1913 the *Cobar* and another ferry, the *Duchess*, were sold by the Wellington Harbour Ferries Company to the Eastbourne Borough Council. The *Cobar* made her last trip to across the harbour on 2 July 1948 (based on information in *Wellington Harbour* (1996), 246, 248, 345).

p. 116
mamuk' tree-fern
Presumably a contraction of mamaku *(Cyathea medullaris)*. The term seems peculiar to Robin Hyde – it was never in general use. [Rawlinson]
  Hyde refers to the mamuk' in several other places in her writing: this, for example, in an unpublished novel: ' The green Durbar umbrellas, enormous and elaborately embroidered, are tree-ferns, punga and lovely mamuk'.'('The Unbelievers', Challis collection, [5] 130); and in an article from her New Zealand travel series, 'On The Road To Anywhere: Part 4, Palm Lilies and a Benedictine. "Sweet Evening" in Opononi': 'Little Waimamuku (christened for the big black-fronded mamuk' tree ferns), is the service car's last oasis in the wilderness before Opononi is reached' (*New Zealand Railways Magazine* Vol. 10, August 1935, 43). The mamuk' in all three instances is described as a kind of boundary marker between the everyday world and another kind of knowledge, signified by the native bush.

p. 117
and takes out The Martyrdom of Man
First published in 1872, by William Winward Reade (1838–1875).

p. 119
'And only man is vile'

> What though the spicy breezes
> Blow soft o'er Ceylon's isle,
> Though every prospect pleases,
> And only man is vile.
>
> In vain with lavish kindness
> The gifts of God are strown,
> The heathen in his blindness
> Bows down to wood and stone.

'From Greenland's icy mountains', Bishop Heber (1782–1826)
Hymns Ancient and Modern: General Hymns, 265.

Hyde had earlier made use of Bishop Heber's hymn, in *Wednesday's Children*: Wednesday and her son Dorset 'went up the beach hand in hand. "What a fool I was," thought Wednesday, "Edward hasn't gone away, here *is* Edward, and the others too." The ribbon of sea-pinks planted beneath the windows of "L'Entente Cordiale," which was a one-storey house at the back, two-storey at the front, not at all bungalow, blew a rainy whiff of spice into the air. Wednesday thought of the Ceylon's breezes hymn. "But here, even man isn't vile," she decided. "Only rather hard to deal with. What jaundiced minds the writers of hymns seem to acquire."' (*Wednesday's Children*, 60).

Man, woman and child; man, woman and child
Augusta's moving epiphany here is counterpointed by her bitter sense of self-betrayal on pages 177-9.

Hyde had used the phrase 'man, woman and child' in *Journalese* in the context of a critique of literary nationalism: 'Now all the Pretty Boys who've been to England once, come home not precisely entrenched in literary positions. . . . We must, they say, develop a purely Colonial style, no family or Windsor ghosts, local colour laid on as thick as a chorine's grease-paint. Sit about singing to tuis and babbling of bellbirds for the term of your natural life, but if you happen to think of something that might have occurred just anywhere in the world of man, woman and child, keep it dark. I hate these aggressively insular New Zealanders' (*Journalese*, 11–12). The phrase also occurs in a letter to Schroder: 'You know for an experienced person I really know precious little about man, woman, or child' (ATL Schroder MS Papers 280: 74, 27 June 1934; in Docherty (2001), 138).

p. 120
Out of the Tower of Babel I save the one word 'Greeting'
Genesis 11:9. This has not been identified amongst Hyde's poems.

Hine, e Hine
This line is the refrain of the well-known love song of Tutanekai to Hinemoa. It was composed by Te Rangi Pai (1868–1916) of Te Arawa iwi. Tutanekai's yearning song of unrequited love goes out across 'the face of the waters' not of Wellington Harbour where Eliza is situated but from the island of Mokoia on Lake Rotorua to where Hinemoa hears it from the rock Iri iri kapua on the shore. 'Kati to pouri ra' ('loneliness is just for the moment'), he sings; 'Noho i te aroha' ('stay with the assurance of my undivided love'). Drawn by his song and the sound of his koauau (flute-playing), the legend goes, Hinemoa swam across the lake to consummate their union. Hyde mentions the legend in *Journalese* 168.
See also 'The Weavers and the Dyers' section in Hyde's *The Book of Nadath*, 33–35.

p. 122
and was now a vegetarian, A.D.G.B.S.
The Fabian socialist writer, George Bernard Shaw was a strict vegetarian. Since discovering ('Anno Domini') Shaw's ideas, Timothy has been a convert.

p. 123
he would teach her Nietzsche when she was a little older
Hyde knew the works of the philosopher Friedrich Wilhelm Nietzsche (1844–
1900), including *Thus Spake Zarathustra* and made reference to his writing and ideas
in many parts of her work. She included a quotation from 'Of chairs of virtue' in the
MS version draft of *Godwits*, page 151, where Nietzsche is mentioned again by
Timothy – though the quotation was removed in the final revision of the novel. A
version of Nietzsche's 'Ubermensch' appears in G. B. Shaw's *Man and Superman*,
which Hyde also knew. In a letter written shortly after her breakdown in 1933,
Hyde wrote: 'I mean to be not merely well but better than ever before. It's useless
to try to get back to normal when one's norm has gone a-hunting like Baal: so I'm
going to have a shot at the supernormal' (ATL Schroder MS Papers 280, 5:71, 12
Dec 1933).

p. 124
London's Martin Eden
See note to page 85 above.

Are the crippled children, then, the sick thoughts of God?
Source not found.

p. 126
Phantoms, or our own face on the gloom
Or phantoms, or their own face on the gloom,
For love of Love, or from heart's loneliness.
From 'Sonnet', Rupert Brooke [Rawlinson].

p. 135
The bitter lines of Iris Tree came into Timothy's mind
Hyde wrote to her literary friend, John Schroder: 'Have you seen, or do you possess,
a copy of the poems of Iris Tree? She is a modern and I have just caught glimpses of
her verse in quotation shape, but cannot get hold of anything complete. What I
have seen has the beauty of bitterness – a dark hard sort of beauty, as cynical as
Byron's' (ATL, Schroder MS Papers 280, 3:30, 28 Sept 1928).

p. 141–2
Little black people living in old, ramshackle huts, by the green edges of an imperious sea
The description in this passage foreshadows the 'houseless men' in the final
paragraph of the novel (*Godwits*, 236). The reference to ambergris here is echoed in
Macnamara's description of ambergris in *Nor the Years Condemn* as 'a stabiliser' that
can 'save people . . . from letting themselves down' (NYC, 309). Hyde also describes
ambergris and 'a Maori weatherglass' in an article on a visit to Stewart Island ('Isle
of the Glowing Sky: Stewart Island and a glass box', *NZ Railways Magazine*, Vol. 11,
February 1937, 27–31, 34).

p. 147
they were camped at Anakawa
In a letter to Eileen Duggan (12 April 1936) Hyde wrote: 'As soon as I can make my doctor let me I am going to Anawata, the Cave of a Thousand Faces. In summer red trees burn there, but in winter red camp-fires, for one sleeps in the cave and presumably eats mussels.' (Docherty (2001), 324-25). Anawhata is on the West Coast of the Auckland isthmus.

p. 151
Our unwalled loves thin out on the empty air
Our unwalled loves thin out on vacuous air,
From 'Town and Country', Rupert Brooke [Rawlinson].

p. 156
I cannot sleep – the night is hot and empty
This verse has not been identified. [Rawlinson].

p. 157
Bernarr McFadden's young men
'A physical fitness guru and publishing genius of the early part of this century, Bernarr Macfadden was a man ahead of his time. Some people also thought he was a nut. Having developed a superb physique through a vegetarian diet and daily workouts, in 1899 he founded a magazine called *Physical Culture*. . . . In it, Macfadden preached the virtues of healthy living, warning readers against tobacco, alcohol and coffee. And at a time when sex was rarely mentioned publicly, Macfadden wrote that it was natural, healthy and enjoyable. With this regimen, he vowed, he himself would live to 150. In 1919 he launched *True Story*, the first confession magazine, followed by *True Romance* and others. In his biggest coup, he bought *Liberty*, a popular general-interest magazine. He was written up in *Time* and *Newsweek*, and at the sight of a press camera he would strip to his underwear to show off his muscles. He gave interviews standing on his head. To preach his doctrine of fitness, he founded a religion he called Cosmotarianism (those with good bodies would go to heaven) and tried to buy his way into political office' (Joseph F. Wilkinson, *Smithsonian Magazine*, December 1997). Hyde mentioned *Physical Culture* in a letter to Schroder dated 1930 (see Docherty (2001), 64).

p. 165
I could make you happy, Eliza, quite easily
A number of phrases and references in this passage and elsewhere in the description of Timothy's feelings for Eliza recur in an unpublished story called 'The Hart Ungalled' (Challis collection) and in many other poems and stories. The sickle-leaved bluegum trees, for example, are a motif that recurs often in connection with the Harry/Timothy figure in Hyde's writing.

Aren't you fond of Rupert Brooke's 'Blanket's rough kiss . . . cool comfort of the sheets . . .'

> Then, the cool kindliness of sheets, that soon
> Smooth away trouble; and the rough male kiss
> Of blankets;
> > From 'The Great Lover', Rupert Brooke.

In your stupidity I found

> In your stupidity I found
> The sweet hush after a sweet sound.
> > [Ten lines omitted]
> And when you thought, it seemed to me
> Infinitely, and like a sea
> About the slight world you had known
> Your vast unconsciousness was thrown.
> > From 'Retrospect', Rupert Brooke [Rawlinson].

p. 168
The sparrows when they fall
Matthew 10:29. The precise phrase Hyde uses may be from a secondary source; but the general meaning is of the value and importance of the least things.

p. 173
How sad it is to be a woman!
How sad it is to be a woman!
Nothing on earth is held so cheap.
> From 'Woman', Fu Hsuan. Translated by Arthur Waley [Rawlinson].

p. 179
'Days should speak,' said the Book of Job
Job 32:7: 'I said, Days should speak, and multitude of years should teach wisdom.'

p. 187
thirty-five or thirty-seven.'
Clearly an oversight on the author's part. The ages 'twenty-five or twenty-seven' should be substituted to synchronise with 'I was seventeen when I got into the very tail-end of the war' on p. 188.[Rawlinson]

p. 190
O, my cinnamon tree! My cinnamon tree!
Source not found.

p. 200
We can go to Dyers'
'Dyers' sounds like 'Myers', the Australian chain of department stores.

p. 207
Children and cherry trees are always ailing
From J. B.Leishman's translations of a poem by Rainer Maria Rilke, 'There Where The Line of Cottages ...' *Poems*, Hogarth Press, 1934. (Published some years after the period in which *Godwits* is set!).[Rawlinson]
In a letter to Lee, Hyde quoted this line in a passage which described her experience in Sydney, adding: 'I *feel* a sense of community sometimes, not only as you'd approve it: more as if the old derelicts with their shabby stories untold, and the children drinking like sparrows at the bubble-fountain and the dead also, tucked away in Grafton Cemetery [in Auckland], *belonged* to me' (Lee Collection 3, 10 March 1936; see Docherty (2001), 195).

p. 208
Sleep, sweet, sleep –
The poet was Rachel Annand Taylor, and the verse should be:
> (Ah sleep, sleep!
> The gods of beauty crave in the Spring
> From out of the world's white flowering
> Some delicate thing to keep.
> Sleep, Sweet, sleep!)

The verse, which Robin Hyde came across in the Sydney Public Library in 1926, haunted her for many years and she quoted it frequently. It came from a poem, 'Four Crimson Violets' in a small book called *Rose and Vine*, published by Elkin Matthews, London, in 1909. Rachel Annand Taylor (1876–1960) was far from unknown in her day, although her reputation as a writer suffered an eclipse after the 1930s. Robin Hyde's misquotation is understandable here, as it is unlikely that many copies of *Rose and Vine* reached New Zealand, or that the poems enjoyed a wide circulation.[Rawlinson]

p. 213
It was her twenty-first birthday, and Cecily was giving her a birthday tea
Hyde wrote to John A. Lee that she had managed to rewrite her autobiographical book down to '21 years of a life' (Auckland City Library, Lee Collection, 2 April 1937). The events of the last chapters of the novel complete Eliza's 'coming of age'. Here, the threshold of adulthood ('they were at the gate of a house') is a bathetic experience for Eliza: 'I was always promised a special [party] for my twenty-first'.

p. 226
John kept his nose buried in This Believing World
By Lewis Browne (1897–1949).

he unfolded Stranger Face *at its centre pages*
The title of Eliza's book of poems is taken from Coleridge's poem, 'Frost At Midnight'. In that poem, sitting alone before a dying fire, the poet's attention focuses on the movement of the soot in the grate. These moving films of soot, according to Coleridge's note to the poem, 'are called *strangers* and supposed to

portend the arrival of some absent friend.' The poet then remembers his schooldays, when homesickness led him to watch those 'strangers' and hope for the visit which they might presage:

> For still I hoped to see the *stranger's* face,
> Townsman, or aunt, or sister more beloved,
> My play-mate when we both were clothed alike!

The schoolboy's list of hoped-for visitors narrows down from the mere acquaintance ('townsman') to his own sister: the person most resembling himself ('we both were clothed alike'). Earlier in the poem too the poet endows the *stranger* with his own mood, recognising that his 'idling' mind is 'everywhere/ Echo or mirror seeking of itself.'(*Coleridge: Poetical Works*, ed. E.H. Coleridge, Oxford University Press: London, 1912, 240). In both cases the *stranger's* face is in some sense the poet himself; just as Eliza's 'Stranger Face' in the novel expresses a new sense of herself.

p. 228
'She stands an instant in the sun'.
With slight alterations in the present text this poem was published as 'The Farmer's Wife' in Robin Hyde's first book of poems, *The Desolate Star*, Whitcombe & Tombs, in 1929. [Rawlinson]

p. 229
There is none of Beauty's daughters
> There be none of Beauty's daughters
> With a magic like to thee;
> And like music on the waters
> Is thy sweet voice to me:
>> From 'Stanzas for Music', Lord Byron [Rawlinson]

p. 230
O Absalom, my son, my son. Would God that I had died for thee, my son Absalom.
2 Samuel 18:9, 14 describe Absalom's death at the hands of Joab. When the news was brought to him David, his father, mourned: 'And the king was much moved, and went up to the chamber over the gate, and wept; and as he went, thus he said, O my son Absalom, my son, my son Absalom! Would God I had died for thee, O Absalom, my son, my son!' (2 Samuel 18:33).

p. 235
That was the wonderful deep mine of souls.
> That was the wonderful deep mine of souls
> [71 lines omitted]
> Already she was no more that fair woman
> Who often sounded in the poet's poems,
> No longer the broad couch's scented island
> Nor yonder man's possession any more.
> She was already loosened like long hair

And given far and wide like falling rain
And dealt out like a stock of various goods.
She was already rooted.
From 'Orpheus. Eurydice. Hermes.', Rainer Maria Rilke.

Translated from the German by J. B. Leishman. The 'library volume' was undoubtedly *Poems* published by The Hogarth Press, London, 1934. (See note to page 207). Except for punctuation Robin Hyde has quoted the lines correctly; however, later books in which this poem appears show that Mr Leishman has revised his translation. [Rawlinson]

Out of the crowd, the faces blind and striving,
Hyde wrote that she had thought of using the phrase 'the people that sat in darkness' as the title of a novel (letter to John Schroder, ATL MS Papers 280: 83 [June – July 1935]). The phrase is from Luke 1:76, 79: 'And thou, child, shalt be called the prophet of the Highest; for thou shalt go before the face of the Lord to prepare his ways. . . . To give light to them that sit in darkness and in the shadow of death, to guide our feet into the way of peace' (see also Romans 2:19). The phrase chimes with 'I move in darkness wholly' in the verse quoted here (and see also note to page 95).
Leggott has identified the lines as part of a poem by Hyde which evolved into the lyric variously called 'Hilltop' and 'Lover'. Drafts occur in the Auckland University Library collection (AU 470.1, 2, 3; AU 596), and Leggott gives two versions in parallel in *Nadath*, xxxv.

p. 236
The thin distributed music of the rain
There are a number of echoes of the poem 'Rain in the Night' in this final paragraph of the novel. See the note to page 75 above.

When she came to the bandstand at Oriental Bay, where great round lights glowed softly like melons
'Round Oriental Bay, water lapping up black by the Parade, seagulls screaming like untamed shrews among the little half-seen boats rocking at anchor, the lights, fat mellow golden ones, are arranged in threesomes. They remind me of Alfred Noyes' bacchanal fruits... "Grapes like melons – nay, clustering suns. . ." ' (*Journalese*, 29). See also note to page 74 above.

more than a King's golden impatient armies might dare
A social order that breaks things into pieces 'dares' not attempt to reintegrate them. In the nursery rhyme, Humpty Dumpty, 'all the king's horses and all the king's men couldn't put Humpty together again.' Here at the end of the novel there is an echo of chapter eight 'Little Ease': 'All the King's horses and all the King's men will never put dismembered buttercup together again' (*Godwits*, 93).

Works cited

A. By Robin Hyde (Iris Wilkinson)

[Short titles for references in the text are given in brackets after each item]

1934 Autobiography. Manuscript written for Dr G.M. Tothill, 1934. NZ MS 412. Auckland City Central Library. (*1934 Auto*).

1935 Journal. Holograph notebook. Derek Challis collection. Copy typed by Gloria Rawlinson. NZ MS 837. Auckland City Central Library.

A Home in This World: An Autobiographical Fragment. Intro. Derek Challis. Auckland: Longman Paul, 1984. (*AHome*).

The Book of Nadath. Introd. and notes Michele Leggott. Auckland: Auckland UP, 1999. (*Nadath*).

Check to Your King: The Life History of Charles Baron de Thierry, King of Nukahiva, Sovereign Chief of New Zealand. London: Hurst & Blackett, 1936. Ed. with intro. Joan Stevens. Wellington: A.H & A.W. Reed, 1960. Reprod. Auckland: Golden Press Pty Ltd, 1975. Rpt 1989. (*Check*).

Disputed Ground: Robin Hyde, Journalist. Ed. and intro. Gillian Boddy and Jacqueline Matthews. Wellington: Victoria UP, 1991. (*Disputed*).

Dragon Rampant. London: Hurst & Blackett, 1939. Rev. ed. with intro. by Derek Challis and critical note by Linda Hardy. Auckland: New Women's P, 1984. (*Dragon*).

The Godwits Fly. London: Hurst & Blackett, 1938. Rev. ed. with intro. by Gloria Rawlinson. Auckland: Auckland UP, 1970. Rpt.1993. Rev. ed. with intro. by Patrick Sandbrook, Auckland: Auckland UP, 2001. (*Godwits*).

—— First Version Typescript and Fragments of Drafts. Derek Challis collection and Iris Wilkinson Papers, AU-B12b. Auckland University Library.

—— MS Version Manuscript. Ex 16, Ex 17, Ex 18. Derek Challis collection.

Houses by the Sea and the Later Poems of Robin Hyde. Ed. and intro. Gloria Rawlinson. Christchurch: Caxton, 1952. (*Houses*).

'Isle of the Glowing Sky: Stewart Island and a Glass Box', *New Zealand Railways Magazine*, 11, February 1937, 27-31, 34.

Journalese. Auckland: The National Printing Co. Ltd., 1934. Extracts incl. in *Disputed Ground*.

Letters to John A. Lee, 1935–39. NZ MS 828. Auckland City Central Library.

Letters to J.H.E. Schroder, 1927–39. MS 280 03-07. Alexander Turnbull Library, National Library of New Zealand, Wellington.

Letters to W. Downie Stewart, 1936–37. MS 985-243, 244. Hocken Library, Dunedin.

Letters to Hardy Sweetman, 1927–28. MS Papers. Alexander Turnbull Library, National Library of New Zealand, Wellington.

Nor the Years Condemn. London: Hurst & Blackett, 1938. Rpt. with intro. by Phillida Bunkle, Linda Hardy and Jacqueline Matthews. Auckland: New Women's P, 1986. Rpt. Dunedin: Otago UP, 1995. (*Years*).

Notebooks, EX 14, Ex 15, Ex 16, Ex 17, Ex 18. Derek Challis collection.

'On the Road to Anywhere: Adventures of a Train Tramp. A Matter of Pipis and Kowhai.' Part V. *The New Zealand Railways Magazine*, 1 January 1936: 35-40.

Passport to Hell. London: Hurst & Blackett, 1936. Rev. ed. with intro. by D.I.B. Smith. Auckland: Auckland UP, 1991. (*Passport*).

'Poetry in Auckland', *Art in New Zealand*, 9, no. 1, 1936, 29-34.

Selected Poems. Selected and ed. Lydia Wevers. Auckland: Oxford UP, 1984.

The Conquerors and Other Poems. Macmillan's Contemporary Poets. London: Macmillan, 1936.

'The Flying-off Place: Stuck on Ninety-Mile Beach.' *The New Zealand Railways Magazine*, 12 September 1937, 43-45.

'The Singers of Loneliness.' *T'ien Hsia Monthly*, August 1938: 9-25. Published under the auspices of the Sun Yat-sen Institute for the Advancement of Culture and Education. Rpt. *Disputed Ground* 347-58.

The Victory Hymn 1935–1995. Ed. with an essay by Michele Leggott. Auckland: The Holloway P, 1995.

Wednesday's Children. London: Hurst & Blackett, 1937. Rpt. with intro. and critical afterword by Susan Ash. Auckland: New Women's P, 1989. Rpt. Dunedin: Otago UP, 1993. (*Wednesday*).

'The Writer and His Audience.' New Zealand Authors' Week 1936. NZ MS 542-06. Auckland City Central Library. Abridged rpt. in *Disputed Ground* 322-27. Holograph copy by Hyde in Challis collection.

B.   Other Sources

Armstrong, Bridget. *The Flight of the Godwit*. Solo dramatisation written and performed by Bridget Armstrong, 1982.

Brooke, Rupert. *The Collected Poems*. Ed. and with a memoir by Edward Marsh. London: Sidgwick & Jackson, 1918.

Challis, Derek. 'The Fate of the Iris Wilkinson [Robin Hyde] Manuscripts', *Journal of New Zealand Literature* 16 1998, pp. 22 – 32.

Docherty, Lisa. '"Do I Speak Well?" A Selection of Letters by Robin Hyde, 1927–39'. PhD Thesis, Auckland University, 2001.

Drabble, M., ed. *The Oxford Companion to English Literature*. Oxford: Oxford UP, 1985.

Frazer, Sir James George. *The Golden Bough. A Study in Magic and Religion*. 1890, 1915; London: Macmillan, 1922.

Gordon, Ian. 'Language' (regular column), *New Zealand Listener*, 21 December 1985, 102.

Johnson, David. *Wellington Harbour*. Wellington: Wellington Maritime Museum Trust, 1996.

Leggott, Michele. 'Opening the Archive: Robin Hyde, Eileen Duggan and the persistence of Record', *Opening the Book: New Essays on New Zealand Writing*, eds Mark Williams and Michele Leggott. Auckland: Auckland UP, 1995, pp. 266-93.

Miles, A.H., ed. *The Sovereign Reciter*. London, Paris, New York, Toronto and Melbourne: Cassell and Co., 1908.

Millay, Edna St Vincent. *Collected Poems*. Ed. Norma Millay. 1917; rpt London:Hamish Hamilton, 1956.

Murray, Stuart. *Never a soul at home: New Zealand literary nationalism and the 1930s*. Wellington: Victoria UP, 1998.

Paul, Mary. *Her Side of the Story: Readings of Mander, Mansfield & Hyde*. Dunedin: Otago UP, 1999.

Sandbrook, Patrick. 'Robin Hyde: a writer at work.' Ph.D thesis. Massey University, 1985.

—— 'A Descriptive Inventory of Some Manuscripts and Drafts of the Work of Robin Hyde', *Journal of New Zealand Literature*, 4, 1986, pp. 21-47.

—— '"Not Easily Put on Paper": Robin Hyde's *The Godwits Fly*', *A Book in the Hand: Essays on the History of the Book in New Zealand*. Eds Penny Griffith, Peter Hughes & Alan Loney. Auckland: Auckland UP, 2000.

Stewart, W. Downie. *The Rt. Hon. Sir Francis H.D. Bell: his life and times*. Wellington: Butterworth, 1937.

Tacitus. *The Agricola and The Germania*. Trans. and introd. H. Mattingly; trans. revised S.A. Handford. Harmondsworth: Penguin, 1948.

Virgil. *The Aeneid*. Trans. and introd. W.F. Jackson Knight. Harmondsworth: Penguin, 1956.